In the Shadow of the Eiffel Tower

Adventure, Intrigue, and Seduction in Paris

Lisa Mortara

Seine Publishing
ISBN 978-0615814537 / 0615814530

Cover photos of Paris by the author
Cover design by Lynne Pierce

The author, 2013

Table of Contents

In Memory of

James Defilippi, my love and companion for over twenty-five years; and Catherine Cardinal, my dear friend who came to love Paris almost as much as I.

In the Shadow of the Eiffel Tower

Adventure, Intrigue, and Seduction in Paris

Foreword

Late 1970s Paris: an era unlike ones earlier or later, when a young woman could explore, unfettered by convention, a city ripe for the pickings, without the multitudes of tourists that saturate the city today. Paris, by reputation, is known as the City of Light, of enlightenment, of openness and tolerance. All true. Yet, that which is hidden, ambiguous, even sinister can be equally fascinating, indeed seductive. If you look long enough, Paris's shadows reveal as much as its light...as I would discover.

1: City of Easy Encounters

I refused to go back to my hotel. Insisted on stretching out the evening in my café until at least eleven o'clock. I mean, it didn't even get completely dark in Paris before then. Besides, what waited for me in that empty, bare-bones room? A book and a cassette player—big deal. Just sitting on a Paris sidewalk was preferable to going to ground early, like a nerdy tourist. I wasn't a tourist, for crying out loud! I had been a student and an aspiring Parisian for at least two weeks.

Café sounds surrounded me. Cups and saucers clinked together. Spoons clanged as they landed in tall ice cream glasses. Chairs scraped the sidewalk, and chatter riddled the air in every direction. I netted the echoes as if with a dream catcher, and breathed in the night's palpably-humid air. You could say I almost felt at one with the city—except for the people.

I didn't have anything in common with tonight's crowd. In front of me, a twentyish-looking couple sat talking with their noses almost touching. Behind me, two middle-agers, with wedding rings, slouched on the same side of their table, their backs against the café wall. Over to the left, a man in a suit sat sipping an espresso, while his little boy dug out the last drop of his ice cream. Everybody had someone. Except me and the guy on my right—he was by himself too. I gave him a distracted glance and then turned to face the waiter who had landed in front of me.

"*Un Orangina, s'il vous plaît,*" I ordered, with perfect diction.

With a nod, he swiveled and strode off towards the bar. French waiters are always in a hurry, and all business.

"You sound as foreign as I do..."

Again, I turned to the guy on my right. Why the hell was he talking to me in English? I issued him a flat, blunt, "Excuse me?"

"I could tell while you were ordering...American?" He produced a freckly smile and leaned toward me.

Unmasked by my accent again! When was that going to change? "Yes," I said, "but I've been studying at the Alliance Française—"

"Your French is good. I didn't mean to run it down. God knows it's better than mine."

He sat back and crossed his Levi-clad legs. He looked pretty young—maybe a few years older than my twenty-two. The way he shoved back his blond bangs and flicked his collar-length hair over the rim of his shirt reminded me of the typical Americans I'd dated back home. I never remained steady with any of them for more than a couple of months. His speech, on the other hand...

"You're English," I said, to show him I could nail an accent as well as he could.

"Right, but I've been living here about a year."

"A year in Paris, and you don't speak French?"

"Pretty pathetic, isn't it!"

More like astounding, I thought...and intriguing. I finally granted him a smile.

"I'm Kevin," he said, "Kevin Smythe. And you?"

I liked his British accent, his cheery smile, the fact he didn't take himself seriously. I doubted he would act like the last jerk who chatted me up in a café. That tango had taken place a few days before, in Montparnasse. There I sat eating an ice cream across from the tall, black, modern Montparnasse tower, when a middle-aged *mec* (great French word for "guy") leaned over and said, "Ah, you speak such good French!" How could he tell when I'd only spoken my order? No matter, I let him make small talk so I could practice my French.

Then he took it up a notch. "How about I show you this neighborhood? Did you know the four famous Hemingway cafés are here?"

A couple of blocks later, I was fully in stride with the language, the reason I had agreed to go for a walk with this old guy in the first place. That and my curiosity about Heminway's haunts. We saw them all right—the Dôme, the Rotonde, the Select, the Coupole—and yet, right afterward, I had to start fighting him off. Arm snaked around my shoulders, lips dogging mine, he murmured in my ear: "It is good, a little love in the afternoon, eh?"

"No," I said, shimmying out of his boa grip. *At least not with you.*

I had made a quick deduction after only two weeks in the City of Light: plant yourself in a café practically anywhere in Paris, and eventually someone will strike up a conversation with you, or make some kind of contact. If you're female, anyway. Paris is a City of Easy Encounters—*quantitative*, not necessarily *qualitative*!

Kevin Smythe, on the other hand, seemed nothing like that middle-aged python, so I made a snap judgment to continue the conversation.

"My name's Haley," I answered.

"Like my compatriot, Hayley Mills!"

Oh, for God's sake, not in Paris too! I had long ago lost count of how many times people trotted out "Hayley Mills" every time I introduced myself. "What a cool name!" my peers would crow. Not too bad as a child, when every little kid envied the screen adventures of Hayley Mills. Now, time had marched on to 1979. I was my own grown-person and I didn't want to hear it anymore, especially the worst of them all: "Did your parents name you after Hayley Mills?" Jesus, what twits. I would have had to be born at least ten years later to be that perky English actress's namesake. And my parents would have been deficient sheep to name me after a movie star. Course, I never knew them because they died when I was two. So who knows?

"Yes," I said patiently, "only I'm Haley Morgan—Haley, with only one y. So tell me, how do you live in a city a year without speaking the language?"

Kevin winked. "Let's say I know enough to get by. Restaurant lingo and the likes."

So another café affair had launched. Good and bad alike, these encounters proved an excellent way to improve my spoken French—much better than school. Not that I didn't take my advanced French classes for foreigners at the Alliance Française seriously. I wanted to "make it" in Paris, like Hemingway, Fitzgerald, and the many other expatriates before me.

Why Paris? Because it was a thousand times cooler than New York or San Francisco, and it positively buried my hometown of Reno, Nevada. I had already made that discovery two years prior, when my aunt and uncle took me on vacation to the City of Light. I fell in love with Paris and felt at home, almost like I had lived there in a previous lifetime. If it sounds corny or hoaxy, so be it. It was true and there was no turning back. I finished my French and history degrees and got the heck out of boring old Reno, much to the ambivalence of my guardian-grandmother who had agreed to my Paris venture, but only on the condition I studied there.

God, I loved my freedom! I scoured the city and soaked it up, like a living sponge in a tropical sea. I adored the City of Easy Encounters so much, I came to a conclusion: if Paris didn't exist, I'd have to create it.

Only one problem remained. I still hadn't made any real friends in Paris, and even the most dazzling place can fizzle at times, and leave you a lonely ember. That's the main reason I decided to take up with Kevin Smythe, an Anglophone to boot. A quality encounter? That remained to be seen.

"I suppose you've seen all the famous sights in Paris," he said, as he dragged his chair closer to my table. "Boulevard Saint-Michel, the Champs-Elysées, et cetera, et cetera..."

"Of course." Did he think I was a debutante?

"Well, they're just tourist traps anyway. How would you like to dig a little deeper?"

That sounded grand. Paris was my apple, and I craved to sink my teeth deeper and deeper into it. This Brit had lived here a year, so he had to know more than me.

"Where?" I asked, trying not to sound too eager.

Again he returned that freckled smile. "I've got a special place in mind—a surprise."

"In which arrondissement?" I said, to drive home the fact I was not a novice when it came to Paris's twenty districts.

"It's in the Eighth. We can take the metro."

Fine. Now I agreed to let Kevin surprise me with the rest.

Paris's subway channeled us under the river, across to the Right Bank, and up to the Arc de Triomphe. From there, a brisk walk took us to a street parallel to the bustling Champs-Elysées.

As we dodged the crowds, I said, "I thought you wrote off touristy places like this."

"Just wait, we're almost there, and you won't even know you're in Paris."

At Kevin's command we finally halted. "Tah-dah!" With a proud grin and sweep of the hand, he indicated the Pub Winston Churchill. "I know the best English hang-outs in the city!"

I shrugged, and let him usher me into the premises. He was right. The Winston Churchill didn't look like Paris. The staid pub, with its somber atmosphere, reminded me of a dark American bar, only more elegant.

We tucked ourselves into a velour-upholstered booth rimmed with smudged brass rails. Stodgy but charming—I could grant it that.

Until about an hour and a couple of club sandwiches later when, along with the rest of Paris, the Churchill began revving up as quickly as the sun sank behind the Arc de Triomphe.

The music picked up and Kevin threw back the ale. I paced myself. Nothing sanctimonious. This particular beer just didn't merit risking a spinning room when I got back to my hotel. As the music pounded, Rod Stewart wailed out from the loud speakers, "If ya want my body, and ya think I'm sexy, come on sugar let me know!"

"You feel at home here," Kevin said, his voice rising above the music. "After a year in Paris, you start missing everything from home."

I smiled politely. "I wouldn't know. Right now I'm loving everything French! American clubs in Paris would be the last thing I'd seek out."

He nodded, blue eyes earnest if a bit bloodshot, smile a little too smug. "You'll see. After six months, you'll be starved for English. You'll be on the prowl, snapping up English-language newspapers and magazines right, left, and center."

Yeah, yeah, I thought. Speak for yourself. It was getting late and Kevin had started waxing sentimental. Before he could get preachy, I changed the subject. "Do you work in the city?"

His eyes brightened. Despite the redness, they even looked boyish. "Ah, that's another secret! I could show you where I work tomorrow." Then he corrected himself. "No, tomorrow's Sunday and it's closed."

I shook my head. "Like everything else in Paris."

"Monday then. I'm off, so I can take you there."

"If you'd just tell me where it is, I could meet you. I know how to get around on my own."

"Right, but then it wouldn't be a surprise, would it?"

Who cared about being surprised? I just wanted to see where this guy worked and how he got a job in Paris. I was trying to think of a polite response, when two men lingering next to our booth distracted me. They kept yakking non-stop, laughing louder and louder.

"I thought you came here to hear English," I said, puzzled over their accent. "I can hardly understand them."

Kevin grimaced. "Just as well. Couple of foul-mouthed Scots, they are." He hailed them brusquely. "Hey! Mind moving on?"

One of the Scots wore his blond hair layered, like Rod Stewart. The tune "Da Ya Think I'm Sexy?" still reverberated in my head when he abruptly stopped talking and whipped around. He slammed his hands on our table, making our glasses rattle.

He glowered at Kevin. "Who the hell da ya think ya are!"

That, I could understand.

Kevin remained calm. "Listen, I only want to carry on my own conversation with my friend."

"What's this bloody git goin' on about?" said the other Scot, his face framed by stringy dark hair.

"We'd just like to converse in peace," I said, trying to keep my distaste for the two out of my voice.

"Oh, American are we?" said the Rod Stewart-look-alike.

"Great!" his mate said. "Fancy havin' a drink with us? Your English bloke's a bloody bore, ya know."

I fixed him with a cold gaze.

Kevin couldn't take it any longer. "You can shut the hell up!"

That encouraged me. "And *you* can kindly get off our table." I glanced down the aisle and saw a waiter. "Shall we order dessert, Kevin?"

The blond straightened, like a dog at attention with his ears pricked. He watched the waiter, who was making his rounds, and then sneered.

His friend's smile turned sour. "Too bad, American lass..."

Rod jerked his head and they swaggered off.

I grinned at their backs and then turned my smile on Kevin. "Well, we got around that impasse!"

"Nice French word, *impasse*." Kevin's eyes flickered back and forth from his plate to me. "You know, you could have got hurt, telling that berk to get off the table."

"Well..."

"Just watch your step from now on, or you'll get in trouble. Let me handle idiots like that."

"I'll keep that in mind next time we're on the verge of another brawl."

He looked past me for a few seconds. Then he struck up some small talk, which included telling me his age: twenty-seven. I wondered if that wasn't to prove his superior experience. Fifteen minutes later, we left.

Maybe I should've given Kevin the heave-ho right then and there. On the other hand, he *was* five years older...and perhaps a little wiser. He had lived and worked in Paris for an entire year, and I definitely wanted to learn about that. So before we went our separate ways, I promised to meet him Monday in the café near my hotel so he could show me his mysterious workplace.

I hopped off the metro at Pont Neuf. My head still buzzed with the evening's events, so I chose the long way back to my hotel, one of those intimate walks where I could mull over my thoughts. Just Paris and me. Across the Seine in the dark, I spotted the Conciergerie, my favorite building with its

Spartan, cream-grey stone façade and triple medieval towers. Midnight had passed, and I didn't give a thought to walking home in the dark. Everybody walked at night in Paris.

A fluttering breeze made the air a smidgeon less dense and humid as I continued across the Pont Neuf, Paris's "New Bridge" some three hundred years ago. What luck, to be living in the center of Paris and strolling home across an elegant work of white sculpted stone...

"BONE SWAHRR!" shouted a couple of drunken young tourists, before I could finish my thought.

I tried to dodge them, but they staggered into me anyway. Agh—another pair of idiots! They reminded me of the Scots. I forced the Winston Churchill fiasco out of my mind and continued across to the Left Bank. Kevin seemed decent enough company...

And I didn't have any other friends...

With that reminder, I wound my way through the narrow lanes of the Latin Quarter, up to my hollow hotel room on rue des Ecoles.

No television, no mini-fridge, no dresser. At least my modest little pad had its own closet-sized bathroom, though I banged my elbows just turning around in it, and risked getting goosed by the walls when I bent to retrieve my shampoo. Still, the place was clean, something my grandmother would have emphasized...despite the instance I found a silverfish in my shower. I had to watch it wiggle in my wad of toilet paper until I flushed it down the toilet. My armoire measured as small as my shower, so that my excess clothes overflowed and migrated to the back of my chair and onto my little wooden desk as well.

In the late 70s, no low-end, fifteen-dollar-a-day hotel room in Paris had a television or a telephone that communicated directly to the outside. For entertainment you either joined your hotel mates around the tube in the lobby, or went to bed and read. Alone. A single room in Paris meant just that—one twin bed. Plus, concierges were akin to sergeants: no one got smuggled past them into the barracks.

So I'd turn in as late as possible, my only companions a book and a cassette player, the latter my most prized possession. Along with the French language, I adored music. I was mad for jazz and the French pop music that wafted from loudspeakers in cafés. People say my father was a music hound. Natural that his passion would rub off on me—except for the fact I never knew him, since I was only a toddler when he and my mother perished in a car crash.

Not to worry, I never got maudlin over being an orphan. The complete contrary, in fact. I don't remember my parents, and it drove me crazy when people dumped their sympathy on me: on "little Haley, raised by her grandmother." Little Haley, the anomaly. The frigging oddball. Now that I had graduated to *big* Haley, those sentimental bear hugs became sparser, thank goodness.

That was one thing I liked about Kevin. He didn't get syrupy or nosy when it came to my background, didn't make me feel embarrassed about being an orphan. In turn, I didn't probe him about why exactly he had become an expatriate in Paris. Instead of Amsterdam, or New York, or New Zealand, for that matter, since he lacked the ambition to learn languages. He seemed to navigate in search of a business opportunity, that's all.

Now, for his surprises...well, the first one left a lot to be desired. Monday came, and I hoped he wouldn't spring another English pub on me.

Native Parisians and expats alike are café creatures. So naturally, after my class at the Alliance Française, I met Kevin at the café next to my hotel. He linked his arm through mine and off we set down rue Saint-Jacques, toward the Seine and the mysterious location of his employment.

Rue Saint-Jacques, narrow and hugged by massive beige limestone buildings, was home to the Sorbonne, and I had made the university's green-domed tower the beacon of my neighborhood. Since we were hoofing it on rue Saint-Jacques, I couldn't resist telling Kevin about the charming way I had found out about the tower of Saint-Jacques across the river.

"I was kicking down the street," I said, "just like we're doing now, when this elderly French lady in a flowery dress stops me. She must've spotted me scanning the area, because she stopped me right on the sidewalk and pointed out the tower across the Seine."

Kevin remained silent.

I went on, feeling my passion would rub off. "You should've seen her. With all these hand gestures, she starts explaining how each corner of the tower represents one of the four Evangelists. She was really nice."

Still no comment. I sighed to myself, and continued anyway. "The lady had these wide, watery blue eyes," I said, "and probably has a century of Paris history under her belt. Anyway, she told me the lion on the tower stands for Saint Mark, the eagle for Saint John—"

"Really?" said Kevin, in a distracted tone.

"Yeah. So I had to go see the tower myself. The thing's like a tall, jagged tooth. Have you ever seen it up close?"

"Yeah, it's old."

Does anything about Paris excite you? I was about to ask him, but we had reached the river, and I saw Notre Dame looming immediately to the right, enthroned on her island in the Seine. The Queen of Paris always mesmerized me. I started drifting towards her, until Kevin retrieved me by the arm and pulled me back onto the sidewalk.

He pointed toward a little enclosed grassy park with bushes. "This way."

I frowned. "There?" My gaze floated back to Notre Dame and her entourage of *bouquinistes* along the sidewalk.

Kevin sighed. "Follow me."

He led me to a recessed area next to the park, and there I saw it— Shakespeare and Company.

He stopped and stood with his hands on his hips. "One of the oldest English bookstores in Paris. The Beat Generation poets hung out here some twenty years ago."

So Kevin did appreciate some history. He even seemed proud of it. I examined the relic. The store's books overflowed its space, spilling out onto tables on the small, rectangular walk in front. Kevin indicated the entrance, and I had to edge in sideways and keep my arms folded to avoid displacing books and people, so narrow were the aisles of this locale.

Books—old, new, used—lay stacked on the floor in every corner. They were crammed into cubbyholes and precariously balanced on the edges of shelves in front of traditionally filed books. Despite the front door being propped open to the afternoon breeze, the smell of dust in the shop commingled with an odor of old, musty books. Above us, gnawed wooden beams braced a ceiling whose plaster was peeling off. It looked as if the place could collapse at any moment.

Utterly charming. "Wow, you actually work here! Do you have any used French novels, by chance?"

Kevin squinted, a freckled cheek screwing up one eye. He flung a few strands of blond hair off his forehead. "French? We probably do somewhere. Organization isn't our strong suit, so I couldn't tell you exactly where. Why on earth would you want French?"

"Maybe because we're in Paris?"

"Then you'll just have to browse around."

Which we did, with no French novels in sight. I did formulate a new opinion of Kevin Smythe, though. Not a bad job at all he had landed in Paris. One I wouldn't have minded myself, if I didn't have to speak English all day.

That evening we went out for pizza, and afterwards we took a stroll along one of the embankment-walkways next to the Seine.

Twilight had risen, and Kevin pointed to a patch of lawn set back from the water. "Look how lovely the grass is here. Nice and soft too."

I looked at the lush lawn so near the river, impressed with another of Kevin's finds.

He wrapped an arm around my shoulders. "Come on, let's sit down. It's ever so cushiony."

I followed him, with a desire mounting in me to top off a perfect day. Sitting turned into stretching our legs out. Stretching led to embracing and reclining on the soft grass. Songs praised lovers on the banks of the Seine who didn't give a damn whether they got caught.

Kevin didn't care either. He was perfectly Parisian in that. Frankly, I didn't either. The City of Light contained its shadows, facets of its private personality, corners not stalked by packs of tourists. Not one pair of feet shuffled by on the walkway, not one voice did we hear apart from our accomplice, the Seine, rolling by in the balmy night, eternal, non-judgmental.

Or did the Seine mock me? Perhaps even warn me about my penchant for taking up with strangers and people my virtual opposites? Maybe I thrived on the stimulation of contrast and new encounters. Truthfully, I wanted to taste all the variety life had to offer before...well, sometimes I couldn't help pondering how my parents died in their early twenties—my age. I just wanted to *live*, without getting serious about anybody.

Besides, now I had a serious relationship with Paris, in many ways much more interesting than people.

Smitten, defined me more accurately. I was in love with both the commercial Right Bank and the intellectual Left Bank. The map of Paris's twenty arrondissements, those sectors into which the city was divided, lay burned in my brain, and I craved to know each of them intimately.

I yakked about my discoveries to anyone who would listen, and persisted even with Kevin. I lived in the Latin Quarter, and once I tried sharing its background with him; how in the Middle Ages that section of the Left Bank already teemed with schools where everyone spoke Latin.

"Yes, that's pretty much common knowledge," he had replied, with an indulgent smile.

Not to be outdone, I unsheathed the fascinating piece of trivia about the ancient Celtic Parisii, who lived two thousand years ago in their little fishing community on the very spot Notre Dame now occupied. He hadn't a clue about that, which made me feel shamefully triumphant.

Trouble was, Kevin didn't give a damn about the Parisii. Stores stoked his passions—record stores, bookstores, various boutiques, and which types would succeed in Paris as opposed to London.

So I ended up pursuing my love affair with Paris on my own. When I was on the Right Bank, those great, sweeping boulevards and avenues punctuated with majestic monuments made my heart pound. From the Opera to the Concorde, and up the Champs-Elysées to the Arc de Triomphe I roamed, admiring Baron Haussmann's mid-1800s designs.

I reveled in the sculpted limestone buildings that surrounded me, with their grey slate roofs and signature wrought-iron balconies, no two designs alike. Crazy as it sounds, the presence of such splendor sent chills through me, a sensation of being enveloped in the past. I figured I must have lived in Paris at the turn of the century, and I could feel the breath of hundred-year-old ghosts. As I explored the stately prospects, Paris's past would swell in my mind in the form of Ravel's "Bolero," and the haunting melody would crescendo in my ears.

No one could relate to this. I tried running my impressions past a couple of my fellow foreigners at the Alliance Française and received polite expressions in the form of question marks. Better than the slack-jawed *Huh*, typical of Renoites. Still, I hoped someday to find a similar soul to share my passions with.

Now, I know some people might wonder: where is this girl's reality? Where does she shop for socks, for instance? Certainly not up on the Grands Boulevards. I only tiptoed through high-end department stores like the Galeries Lafayette behind the Opera. And then only to gawk at the heavy, enameled balconies of the upper floors that reminded me of sagging wedding-cake frosting, or to marvel at the store's dazzling glass cupola.

I came down to earth in lower-end stores, like the Samaritaine, a department store just as old as the Great Ones, but much more suitable to my budget. Even in the Samaritaine I fantasized about the past. While I walked across the creaking parquet, I wondered just how long those wooden floors had been talking. Did they groan under Debussy's boots? Did they complain about Hemingway and Fitzgerald traipsing across them? Anyway, if I lost my umbrella (maddeningly common in a rainy city like Paris), Samaritaine would come through with a nice little economical model.

Never on Sunday, though. It was closed—like everything else in Paris, minus churches and museums, which I had grown tired of trailing through. Besides, churches and museums left me feeling lonely. I could relate to Juliette

Gréco's song, "Je hais les dimanches"—"I Hate Sundays." From a lone distance, I would watch couples exit Mass arm in arm; see them merrily cross the street to a café for an intimate, cheek-to-cheek lunch. I swear, cheerful sights like that sometimes depressed me—gave me the *cafard*, as they say in French.

Then I stumbled across a gold mine. A find that surrounded me, and hinted I would never be lonely again on Sundays in the City of Light. I discovered Paris, City of Cinema.

If I had inherited my passion for music from my father, my mother must have left me her love of movies before she and my father were obliterated from my life. My grandmother told me she had been mad for the movies, even wanted to be an actress. She starred in school plays, had a cast of friends off stage, and always told witty jokes...nothing like me. But I wasn't jealous: I was the one speaking French and living in Paris.

In Paris, you could see every film from every country in the world. I soon realized that hundreds of screens were woven from Right to Left Bank, and discovering their different styles gave me the thrill of being a kid again in Disneyland. On the Champs-Elysées I found large, regal, fifty-year-old art deco marvels, with plush-carpeted "Salles Prestiges," the enormous halls where they showed first-run movies. Then there was the Left Bank, my home, which amounted to nothing less than a cinema Mecca, with modern multiplexes in the Odéon district and little hole-in-the wall studios tucked away in the Latin Quarter.

With Kevin, I watched vintage works like *Psycho*, *Dr. No*, and *Harold and Maude*. On my own, I sought out French films, Italian, German and Japanese flicks, all subtitled in French of course. I loved going to the movies alone in Paris. I would settle into one of those maneuverable easy chairs, lounge back in the cool, cozy darkness of the auditorium, and let the language and the images spirit me away, as if the movie played just for me...

When Kevin invited me to the cinema, it was always for a movie in English. One Sunday he wanted to see *Grease* on the Champs-Elysées, that tourist bazaar.

"Come on, Haley," he said, trying to coax me into it on the phone. "You can get your French practice in reading the subtitles." Which was true. Keeping up with the flashing French sentences was like trying to swim alongside Mark Spitz. Still, *Grease* didn't interest me.

"You know," I said, "over at Odéon they're showing *Diabolique*, with Simone Signoret."

"French classic in black and white, I suppose."

"I don't think it's in color."

"I'd have to wear my thinking cap, wouldn't I?"

"You've lived here a year. I doubt you'll have to bust your brains."

"Wouldn't be exactly relaxing either. Especially for Sunday."

I was using the phone at the hotel's desk and the concierge kept shooting me sharp looks. I always found him impatient and impersonal, and tried to have as little to do with him as possible. Now I needed to get off his precious telephone.

"I'd rather see *Diabolique*. Sorry."

"...No problem, enjoy your film. We'll talk later."

That sounded reasonable—kind of like, "Do your own thing." Kevin's tone, on the other hand, didn't convince me. His voice sounded a touch high and his speech clipped. He was miffed...probably. I hated ambiguities like that. I didn't know where he stood, and it made me restless. For a distraction, I decided to plunge into one of my discovery walks, since my movie didn't play until late afternoon.

My grandmother would be proud of me. Not for choosing such a pure pursuit as a constitutional, as she would call it, but for the lunch I would consume beforehand. My whole childhood had been, in her words, one big battle to make me eat. I only wanted to play, and couldn't be bothered to remember when it was lunchtime. God forbid if she had to come looking for me and crane her neck to spot me in a tree. Then Gram would put me under house arrest, where I would be condemned to clean my room for the rest of the afternoon. I never lived to eat and had only started to enjoy eating to live when I was about fifteen. At twenty-two I had barely begun to discover the delights of food, particularly French food.

After a marvelous *salade de crudités* (Gram would have applauded the healthy choice) in a café under the arcades of rue de Rivoli, I crossed the street to the Louvre. Sunday offered plenty of people to watch, and I planned to make a sweep all the way down to Place de la Concorde.

I quickened my march through the dusty grounds, skirted the little arch called the Carrousel, and scooted around the big basin of water where I expected to find children floating their toy boats. Only, no children appeared. No kids, nor their admiring parents who usually relaxed in the green-iron chairs encircling the water.

Very odd for a Sunday.

I moved further down the sandy alley of the Tuileries Gardens, ready to cast a sunny smile at the hippy-types who frequently lounged on the grass under the plane trees. (signs prohibited the behavior, but they didn't care). And yet, I didn't see one shirtless member of the counter culture camped on the prohibited lawns.

Then, another anomaly. Music suddenly rose through the gardens and trumpeted skyward through the leaves of the plane trees. "Saber Dance," I identified from one of my father's albums. I looked up and discovered loudspeakers firing the spirited song down to Place de la Concorde. Excited, I picked up my pace and hurried through the rest of the Tuileries, toward the dirt ramps overlooking the Place.

I could barely make anything out through the thick crowd, so I zigzagged in to get a closer look. All entrances to the famous square with the Egyptian obelisk stood barricaded, and pockets of police mulled about, chatting among themselves or responding to crackling radios.

"What's happening?" I asked a *mec* in the crowd.

"The arrival of the Tour de France, *bien sûr!*"

"At the Concorde?"

"Of course! Any time now the cyclists will come barreling down the Champs-Elysées. Mademoiselle must be patient."

Good advice, but none that I could follow. I couldn't last half an hour in idle mode and I hated feeling hemmed in. Crowds congregated next to the Seine on the left and on rue de Rivoli on the right, so I wheeled around and threaded my way back through the Tuileries, to the Louvre whose entrance was free on Sundays.

Normally that meant teeming, oppressive humanity. Not today, for the Tour trumped the Louvre, and I decided to scour more of the biggest museum in the world under one roof while it remained relatively deserted. To tell the truth, free admission meant even more than I've let on. My grandmother kept me on a meager allowance, and Paris was proving very expensive. So I took advantage of every freebie I could.

I entered the museum on the side of the courtyard, whisked past all the high-profile collections I had already seen, and headed straight for one of the wings off the beaten track. There, I found myself alone in an empty corridor of the ancient palace, where the only echo of heels on parquet was mine.

A slight thrill pricked me as I advanced down the hall, for it got darker and dustier the deeper I went. I wandered into a shadowy chamber and faced a jumble of old furniture. Mostly Louis XV or XVI I figured, as I examined the feminine curve of the legs. Not that I claim to be an expert, but about a week earlier I had visited a little museum devoted entirely to eighteenth-century furnishings. Anyway, here sat all this museum overflow, with no showcasing or informational plaques. A beam of light from a window pooled on a desk, spotlighting a solid layer of dust on gilt. I stared at it for a moment, feeling a funny, shared sense of aloneness. Then I left the abandoned desks and bureaus and returned to the corridor.

I had discovered a storage wing and wondered if this could be the part of the old palace where a certain king (I couldn't remember his name) practiced his hunting—indoors, of all things. Servants would lay dirt and trees to forest the hall, a fox was let loose, and off raced the king on horseback. Something more surreal than outrageous.

I tried another room. Cool, dark, and dusty as well. Its walls were blanketed with old tapestries; Renaissance, they seemed, given the ruffled collars worn by the woven characters. They hung huge and somber, and each covered almost an entire wall. Again, I found no information about them, and like the neighboring furniture, the tapestries seemed abandoned to collect dust rather than admirers.

I stepped closer to one. On horseback sat a man, ready to resume impaling an already buckling, agonized stag. The youthful hunter flashed a lance and a luminous smile. A chilling smile, like a mad full moon against the night. An eerie feeling began to creep into me and I stepped back. My eyes hurt, for some reason, as if assaulted by the image, and I could feel sweat dampen my hairline. Then my insides started to writhe, and I gasped and hurried out of the ghostly chamber that had wrapped around me, squeezing me until I could barely breathe.

I fled the Louvre and walked and walked, expanding my lungs with gulps of fresh, sun-warmed air. Finally, I ended up back at the east end of the palace where I faced the little Gothic church, Saint-Germain l'Auxerrois. What the hell had happened to me? Something alien had invaded me. I gazed at the limestone Auxerrois with its lacy, sculptured façade. Somehow the light, airy-looking structure comforted me, and I was able to move on. I crossed the street and headed east on rue de Rivoli, past tourists still clamoring for a glimpse of the bicycle Tour.

The sparser the crowds got, the lighter I felt, almost as if nothing sinister or oppressive had ever taken place. So I rambled on, and wrote off the whole thing as a bizarre fluke. I reclaimed my explorer's hat and my aim of absorbing every sight, sound, and smell around me.

I didn't care which way I went, and took a random left on rue Saint-Denis. Jeez, the sidewalks were narrow. If I wasn't careful, I could stamp on the foot of one of the girls poised in the doorways. Hmm...one was bound in black leather, lace, and heels, another in a short, tight satin dress. Lipstick, mascara, and rouge looked spatulaed on them like...whores. *Bien sûr*, that's what they were—in all the splendor of broad, sunny daylight. Nothing shady, nothing secret, not a speck of shame emanated from their bold eyes and bodies. Just charming little smiles, cast with a flick of the chin, like blown kisses. Stunned, I stuck to the street, until one sent a kiss my way, along with, "*Salut, ma petite!*"

That's when embarrassment got the best of me and I ditched rue Saint-Denis, found a phone booth, and called Kevin. I didn't even care about my movie. This discovery was too exciting to keep to myself.

"Yeah," he said airily, "I found rue Saint-Denis eons ago. But it wouldn't have been exactly gentlemanly to propose it to you, would it?"

I tapped my fingers on the top of the phone console. "Listen, I want to see *all* of Paris. So if you've got any colorful ideas, tell me, or I'll have to find them on my own."

"Slow down, Haley! If you're game for that kind of thing, I've got the perfect place. Ever been to Place Pigalle and Montmartre?"

"No, but they're on my list."

"All right, that'll be your next excursion, courtesy of tour guide Kevin Smythe. Tomorrow night, then?"

"Yeah, shall we meet there?"

"Nooo. We'll meet in your café and go together. The area's a bit dodgy at night."

That qualification intrigued me, and the next evening about ten o'clock, we embarked on the metro for Place Pigalle. I concentrated on the passengers in order not to miss anything "dodgy," but it takes half an hour to get to the other side of Paris, and for the first fifteen minutes of our trek north all I noticed were the usual sober, impassive subway faces.

We had to change lines, but thank God it wasn't rush hour when thirty bodies stuffed in a train with no air conditioning quickly wilts you and you hope no stranger's clammy skin grazes yours. We waited on the transfer platform where a cool draft of air shot through from some entrance or vent and dried my perspiration. I sniffed the sharp scent of metal and greasy machinery. Nothing unpleasant—they just reminded me I was underground.

When we caught the train north, things finally started to change. A swelling stream of minorities—Africans and Middle Eastern types—began adding color to the interior of the blue and white metro train. Immigrants from the ex-colonies. Paris offered an opportunity for everyone. I wondered what dreams they chased here.

"Is this what you mean by dodgy?" I asked Kevin, nodding at the variety of complexions as we emerged at Place Pigalle.

"No, no," he answered with a mysterious tone. "Just wait and see."

I didn't wait long. Barely two paces from the metro exit, I spotted a very tall, nail-thin black woman dancing in the middle of the neon-lit street. Her shiny, straight hair and red dress swung along with her twirls, and her bright-red lipstick gleamed in the night. Still, dancing in the street didn't seem terribly strange...

Until she launched into song: "I feel pretty, oh so pretty, I feel pretty and witty and gay!" But instead of a *West Side Story* soprano, I heard something in between a tenor and a baritone resonate from her, or rather *him*. After the momentary shock, I zeroed in on his accent, American. Then he paused his song to announce in a high voice:

"I'll show them. Show you all! Broadway here I come! If I can make it there," he sang, "I'll make it anywhere, it's up to *me*, New York, New York!" He held the last note so long, all of us bystanders burst into applause the moment he left off. Then he curtsied, slowly, deeply, eyes closed, with one bare knee brushing the asphalt. He stretched his lean brown arms wide, in swan dive form, and bowed his head. When he rose, he winked—at me, I could have sworn—and then danced off into the night.

That was my initiation to Place Pigalle. In every direction, neon flashed *Sex Shop*, *Sex Show*, and the like. Proprietors or their employees manned the sidewalk to hawk their erotic wares.

"Come right in!" a mustached hawker called to us in English. "Experience a live sex show." He eyed me. "Men *and* women." I linked my arm in Kevin's and we walked past him.

We weren't out of earshot when I heard him shift gears: "*Entrate, entrate, ragazzi!*" I looked back and saw another pair of tourists in his sights.

"Do they speak every language in the world?" I marveled.

Kevin laughed and squeezed my shoulder. "Just about!"

Down the sidewalk I heard a third language. A couple of German-speaking men were surveying the merchandise of a sex-shop window, mostly flesh-pink gadgets resembling phalluses.

"*Willkommen, willkommen,*" said the vendor in a droning voice. A cigarette hung from his lips and his expressionless face sagged like a burdened bag. As Kevin and I strolled by, his fine-tuned ear caught us chatting and he changed to English. "We have products for ladies too, Mademoiselle. And very sophisticated games. The Kama Sutra card game, for instance—very refined."

No change of expression or tone of voice from this *mec*. Remarkable, I thought, after such a speech.

"Let's move on," I said to Kevin, who had lingered at the window. When I looked at the Germans, they were grinning at me, the asses!

Kevin slipped me a wry smile. "Shall we try another street?"

Honestly, I'd had my fill of Pigalle. The only thing worth seeing in the whole circus had been the black dancer. I truly hoped he could make it in some way, singing or dancing in his beloved New York. Just like me in Paris. In what capacity? I had no idea. I didn't know how far I would have to go either. I just knew I would do whatever it took to "make it"—whatever that meant.

"How about we move on to Montmartre and the artists' hangout?" I said.

Kevin stopped and frowned. "Well, the only problem is, there isn't a metro stop up there. We'll have to walk. And it's not a direct route."

I sighed. "In other words we could get lost."

He shrugged and shoved his bangs back. "I could get us there quicker in the daytime. We could have a drink somewhere instead. Save Montmartre for another day?"

The drink became two for me and three for Kevin. How those sweet rum cocktails go down smooth on a hot summer night! La Belle Martinique, a bar off Place Pigalle, displayed a tropical flair (the plastic palm trees were on the tacky side, but still admissible) and reggae pulsated in the background. A black woman danced between the round tables. She wound her way around our table as well, pink-knit dress stretching to accommodate the gyrations of her large hips. Pendulous earrings matching her dress and lipstick dangled rhythmically. The more I watched her thrusting hips, the more I wanted to dance myself, what with the restless reggae and my second rum-charged cocktail pounding through me.

"We ought to dance," I said to Kevin.

"Don't be daft. Haven't you noticed we're the only white people in here?"

I started to raise a tipsy objection, but he cut me off: "Besides, look what time it is."

I peeked at my watch, and sobered with a start. 12:15! The metro stopped running around 12:30, when the grilled bars came clattering down.

We abandoned La Belle Martinique, raced back to Pigalle, and plunged underground, where we scrutinized the big subway map plastered on the entrance wall. Thirteen tangled, color-coded train lines represented the bowels of Paris.

We were still studying the wall map when Kevin said, "Would you consider spending the night at my flat?"

I straightened and looked at him. A tingling began to seep through me. "I thought your concierge doesn't allow over-night visitors?"

The fact was, I had yet to lay eyes on Kevin's studio. He had informed me about the obstacle to romance posed by his matronly concierge. I pictured her with half-moon spectacles and scathing eyes that peered over them, glaring at visitors like a nun.

"Ah, but I've got a new concierge and I've been studying her habits." He shot me a crafty smile. "About now she'll be watching television behind the counter in the back. We can slip into the lobby and head straight for the stairs. Are you game?"

"Mmm." The pulse of the Martinique bar started mounting in me and I didn't want it to stop. Reggae rhythm surged through me, and I could almost feel the thrusts of the black dancer. Kevin and I had failed to dance in the bar, but we could do a bit of tangoing at his place...finish what we had started that time down by the Seine..."Okay, what's the trick?"

It turned out to be me crouching down and duck-walking past the desk, while next to me Kevin gave a cheery *"bonne nuit!"* to the concierge. She remained riveted, as Kevin had predicted, to her program within the sanctum of her little room behind the counter. She did, however, return a distracted "good night" to Kevin. French people are never remiss in that.

Once we hit the door and started up the stairs, I started thinking. Kevin had a rude and condescending streak, and his latest offense returned to mind. I stopped dry. "Hey, why were you afraid of dancing in that bar? You were really rude about it."

He turned to me from the stair above and put a hand on my shoulder. "Haley, old girl, I know this city better than you. Come on, let's not spoil things."

Choices. Too late to ponder them. The metro was closed, and I lived across town from Kevin's Right Bank building in the Tenth arrondissement. I resumed the stairs, thinking he may know Paris better at this point, but that I would soon surpass him.

By the time we reached Kevin's floor, I felt flushed again and for some reason a Brigitte Bardot song started bouncing in my brain—something about how life is magnificent, so why complicate it with hesitations? I agreed. I lived in arguably the most romantic city in the world. I wasn't in love with Kevin, but after our dalliance by the Seine, I thought he could be a good lover...for at least one night.

The next morning I overslept and missed my classes at the Alliance Française.

For the first time.

"I never cut a class in college," I told Kevin over coffee and baguettes.

"Bravo," he said, in a teasing tone. "So you miss class once in a while. What's the big deal?"

"Nothing...as long as I don't make a habit of it. Once in a while, sure...I just can't drop out, or get kicked out."

Kevin reached over the breakfast table and roughed up my hair. "Cheer up. You're not going to get kicked out. The school doesn't care whether you show up as long as they're cashing your checks. Why do you care so much, anyway?"

I smiled at him. The eve's tumble had been good...better than I had anticipated. What passion Kevin lacked in conversation, he made up for in love's language of touch...of taste...a sexual elixir. My first in Paris. I still hadn't *fallen* for him, but I felt I could try opening another part of my life to him. "Well," I began, "if I quit school, my checks from my grandmother dry up. And that would be the end of Paris."

Kevin folded his arms and nodded. "I see. You've got be a good girl and get good grades. I have full confidence in you."

It was a rare meeting of the minds, and I went on to further explain my financial situation. My grandmother approved of my perfecting my French, provided I studied. Granted, at twenty-two I could do what I wanted, and yet there was the little matter of my trust fund. My grandmother had set it up after my parents died, and she administered it with stipulations. In short, if I continued my studies, Gram would subsidize me with her own money. When I turned twenty-five, I could take control of my funds.

So Gram kept me on kind of a leash, albeit with at least 6000 miles of slack. If I quit school, I would be cut off and have to return home and get a job. When I told Kevin, his attitude softened with true sympathy. People always take you more seriously when money's at stake.

So I preferred education...for the time being.

School for foreigners in Paris proved fun and pressure-free. Kevin was right. I doubt many people cared who skipped class. Still, I felt one of my teachers did, and I didn't want to disappoint him—not eager Professor Bertalot. He was old, at least sixty-something, but I never met anyone more enthusiastic for the French language.

He gave his heart and soul for proper pronunciation. "CODOP," (pronounced "kudup") we learned to repeat after him. "CO," to get our lips out there like a chicken's: "CO, CO, CO." Then, "DOP, DOP, DOP," to reel them in. "They represent the two basic directions in which you move your mouth in French," he had explained. "Lips out, lips in, lips out, lips in!"

Short, bald, with sparse grey hair on the sides of his head, the man might not have looked virile and exuberant. Yet he was a marvel of geriatric energy, the way he got in every student's face at least once during a ninety-minute class. Many students had pronunciation problems, considering they came from umpteen different countries. There was an Iraqi, about my age, who asked me to repeat vocabulary for him. He had sharp black eyes and thick black eyebrows that projected a dark sternness when he was concentrating. Then he would turn and smile at me, and a huge glimmering grin made him look like the most cheerful, friendly person you could know. He loved the Western World and probably soaked up Paris as much as I did. Or seemed to. You never know about people.

I learned that the hard way.

One afternoon I stopped for coffee in my usual café near school on boulevard Raspail. There I sat on the café terrace with one of my texts, grinding away at grammar exercises. That was the homework my second teacher always dumped on us. I couldn't understand it. This man had to be thirty years younger than dear old Professor Bertalot, but I'll be damned if youth equaled enthusiasm in his case. Blond and blasé, head buried in his book, he slouched over his desk and rarely looked at us, much less left his post to engage anyone. The only time he permitted himself a smile was when a student made a mistake. Then he would laser a smirk or a grimace at the poor, offending slob who had mucked up the precious subjunctive. Otherwise, he just called on us to review grammar exercises, with the pace and tone of an assembly-line robot.

The contrast between my two teachers didn't end there. Professor Bertalot always wore a dark suit and vest. His immaculate white shirt gleamed at the cuffs where two gold cufflinks winked. With his red tie and bright smile, he was the morning sunshine and could dazzle any student who had the early-morning blahs. Grammar *mec*, on the other hand, fashioned himself a hippy. He had the long stringy hair all right, but as far as *his* cuffs were concerned, I wished he would roll them up and spare us their grime. Normally, I wouldn't have minded slovenliness; it's just that hippies weren't supposed to look down their noses at people.

It was tempting to postpone grammar homework until evening or late at night. But then my self-discipline tended to desert me all together, and the thought of receiving one of the *mec's* exterminating smirks made me cringe. So, on the café terrace across from boulevard Raspail's median of shady trees, I got down to work...for about two minutes.

"Excuse me, are you a foreign student?" I heard vaguely in English, as if a fly had navigated too close to my ear. I glanced to my left to see who had sat down, and saw a guy about my age with glasses and a dark complexion.

"You study French grammar," he clarified, in an accent I couldn't identify.

I put down my pen, barely containing an exasperated sigh. "How did you know I speak English?"

He gave a slight smile. "I guessed. Anyway, it is the only foreign language I know, except for a little French." He pulled his chair closer. "I have only been in Paris a few weeks."

"Studying as well?" I asked, with polite hollowness.

"No, I work...for my uncle. He owns a Greek restaurant near Place Saint-Michel. The Poseidon."

"You're Greek then?"

He practically hurled his response at me. "Yes, from Crete!" Then he lowered his voice to almost a whisper. "Some people think I am Iranian. They keep me away because of the Shah."

I had heard about the Iranian emperor being overthrown by Islamic extremists, but it hadn't much interested me until now. Unfortunate that people discarded this fellow like an exotic but putrefied fruit. He looked sad, as a matter of fact.

"What is your name?" he went on.

I hesitated for a split second, just long enough to ask myself whether I wanted to get involved with yet another English-speaking foreigner. Too bad the thought didn't flit through my mind faster, because the Greek's eyes suddenly darkened, and then darted to his lap.

"Haley, my name's Haley," I blurted, ears burning with embarrassment.

His black eyes popped up, like corks from under water. "I am George, *Yiorgos* in Greek," he said, a shy smile leaking back out. "Would you like to take a walk?"

Well, that was it. I shut my book while keeping a polite smile pointed at this mournful kid from Crete. He looked so wronged, how could I refuse him? I could, on the other hand, turn the situation to my advantage.

"Ever heard of Ernest Hemingway and F. Scott Fitzgerald?" I asked. When I received a blank stare, I went on. "There are some famous cafés around here that are really old, but neat. Just down boulevard du Montparnasse. We could go see them…"

George smiled with his mouth, but his eyes seemed guarded. "You are kind," he said. "I will buy ice cream there."

The Hemingway cafés still awaited my exploration. When I had last waltzed along boulevard du Montparnasse, it was with that middle-aged French lecher who had pounced on me before I could get a feel for the four landmarks. I couldn't help thinking about that as George and I started our stroll. Fortunately, the French are faithful to their cafés, so he probably stayed up at the corner of rue de Rennes, "fishing" where we had met.

Strange, but as we explored the neighborhood, I started to feel a slight affinity with this Greek. Like me, he appreciated interesting architecture, and we both fancied the viney wrought iron that grew from balconies all over Paris. Here in Montparnasse, certain corner buildings were capped with stylish grey domes.

"That one looks like a Prussian helmet," I said, "spike and all."

"And that one, the hat of a witch," said George, as we wove through the quarter full of leafy plane trees.

"A lot of Alsatian restaurants here," I pointed out, as we dodged a sidewalk billboard advertising sauerkraut, ham hocks, and pork sausage. "Basically German fare. The French have those provinces that used to belong to Germany."

"Yes, from the Wars. Do you like pork?"

The nonsequitur puzzled me, and I slowed a little. "Yeah…you?"

"I'm not used to it," he said, frowning. "My father does not like it."

"Oh," I said, still wondering about the relevancy of the question.

After exploring the architecture of a couple of more side streets, we reached the Hemingway cafés, and I launched into the subject at hand. "Fortunately for Fitzgerald and Hemingway the four cafés are neighbors, so they didn't have to teeter far in their tipsiness!"

George's eyes narrowed. I started to explain and then decided against it. It's hard to translate humor.

I wanted to sit in the open air and suggested the Rotonde, which faced the Dôme on the opposite side of the street. At the same time, I wanted to retreat from the sidewalk traffic, so I led us into the recessed area under the terrace roof. There, I could still feel the summer air, perceive bustling city sounds and watch the parade of people on the sidewalk without seeming nosey.

Before we ducked into the Rotonde, George pointed out the Dôme's corner cap across the street. "That one looks like the hat of an ancient Mongol. All it needs is hair!"

I knew he meant *fur*, but I didn't correct him. I just laughed, and enjoyed being able to finally share Paris's charms with someone.

From our vantage point, we could see right into the Dôme's terrace across the way. "I know what we can do next," I said, after licking the last drop of ice cream off my long spoon. "We can cross the street and have something else in the Dôme. I'll pay this time." I watched George retrieve a last dribble of strawberry ice cream and waited for his reply.

It took a few moments. First, he dropped his spoon with a clink into the glass, and then he slowly dabbed his lips with his napkin. Finally, he said, "All right, but I will pay."

"No. My idea, my treat."

"I must insist, Haley."

I studied him as he removed his wallet and pulled out a bill. Old-fashioned type. Then I shrugged. "Okay."

So, like Hemingway and company of old, we barhopped across the street to the Dôme, where I ordered a coffee in order to indebt myself as little as possible to George. I liked French-style espresso. The demitassed portion was small, but concentrated and rich, and it was the cheapest thing on the menu—the minimum you could order in a café and still have rights to camp there all day, if you wanted.

George opted for tea, and things went silent.

I checked my watch. "If we were like the Roaring Twenties set, we'd be on to cocktails by now. What do you drink in Crete for a fun time?" Serious orbs surveyed me from their wire-rimmed spectacles. "Greek coffee...I don't drink alcohol."

"Oh."

For a second he lowered his eyes. Then they shot back up. "I know Greek food though..."

"Yeah? I've tried gyros."

"My uncle makes that!"

"I'll have to try your restaurant."

"Where do you study?" he asked me, out of the blue.

"The Alliance Française, over by the café where we met."

"Everyday until this time?"

"Except weekends."

"Then I hope to see you again in the neighborhood. My house is in boulevard Raspail. Where do you live?"

Hang on, I said to myself. How did this sad, timid kid get so bold all of a sudden? I made my answer as vague as possible. "In the Fifth."

"The Fifth arrondissement?"

"Uhuh."

"This is interesting," he said, his smile swelling. "I live in the Sixth and work in the Fifth, and you live in the Fifth and study in the Sixth!"

Quite a coincidence. And that, I decided, was the only personal thing this moody *mec* would know about me.

I slapped a hand on my book. "Speaking of studying..."

"I was thinking of dinner," George said. "Would you come with me this evening?" His eyes had turned to burning coals. I was stunned by the about-face and needed time to figure out a way to let him down.

He leaned toward me. "I can come for you. You choose the hour. A restaurant of your choosing too—"

"There's no way tonight. I'm already busy..."

"Tomorrow evening then?"

"...Difficult. There's this project I have to do for school..."

"You don't like my company." The statement came low, like an ominous breeze, and had a stronger impact than if he had roared at me.

I felt helpless and tried to lean back without appearing offensive. "Of course I like your company. Let me come to your restaurant first. Meet your family and all..."

"I am not sure they would welcome you." Same soft, even tone, same burning look.

The contrast within him rattled me and I stared at my cup. When I looked up, the burning coals were spent, and his eyes began to water.

Nom de Dieu! I thought he might start to weep. "I'll...I'll come to your restaurant..."

George began to edge out of his seat. He rose stiffly.

"Place Saint-Michel, right?" I asked. "Your restaurant?"

For an answer, I received the back of George's head and its short-cropped black hair, shaved up the back and sides. Old-fashioned there too, I thought distractedly, as I gaped at his departing back.

"Why do you give crackpots like that the time of day?" Kevin asked over the phone. On he blathered, warning me that Paris was full of predators and that I had better be a lot more careful and discriminating about whom I chatted up in cafés (as if I were the one who always started these conversations!).

"Really." I was sitting on the little wooden bench in my hotel lobby's phone booth. The telephone booth had a matching wooden door with a peek-window and a small counter hosting the grey telephone, whose mechanical counter ticked off the minutes at audible intervals—my minutes.

"Forgotten how we met?" I asked. "According to your advice, I should never have given *you* the time of day."

"That's different. We come from similar cultures. But never mind. There's a new disco I want to take you to. The Cool Tattoo over in the Marais. And don't worry, it's not just for British and Americans. French go there too."

After I hung up I wished I hadn't told Kevin about George. How could I expect anyone to fathom an encounter I couldn't make heads or tails of myself?

George's bizarre behavior continued to mystify me, but I managed to shake off those thoughts and substitute them with Kevin's news. Cool Tattoo: what kind of name was that? The only people I imagined with tattoos were sailors. I hoped Kevin would prove right, and that I'd meet some French people in this new disco.

The Cool Tattoo was located in the Marais, a Right Bank neighborhood I hadn't investigated yet. So the next afternoon I decided to explore the area before our date. I had heard about a museum there devoted to the history of Paris. Before I could find it, though, I discovered a scene that made me think I wasn't even in the city.

I saw men in yarmulkes. Men with beards, black hats and suits, with ringlets bouncing aside their cheeks. They all bustled through the lanes, seeming quite at home—because they were. I had stumbled onto the Jewish quarter of Paris. As I laced through the thread-narrow streets, my head rotated like a beacon light, observing every little detail: balconies, roofs, a green car...until I slammed right into an Orthodox Jew in person. His hat flew off, and he squatted in his black suit to retrieve it. I stood there paralyzed, as if I'd run down a priest. When he sprang up, he only reached my shoulder, and his red curls were still bobbing.

He adjusted his black-framed glasses and spread his hands in a plea. "You must pay attention when walking!"

"I know," I said. Then I went on, just to keep my French running. "Sorry, but I was distracted by this strange green car that looked like an insect—"

"The old Citroën! I saw it too—a '69 DS. It would turn anyone's head!"

"Actually, I came here to see the Musée Carnavalet..."

"Splendid museum. Not far, and there's an excellent café in the vicinity. Let me show you."

Whatever made his friendly attitude appear—talk of the car, my interest in Paris, my accent—I decided to let him be my guide.

That evening, when I shared my day with Kevin, I skipped the encounter with the little Orthodox Jew.

On the surface, you would think the Cool Tattoo dated back to the nineteenth century. It held hard and fast to the law Professor Bertalot had told us about: businesses could remodel a building's interior, but they could not touch Paris's beige limestone, balconied façades. History is sacrosanct in France, and I was grateful. Then I entered the Cool Tattoo and witnessed the law's inverse.

Posters of Andy Warhol's Marilyn Monroe and Campbell's soup plastered the walls, and a sea of youths crowded the place dressed in the usual bellbottoms and vests, platform heels and miniskirts. Some lounged about on low, spongy-orange couches fronted by yellow plastic tables, while others stood in pods. They jabbered non-stop in English, yelling to compete with a booming Bee Gees record. I thought I'd been transported to New York or Los Angeles.

Kevin and I found a vacant sofa and sank into it. Then we marked our territory with Kevin's pullover sweater and got up to dance. What else could you do in a place like that?

Except, the dancing didn't go too well. A damned strobe light lit the disco floor and its swirling flashes started making me seasick. Light and shadow alternated, simulating changes in speed that sent my equilibrium into a storm. I refused to be a killjoy and endured it, the way I always did at home. But why on earth had the torture device made the journey all the way across the Atlantic?

Even worse, the Cool Tattoo's dance floor had the dimensions of a closet. So by the time the DJ with an afro unleashed the Cars' "Let's Go," I was dizzy and moving too close to my fellow dancers. I almost hit somebody on my left who advanced like a jerking movie reel. So I shifted, and instead rammed a girl on the right.

After "Let's Go," I retreated. I let Kevin scurry off to get us a drink and plunked myself on our sofa. I let my head flop back on the cushions and my eyes close to calm the turbulent sea in me. My ears stayed alert for a stray French word, but no such luck.

I must have sat that way for twenty minutes, and was about to call it quits when Kevin finally returned. Only he wasn't alone, and I shot out of my slouch.

"Sasha," Kevin said to the beaming girl with bobbed-brown hair, "meet Haley." He grinned, and they both dropped onto the couch, Kevin in the middle. "Sasha's from New York."

"*Sasha*," I said, mustering a bit of cheer from my nauseated being. "Isn't that short for Alexander?"

"Alexandra in my case. Alexandra Rifkin," she said in a pleasant voice. "Were you named after Hayley Mills, by chance?"

"Sasha's only been in Paris a couple of weeks," Kevin said, before I could express a big fat *No!* "I told her we'd take her under our wing."

Great, another Anglophone. I sighed inwardly, and then chastised myself for lack of charity.

"Kevin's very generous and considerate," said Sasha, with a merry smile.

"Nonsense, I've always wanted to add a New Yorker to my list of mates."

"So, you're finding your way around Paris all right?" I asked Sasha, in hopes of receiving a solid *yes*.

"Sort of. Outside of my hotel most people don't speak English. But I've made it here twice at least." Her arms swept out as if to give the disco a big hug.

"Twice," I echoed flatly.

"Well," she said, "it's not Studio 54, but it'll do for now."

"Studio 54—you've got in there!?" The way Kevin gasped, you'd think Sasha had been invited to the White House.

Her eyes gleamed a catlike golden-brown. She lifted one dark brow, the kind that are thicker above the eyes near the nose, and then arch up and out, thinner. "Sure," she answered. "You just have to know the right people."

"And they would be...?" said Kevin.

She shrugged. "John and Caroline Kennedy, to name a couple."

"Wow!"

"No big deal," said Sasha. "Their mother works at the same publishing house as mine."

Don't choke on that beer, Kevin, I said to myself. She's only been in the City of Light two weeks and has already rushed twice to this American mock-up. "Interesting," I said, trying to sound nonchalant. "What are you doing in Paris?"

"Studying cuisine at the Cordon Bleu. Kevin says you're at the Alliance Française."

So, they had already become chums at the bar. "Did he tell you he works at Shakespeare and Company?" I asked.

"Yeah, cool, isn't it!"

"I haven't told either of you what I really want to do," Kevin said. "What I *plan* on doing."

We peered at him.

"Eventually," he drawled out, "I'm going to buy or lease a place like this. Start my own club. Call it The Roundabout, or something more clever."

"Be sure and let me know when it opens," said Sasha. "I'll be the first one in the door!"

I forced a gracious smile at Sasha and then turned to Kevin. "Sounds like something you'd be good at." I couldn't think of anything else to say, so I sat back. Then something distracted me. The DJ was finally playing a French song. I concentrated, trying to block out the noise.

"Do either of you know this song?" I asked.

"It's French," Kevin said. "Never heard it before."

Sasha shook her head.

I listened hard. A bass voice sang, *Quand on a du feu,* I was almost certain. It meant, "When you have a light," like a match or a lighter. Catchy melody, I thought, before the rest was sucked into the whirlpool of disco noise.

Kevin and Sasha blabbered away, with Sasha still prating on about Studio-frigging-54 and how she had witnessed America's most darling two Kennedys sniff coke. That led to the story of how she happened to collide with Jackie Onassis at the publishing house where the American icon and Sasha's mother worked as editors. Sasha was in the building and had to go to the bathroom.

"I hauled into the ladies room with a stack of books my mom wanted delivered to the car. I got in the door, but the books blocked my view of feet under the stalls. So I dumped them on a table and charged into a stall. Guess whose?"

Kevin and I exchanged looks.

Sasha smiled, no doubt to prolong the effect of her pause. "Jackie O's!" she finally said. "I hit her square in the face with the door. Evidently, she'd just unlatched it. Boy, did she ever tear me to shreds! I thought she'd call the police! I tell you, you don't wanna screw with her!"

I have to admit I found the story funny...providing it was true.

"Yeah," Sasha dragged out, "she really gave me hell, especially since I practically threw her out of the stall."

Kevin and I stared at her.

"I had to go bad!"

"Hey," I finally spoke up. "Why's this place called Cool Tattoo?"

She pointed toward the disco floor. "Because you can get tattooed in the back, behind that curtain. I almost got one last time I was here."

Kevin's eyes shifted from the curtain to Sasha. "And this time?"

"Well...I'd like to try it..."

Her hesitation left the door open and I barged right in. "*Try* one? They're permanent."

Kevin frowned at me. "Don't be a wet blanket, Haley."

"She's not," Sasha said. "I've considered that." Then she lowered her voice. "But, I've got this super idea for a tattoo—nothing big or gaudy..."

We watched her.

"Yes, go on," Kevin said.

"It's a secret. You'll have to wait and see."

"Well, get on with it!" said Kevin. "Have another drink, it'll help you take the leap. Haley, you could use another one too—get out of your head!"

I ignored him, just as he ignored my full glass of beer sitting on the little yellow table in front of me.

Sasha smiled at him and lightly licked her lips. "Thanks, but I don't need a drink to make up my mind. A little company would be appreciated, though."

Their eyes met. "Company...?" Kevin said. "You want me to do it too?"

"Definitely." She crossed her arms and gazed at him with wry cat eyes.

Kevin stiffened. He tossed back his remaining ale and slammed the glass on the plastic table. "I'm in." Then his eyes widened. "Hang on, I don't know what kind of bloody tattoo to get!"

Sasha hooked his arm. "You'll think of something. Come on!"

Out of convenience, I could say Kevin and Sasha didn't even toss me a backward glance. Then I could have dismissed them from my company all together. But that's not what happened. They both sent me inviting looks, called my name in unison and urged me to follow. I just nodded and told them to go on without me. And they did.

I sat for a while, trying to decide whether I really was a wet blanket. Why didn't I go with them, if only to watch? Because I loathed the idea of following Sasha like a puppy dog. Age-wise she had a couple of years on me, but with only two weeks of Paris behind her, was I to let *her*, an *American*, take the lead for a stupid thing like a tattoo?

Anger sunk its claws into me. Then it mutated and I started feeling down, enveloped by the *cafard*. Nothing worse than not getting on with people. I tried to dismiss the whole business. The loud speakers were belting out the Bee Gees again. I watched the dancers in their strobe-lit spasms. Anger started to creep back. Then...

Ouais, I heard. That slack, casual French form of *oui*. No one said it in school, but young people cast it around the cafés. Which meant...

With a bound, I was on my feet, staring at a French trio behind my couch. Two men and a woman in their early thirties, or so, stood chatting. One of them would utter a word or two and then let out a breathy, bored *pfff*, a French way to express indifference or disdain. A natural reaction to this place, I thought.

The three of them radiated style, the men in suits with wide lapels and flared trousers, the woman in a tight white sweater and black miniskirt that seemed to melt over her hips. They might have just stepped out of *Vogue*, and I felt painfully un-chic in my ordinary bell-bottom jeans and matching navy-blue, boat-neck tee shirt. I looked down at the only thing stylish about me—my blue suede shoes.

And yet, what did I have to lose? *"Excusez-moi,"* I started, unsheathing my best French. "I was trying to find something different to drink." I nodded at the lone girl's glass and the pinkish-gold liquid that sparkled in it. "Is that good?"

"Papaya juice, gin, and champagne," she said. "Quite good."

"That's because it's the only thing here not American," said one of her male friends.

"You're not American, are you?" asked the other *mec*, looking worried.

"Well...never mind," I said to reassure them. "I'm sick of this place too."

"Why not have a drink with us?" asked the considerate man.

"Or better yet, a smoke outside," the confident guy suggested, eyes sparkling with a kind of irony.

"Mmm..." said the girl.

I scanned the bar: smoky as green wood burning in a fireplace with the damper down. Why bother to step outside? I eyed the three of them again. "Oh," I said, when it finally hit me.

"*Ouais*," said the confident one. "And after that who knows?"

I glanced at the kinder fellow, who shot me a wide-eyed grin, brows bouncing up and down. Then I caught the girl's shrewd smile.

"All right," I said. Their plan had to be better than waiting for Kevin and Sasha. Or going home alone.

I had sworn off marijuana some years earlier. Cannabis, as the French call it, had almost gotten me killed, an experience that culminated with my friend falling out of the car she was driving and I having to leap over to steer it off the road. Thank God for bench seats.

Here, however, I wouldn't have to drive anywhere, and if I didn't look chic tonight, I could at least act cool in front of these sophisticated types.

So we filed out of the Cool Tattoo and over to a little side street, some dead-end *ruelle* no bigger than an alley. Not a human face in sight. Only a scrawny cat that prowled in and out between parked cars.

I accepted the second hit off the joint, and my throat filled with fire. Tears battled their way out, and I only hoped the night would veil them.

"Are you all right?" the nice *mec* asked.

"*Oui, oui, bien sûr*," I squeaked, strangling a cough. Jesus, I felt like a little kid who sneaks a sip from someone's abandoned glass of whiskey and receives a kick in surprise.

Funny, what can pop into your mind at moments like these. My pooling eyes made me think of George, the Greek from Crete. Eyes watered easily; maybe he hadn't been crying after all.

The next time the joint came round, I tried to inhale more air than smoke, and when the cocky guy finally stamped out the roach, I indulged in a silent sigh.

"We could go back to my place now," he proposed. "The car's right around the corner."

Scenarios looped through my head. We would speak French all evening...listen to French music...laugh...

Then the cat yowled from the gutter. A car had started up, and its refracted lights emanated from the feline's eyes. I flinched.

"Come with us!" the friendly *mec* said. "It'll make a proper group of two guys and two girls."

"*Ouais*," said the woman, aiming a seductive smile at me. "We'll open some champagne..."

I watched the three of them. They all looked so eager. And the woman seemed to exude sex. "I don't know...I'll have to tell my friends back at the disco..."

"*Faut faire confiance*," said the confident *mec*, with a rakish tilt of the head.

Confiance? Somehow, he didn't make me feel very *trusting*.

"*Y a rien à craindre, ma petite*," said the woman. She stepped closer, and I smelled the scent of perfume mingled with herb.

Nothing to fear...?

All three pairs of eyes glinted in the silver moonlight, and I shivered. August had arrived, chilly evenings in its train. I rubbed my bare arms.

"You're cold," said the woman, in a sensuous voice. In another flowing step, she reached me and started rubbing my shoulders with soft, slow caresses. "Come with us. Our car's not ten paces away."

Monsieur Confident watched us with a wolf smile. The humble fellow grinned and nodded at me. Then the images escalated. Their pale, moon-lit faces became the spot-lit tapestry characters from the Louvre. Their grins gleamed against the shadowy night, making me shudder. Must be the dope, I thought, as I glanced around the blind backstreet. No one but us. Even the cat had disappeared.

The *mecs* stayed silent, and the woman's soft, fine-boned hand lingered on my arm. Probably a calculated move, entrusting me to their girlfriend.

Her warm whisper penetrated my ear. "Come get warm, *chérie*, with a nice relaxing drink."

Somehow I didn't have the strength to back away. I felt weak and rubbery, as if under a spell.

Again, I resorted to Kevin and Sasha. "I really shouldn't abandon my friends..."

"Ooh," said the kind fellow, face drooping into a sort of amused disappointment.

The woman gave my arm a feathery tickle and then released it.

"Sorry, I've got to get back," I said.

The *mec* with the wolf smile shot me a smirk. "Don't be so bourgeois. This is Paris!"

Bourgeois: is that what we Anglos amounted to? My face burned from ear to ear, and I only hoped the night covered my embarrassment. "*Au revoir,*" I said, and turned away from them.

That was the worst—having to show them my back. Certain, as I walked away, that they were mocking me—the provincial American.

Cooler days and nights marked not the only change in August. The shift in air ushered in something rather unexpected as well. One morning I checked into my grammar class at the Alliance Française and found a message waiting for me.

"For you, Mademoiselle," said my teacher, waiving a white piece of paper without looking at me. The sloppy, hippy *mec* didn't even bother rising from his slouch.

I sat down at my wooden desk, unfolded the note and read: *A message awaits you at the front desk.*

Jeez, I complained to myself, they could have sent it directly here. I hadn't time to retrieve it right away, so throughout class I speculated on its contents. I even lost my place when grammar *mec* called on me to express a hypothetical situation in French: *in the case that...*

"*Pardon*," I said, surprised.

He shot me a smirk, strings of blond hair hanging over one eye. The Italian girl next to me pointed to the correct place in my text, and I recovered. As soon as class ended, I scooted out of the room, down the hall, and over to the front desk.

"Ah, Mademoiselle Morgan," said the middle-aged secretary, after I presented the paper to her. "You've had a visitor. A certain monsieur called *Georges* Abdi."

The French pronunciation of 'George' disconcerted me, and her officious frown set against a flame of red hair didn't help either. I only managed to squint back.

"He said you knew him...speaks with an accent, maybe Greek."

I almost slapped my forehead. "*Oui, oui, oui !*" I said. "I've met him...uh..."

When I didn't go on, Madame's French came hammering: "He declined to reveal the nature of his visit. Expressed he would call on you again. He even asked for your address. Of course, we don't produce such information..." She shook her head and gave me a sharp, suspicious look.

"*Ah bon, très bien—merci, madame, merci!*" I repeated, backing away with a weak smile.

School had ended, and I exited the building mystified. Why in the world had George come to my school? The Alliance Française was the only reference point I had let slip during our strange encounter, and he had remembered it. What did he want?

I couldn't provide an answer, so I took off walking, no aim other than to dismiss the bizarre business. I managed to do that, and yet I still found the air in the city mutating in a mysterious, intangible way. The notes of the symphony that was my Paris slid from major to minor, with variations of sevenths. That's the only way I can describe the unease and melancholy seeping into me.

Part of my discomfort consisted of the Sasha-Kevin duo. Whenever I saw Kevin anymore, Sasha the blowhard tagged along. The Anglophonic circle wore down my patience. I wanted French friends, people to talk to and who could perhaps help me establish myself here, so I could make something of myself in the city I loved. No one could accuse me of not trying. According to Kevin, I was *too* outgoing. Yet every one of my French encounters had fallen flat, and I felt like a hamster on its play-wheel.

My wanderings took me to the Right Bank, where Paris finally began to work its old magic on me. Something about those magnificent boulevards and avenues always pulled me out of a dark mood, or transformed it. That's what happened when I hit the avenue de l'Opéra. The street leading to the famous opera house opened to me like a time portal and I felt a yearning for Paris's past. Sure, cars buzzed up and down the wide, regal thoroughfare, yet my imagination transformed them into horse-drawn coaches, clip-clopping up and down the rain-damp road of an impressionist painting. The stately, stone buildings with their august-grey roofs and frilly wrought-iron balconies still stood from those turn-of-the-century days. And again it seemed I had lived here once upon a time; only the essence of La Belle Epoque hovered out of my reach, on a different plane.

Gliding on a different plane, but almost touching...yes, that's what it felt like. I experienced something like it at home when I would examine 1950s black-and-white photos of my parents. One snapshot showed them smiling in a restaurant, accompanied by the typical cocktails and filterless cigarettes of the time. A subtle, mysterious smile floated from my father who was dressed in a double-breasted suit, half a cufflink peeking out from his left sleeve. Who knows what that smile meant or what the man was all about? That's why I couldn't wring out a tear for him or my mother. I didn't remember them and had never known them. How could I feel the loss of something I never remembered having? Was I supposed to sob over the death of my great-great-grandfather? No difference...well, almost.

The Opera reared gigantic as I closed in. The imposing creation expressed a clutter of architectural styles—Roman arches, Corinthian columns, winged-victory statues—and sat at the top of about ten cement steps. After climbing them, I halted to scan the tall wooden doors peaked with short glass panels.

This was the first time I had approached the iconic Opéra and didn't know exactly how to proceed. So I gave a tug at one of the massive doors to see if it was locked. It opened, and I walked into a shadowy lobby. I stood alone on a cold marble floor and faced four statues, white and marble-looking themselves. Handel, Gluck, Lully, and Rameau, I discovered once I read their name plates. Upon inspecting these four gods of classical music, I stood back to take in the whole scene, and that's when I began to notice how dark the lobby was, and that only I and the wigged titans occupied it. I backed up again and hunched my shoulders. The shadows seemed to hover closer, creeping up on me like black fog. The darkness magnified the statues' whiteness, and Lully's frozen frown intensified, snarly and aggressive. I knew it had to be my imagination, but I couldn't help it: Lully seemed ready to step down from his pedestal. A painful constriction started to grip my chest and I had to look away. I turned, and without looking back, I fled, my steps echoing on the marble floor, the heavy wooden door thudding shut behind me.

Back on the steps, I devoured the cool air, inhaling greedily, heart pounding. I descended to the sidewalk, still breathing hard. So, the curious sensation I had experienced in the Louvre was *not* a fluke—more like a regression, almost as if I were six years old again and scared of the dark. Frightened of some monster. I shivered. Where the hell had this thing come from and what was I to make of it?

I shook my head and looked skyward, trying to bask in a spot of tepid sunshine, although the pale sun did little more than tinge the vault a whitish-grey. Whatever new nickname Paris might acquire in the future, it would never be City of Sunny Skies. To distract myself, I thought of what Professor Bertalot had told us about the City of Light. That the nickname came about from the spaciousness created with Baron Haussmann's overhaul of streets and architecture in the mid-1800s. Wide boulevards replaced many narrow, dark lanes to let in simple daylight. Buildings took on a lightness of shape and angles...

The digression was working, and I started feeling lighter myself. The strange and ominous phenomenon that had visited me twice now stuck to the back of my mind, but I couldn't crack it so I threw up my hands and headed east. Plane trees bordered the boulevard like green troops lined up for review.

A green city bus whistled by, and its windy wake lifted the summer leaves in a rustle. A breeze followed, keeping them astir. Restless, like me.

I checked a street plaque on the side of a building. The same boulevard was changing names almost every block. Buildings became plainer. They lacked sculpture, though they still were stamped with signature grey roofs and imaginative ironwork. It seemed I had entered a territory devoid of anything resembling a tourist attraction, not even a rack of postcards at the newspaper kiosks.

Suddenly, a great alien monument appeared in the middle of the intersection, startling me by its sheer unexpectedness: a huge sandstone arch dedicated to Louis XIV. The chiseled Sun King sat near the top on horseback, dressed as an ancient Roman, yet identifiable by the long curly wig cascading over his shoulders. About a block later, another megalithic arch materialized. On this one Louis XIV played the Homeric hero, disrobed with sword in hand, still preserved from anonymity by his flowing wig. Not one of these monuments had I seen on the postcards of tourist Paris. I turned left and plunged north, farther and farther from the city's center, thrill of the unknown urging me on. I welcomed the sensation, the slight tickle of fear that I could get lost. Better the unknown that I would eventually face, than an intermittent phobia I could do nothing about.

As I meandered along, I noticed that people spoke less French and more...Arabic, it had to be. Yes, I had ended up in the northern Arab neighborhoods where I didn't understand a word or a gesture. Speech sounded like a rush of consonants with no vowels. Spicy smells swirled in the air, sweet and woody, like edible incense. I saw *couscous* stamped on restaurant marquees in French. Complexions got darker, many men with mustaches and heavy eyebrows, but the dress remained French. For some reason, George popped into my head again. He wasn't Arab, but his black hair and swarthiness led people to mistake him for Iranian. I couldn't clear my mind of his sad, watery eyes, much less his visit to the Alliance Française in search of me.

Mine did not amount to the average tourist experience, which made me happy that I no longer counted as a visitor. Paris had started to absorb me as part of the living, morphing city, for good...or otherwise. Did my strange "art terror" also make up part of the city that had swallowed me up? I didn't know...

Umph! Someone ran into me, or I him.

A man with a black beard and arms full of packages stood glaring at me.

"*Excusez-moi,*" I muttered.

He smiled sourly and looked me up and down, without saying a word. He didn't even bother to back out of my personal space—just stood there staring at me, like I was supposed to do something.

"*Excusez-moi*," I said again, and shifted out of his way to continue along my path. His eyes turned to follow me, and as I walked away, I peeked back and found his black eyes still nailing me with disdain. *Creep*, I thought. Well, maybe I didn't quite feel at home here, in this part of Paris...

With that in mind, I decided to hook right and snake back south. To where the aroma of fried foods dominated the air. Crêpes, croques, fries, omelets—cooked and eaten on the sidewalks of *my* Paris.

The return to the river reminded me of the present. Again, Sasha and Kevin intruded on my thoughts—they and their tattoos, the idiots! Sasha now sported a miniature Arc de Triomphe engraved discreetly on the underside of her knee. Kevin, on the other hand, had the macho in him stamped right on the inside of his bicep—a little obelisk, mimicking the towering Egyptian monument in the middle of Place de la Concorde. A phallic symbol if I ever saw one, to go with Sasha's arch. Their inside joke didn't fool me.

I have to confess something about Sasha, though. She liked to show off, and that bugged me, but she hadn't turned out the snobbish Manhattanite I had feared...or *wanted* her to be, which would have given me excellent reason to reject her company. As of now, for better or worse, I continued to tolerate her.

At twilight I reached my side of the Seine. The mix of melancholy and nostalgia had returned to linger in me, and I cut over to the back streets near the Panthéon to prolong the mood, to feel the past, La Belle Epoque, mesh with the city's limestone buildings. I slipped into a tiny side street next to the Sorbonne and just trailed along, every so often brushing my fingers against the Sorbonne's body of cool, smooth stone. Claude Debussy's "Sounds and Scents Swirl in the Evening Air" began to play in my mind, and the echoing piano chords filled me with another sensation of déjà vu. Yes, I had to have heard the piece at the turn of the century, right here in this little *ruelle*.

I left the Sorbonne and engaged a hilly, serpentine old lane about as wide as a ruler. It probably hadn't changed since Debussy's time. Houses, crowded and crooked, emitted a golden glow: modern light today; fire and gaslight a hundred years ago. A dog barked from a doorway on the darkening sidewalk opposite me. "*Silence!*" followed from a window. I smiled at sounds that could just as likely have wafted through the air a hundred years ago. Then, shivering from the chill left by the fleeing sun, I headed back to my hotel with only thoughts of Debussy to keep me company.

2: El Dorado on the Water

Odéon was one of my favorite Left-Bank neighborhoods...ordinarily. I loved its cinemas, the modern multiplexes the quarter offered. I couldn't wait to sink into one of those black-leather easy chairs and buy a box of my favorite caramels from the candy salesgirl who covered the auditorium on foot before the film like a peanut vendor at a baseball game. After that, I would relax and enjoy the show...usually.

Normally I didn't even mind standing in line for my ticket because it gave me a chance to check out one of my favorite statues—Georges Jacques Danton. Star of the neighborhood, his statue stood obscured by the dense leaves of Paris's ubiquitous plane trees. I had to maneuver under them just to have a gaze at the hero of the French Revolution. There he posed on his plinth, feet planted widely apart, arm sweeping out to make some dramatic point. In summer the Noble Man's black statue was often ignobly striped white with pigeon goo. Poor Danton. Though if he were alive, pigeon droppings would be the least of his worries. After all, the guillotine awaited him.

I was not slated for the guillotine today, but I had my worries. I tried distracting myself by rereading the engravings on Danton's pedestal before I stepped into line at the cinema complex behind it. I tried contemplating one of the great man's sayings, "After bread, education is the first need of the people," but I couldn't concentrate. As much as I loved going to the movies alone, this particular evening I should not have been solo. Kevin, Sasha, and I, had planned to go together.

It started with a perfectly normal prelude to a movie and dinner. We sat innocently sipping coffee on a café veranda, the three of us hunched together, poring over a *Pariscope* for movie times and locations.

Kevin proposed the Champs-Elysées and a movie in English. A hamburger would follow at the nearby Pub Winston Churchill and crown his evening brilliantly. Sasha seconded it and couldn't wait to see this new Anglo restaurant where she could swim in burgers and beer.

I kept my eyes on the Pariscope. I flipped through the little magazine with determined fingers, panning for a French film they might find acceptable. To change the subject, I complained about the coffee and pointed out how much better I'd found it in that café in the Marais where the little Orthodox Jew had led me after we collided on the sidewalk. "Great coffee," I emphasized, after telling the story.

Sasha cackled. "You didn't see him coming because he probably only came up to your boobs!"

"About my shoulder, really," I said, proud of my anecdote.

"Whatever," she said. "He was a real *mensch*, showing you the sights."

Sasha was Jewish herself and loved displaying her knowledge of Yiddish. I had to admit it amused me when I didn't think she was showing off.

Kevin always got a kick out of the colorful lingo. This time, however, he neither laughed nor smiled, and I could see the pink skin under his freckles turning red.

When he spoke, his voice was cool and even. "You let him guide you around the Marais?"

I shrugged. "It patched up an awkward situation. He could've cursed me out for slamming into him."

"Well, perhaps he should have."

"...What?"

Kevin leaned in. "He should have cursed you out, then maybe, *just maybe*, you'd think twice before chatting up foreign blokes you don't know—on the street of all places!"

Sasha intervened. "Hey you two, we've got a movie to pick out..."

Kevin mowed on. "I can't believe how many times this happens! I mean, is that your goal? To rack up a kilometric list of *guys* to brag about when you're back in America?" With a disgusted grimace, he flopped back in his chair.

Sasha sat back, spying us with thoughtful eyes.

I sighed, and with as much disdain as possible said, "No, bragging about conquests is what you *blokes* do!" I shoved my demitasse forward and pushed my chair back. "Sasha, why don't you go on to the movies on the Champs-Elysées. I'm going to see something somewhere else." With that, I left the café, ducked into the nearest metro, and headed for Odéon.

Once I bought my ticket and got seated I still couldn't focus. That's my problem. When I blow up, everything around me goes blurry. My mind pushes everything out, including the things in my best interest or those I ordinarily love.

First, I spaced out during the Darty ad. Darty specializes in appliances and electronics, and its honking blue and yellow cartoon truck—DARTY stamped on it in big, thick red letters—zooms to rescue people with appliance troubles. That spunky little truck made its appearance before every movie I ever saw in Paris, but this evening it drove right across the screen, and I barely noticed it.

I stewed straight into the film, my mind a churning cement truck that turned my row with Kevin over and over. The French language in the movie, so beneficial to me, went flying to the wind, and because I couldn't concentrate on the dialogue I lost the plot as well.

After the movie wound down and the house lights rose, I started whipping myself for not canning my resentment of Kevin for the duration of the film. Furious, I reached down to yank my purse off the plush-carpet floor.

It wasn't there...

Perplexity, and then panic overrode my anger. I looked under my seat and checked under those nearby. Nothing. My mind raced for a way out—a benign mix up?—in vain. Along with my purse, my passport, traveler's checks, and French francs had vanished. I rubbed my forehead as if my tense fingers could reach right through my skull and shake my brain for an answer.

Nowhere else to search. *This can't be happening*! A brisk stride up the aisle through the auditorium door landed me in the lobby. I scanned the milling crowd. Who had stolen my purse and when? Certainly no one here; the thief had to be long gone. I sighed and let my shoulders sag. Then I took a deep breath, drew myself back up, and approached the only man in the place wearing a tie. A young guy, no older than me, he stood talking to the ticket taker. I gauged his warm smile as a good sign and edged closer, waiting for a lull in their conversation. He turned to me, the residual of a laugh animating his eyes.

"Is there something I can do for you?"

"Someone stole my purse," I said in nervous French.

"Where?" His urgent tone heartened me. "In the auditorium?"

I nodded desperately. "I had it on the floor next to my seat. When the movie ended, it was gone!"

He sent one usher to scour the auditorium and another outside. I didn't expect my purse to materialize, but things were moving forward and I relaxed a little.

He had just told me his name, Luc Perri, when an employee came sailing back inside. I couldn't believe it, but there I saw it in her hand—my purse! It had ended up in a trash bin behind the cinema. I pounced on it—and soon lost hope again. No money, no traveler's checks, no passport. I almost wanted to fling it back in the trash, when...I spotted my picture. For some reason, the thief had left my student identification card.

"That's very fortunate," Luc, the manager, said. "With at least one form of I. D. , I believe you can replace the others. You'll have to go to the bank for your traveler's checks. Of course, you'll have to get a photo and take it to the embassy for a new passport—you're American, aren't you?"

Overwhelmed by the tasks in front of me, all I did was nod at him. I didn't even care that my accent had again given me away.

"I can help you," he said. "Take you to the bank and things—disgraceful, this happening here in the cinema. I could pick you up tomorrow morning...?"

I felt like a sheep. I'm not even sure I kept my mouth closed; it could have been hanging open as wide as my eyes. Then my mind snapped to attention. *This matter could be taken care of much more smoothly with a Parisian showing me the ropes, especially a kind and capable fellow like this manager.* So I gave Luc Perri my address and we established a rendezvous for the next day. My French was swimming along, performing butterflies and backstrokes, when a man entered the lobby, bypassed the ticket taker, and came straight to us.

"Thierry," Luc said. "This is Haley. She's an American who's had her purse stolen here."

"Ah, what rotten luck," said the new *mec* who looked about Luc's age but surpassed both him and me in height by about a head. "Have you reported it?"

"Not yet. I'm on shift through the last showing. Maybe you could accompany Haley (he pronounced it Ailý) to the commissariat."

Just noticing that pronunciation detail made me lose the thread of the conversation. "*Pardon?*" I said, frustrated.

"Oh, sorry," Thierry said, and commenced to speak almost flawless English. "My friend Luc asked me to accompany you to the police station to make a complaint...a report, I mean. In France it's the opposite of the States. There, the police come to you. Here, you go to the police."

I smiled at both of them. Given a mess like this, I couldn't believe my luck.

"*Bon*," said Luc, returning to French. "I'll finish up here. Come back when you've taken care of the police business."

During our walk to the police commissariat, I asked Thierry where he had learned to speak English so well.

"I studied it in school. Then I went to Michigan where I was able to practice it. I spent three months there with some American friends, hiking, swimming, kayaking on the lake—a real blast!"

A real blast, I repeated to myself, with a sting of envy. The *mec* even knew slang. I would have to do better with French, I decided. No reason not to learn it better than Thierry had English, what with me living here.

We sat in the stuffy, smoky commissariat of the Sixth arrondissement for practically an eternity. First, we waited on a bench in the lobby. Then we moved into a policeman's office. Thierry blithely translated as the officer tapped his typewriter keys with two yellow, nicotine-stained fingers. A filter-less cigarette dangled from his lips.

Finally, I squared my shoulders and plunged in with my own French. I could understand almost everything, especially since the cop kept repeating his questions. By the time he lit his third cigarette, the report came rolling out of the typewriter. Amazing, with all his squinting against the smoke he could see what he'd pecked out. Combine that with the blowing and flicking of fallen ash—off the typewriter, off his lap—it was a miracle we got out of there at all.

He hacked up some phlegm as he herded us out of his office. "Of course, Mademoiselle, the chances of finding your possessions are remote."

"*Bien sûr*," I answered, in cynical agreement.

"There are a lot of these thefts," said Thierry afterwards, enunciating *these thefts*, no doubt to make his th's sound right. "So the police get a little jaded about the procedure. But at least you have a copy of his report to bring to the American embassy for a new passport."

"I'll be surprised if that desiccated, smoke-cured cop wrote it right. How do you say *desiccated* in French?" I confess, I was trying to test Thierry's mastery of English. A bit base, I know, but I wanted to glean what he had learned in school in addition to his Michigan slang.

"*Desséché*," he fired back.

Thierry had learned plenty, I found out as we killed time in a café waiting for Luc to close the cinema. Thierry had studied Latin, ancient Greek, plus the classical literature of both languages. He had passed his high school *baccalau-*

réat—his "bac"—in these subjects, after a series of exams requiring reading, writing, and orally analyzing ancient texts. Impressive.

"What about Luc?" I asked, as Thierry jotted the Greek alphabet in my notebook—yes, the considerate thief had left me that too.

"He's always preferred business," Thierry said, his pen forming a theta. "He hasn't taken his exams yet." Then his head popped up. "It will be cool, all of us going to the embassy tomorrow. And I thought my American adventure was over after Michigan!"

Not until after midnight did Luc, with Thierry in the back seat, ferry me back to my hotel. After I watched Luc's sporty orange Lancia disappear down rue des Ecoles, the chain of extraordinary events burst in my brain. For a moment I just stood there on the sidewalk, trying to comprehend each individual link. I had made a date with not only one, but two Frenchmen. I had cruised through Paris with them in an Italian sports car. Losing my money and passport? Even that would have dissolved into a lark, if money hadn't already been tight.

The thought grounded me somewhat, and I entered the hotel cursing the low dollar and the expensiveness of Paris. I had almost reached the lobby stairs when the concierge called me to his desk, waving a folded piece of paper. "Message for you, Mademoiselle."

"From who?" I asked, taking the note. I scanned the handwriting and answered myself with a sour "Oh." I started up the stairs, reading while climbing. Small block printing revealed a left-handed apology from Kevin. So he was sorry about the row. And yet he couldn't resist adding a caveat: "Haley, I fear you are not being careful when you befriend strangers like that. With the dangers involved, you could reap some severe consequences."

I wadded the paper into a ragged ball and dropped it into my dinky wastepaper basket as soon as I entered my room. To give Kevin's concern its due, how did he want me to conduct my life in Paris? He condemned me for reaching out to foreigners while all he did was play it safe with English-speaking girls. At least I had made friends with some French people—a pretty trustworthy pair of fellows at that. What had he come to Paris for?

Oh yes, to open a disco for Anglos. Kevin wanted a partner to front some of the money and had even urged me to invest in his "sure thing." As I changed my clothes, I regretted having told him about my trust fund. He knew I couldn't help myself to it until I was twenty-five. Even then, why would I waste it on his operation? He didn't trust me with my choices and judgment so why should I trust him?

Finally, I forced myself to stop pacing and sit on my twin bed with my back propped against the headboard. I'll not be getting back to Kevin Smythe for a long while, I said to myself coolly. With that, I crossed my feet and let my mind drift back to replay my recent adventure.

The next morning Luc and Thierry pulled up in front of my hotel in the orange Lancia. It turned out Luc's father was of Italian origin (hence the surname Perri, an Italian version of Perry), and both father and son fancied Italian cars.

Luc and Thierry insisted I sit in front, while Thierry sprawled out in the coffin-sized back seat, feet up sofa-style. We sped down boulevard Saint-Germain, first to Barclay's bank to replace my traveler's checks and then to a *photomaton* (one of the many curtained booths planted round the city, where you pop a coin in the machine and sit for an instantaneous passport mugshot). Finally, we proceeded across the river to the American embassy in the Eighth arrondissement for the processing of my new passport. Between stops at the bank and the embassy, lunch and café pauses, we devoured the day as if it were a banquet. I would show Kevin consequences!

Another round of fireworks went off the following day when Luc and Thierry invited me for a day trip to Normandy. We all piled into the Lancia and struck north on a road hugged by lush, grassy fields that flashed a deep, rich green under the overcast sky. I guess I'd been cooped up in the beige-and-grey city too long, for the green waxed almost psychedelic.

Luc and Thierry chattered the whole way. I was hooked on scenery.

"*Ça va*, Haley?" Luc would ask every so often. "You're so quiet."

"*Oui, oui, ça va très bien.*" Everything was excellent, I told him. How could anyone here understand my silence, the hypnotic effect of green on a girl used to the sagebrush and tumbleweeds of Nevada?

By the time we reached Honfleur on the English Channel—La Manche, in French—the sun decided to have a peek from the clouds and then retreat once again. The darkness of the sky and sea matched the town's rugged, grey stone buildings, and for some reason the somber mood made me think of money again. So far, Luc and Thierry hadn't let me pay for anything and that didn't sit well. I didn't want them to consider me a charity case.

We stopped at a café across from a dock clustered with merry boats. Crêpes and hard apple cider was the specialty, and I planned to treat my friends to lunch with the fresh money I'd cashed from my new traveler's checks.

"If you like crêpes and cider," Thierry said, "you'll have to try them in Paris where the Breton émigrés make them."

"He ought to know," said Luc, "his grandparents are Bretons and they have an apartment in Montparnasse."

"We'll have to make the most of that," Thierry said.

Luc agreed. "*Absolument*—our next meal will be in a restaurant in Montparnasse."

Thierry raised his dark eyebrows. "I meant more than that."

"What?" Luc asked.

"I'm working on it," Thierry replied. "Give me time."

I filled the pause. "Well, until then, I'd like to pay for this."

"No, another time," Luc said. "We invited you."

"Wait until we're back in Paris," Thierry said.

I didn't argue, for fear of ruining things. I just observed Thierry for a moment and then turned my gaze to Luc. That was the moment I realized he looked like me in a way. Same height and wavy, chestnut-brown hair. He also had round, hazel-green eyes, expressive to the point they could never look impassive. Medium complexion, neither pink, nor olive...we could have passed for brother and sister.

"Come on you two," he suddenly said, slamming the door on my reflections. "We can't waste the whole day here."

That's where Luc and I differed. My language skills benefited plenty from chitchatting in cafés. The sun had come out again and the water sent shimmering reflections of yellow, red, and blue boats to cheer the atmosphere. Why the hurry?

We drove to some grass-covered cliffs. Black-and-grey clouds had returned to marble the sky, and when we exited the car, wind whipped our hair relentlessly. Luc and Thierry led the way on foot toward the sea, over a sandy path bordered by tufts of light-green grass flattened by the gale. We had left charming Honfleur for a lashing of cold, salty wind.

I had barely finished my internal complaint when we reached the edge of the cliff, and I gazed down at the raw beach hundreds of feet below. Its coarse sand lay strewn with black jagged rock. Then I shifted my view down the beach, and almost staggered in disbelief. Something fantastically familiar stood on the shore. A promontory of the cliff stretched seaward and descended into the water like a pillar, rough, thick, and chalk-white.

"Etretat," I whispered in awe. I had seen the arched-white cliff in art books and viewed the original canvas in a Paris museum. But witnessing Claude Monet's actual inspiration in person...well, it was like meeting a famous actor I had admired for years—art translated back into life, a ghost come alive in flesh and blood. Just as Luc and Thierry had appeared out of nowhere and were beginning to flesh out Paris for me.

After we got back to Paris, before my friends left me at the hotel, we established yet another rendezvous for two days hence. As I climbed my three flights of stairs, I speculated on what our next date could hold. I tried forcing myself to appreciate the little hiatus. I could return to school for one thing, having skipped a couple of days.

I didn't give a hoot about cynical Monsieur Grammar's class, but there was dear, grandfatherly Professor Bertalot to consider. I didn't like disappointing such an enthusiastic man or leaving him to wonder, maybe even worry, about my whereabouts. He called on me so often, he might even depend on me, I thought, and he was probably the only local person who cared about me.

My brain was bubbling over with these thoughts when I unlocked my door and punched on the light...

And stared hard...at a room that wasn't mine. The odd-colored bedspread, the alien bottles of beer on the desk, the black wingtips under the chair, all provided disorienting proof.

I backed out quickly and slammed the door. The plaque at the top read: number 35. Dizzily, I verified my key. "33," I said aloud, baffled. The concierge had indeed given me the correct key. In three paces I reached room 33 and opened it. Familiarity greeted me, everything in its right place, including my Evian water bottle and cassette player on the desk, and the unsteady stack of tee shirts piled on the back of the chair.

I closed the door and stepped back into the dimly-lit corridor. I looked left and right, and then slipped across the hall to room 34. I glanced around me again, sucked my breath in, and tried my key in the lock. A tingling ran up and down my spine and I closed my eyes, for my key turned and turned, and the only thing that remained was pushing the door open. What would I say if I found someone lounging on the bed in his underwear? Worse than that embarrassment, how would I explain my clandestine entrance?

Irrelevant, I thought. If the room were occupied, someone would already be on his feet, barking the alarm. I nudged the door a hair. Darkness met my eyes. Thankful, I closed the door and relocked it. Then I stepped back into the middle of the hall and waved my key in the air by its heavy-metal, paper-weightish holder. "Cheap asses!" I said out loud. Every key and lock identical!

I wanted to confront the concierge, but what could he do about it, since he didn't own the place? The next morning it took three cups of strong French coffee to blunt the hammering in my head. From midnight on, all I had done was open and close my eyes like blinds, picturing the most bizarre of strangers blundering into my room. I swear, I heard the floor creak outside my door all night long. When not worrying about that, I ruminated over where to go. To another hotel, to be sure, but which one? How could I know the next hotel wouldn't pull the same cheap trick? I would have to ask the clerk point blank if one key fit all—way too embarrassing, plus awkward in a foreign language.

At least I can say a silver lining presented itself. I now had two good explanations for part of my school absence. After class on the first day back, I learned that dear Professor Bertalot had indeed been concerned about me. I gazed down at the old man who measured only about 5'5", but whose eyes shone like black onyx.

"Someone stole my purse," I told him.

"*Bon Dieu!*" he said, clasping his smooth pate with a slap.

"It didn't turn out too bad," I said, "but I lost a lot of time replacing my passport and things." I purposely remained vague about the "time" I had lost.

"You should have come to me. France is such a tangle when it comes to bureaucracy. Hundreds of wires going in different directions," he said, waving his hands about his head, "and you have to chase them all down..." Then the hands calmed and alighted on his signature, cheery-red tie. He cleared his throat while straightening it. "Would you by chance need money, *ma chère*...to tide you over...?"

"Oh, thank you, Professor, but I've already replaced my traveler's checks. Thank you again for asking, though!" I went all tender and embarrassed at the same time and felt a cramp of guilt about my outing to Normandy. Still, I had to profit from this touching moment...advice, I told myself, ask him for advice!

"What I'd like to ask you, though...Well, you see, along with getting my purse stolen, I've just found out that all the keys and locks in my hotel are identical, which means—"

Both hands flew to his bald head. "I know exactly what that means—anyone can enter your room! Oh, I know that type of hotel..." He stopped discreetly.

I shifted my weight uneasily, embarrassed at having ended up in a cheap joint like that.

"Listen, *ma chère*," he said. "I know a hotel on the Right Bank that I can vouch is clean, *safe*, and economical. A former pupil of mine owns it, a charming Algerian gentleman named Madani, as bright and eager when he was here at the Alliance Française as you are...oh, must be at least ten years ago now. *Mon Dieu*, how time flies!" He cleared his throat forcefully. "At any rate, I shall gladly contact him on your behalf if you wish to change hotels."

Thank you, you dear, dear, man! I said to myself. And I expressed it and expounded on it in French, albeit without the *dears* and with quite a lot of stuttering.

An additional day and sketchy night I endured in that farce called a hotel. I had to wait until my date with Luc and Thierry, for neither of them had given me a phone number. Just as well, since I dreaded talking on the phone in French, a source of anxiety rivaling my two sleepless nights. I always had to ask people to repeat things. Then if they threw a telephone number at me to field, I would break into a sweat. Here, people never lob numbers at you one by one. They fire them as if from a Gatling gun. Instead of five-three-one, they shoot: *five hundred thirty-one*. Even worse, they launch numbers over sixty-nine in that crazy French system of counting: *sixty plus ten,* for seventy; *four twenties,* for eighty; *four twenties plus ten,* for ninety—a nightmare over the phone!

When Luc and Thierry came to fetch me, I greeted them each with the twin-cheeked kiss Luc had initiated our last meeting. Suitcase in hand, I started reeling off my surreal hotel story as we stowed my gear in the trunk.

"*Faut se méfier à Paris*," Luc said in the car. In other words, watch your step in Paris. "It's a big city and there are a lot of shady people around."

"It's not like they lurk on every corner," said Thierry from the back seat.

"I know. I just mean you have to stay on your toes. If I recall, your grandmother got robbed coming out of the bank about two weeks ago."

"How did that happen?" I asked, picturing a dark man with a revolver, ready to attack Thierry's elderly grandmother.

"Two guys on a motorcycle drove up next to the sidewalk," Thierry said. "The one on the back snatched her purse and they drove off."

"At least they didn't pull a gun on her or anything," I said.

Thierry laughed. "In Paris we don't have what you call *muggings* in the States. Pick pocketing and purse snatching are the specialties here. Unlike

New York, where they broke into Luc's dad's hotel room when he was out—literally broke the lock. And he was staying at the Pierre!"

Jesus! I had slept serene as a cat on a heating vent for over a month in that scam of a hotel in the Latin Quarter. No one had taken as much as a pencil from my room. Still, I was glad to be moving.

To my new address: the Lux Hotel, Right Bank, rue du Roule, squarely in the First arrondissement. The middle of the dartboard. The dead center of Paris, two streets east of the Louvre and two blocks up from the Conciergerie, my favorite building.

When we arrived, Monsieur Madani, the Algerian owner, was nice enough to take my suitcase up to my room on the second floor. Once he dropped it off and left, I nonchalantly walked back into the corridor. I made sure he was gone and then, key in hand, I hopped across the hall and got ready to perform the drill. I looked left and right, and then plunged the key into my neighbor's lock, an excuse ready that I was a newcomer who had mistaken rooms. No need for it, thank God. A twist found my key blocked by sturdy metal. I yanked it out and with a silent "whoopee," lunged back into my room, closed the door, and leaned against it with a sigh.

I observed a room no bigger than my quarters on rue des Ecoles. In place of white walls, though, delicately-flowered wallpaper surrounded me—a little too girly-girl, but it would do. On the other hand, instead of a window overlooking a dull, dim inner courtyard, I had a luminous view of the street below. I could even see a corner of the turn-of-the-century Samaritaine where I bought my basics. Above all, I possessed a key and lock of my own, all for three dollars a day more. Gram wouldn't mind subsidizing the balance, not with my safety at stake.

On second thought...I wouldn't mention my safety. I wanted no bad impressions of Paris channeling her way. No, I'd have to invent some other excuse for moving. Convenience in terms of school or some such rot. I'd think of something. Professor Bertalot's recommendation would help. I tossed my suitcase on the desk and dashed downstairs. Other observations could wait; Luc and Thierry could not.

To celebrate my reversal of fortune, I invited them for coffee. About time I got to reciprocate. During our two-block walk down to the Seine, I oriented myself. Metro stops Pont Neuf or Louvre would be my stations. Down on the Quai Mégisserie, we passed a little pet shop where songbirds in wicker cages charmed the pedestrians on the sidewalk. I chose an outdoor café within earshot of the birds where I could also gaze at the Conciergerie and its three medieval towers. The Seine, its ancient island and bastion, the songbirds...a familiar tune wafting out of the café...

The bass voice rang sonorous and energetic, the melody cheery and upbeat; it was the record from the Cool Tattoo. "I like this song!" I said.

"Quand on a du feu," Luc said it was called.

As usual, Thierry had to translate: "When you have a light."

"I know," I said, trying to mask my irritation. "What does he say after that?"

Luc repeated more of the French lyrics and I blocked Thierry before he could translate.

"I've got it," I said. "If only he had his lighter or a match, he could win the girl who pulls out her cigarette."

Luc offered his own rough translation. "He says: with a lighter he would have genius."

Thierry quickly polished it. "No, no. It's more like: all you need is a match and the sky's the limit. Opportunity meets preparation, in other words."

I thought of throwing out something better, but nothing came to mind. Plus, I didn't want Luc to feel inferior. Thierry's "opportunity meets preparation" seemed insightful, though. Kind of a definition of "luck."

"It's Joe Dassin singing," Luc said, back to French.

"I like him," I said. The singer's voice sounded like deep chimes. I didn't know how to express that in French and I didn't want to ask Thierry.

"Joe Dassin's your countryman," said Luc, "but he's lived here most of his life."

"He's the son of Jules Dassin," Thierry said. "The American director who got black-listed during the forties and Fifties. They immigrated to France and Jules Dassin started making movies in Europe."

"Joe is completely American," Luc said, "but he sings and speaks French like a native. No accent."

No accent, I repeated to myself, envy stinging me.

"If you'd like," said Luc, "I've got some of his records you could listen to."

"...Sure," I answered, and we exchanged brief smiles. Then our gazes drifted back to the banks of the Seine across the street, and to the rows of *bouquinistes* displaying old books and posters on the sidewalk. Pedestrians idled past, some pausing to browse them.

Thierry finally broke the silence. "Did you happen to visit the little maze next to Place Saint-Michel when you were staying on the Left Bank?"

"No," I said, "but I've been close if it's near boulevard Saint-Michel."

"How about a little tour of the place?" he asked.

If this was a competition, Luc had closed in fast and direct with his 'invitation to listen to his music. Thierry lingered, taking his time...circumspect.

Parking is tricky in Paris. We retrieved the Lancia from rue du Roule, and with Thierry in the back, long legs splayed out, we crossed the Seine into the neighborhood of Place Saint-Michel. There, we commenced trolling for a parking place. Finally we homed in on a spot, but it appeared too short for the Lancia. No problem for Luc, who made space anyway and backed in, tapping the car behind him with his metal bumper. Then he nudged the car in front until he jockeyed into a position. I glanced behind for Thierry's reaction, and found him looking relaxed and impassive. I smiled to myself. In Paris, no doubt, this maneuver was as normal as jaywalking.

Place Saint-Michel rang a bell with me...in an off-tune way...familiar, yet awry. I couldn't remember the reason, and when we got out of the car, I just followed the boys.

The maze next to the Place turned out to be a tangle of paved foot paths thicketed with a host of ethnic restaurants, many Greek and Middle Eastern. That jogged my memory again, and as we wound our way along paths wide enough only for a horse a hundred years ago, curiosity swelled in me, along with a slight sensation of dread...

Throughout the little labyrinth, restaurateurs barked their fare, like the hawkers of the sex shops and cabarets at Place Pigalle. Exotic aromas escaped from open doors and food gaped from window encasements. I saw culinary wonders such as whole, big-eyed fish resting on ice, fresh kabobs on beds of lettuce, and multicolored blocks of sweets blanketed with powdered sugar. A mustached man in one doorway boasted of the best Greek brochettes in the city. As we strolled past, I eyed him uneasily. Then I caught the name *Acropolis* on his building and, with relief, moved on.

We turned a corner, and a savory scent of barbecued meat drew us to the window of yet another Greek restaurant. We stopped to scrutinize its contents. Next to the window stood a hawker in a white shirt and black trousers, who at one point quit speaking French to passersby and started conferring with a colleague in a different language. I figured it was Greek, and peered inside the doorway. What I saw gave me start.

A young man was setting tables. I could only see his profile, yet I was sure I recognized him. Black hair shaved up the back and sides...wire-rimmed glasses. He turned, and I froze for a heartbeat. Then I jumped back into the middle of the street. My eyes shot up to check the restaurant's sign—the *Poseidon!* Luc and Thierry had continued on ahead, so I hurried to join them, repeating to myself: Did George see me?

George, the Greek from Crete. Picturing his teary departure from the café Rotonde made me groan. The reminder of his visit to my school made me squirm inside. After a comfortable number of paces, I looked back. Thank God, only the hook-nosed hawker stood in front of the Poseidon.

Luc and Thierry stopped to wait for me.

"Have you ever eaten in the Poseidon?" I asked, pointing back at the restaurant.

They glanced at each other and shook their heads.

"Why?" asked Luc. "If you want to eat Greek, I know an excellent restaurant— "

"I didn't mean that...I've met one of the Greeks who work there..."

Luc cocked his head. "The Poseidon? It's a Greek restaurant but they're not Greek. Those two weren't speaking Greek, were they, Thierry?"

"Nope," Thierry answered in English. "Some kind of eastern language."

"Not even modern Greek?" I asked him, figuring his expertise might be limited to ancient Greek.

"No, no. I've heard plenty of modern Greek and those guys were speaking something else. Something Middle Eastern probably."

They both eyed me with curiosity.

I shrugged casually. "It's nothing. Just wondering about non-Greeks running Greek restaurants..."

"Not so strange," Luc said. "Greek cuisine's very popular in Paris."

He began to elaborate, but I lost most of it because my mind wouldn't let go of George. What sort of people were they at the Poseidon? Why did George tell me his Greek family ran the restaurant?

I finally had to pay attention because Luc and Thierry now proposed we dine in a Greek restaurant in another neighborhood.

Deep into the Fifth arrondissement we shuttled, to a tiny district called Mouffetard.

"How did I manage to miss this place too?" I said, as we got out of the car. "Both places we've seen today are about a fifteen-minute walk from my old hotel."

Luc grinned. "Well, we're here to remedy that."

"Have you noticed the cobblestones?" Thierry asked me, as we started a walk around the Place Contrescarpe. "They're practically the only ones left in the Latin Quarter. During the 1968 student riots people dug them up and hurled them at the police, so the city replaced almost all of them in this quarter with asphalt."

"Thierry should be teaching history," Luc said. "He can tell you the name of Charlemagne's horse."

Thierry ignored the joke, and went on, "If I'd been old enough at the time, I might have demonstrated too. I wouldn't have resorted to violence, just protested for reforms."

"I wouldn't have done either," Luc said.

I sensed some heat developing between my friends, so I changed the subject. "Looks like Haussmann never laid hands on this neighborhood a hundred years ago." I scanned the peeling plaster on the walls of the Mouffetard's old buildings. They seemed impoverished, deprived of the sculpted façades and elegant balconies adorning the great avenues and boulevards. "This place has the charm of a country village."

"Exactly," Thierry said. "Haussmann left many neighborhoods alone. Little pockets of old France like the Quartier Mouffetard have survived all over Paris. People have always valued them because, just as you said, they maintain an atmosphere of village life—"

"*Bon*," Luc said. "Time for dinner, I'm starved."

Luc didn't bother with the sidewalk. He strode down the middle of rue Descartes. When the rumble of a vehicle approached, he simply hopped onto the ribbon-thin sidewalk and let the car pass. Then he glided back into the street—one fluid movement, the repetition of which resembled a weaving dance.

We stopped in front of LES OLYMPIADES, a sign posted above the restaurant door in that pseudo Greek style with the E's looking like sigmas. We entered, and Luc and Thierry introduced me to the owner—a *real* Greek, with broad, bulky shoulders like Hercules. Mandolin music trilled through the establishment, providing a soundtrack for the murals depicting Greek dancers. All of it spirited my imagination off to a country whose myths I had loved.

After we got seated, Luc and Thierry launched into a conversation about food, and I had to concentrate to keep up. Astounding, the way they rated wines and dissected the subtleties of foods I had never heard of. Normal enough, if they had been a pair of mature bonvivants instead of a couple of nineteen-years-olds! They were three years younger than me, but in experience and taste they seemed twenty years older than any guys I had known in the States. Luc already managed a cinema. Thierry didn't work, yet his worldliness exceeded most Americans who were thirty, let alone nineteen. They did both live with their parents, however—one equalizer!

Suddenly, a rush of resentment filled me. I flashed on myself as "Little Haley," babied and brought up by her grandmother. "She's all that remains of her parents," relatives would say. "Such vibrant people they were," friends would comment. *I'm not my parents*, I longed to tell them. God, I felt behind in the game of life. With Luc and Thierry I could learn a lot about becoming worldly, and learn it fast.

So I got back to listening to my friends converse about Greek food. We had to try a little of everything, Luc insisted—dolmades, spinach pie, brochettes of pork, veal, and beef. And we couldn't pass up Greek wine.

"*Oinos*," I said, reading the Greek characters on the bottle they chose.

Thierry translated: "*wine, in ancient Greek.*"

I delighted in being able to read it for myself, having remembered Thierry's scrawled Greek alphabet in my notebook. The wine itself, on the other hand, tasted like a chemical spill.

"This reminds me of...(what was the word in French?)...turpentine," I finally said in English. So much for worldliness, but I'd never sampled a fouler drink. They didn't understand "turpentine," not even Thierry, which pleased me deep down. So I told them it tasted like chemicals, and they laughed.

"It's retsina," Luc said, his eyes candid and inviting.

Thierry's expression remained subtle when he smiled. "What you taste is actually resin from pine trees," he said. "They put it in the wine to give it that, uh..."

"Flavor of paint thinner," I said in English.

After Thierry translated, Luc smiled at me, holding my gaze. "You said you knew that fellow from the Poseidon...the Greek restaurant at Place Saint-Michel..."

"The guy inside setting tables," I said, wondering at the question. "I met him in a café and he told me he was Greek, from Crete."

I listened eagerly while Luc and Thierry tinkered with that. Thierry's dark-brown eyes went skeptical and Luc shook his head.

"Highly doubtful," Thierry said.

"Unless he's a Greek working for the Middle Easterners who run the restaurant," said Luc.

"He told me his uncle owns the place," I said.

"Back to being highly improbable," said Thierry.

"Hold on," said Luc, arching his back. He carried himself like a model, whereas Thierry had a more relaxed posture. "Let's ask the owner of this restaurant what he knows about the Poseidon."

When the tall, muscular Greek came by our table, Luc stopped him and explained our mystery.

The owner began rubbing his chin. "Poseidon, Place Saint-Michel...yes, I've heard of it. I believe the owners are Kurds...or Iranians."

"No possibility they could be Greek?" I asked, stunned by the Iranian theory.

"Definitely not Greek." The owner smiled at me, revealing a gap between his front teeth. "If you want good Greek food, you do well to stick with a Greek owner," he said, squaring his massive shoulders.

After he left our table, Luc leaned toward me. "Better watch out. Got to be on your guard in this city."

I tensed and waited for another lecture on the dangers of café encounters, but Luc's advice stopped there.

"The problem is," Thierry said, "people here think Americans are naïve. They get it from American films and TV. They don't understand that they're really just open and sincere. How do you say...*guileless*, but smart at the same time. At least the ones I know in Michigan."

I smiled at him.

"That sounds like Haley too," Luc said ("Ailý," he continued to pronounce my name, a quirk I had become fond of).

I met Luc's eyes, and for a second I held his soft smile. Then I released it and glanced at Thierry who had just lit a cigarette. Through a stream of smoke he projected a serious look, perhaps an expression of aloof interest.

When we left the restaurant, a low flame licked the quick of me, and it grew hotter as we glided along in the Lancia into the Fourteenth arrondissement. During dessert I had revealed my love of jazz, and Thierry suggested a piano bar. The next thing I knew, we were on our way to the hotel PLM and its Bar Tahonga. My every wish seemed to be either Luc or Thierry's command. I felt an electric power and speed inside me, as if my blood were accelerating along with the Lancia, and my life transforming right then and there.

We settled at a table in the PLM's intimate bar, a glass-encased cocoon that jutted out of the building over the edge of the sidewalk.

Thierry explained the acronym. "A lot of people think PLM stands for Paris, Lyon, Marseille. That's the train route to the south of France."

The light ebbed low and golden, and bluesy jazz surged in waves from a black pianist with a resonant, soulful voice. Entranced by the sensuous atmosphere, I vaguely heard Thierry continue.

"PLM actually stands for Paris, Lyon, *Méditerranée*," he said.

"You're sure it's not Marseille?" Luc asked.

"Positive."

Their conversation faded as the music swelled and hypnotized me. The earthy singer sent out deep, quavering tones, while her piano followed in syncopated stutters. "A week in Paris, will ease the bite of it..." I closed my eyes and savored the cool melancholy of "Lush Life." And I thanked the stars for my life in Paris, which was no mere week.

"She sings American jazz pretty well, don't you think? Thierry asked. "Mmm," I said. Then suddenly I stiffened. The singer had swung into "Blues in the Night." *Nom de Dieu*, that song transported me straight out of Paris and back to my earliest childhood in Reno.

I remembered riding at night in a huge, finned 1950s car. The radio crackled, and then sent the same "Blues in the Night" to lull me on the big bench seat in the back. In the inexact, abstract painting that was my memory, blue notes seemed to flutter from the green glow of the radio light. They penetrated the inky night, and rode the air over the front seat toward me. In this memory I always saw a driver through the watery ink, and someone in the passenger seat. They never turned around...maybe they were my parents...my memory could almost grasp them through the music.

Then, in the same memory, oncoming headlights would rush at me out of nowhere. They blinded me like flash bulbs: white, red, orange lights, one after another, non-stop—I had to duck ...before the surreal scene receded like a tide.

Perhaps the memory amounted to sheer fantasy. Still, something had planted that image in my mind from childhood, like a recurring dream. I shook myself. I was back in Paris at the Bar Tahonga, treated to soul-strumming standards by two French nineteen-year-olds. Wild, and practically surreal itself.

Two days later, Luc formally invited me to his home to listen to records and have lunch with his family—another milestone. About half an hour before time to leave my room, I felt I could fly down the stairs on pure euphoria. My nerves started ping-ponging all over the place as I finished getting ready, and when my phone buzzed, I thought someone had shot a gun. Why was Luc early? I lunged at the receiver and yanked it up. Silence was my initial response to Monsieur Madani's communiqué. "*Bon, d'accord,*" I finally said grudgingly. Then I dragged my feet down the two flights to the ground floor, riding on lead rather than ether—searching for a way out. With a sigh, I opened the door to the lobby and greeted Kevin.

"Where in bloody hell have you been? I had to practically bribe them at the Alliance Française to get this address!"

I glanced at Monsieur Madani behind his counter, head slightly lifted from his newspaper. When I first met him, he told me he didn't know English, but I pulled Kevin into the stairwell anyway and let the door swing shut.

Kevin thundered on. "What, you just disappear off the planet without a word?"

I shrugged. "I moved hotels, that's all. So the Alliance gave you this address?"

"They gave it to Sasha actually—we thought it better for her to ask. Still, she said it was an ordeal getting it."

I tried to appear detached. "Well, now you have Sasha to keep you busy. After that rude scene and the note you sent me, I figured we could use a break from each other."

Kevin shook his head. "That's ridiculous! Sasha's not a *replacement* for you. And you're confusing the issue. What I said in the note was for your own good. Because I care about you! You could've at least let me know you were all right."

He had me there. Funny, though, I wasn't angry with Kevin anymore. And I really should have informed him of my whereabouts. He did seem concerned about me.

I decided to set things straight. "Sorry I made you worry, but you've got to stop telling me how to live my life. If I talk to people in cafés, that's my business—I'm not your little sister. You're always saying I've got to trust you. Well, it works both ways." There, I felt better. Now I braced myself for his counter-argument.

Instead, he just watched me, eyes grave, arms crossed. Then he dropped his hands and said, "Of course I was wrong to tell you what to do. I just don't want to see you in trouble—or hurt. Forgive me? Let bygones be bygones?"

Astounded, I stepped backwards and almost fell onto the stairs.

He lifted his hands to catch me and I threw mine up to assure him I was fine.

"Listen," he said, "Sasha and I are taking the train over to Versailles tomorrow. Come with us."

Kevin's cheery, freckled smile was back, the look that had attracted me the first time we met in the café on rue des Ecoles. He was still my friend, and I gave in. We established our rendezvous and I started back upstairs. About three steps up, the door to the lobby swung open behind me and Monsieur Madani called to me: "Monsieur Luc has arrived." I turned around and noticed a subtle smile pulling at the corners of his mouth.

Luc had just missed us arguing, thank God. On the other hand, I would have liked to see him and Kevin cross paths in the lobby—just for kicks.

Luc had a colossal record collection. So did his father. Monsieur Perri gained my graces that first meeting when he showed me his Stan Kenton and Artie Shaw albums. I told him about my father, who was a big-band and opera fan, and next thing I knew, he guided me to a framed photo on a living room table. The old sepia and white image showed Monsieur Perri's grandfather and Giuseppe Verdi, opera icon, standing side by side. Both wore beards and expressed sober stares in nineteenth-century fashion. Another frame, next to the photo, exhibited Giuseppe Verdi's own handwriting in a letter to Grandfather Perri. My own father might have prized them both as well.

No doubt about it, an air of importance hummed in the Perris' Montrouge home. Just south of the Fourteenth arrondissement, Montrouge became my first sampling of a Paris suburb, or *banlieue*. Montrouge had a modern feel and so did the Perri house: wall-to-wall carpet; sharp-cornered, straight-legged furniture; the latest stereo equipment perched on a glass table.

From the kitchen drifted the aroma of warm herbs, followed by Madame Perri who swept us into the dining room. She was as kind as her husband, yet as hyper as he was tranquil. When I hesitated at sopping up my remaining sauce with good French bread, she urged me on. "Go ahead, Haley, that's what bread is for!"

When I told her she must have a secret recipe for her succulent roast potatoes, she practically broke into song—"No secret whatsoever, Haley, dear!"—and started rattling off the recipe.

Luc grinned, and I started thinking I had discovered the perfect family. Candid, friendly, no maudlin pats on the head about my deceased parents...

Then, into the doorway popped a head, followed by the rest of first-born Jeanne Perri. She had arrived late for lunch. Luc had told me about his sister who was seven or eight years his senior, and a law student at the Sorbonne. Politeness oozed from Jeanne, particularly after a faux pas.

She no sooner got seated and introduced to me, when out of her mouth flew: "Are your parents fans of Hayley Mills?"

A mortuary silence ensued, followed by Madame Perri's whispered explanation that I was an orphan. Needless to say, my mood sank.

Jeanne turned all milk and honey. "I'm sorry. I only mentioned Hayley Mills because I love the name, and the actress too..."

The warm comeback didn't quite convince me, and Jeanne's smile seemed cool. Had she mocked me, or had she just tried to make conversation?

By the time lunch was over, I had rallied nicely. Sitting Indian-style on the living room carpet, Luc and I sifted through records to sample. Jeanne made spotty appearances, although I didn't know why since she was considerably older than us. She never sat down, and with her glasses and silk scarf, she emitted the kind of poshness I associated with studying at the Sorbonne.

When she left the room, Luc complained. "She's always showing off with some legal crap."

I didn't care. At that point my fascination lay with Joe Dassin. The first French singer I had developed a passion for was ironically born in America. Luc said he had grown up in the States, England, France, and Switzerland. I would have sold my U. S. citizenship to lead that kind of life, and I felt envy mount in me like lava. Jeez, I thought, I need to get a hold of myself. I still had time to make something of myself.

I let Luc distract me with a little Francis Cabrel, a *mec* born in France but bent on the blues—just the opposite of Joe Dassin. Cabrel sang of bars, bourbon, and Southern Comfort. Luc told me that Francis Cabrel, along with Jimmy Buffet, was one of Thierry's favorite singers. *Thierry*. His absence from our little team suddenly struck me as off-balance.

It wouldn't last long.

"By the way," Luc said, as if reading my thoughts, "Thierry and I have a little trip to propose to you."

The idea came out of nowhere, and I stared at him.

"A two-day visit of the Châteaux of the Loire," he said. "We could leave early Saturday morning and get back Sunday evening. You wouldn't even miss school."

"Wouldn't you miss work?" I asked, still a little surprised.

"I'll be on vacation for three weeks, and after that I'm starting a new job managing another cinema."

The thrill of a new discovery shot through me like electricity. "I'd love to go!"

"Go where?" In the midst of washing up, Madame Perri had swung into the living room to pick up a couple of stray glasses.

Luc filled her in matter-of-factly, as if informing her of his latest work schedule.

"Now you boys act like gentlemen with Haley!" she said.

"I'm sure Haley can handle herself, *Maman.*" The voice came from the doorway, where Jeanne had peeked into the room again.

Her comment disconcerted me. Did I look tough...unattractive? Had I just been insulted? Or had Jeanne simply given me a compliment on my savoir-faire? Perhaps, she meant to insult Luc and Thierry...How could I tell?

Versailles is a monster: a palace, a park, a town. In one afternoon you're lucky to see a sliver of the palace and park, let alone burrow into its looming woods. Kevin had been there, seen a fraction, and insisted on being our conquering guide. I figured I owed him the company after having made him worry about me for two weeks.

He bebopped into the Lux Hotel lobby late Sunday morning to pick me up, dressed in shorts and a tee shirt. No one, including Kevin in his normal state, wore shorts in Paris, save little French boys and American tourists. Kevin took our outing as seriously as a boy scout.

I gave his pink, blond-haired legs a little grin. "Where's Sasha?"

"Waiting in the car so we don't get a ticket."

Kevin had borrowed the car from a work friend. Much more cost-effective, he told me, than three train tickets, and infinitely more flexible.

What greeted me next to the curb was a clunky, alien-looking Deux Chevaux. Its gearshift jutted from the dashboard like a robotic appendage, and it shifted with a heavy, metal-on-metal rattle. Kevin cranked at it and met the challenge, ferrying us bumpily to Versailles. Sasha sat by his side with a map, navigating. I didn't care that I was relegated to the back. The sky beamed blue for a change, and I had found myself a new trio whose reverse-gender proportions delighted me. With my new attitude, I even viewed Sasha, all cozy in the front seat with Kevin, from a positive angle. She proved a regular card sometimes.

"I read in the New York Herald Tribune," she said solemnly, "that Prince Charles fell off his horse during a polo match last week."

"Well?" said Kevin, squinting at the road.

Sasha answered matter-of-factly. "I just wonder if he manages to stay on when he's with a girl?"

"*Ha, ha,*" Kevin responded to our girly sniggers, though in the rearview mirror I caught a slit of a smile.

We parked and started walking. Blessed sun streamed over us as we traversed the great cobblestoned courtyard of what Louis XIV had designed to be the world's biggest palace. We passed the equestrian statue of the Sun King himself, his sword fending the vault of blue sky.

Then we entered the palace and started our visit. I marveled at the Hall of Mirrors whose seventeen looking-glasses faced the windows and sent shimmering reflections of the countryside back into the hall.

"Do you think Louis XIV needed all these mirrors to accommodate his exponential ego?" Sasha asked.

In Napoleon's bedroom she surveyed the extravagantly canopied, albeit markedly short bed. "Do you think he came up short in every department?"

No wonder Kevin liked her so much. With her feline eyes and high, flinty cheekbones, she had the air of a saucy Katharine Hepburn at twenty-five. I felt awfully young.

Outdoors, sculpted fountains sent jets of water into their basins. A statue of Apollo surged from the tide in one of the biggest pools, driving his horse-drawn chariot to herald in the day.

We meandered on, and approached a gargantuan acreage of mature, robust trees. The woods dwarfed the palace and reminded me that autumn had indeed arrived. I'd hardly noticed the gradual change from green to gold in Paris. Here, the variety of late-September leaves enveloped me in a forest of stained glass.

My break from Sasha and Kevin had decidedly helped our friendship. The three of us roamed about like best pals, joking and capering in the sunshine.

We even trespassed onto lawns designated off-limits to perform an occasional cartwheel. We got on so well, we hardly kept track of which way we were going and started weaving through the trees, plunging deeper into the forest.

"All right, who's hungry?" Sasha began pulling packages out of her big purse. "I made sandwiches. They're small—I didn't have much room."

It didn't matter. Kevin and I practically pounced on them.

We had to stand and eat since the ground felt damp from a recent rain.

"It smells like mushrooms," I said. "Almost as if they're in the sandwiches."

Sasha looked blank. Kevin appeared alert and then nodded his head at the pungent fungal odor.

I explained my remark. "My grandmother used to take me mushroom hunting when I was a kid, in the woods along the Carson River—always after the first fall rain. We'd have a picnic, kind of like we're doing now, and we'd come home with a carload of mushrooms my grandmother would pickle and use for cooking." I trailed off when I noticed Sasha's skeptical smile.

"So you never worried about getting poisoned?" she asked.

"No...my grandmother knew which ones to pick."

"Hmm..."

"She wasn't raised in Manhattan, Sasha. She knows rural Nevada."

"Eat up girls!" Kevin said. He had finished his sandwich and looked ready to push on.

I didn't want to let Sasha get the upper hand. "I bet I can spot mushrooms somewhere in these woods. You look for lumpy, cracked soil around the base of trees."

As a matter of fact, after about five minutes I found a clump of crumpled soil next to a tree. I scooped off the damp dirt and there it lay—a big beige blossom.

Sasha marveled at it.

"I don't know what kind it is," I said, "poisonous or not, but I can flush out some more."

Before I could get started, both she and Kevin wanted to join the game. We decided to bet on who could sight the most mushrooms. We each kept tally of our finds, working on the honor system. The losers would have to foot the gasoline bill for the trip.

I stalked the woods, elated. I had surpassed even Sasha, and for once my provincial background had paid off.

We dug deeper into the shadowy woods, calling out our respective tallies from our various locations. Musty odors of cracked, decaying timber and wet wood and leaves made the provincial and the worldly Haley meld in my mind. They seemed at peace...until at one point, I looked skyward. Through holes in the quilt of leaves above, I noticed the sky had assumed that purplish-bruised look that signaled encroaching dusk. I called Sasha and Kevin in to regroup so we could think about getting out. Not an insignificant challenge, it turned out.

We were lost, pure and simple.

Kevin marched us around, to no avail. Sasha, in her tank top, started hugging her arms and complaining of the cold. Kevin, who would never call attention to any goose bumps of his own, muttered, "bloody game." I had won the game, but I quickly made it clear I would contribute gas money regardless. Whenever we got out of this labyrinth worthy of Daedalus.

I swear it gets dark fast when you're lost. We trouped together and tried different directions. Then Sasha's laments turned into serious anxiety, verging on panic.

"Stop—we're digging ourselves in deeper!" She ran her hand through her hair, squeezing dark handfuls.

"Calm down, Sasha," Kevin said gently, and draped a bare arm around her shoulders.

Thank God this outing wasn't my idea, I said to myself. I started rubbing my own bare arms and commenced pacing about. I tried to ignore them, but I could hear Kevin whispering something in Sasha's ear.

Then she flung his arm into the twilight. "We've got to do something!"

I edged further away and looked for something familiar to set us in the right direction.

"We're not as smart as Hansel and Gretel," Sasha said. "We couldn't even manage to leave a trail of crumbs!"

"Not true," said Kevin. "We ate those sandwiches somewhere around here so keep your eyes sharp."

"Oh sure, in the darkness!" Sasha reigned when it came to emoting.

I couldn't spot any crumbs, but I did sight a small mound of crinkled earth near a tree and couldn't resist digging at it.

"Haley, let the damn mushrooms go," Kevin said, with a loud sigh.

Sasha was blunter. "For Christ's sake, Haley, it's because of those fucking mushrooms we're in this mess!"

I had stooped at the base of the tree, and when I shot up to defend myself I saw a light shining at us. I froze. We all did, until we figured out it was a flashlight and that someone had to be behind it.

"Over here!" Sasha yelled, bouncing up and down like a silly cheerleader.

"*Ici!*" Kevin translated into French.

When a uniformed guard reached us, both my friends looked to me for the French to get us out of the jam. Too bad I didn't have the luxury to gloat. I started speaking immediately, only to be cut off.

"What are you all doing here in the dark?" asked the guard behind his flashlight.

"Just strolling," I said.

"And all these uncovered mushrooms? What were you planning to do with them?"

"We were trying to identify them—that's all," I said, squinting at his light.

Kevin finally pitched in. "That's right. It's a game, you see." That was the first time I heard him speak more than two words of French.

"A game?" said the forest guardian. "This is vandalism of the property of the French Republic. Or, perhaps you were going to steal the mushrooms..."

He shined his light in my eyes, so all I could make out were some kind of military hat and boots. "You're all English?" he asked.

Our awkward pause didn't help our cause.

"Come with me right now, all three of you!" He pointed the way with his flashlight and we followed.

"At least we're getting the hell out of here," Sasha said.

When we reached a break in the woods where a shard of twilight sliced through the leaves, the guard extinguished his light and came into focus. Middle-aged and mustached, the only thing distinguishing him as a forest guardian, apart from a brimmed cap and military boots, was a massive hunting knife strapped to his belt.

A few seconds later, two more hatted and booted men with knives at their sides stepped into the light. Our mustached guard conferred with them quietly in a voice far too low for my comprehension.

Then he turned back to us. "We're taking you to the commissariat."

Sasha slapped her hand on her hips. "Holy shit!"

Kevin placed himself between the guard and us. "But we've said it was a game...nothing stolen." He displayed his empty palms.

"That's because I stopped you in time," the guard said, eyes impassive.

Kevin looked back at me.

I summoned some saliva to my dry mouth and stepped forward. "We didn't mean any harm. We were only counting the mushrooms. I mean, it was a contest to see who could spot the most. We had no intention of taking any...not one...we don't even know if they're poisonous...then we got lost..." I halted and started chewing my lower lip. I regretted the bit about the mushrooms possibly being poisonous and feared he might think that was the only reason we didn't steal them.

Then, out came the guard's hand. "Your purses, please."

"What!" said Sasha.

The other two guards stepped closer, hands on their hunting knives.

I handed over my purse. "Give him yours too," I told Sasha. "Let him check it, then maybe he'll let us go."

Kevin interrupted. "Hang on a minute. Haley, ask him if they have badges or something...some I.D."

I asked, but the mustached *mec* ignored me as he picked through my purse.

"Now yours, Mademoiselle."

Sasha's jaw tensed and her eyes oozed contempt. "Fine!"

I faced the guard again. "I asked you if you had any police identification."

Again he ignored me. The ransacking of Sasha's purse complete, mine anchored under his arm, he finally raised his eyes. "Perhaps you'd like to spare yourselves that unpleasant trip to the commissariat."

Kevin, Sasha, and I exchanged frowns.

Kevin shifted his weight. "How?"

"Let's say by paying the fine for disturbing the Republic's terrain right here and now."

Kevin backed closer to us. "I'll ask my friends," he said, in a very reasonable French tone.

With a flick of his chin, the guard gave the go-ahead.

"They're not real guards," I whispered, as soon as Kevin turned around.

"Right," he said. "We've got to convince him to give your bags back, make it seem you're getting money out to pay him. I'll pull out my wallet as well."

"And then?" Sasha asked.

"We run for it," I answered, steeling my nerves.

"Exactly. Toward the remaining light in the clearing."

"Are you crazy?" Sasha said. "They've got butcher knives!"

Kevin spread his hands. "Calm down, we're in Versailles, not Central Park. I'm sure the knives are just a bluff. Once we're in the clear, we'll certainly see other people."

I agreed. "The phonies probably have an escape vehicle. Which means there has to be a road...and maybe other motorists."

"*Bon!*" barked the guard, sending my heart into my throat. "Is it the commissariat, then?" His accomplices said nothing. They just held their ground and squeezed their knives.

"Let him arrest us," Sasha said. "Let them lead us into the open. People will see us and we'll scream for help."

Kevin and I exchanged glances. "Call their bluff," he said, nodding at Sasha.

"If there really *are* people out there," I said. My mind grappled for a way to get our purses back. "I don't hear anything."

"*Allez, venez!*"

Our heads whipped back. "He wants us to go now," said Sasha, sounding resigned.

"We'll pay the fine and go from there," Kevin said, deciding for us all.

It made sense. I doubted the bastard would return our purses without us agreeing to pay his fake fine.

Kevin faced the ringleader. "We're paying." His hand moved to his front pocket.

"Slowly!" the guard ordered.

"We have to get our money too," I told him, pointing to our purses lodged in his big, beefy hands.

He smirked, the first trace of expression to escape his cold, leathered face.

"How do you know how much the fine is?" he asked me.

I gnawed on my bottom lip again. Out of the corner of my eye I could see Kevin standing grim.

"One thousand francs," the guard finally told us, looking stern again.

About two hundred dollars, I rapidly calculated.

Kevin nodded. I reached for my purse, half expecting him to jerk it back and take the money himself.

Instead, he turned them over to us. I glanced at Sasha. Her eyes had steadied and regained their shrewd air. The guard's partners started checking their watches and pulling up their collars, engaging in those routine gestures that signal it's time to move on and enjoy the spoils, until the next hunting expedition. I started to feel hopeful, until one of the thugs planted his hand firmly on his knife again and stared at us.

My sweating hands managed to fish 200 francs out of my wallet—forty dollars. Sasha pulled out 300. That left Kevin to produce the balance. He thumbed through his bills several times—350 francs. The guard snatched our money and Kevin's wallet, checked the contents, and then threw it back at him, disgusted.

"The rest!"

"I've got some change," I said.

"We don't take change!" After recounting the insufficient funds, he turned to his cronies. Another conference.

Kevin whispered to us. "Listen, it's almost completely dark. We've got to make a run for it."

I nodded firmly. Sasha did so wearily. Kevin gave the final strong nod. "Go!"

I sprinted toward the clearing. Out in the dusk, I dared not hesitate. I saw a dirt road and flew toward it, my feet practically pedaling air.

"Haley!" I heard Kevin shout. Heart hammering, I turned and saw Kevin waving at me. I felt like a car charging at sixty miles per hour, with someone just releasing the gas pedal; it was hard to slow down.

Kevin and Sasha caught up with me.

I took staggering breaths. "Where'd they go?" No vehicle occupied the road.

"They hung back, I guess, and crept off into the woods," Kevin said, dropping Sasha's hand.

Sasha began pawing through her purse. "We've got to find the real police and report this nightmare."

Sasha, Sasha, Sasha! I said to myself. I'm the worldly one in this situation. I made my point gently to her. "It's not likely we'll get our money back…"

"The money's peanuts, Haley. It's my credit cards I've got to do something about."

My ironic smile wilted.

Kevin's hand flew to his shorts' pocket and ripped out his wallet.

"He's stolen my Visa—sodding bastard!"

"You're lucky," said Sasha dryly. "They got my Visa, my American Express, my Diners, and my Carte Blanche."

Oh là là. The phony guard must have slipped them out while he rifled through our stuff, or when he granted us the three-way huddle. I checked my purse. Everything was there (I owned no credit cards) except my forty dollars worth of francs. More than peanuts to me.

We hiked back to the palace and reported the heist to security. They told Sasha and Kevin to deal with their credit cards Monday morning and said they would do everything possible to get our money back. They did sound adamant, what with the safety of tourism at Versailles at stake, and they seemed particularly concerned with the phonies impersonating law enforcement officers.

The drive back to Paris was a funeral procession. Kevin and I exchanged a few upbeat utterances while Sasha sat in the back, mute. I told her I'd help her replace her credit cards—accompany her to the American Express building, to the bank, et cetera. Kevin said we would all go together, to which Sasha finally mumbled a "thanks."

We arrived in Paris from the south, so Kevin deposited Sasha at her Left-Bank hotel first. It neighbored the Eiffel Tower and flew a line of flags, U. S. , British, and Canadian, to name a few. No wonder there was always an English-speaking concierge on duty.

Unlike my homey little Lux where I'd sooner bet on Arabic wafting through the lobby. As Kevin taxied to the curb, I offered to run up to my room for gas money.

"Never mind," he said, "I'll take care of it. And don't worry about Sasha. I'll take her to the bank tomorrow—I've got to go as well—and to American Express and Carte Blanche and Diners Club. Her concierge will know where they are."

"American Express is right by the Opera," I said. It was all I could think to contribute.

"Keep in touch!" Kevin said, before I closed the door. Then he chugged off in the Deux Chevaux and made a u-turn in my short, narrow street, two wheels bumping over the curb.

Frustration and emptiness filled me as I watched Kevin drive off, as if I'd suffered some kind of setback by hooking up with him and Sasha again. I needed to move forward. Just the thought of Versailles caused my whole being to bristle. Not due to our robbery, but because Sasha acted like a turd about it and Kevin tolerated her snotty attitude. The two of them deserved each other. I did not.

Fortunately, I had Luc and Thierry to work magic on me. The weekend arrived and we prepared to set out. Destination: the Châteaux of the Loire. We would explore the Loire Valley in search of châteaux. Following that, we would sojourn, as Thierry put it, in his grandparents' apartment in Paris the four days or so of their holiday absence. If the second part sounded kind of crazy, so be it. If I missed a day or two of school, it would count as part of my education and transformation.

Thierry had told me he always took care of his grandparents' place when they were away. Space abounded in the flat, so I would have my own room. In the ether where I orbited around my friends, a sofa would have suited me.

To top it off, that thoroughly decent Monsieur Madani, who had insisted I drop the *monsieur*, decided to waive my room charge during my absence. If the hotel filled up, he would simply stow my large suitcase and rent the room until my return. You could call that a blessing since I was spending money as if I had pockets as deep as Sasha's.

The cool, crisp air stung my face when we stepped out of the Lux that Monday morning, Luc swinging my maroon-leather tote bag. The three of us practically tap-danced with enthusiasm down the sidewalk. When we reached the orange Lancia, a piece of paper clamped to the windshield with one of its wipers awaited us as well.

Thierry snatched it up. "*Merde, un P-V!*"

The obscenity—"Shit, a ticket!"—would have made me laugh, if I hadn't been the one to cause the delay by dilly-dallying in my room. Luc took the ticket from Thierry and scanned it.

"It's my fault," I said, "getting downstairs late. I'll pay for it."

"No way!" Luc said. With boyish glee, he tore the ticket into three strips and let them flutter into a sidewalk trash receptacle.

I laughed and Thierry smiled.

"Won't you get in trouble?" I asked.

"Bah, I do it all the time. *Je m'en fous, hein.*"

Luc didn't give a damn. I don't know which delighted me more: his tearing up the ticket, or the increasing amount of slang, obscenity and profanity I was understanding. At any rate, my spirits shot back into orbit. As we peeled off in the Lancia, the voice of Joe Dassin boomed from the speakers, singing "Côté banjo, côté violon. "I faltered at some of the words, so Thierry dished up a translation as usual, telling me how the song mirrored Joe's own life. Banjo in San Francisco, violin in Paris. Jetting back and forth across the Atlantic, blazing a life on two continents. Perfectly bilingual and reveling in the best of both cultures. For a few guitar beats envy got the best of me, and I wanted to cry at how late I had gotten my start here.

Then, Luc distracted me. As we coasted through the countryside, one of those long, straight stretches of narrow road presented itself, with an honor guard of majestic trees lining both sides. As we passed through, like the Président of the République, Luc shifted into fifth and slammed the gas. 200 kilometers per hour the needle read, over 100 miles an hour on a two-lane country highway. And who wore seat belts? Straplessly naked, we rocketed forward, trees zinging past in reverse. Then, Luc started tapping the brakes. The Lancia stuttered, but refused to sway.

"See how good these brakes are?" he said, relaxed and gloating.

I gulped and nodded.

"We get the message," Thierry called from the back seat, hands cupped megaphone-style.

Luc let up, taming the car back to a reasonable thirty kilometers per hour, or so, over the speed limit. He flashed me a quick smile, hazel eyes dancing.

When we reached Chambord, our first château, Thierry took over. "A Renaissance château," he began.

"Private hunting lodge of François I," Luc said. "See, I know history too."

The "hunting lodge" was the biggest palace I had seen apart from Versailles. Immense, white, with robust towers and multiple spires, it glistened in the sun's generous mood. Vast, manicured lawns encircled it and dirt access roads wound into unending tracts of woods. My imagination could easily conjure up a dicey adventure in that forest, and I decided to recount my escapade at Versailles.

"You got robbed again?" Thierry said, as we walked only about one thousandth of the way around Chambord.

"Yeah, but they only got a couple hundred francs." I minimized my misfortune so they wouldn't feel sorry for me, though the loss of that forty dollars continued to chafe.

"Still," said Thierry, navigating my undercurrent, "200 francs goes a long way."

"Some good news, though," Luc said. "Because of what happened to you in the cinema, they're flashing a big warning on the screen before each film: LADIES, KEEP YOUR PURSES IN YOUR LAPS! And they caught a thief in another cinema in the neighborhood smack dab in the act of hooking a purse. Maybe the same guy."

"How did they catch him?" I asked.

"Ha! Evidently, he'd unwound a series of metal coat hangers, then twisted them all together into one long hooked implement. He was on his hands and knees in the dark, poking it under the seats in front of him to snag a purse. An usher surprised him and they called the police."

"Wow," I said. "And because of me there's a warning before every movie!"

"Okay, let's go San Francisco," Thierry rhymed in English. "I feel like driving."

I had never seen Thierry with a car, but Luc evidently indulged him with his. Thierry took the helm en route to the next château. Given his phlegmatic nature, I predicted we'd be in for a sedate drive to Azay-le-Rideau.

Not even close. Thierry loved to take on curves. He skidded around one so sharply, I pitied the famous Lancia brakes. At the same time, an air of tranquility rivaling nirvana floated around him. Shoulders loose and relaxed against his seat, a cigarette dangling from the corner of his mouth, Thierry the dark-eyed classical scholar reminded me of Marlon Brando on a motorcycle. He cornered one curve so fast, he had to jerk up the handbrake as we smoked around it.

"What the heck was that maneuver?" I asked.

He babbled a bunch of mechanical jargon at me that went right over my head in French. He couldn't even muster a translation, which made me grin inside. As did my conclusion about his driving—he refused to be outdone by Luc.

"After we see the next château, it'll be your turn to drive," said Luc, as if reading my mind.

My smugness dissolved. I hadn't driven a manual transmission since I first learned to drive, and I wondered about the lame performance I would give. I continued worrying about it as we drove into a secluded niche in the forest. There, I witnessed Azay-le-Rideau, and my angst shrank away. The petite (compared to Chambord), white château glittered on an inlet of water. Surrounded by thick woods in colorful transition, it struck me as a diamond set off by golden topaz and garnet. Luc and Thierry had to practically haul me away from the jewel.

"Come on," Luc said, "we've got to get to Tours and check into the hotel. Your turn to drive, remember?"

Another reason I was in no hurry to leave. I chuckled nervously. "Yeah, right."

"Seriously, you have a go at it."

"You better take him up on it now," Thierry said. "He may not feel this generous again until next September."

I hadn't manipulated a stick shift and clutch in at least six years, but my pride wouldn't let me back down. I took the leap and spent more time jerking us around than propelling us forward. Stop-go, stop-go. We lurched along while I searched for the right gear as if I were shifting in a bathtub. My only consolation was I didn't stall the car.

Later on, as I got settled in my hotel room, I thought I could still hear Luc and Thierry laughing about it. Our communal door stood open and I strolled into their room to jokingly complain that enough was enough. Instead, the words froze on my lips, as I saw them trampolining on their beds. Up and down they jumped, sparring with jabs aimed at knocking each other to the floor. The gap in sophistication between my nineteen-year-old friends and me narrowed on the spot.

And yet, they continued to educate me. On our promenade around Tours we stopped to watch a game of *boules*, which they had to explain to me. From some loudspeaker flowed Joe Dassin's voice again.

"It's 'L'été indien,'" said Luc, with the song's title.

Thierry added a translation. "It means Indian summer."

Completely unnecessary. Not only could I translate it myself, I was able to understand much of what Joe sang. He crooned of strolling along a beach with a girl, never feeling so happy. Later on, he would remember every detail of that colorful Indian summer day that would define his life. I felt the same way about my friendship with Luc and Thierry, and our odyssey continued to unfold when we moored back in Paris and took up residence at Thierry's grandparents' flat.

If Luc played leader of our little trio, always keeping the game going with something new to propose, Thierry had a brilliant idea or two of his own. He and I had a couple of things in common as well. Like me, he was an only child and we both bore names of famous individuals. Thierry's surname, Kérouac, distinguished him.

Our attitudes toward our names, on the other hand, differed dramatically. While I hated being compared to Hayley Mills, Thierry loved people asking if he was related to Jack Kerouac. He even claimed distant "cousinship" with the deceased American hero of the Beat Generation. "Entirely possible," he once told me, since one of his ancestors had immigrated to Québec a couple hundred years ago. A more recent branch of the Kérouac family then moved back to their native Brittany and on to Paris. End of story, except Thierry continued to delight in being taken for Jack Kerouac's relative.

Thierry's grandparents' home in Montparnasse radiated the spirit of old France. The first evening, I tiptoed around the place like a trespasser. In the armoire in my room, I caught a whiff of mothballs. In the living room I examined the tall glass doors that swept open onto a narrow balcony, styled with that viney wrought iron I loved. With its Empire furniture, the abode suggest-

ed a sedate, dignified generation whose stillness was amplified by the ticktock-
ing of a large, art nouveau table clock.

My own grandmother jumped to mind. She had no idea I was staying here,
knew nothing about the Loire trip. I had barely told her about Sasha and Kevin
since I only called her about once a month. My friendships, I revealed gradually and discreetly. Other subjects, like my little getaways, I avoided. Who could
expect her to understand my traipsing around France with two guys I had only
recently met?

Old France notwithstanding, the Kérouacs' flat basically served as a camp
bed. Not one second of our precious independence did we squander. No time
to sleep, let alone play house, or even reflect. From French jazz joints to Brazil-
ian nightclubs, fresh discoveries blossomed off the tourist trail every day and
night.

After two nights of clubbing, we decided to treat ourselves to a chic dinner
out. Somewhere unconventional, Thierry suggested, out of town even, like the
Charles de Gaulle airport.

"It's brand-new and state-of-the art," he said, during one of the brief moments we sat in his grandparent's living room. "Wait till you see the bowels of
this airport. Translucent tubes transport you on people-movers from level to
level, like something out of 2001, A Space Odyssey!"

"We can dine at Maxim's, then," said Luc.

"But Maxim's is in downtown Paris," I said.

"It's got an airport branch," said Thierry. "Not as chic as the original, but
not as expensive either. Maxim's in rue Royal costs les yeux de la tête. How do
you say that in English? Both your eyes?"

I had to resist a smug smile. "Not quite. More like, an arm and a leg."

Luc laughed, and Thierry nodded, registering the idiom in his encyclopedic
brain, no doubt.

Settling on an upper-middle-class relation of the hundred-year-old Maxim's, suited me fine, considering I was hemorrhaging francs converted from an
anemic dollar. You'd think I resided in an Eiffel-Tower hotel like Sasha, the
way I was spending. After two days of this spree, I really started to worry.
When I thought of the two hundred francs lost to those park pirates, my
mouth tasted like rusted metal—the flavor of blood from a cut lip. *Christ, I
could buy four or five meals with that forty dollars!*

Still, I couldn't resist any part of this adventure, and I insisted on financing
my share of nightclubs, restaurants, and every other expense we racked up

while painting Paris. Maxim's at the airport, my initiation into haute cuisine, I considered no exception.

According to Luc, no one should be ravenous, or even hint they're hungry when frequenting a place like Maxim's—that would be extremely un-chic.

"They'll serve you spare, esthetically-pleasing portions," Thierry said.

"Yes," Luc said, "but leave a little food on each change of plate."

"So they don't think I'm a starving peasant!" I said with a laugh. My observation came from history. Deep down, I thought, *if I don't slow down I could end up one.*

"These days," said Thierry, "it's so you don't look ravished just to be there; like it's a once-in-a-life-time opportunity. You've got to appear *désinvolte.* Uhm, in English that would be..."

"Nonchalant," I said, beating him to the translation.

"Not quite...more like *detached.*"

A hair's distinction, I thought, preferring my synonym to Thierry's.

At any rate, when we got to Maxim's, I followed their advice and played the high-cuisine game. Luc ordered a Gevrey-Chambertin, one of Burgundy's crown wines in quality and price. He sniffed the cork and swirled the wine in his glass. Swished the robust red around his palate and finally let the waiter pour.

Everything seemed normal, until about five minutes later when he began to frown. The waiter had left, so Luc conferred with Thierry. Thierry took a careful sip, all the while maintaining a thoughtful expression. Then the corners of his mouth turned down and he shook his head, expelling a "*bof*" of discontent.

"See, it tastes like cork!" Luc said. "Try it again, Haley. See if you taste it."

I didn't know cork from cask, but I grappled with the bouquet all the same.

"Uh...yes, I think so..." I said, squinting at my glass, as if a crumb of cork might surface at any moment.

"Very subtle," Luc said, "but it's there, right Thierry?"

Thierry gave his palate another bathing, lifted his dark eyebrows and pronounced: "An insidious infiltration of cork—no doubt about it."

"Right," Luc said, "and that's unacceptable. Garçon!"

Given the wine's price and status, I understood that nothing short of perfection would be admissible. The waiter arrived, and before he even finished listening to Luc, he took off to fetch the maître d'. The latter's arrival, complete with his own glass, ignited a brush fire, and the French accelerated along with the heat. I held my own and identified where to insert my "*oui*" as witness to our case. Face reddening, the maître d' poked the wine menu, indicating the venerable Gevrey-Chambertin's price. From my chair, though, I couldn't make the figure out. Luc had chosen the wine as his treat, therefore he did most of the dueling, with Thierry his second.

His hands chopped the air, as he made *his* point about the Gevrey's price. "It shouldn't include a flavor of cork!"

"You're delirious!" responded the maître d', having performed his own tasting ritual on the Chambertin. "There isn't as much as a hint of cork!"

"I'd say it's more like *echoes* of cork weaving throughout the wine," Thierry said in a placid tone, compared to Luc's more fiery, Latin nature.

"How do you two dare accuse a wine of this caliber! What do you know at your age?"

Luc battled back. "We know cork when we taste it. I've tasted it even in good champagne. Just a couple of weeks ago, at home, we got a cork-contaminated bottle of Veuve Cliquot."

The maître d' finally gave Luc a smile, though it was in the form of a sneer. "*Veuve Cliquot!* Shows you're just kids—*des debutants!*"

Thierry shrugged. "Kids with bank accounts."

I had to chew the inside of my cheek to keep from laughing at the outraged maître d'. No way this high-strung *mec* was taking the wine back. Lips curled, he glared at Luc and Thierry for a couple of seconds and then turned his back on us.

After he'd taken himself off, I ventured an opinion to rescue our mood. "It's actually not that bad...I don't mind drinking it."

"We've got to leave it," Luc said, a frown of frustration creasing his brow.

"Otherwise we'll lose all credibility," said Thierry. "But I wonder, after we leave, whether that boor'll cork the bottle and take it home..."

"That'd be a royal screwing!" Luc said.

Thierry sat back and crossed his arms. "At least we'd be vindicated as the ones with superior taste."

That produced a grin from me and a laugh from Luc, which restored the cheer I had wanted back. We wound up the dinner abandoning the Gevrey-Chambertin in style, along with other remnants of the meal.

There it stood on the table, out of its nesting basket.

Until I reached for the bill. Usually, Luc either commandeered the check and designated what Thierry and I should chip in, or he would assess the bill in concert with Thierry and then tell me what I could contribute. I suspected I didn't always pay my full share, and sometimes Luc and Thierry refused out-right to take my money. This evening I decided to snatch the bill and check it myself, because I wanted to pay for part of the disastrous wine venture.

To this day, I don't know whether it was purely accidental or a subconscious gesture. Out flew my hand to swipe the bill and down went the Gevrey-Chambertin onto its side. A purple stream flowed onto the white-linen table-cloth.

Luc and Thierry leaped to rescue the bottle, but I stopped them. "Wait! Let as much spill as possible!"

They smiled, and that encouraged me to lift the bottle's base. Luc nudged out a few more drops and finally called the waiter.

I made my eyes as big and candid as possible to address his frown. "Sorry about that. It's all my fault."

I felt a touch of pity for the guy, and then dismissed it when I realized he would be changing the tablecloth anyway. Especially at those prices. I never did find out the cost of the Gevrey-Chambertin, for during the chaos of the spilled bottle, Luc had swept in for the bill. With that, we left Maxim's, our mood substantially buoyed. Before I melted into sleep that night, I barely had time to tell myself I was the luckiest person on earth...I couldn't even remember what it was like to be lonely...

By day we jumped around the city, from *quartier* to *quartier,* on that checker-board of arrondissements.

About the fourth day of our little adventure we alighted in Montmartre, where I finally got around to exploring the famed artists' quarter. It turned out a disappointing nest of carnie barkers with too many *mecs* hawking their talents at portraits and caricatures. Fortunately, the towering white basilica of Sacré Coeur also inhabited the neighborhood.

Reverence filled me as I entered the church and faced an enormous fresco of Christ on the domed ceiling. Framed in golden rays, arms spread wide to encompass his flock, He projected omnipotence and radiated power from one of the loftiest elevations in the city. From this throne, I mused, He could monitor His Parisian subjects from Pigalle to Montparnasse.

He could also monitor me. "Superstitious" rarely described me, but just contemplating this God-image sent a twinge of guilt to the base of my brain. By now I should have signed up for the fall session at the Alliance Française. I had missed a couple classes at the end of summer session and now this furlough with Luc and Thierry. That made how many skipped classes...four, maybe?

Back in the car, I shoved the concern under my mental rug as we bulleted down to the Champs Elysées—only to feel it buzzing around my ears again like an annoying mosquito when we ducked into the round, porthole entrance to Lido Musique. I shouldn't have been music shopping, considering the state of my finances. But the hell with it, I told myself. I wanted to treat myself to some French music, my first cassettes after finally having targeted my tastes.

A Joe Dassin album, something by Serge Gainsbourg, a sampling of Françoise Hardy filled my hands, the cassettes clicking against one another as I paid and swung the bag out the door. Funny, how you can *will* the act of purchasing something to make sense. And it did, until I found myself on the sidewalk. Then, a cigarette-sized hole of guilt started burning around the general area of my esophagus.

I didn't want to mention my problematic spending habits to Luc and Thierry, so I brought up school.

"Don't worry about it," said Luc. "*We're* teaching you French now."

True, I told myself.

"Come on," Thierry said. "We'll continue your education on the Left Bank. You still haven't seen one of the most chic cafés in Paris."

By the time we reached the historic Deux Magots, my heartburn had vanished, and my mind had floated back to the heady ether-sphere like a hot air balloon. A white-aproned waiter brought me coffee in my own little posh, silver pot. And as we lounged in one of the leather booths with polished brass bars, Thierry rattled off a list of celebrities who frequented the café.

"If we sit here long enough," he said, "we could run into Jean-Paul Sartre and Simone de Beauvoir."

Now this smacked of true education. Imagine, having coffee next to Sartre, the founder of existentialism and probably the most famous philosopher in France.

"Thierry's got high hopes," said Luc. "The man's older than God."

"Remember, I saw Sartre in here three years ago," Thierry said, with a slight frown.

Luc smiled and shook his head. "I know. It'll haunt me on my deathbed."

Thierry's olive skin turned dark red, and I saw a flash of irritation in his eyes. He turned away from Luc and concentrated on me. "You might see

Juliette Gréco here too, if you come often enough. It would have been more likely in the Sixties, though."

I didn't know that era in Paris. Instead, I focused on Luc's bantering. Like a boxer, he danced around Thierry, delivering short jabs. He didn't quite land a punch. Not in front of me, anyway.

I scanned the room. No celebrities in sight. On the other hand, I probably wouldn't have recognized one if he or she had marched in and squeezed into our booth. I glanced at the door. Who knew, maybe Joe Dassin might walk in. Then I squinted...someone familiar indeed was filing into the café. An individual of far more consequence to me than any French celebrity.

Short black hair parted on the side, wire-rimmed glasses, slouching shoulders. I blinked to be sure...yes, none other than George the fake Greek, following three people into the café. I reminded myself of the Deux Magots' location, just a little east of Boulevard Raspail where George had said he lived.

I crossed my legs, recrossed them the other way, sat on my hands, all the while tracking George with my eyes. Judging by their looks and ages, I figured his companions were relatives. The leather booth creaked as I slid down and then back up. George had left the three others to settle at a table, and turned my way. Luc and Thierry had stopped talking.

"It's George, the so-called Greek from the Poseidon," I told them quickly through my teeth. Then I displayed my most genial smile. Out went my hand. "George! Good to see you again. These are my friends Luc and Thierry."

The three exchanged stiff handshakes. George produced little more than a nod and a grunt during the two seconds his eyes strayed from me.

"Your uncle and aunt?" I asked, nodding toward the table where the trio had seated themselves.

"Yes, and my cousin," he replied in English. "I must return to them."

His eyes studied me; they seemed more stoic than sad this day. "I may see you again, Haley," he finally said.

I responded with a stutter. "Uh, yeah...quite possible."

With another curt nod, he left us.

Thierry frowned. "Peculiar *mec*..."

"I don't trust him," said Luc.

I watched George rejoin his family. "He's harmless. If you two had seen him when we first met..."

I couldn't resist recounting the story of George and his sad eyes moistened with tears. It netted shock, and then snickers and barbs from Luc and Thierry.

I regretted my impulsiveness and decided *not* to tell them about George's visit to the Alliance Française.

"He said he had to leave, but who asked him to stay?" said Thierry.

They laughed while I observed George. His shoulders sagged and his dark eyes drooped, the way they did when I'd met him before. His aunt and uncle and his cousin chattered on in Iranian or Kurdish or who-the-hell-knew-what language. He hung back, pensive and detached, some bizarre force field dividing him from the social buzz...

Luc snapped his fingers. "Haley, are you with us?"

"...Yeah, sure," I said, and forced myself to file George, the enigma, away for the time being.

Luc sprang off the diving board and cut cleanly through the swimming pool's aquamarine water. A dip suited our mood, a kind of ritual to mark the end of summer, along with the last day of vacation together. Amidst the flurry of activity, I did manage to get over to the Alliance Française and enroll in autumn classes. To insure my finances didn't dry up, I also obtained a certificate of courses completed to send to my grandmother in the States. And just maybe, with that concrete proof of my accomplishments, Gram might loosen her purse strings a little more. I would have to feel the situation out next time I called her. Now that I had taken care of business, I concentrated on fêting myself on this last day of freedom.

The swimming pool crowned the top floor of the Nikko, an upscale Japanese hotel on the Left Bank. For a fee, non-guests could shoot to the top in the elevator and splash the afternoon away. Despite this lingering day of Indian summer—*l'été indien*—and the hotel's sunroof rolled open, we were the only souls there.

I lazed on my towel at the side of the pool and watched my friends dunk each other and race through the water. In their swimsuits Luc and Thierry cut a contrast I couldn't help analyzing, as I lay propped up on one elbow. I found Thierry predictable in his mid-thigh, American-style trunks. And Luc, well, he played it suave in his quasi Speedo. At nineteen, Thierry had already sprouted dark chest hair, while Luc's chest shone smooth as a statue of a Greek god. Even in street clothes they clashed. Thierry roughed it, occasionally, in jeans and tennis shoes, whereas Luc lived in slacks and collared shirts. The only style they shared were haircuts that fashionably brushed their collars.

Luc acted athletic, diving and propelling himself through the water with as much jubilance as a dolphin. Burdened with more height and bulk, Thierry created heavier water resistance. Of course, I had no room to talk, having never bothered to learn that coordinated breathing and stroking rigmarole. Pure instinct and will kept me afloat and moving. Kind of amazing, since I had grown up without ever taking a formal swimming lesson. I could credit that oversight to Gram, since she never learned to swim herself.

Luc and Thierry finally climbed out of the pool to join me. "We've got to seriously dry off now," said Thierry, stretching out on his towel next to me. "That's if you still want to make the museum."

"Haley?" said Luc on my other side.

For a moment I gazed at his glistening chest. "Sure...I was just thinking about the great time I've had this week." A blur of fun had carried me like a magic carpet. No time to think, until now.

Luc lifted himself onto his elbow. "*Ouais.* Thierry, why can't you convince your grandparents to stay away for a month or so?"

Thierry didn't budge from his back. Eyes closed he answered, "How nice that would be."

Luc and Thierry volleyed more small talk. They discussed the new cinema Luc would manage when he went back to work, a bigger, and more up-scale theater. I savored the moment, relishing the warmth my two friends radiated: one, a reflective, studious type, into America and the blues; the other, extroverted and ambitious, full of drive and savoir faire. Like me, both loved laughs and zany antics. If I had to choose only one, it would be like having to give up half of Paris. Still, as I lounged on my towel between them, I noticed one lay a little closer to me. Just enough that his bare arm grazed mine...Luc. And when I felt the wet friction, the current pulsing from his damp skin, I didn't pull away.

Dry, changed, and charged, we cruised north into the Sixth arrondissement to the Eugène Delacroix museum. Tucked away in a building off little Place Furstenberg , the painter's final workshop had become the setting for exhibiting some of his work. Without Luc and Thierry I would never have unearthed this museum.

Nor would I have discovered a secret.

The lighting waned low and shadowy, a complement to Delacroix's somber subject matter that included wild animals devouring prey, martial scenes, and massacres. The three of us started examining the paintings together, but soon typical museum behavior took hold and we began to stray off separately.

I drifted into a dimly-lit room. I stopped before a sketch of a lion devouring a gazelle, to which I curled my lip and moved on. I passed other drawings and then moved on to an oil painting. It was small enough to fit on my bedroom wall, but its darkness magnified the content.

Dante and Virgil in Hell, the plaque read. The two protagonists stood in a boat surrounded by a black sky and roiling sea. Stark-white naked men with ferocious faces grasped the boat's sides as they swam. One man was gnawing on the boat with vicious teeth. The contrast of dark and light, the violent expressions...I started to squirm. First my heartbeat quickened, and then my breathing. I turned to another wall. No use, more dark, violent paintings— wild animals, war, death. Again I pivoted, and squinted in order to screen my eyes from the painful black, red and orange flying at me from the canvases. Through the slits of my eyes I navigated to the exit and made it into the next room. Luc and Thierry stood chatting. I sagged with relief.

"What's wrong?" asked Luc. "You look pale."

The pounding within me started to ebb. "Nothing, I just need some air. Awfully stuffy in here."

"You look like a bed sheet," said Thierry.

"I'm okay."

They exchanged glances.

"Really, I'm fine, never mind."

It was partly true. The fear receded as soon as I approached people. I experimented by examining the portrait of a soldier whose face gleamed white against his black fur hat and the dark background. The contrast made me wince a little, but caused no additional distress with Luc and Thierry nearby. Nor did any other violent scene in the room.

I thought about the other museums I had visited. The Louvre displayed the most grisly painting by Eugène Delacroix I had ever seen. That huge harem massacre, with assassins slaughtering people and horses. One man threatens to slice a woman's throat, while the pasha lies back on his enormous red bed and watches. Nothing assailed me in that grand salon, because, I figured, tourists abounded...

Suddenly, a powerful image rose from the fathoms of the ocean representing my childhood. With my grandmother, I remembered perusing an old book on the history of the Earth. When we would flip to the section on dinosaurs, a chill would shoot up my spine. The beasts' hides shone scarlet and black against a murky jungle. The eyes of the Tyrannosaurus Rex glinted crimson, and shreds of flesh hung from its stiletto teeth. As long as I leafed through the book with Gram, I remembered enjoying the thrill. Alone, I could barely crack the volume. I had to peek at the monsters and then slam the book shut, breathless with primeval fear ... Why?

"Maybe we should leave," I heard Luc say.

I stared right through him. "No, I was just thinking..."

I explained my bizarre phobia, at least what I thought amounted to a phobia, and Luc looked puzzled.

Thierry immediately agreed with me. "It's a phobia, all right—a feeling of being overcome by a work of art to the point of rapid heart rate and even fainting."

I gaped at him.

"I just read about it," he said. "Stendhal was a nineteenth-century French writer, the first to record the experience. When he was in Florence, he was taken by extreme rapture when looking at the art. The ecstasy made him feel like life was being drained from him."

"Only with me it's an entirely negative sensation," I said. "It's like I'm being attacked by the paintings, and it only happens when I'm alone."

None of us knew how to interpret it. We left the museum and soon I was distracted by the fact our spree was coming to an end. We celebrated the last dinner of our vacation in a Breton crêperie in Montparnasse, and for two hours the crêpes, the galettes, and rivers of hard apple cider kept my mind off having to return to my hotel.

But time cheats you. Around ten o'clock Luc and Thierry dropped me off at the Lux and returned to the folds of their families. Monsieur Madani, who reminded me to drop the *monsieur*, installed me back in my old room that had only been occupied once while I was absent.

I closed my door and surveyed the uncomfortable emptiness: twin bed, narrow armoire, skeletal desk, high radiator—that was it. When I thought of my friends and me in Thierry's grandparents' home, loneliness swooped down on me with a vengeance. It carved me out hollow and left me almost nauseous. I clasped my head and shook it—incomprehensible, that my feelings could turn on me in the space of a few days! I felt so down, I didn't have the ambition to unpack my tote bag and suitcase that sat on the thin carpet. Madani, kind man, had invited me to watch television with the other guests downstairs, so I turned my back on my luggage and slammed the door.

Down in the breakfast room that doubled as a parlor, the only thing that saved me was a comic romp on TV. Madani slipped in and out, pausing to chuckle at a segment or two. He always stood, and the presence of this thin, middle-aged Algerian gentleman kindled a spark of home. Night and day, he guarded his hotel, with only occasional relief from his brother. I never saw his wife, but once in a while in the afternoon I would come home to see his two sons, chattering away while penning their homework at the breakfast tables. Cute kids, Malik and Karim. They too infused a cheery feeling of home into the place. Malik, about twelve, wore oversized glasses whose thick black frames tilted crooked on his narrow face. I would joke with him and Karim (about a year younger) and tease them whenever I saw them hanging about the hotel.

Too bad they weren't there the evening Luc and Thierry dropped me off. Still, I survived. As I got into bed, I jazzed myself up to go back to school the next morning. After all, I had to keep improving my French and master it better than Thierry had English. I had to get ahead, if I were to make something of myself in some kind of career or job here.

While Luc was still on vacation, the three of us continued hopscotching about Paris and day tripping out to explore castles—Blois, Pierrefonds, Fontainebleau. Driving the sports car impassioned me, and Luc indulged me. I tackled every terrain, enchanted with the orange wonder's spunky pickup and tight traction. I loved shifting gears (smoothly now), which delivered some kind of release I didn't understand, almost as if I had merged with the car and its power. I relished squeezing around curves, downshifting for hills, turning on a dime, and slipping into a sliver of a parking space like a shadow. The Lancia meshed with my restlessness—swift, energetic, packed with potential— whose appetite for life could threaten its grip on the ground as it raced towards whatever rally life held.

"Keep in touch," Kevin had reminded me the night he dropped me at my hotel after the Versailles fiasco. Not a peep had he made since then. Instead, Sasha called me. "Come out for coffee, Haley, we've gotta catch up." Curiosity nudged me and I agreed. I had glimpsed the outside of the palace she inhabited near the Eiffel Tower. Now I wanted to peer inside, so I suggested meeting her there.

When I entered the lobby, I witnessed everything imaginable in a four-star hotel. Huge, gaping lobby, with dark-wood wainscoting and polished mahogany desks that made Madani's desk look like a ticket counter at the cinema. The clerks behind them, in formal black, reminded me of undertakers, with their hushed voices, lifted eyebrows and half-closed eyes. The floors shone with veined marble, covered in places with flowery oriental rugs, and personnel strode here and scurried there to accommodate every need, even whim, I imagined, of the guests. I found the whole scene amusing, and hoped the bellboys wore rubber soles, so as not to slip on the slick marble and break their necks.

I was early, so I settled in a leather armchair to wait for Sasha. I sifted through some newspapers on the glass table next to me: English, Italian, German, and finally the French *Figaro*.

An article snagged my eye: the Shah of Iran had contracted lymphoma and sought admission to the U. S. for medical treatment. That made me think of George, and I wondered if he still passed himself off as Greek instead of Iranian or Kurdish, or whatever he really was. I thought about his tears, his approaching me in the Deux Magots when I was with Luc and Thierry, and his attempt to get my address at the Alliance Française. Interesting, that he didn't mention that in front of Luc and Thierry. *Who the hell was he, and what did he want with me?* The urge to get to the bottom of the mystery seized me, and I started daydreaming about just how I could investigate the matter, when Sasha appeared.

"You found it," she said blandly.

"Sure," I replied. "I've been in this city long enough to track down most anything." When she didn't respond, I wondered if I'd come across as bragging.

Sasha looked weary, her golden-brown cat eyes dull for a change. "Come on," she said, with a tired smile, "I'll show you my room and then we'll go."

Strange, I thought of Sasha's terseness.

I followed her into an elevator almost as capacious as my entire room at the Lux. I estimated enough space for four people and all their luggage—astounding, considering most elevators in Paris were as narrow as an armoire.

By the time Sasha and I entered her room, I thought I had been transported out of Paris and into the Saint Francis in San Francisco, or some other swanky hotel: thick, deep carpet, a king-size bed, a television, a refrigerator, and a desk reminiscent of the furniture in the Louvre.

"Not bad," I said to her. "What more could you ask for?"

She shrugged. "A kitchenette."

I laughed. "There's room for it!" Again no response from her. I walked to the window and pulled the sheers aside. The Eiffel Tower hogged the cityscape. Nothing here reflected my Parisian world—not the room, not the impersonal lobby, not the view.

"Let's go," she said, voice still bland.

For a moment I frowned at her. Then I thought, *fine with me*. I didn't want this atmosphere rubbing off and turning me back into a tourist.

I suggested the Flore, an upscale café whose allure rivaled that of the near-by Deux Magots. I reckoned it would impress Sasha, and the Flore adhered to the same unwritten law governing all French cafés. Once you ordered as little as a demitasse of coffee, the table was yours until closing time. We settled in on the covered terrace, and I waited for Sasha's reaction to the leafy, ritzy neighborhood of Saint-Germain.

To my disappointment, she made no comment.

"Been out in the woods lately?" she asked, instead.

I frowned. Then I figured out she was referring to Versailles, so I smiled.

"Haley, I never did apologize for blaming that nightmare on you."

That kind of touched me. "Don't worry about it. Did you get your credit cards taken care of?"

"Yeah, no problem..." Her voice trailed off, and for a moment she seemed to stare right through me.

I shifted in my chair and sipped my espresso. I noticed she hadn't touched her café au lait.

Suddenly, she snapped to attention and leaned in. "Haley, do you think Kevin's responsible?"

I blinked. "Responsible for what?"

"Would you trust him with your money, for example?"

"With my money? Oh," I said, "you mean his disco idea."

"I take it he's asked you to invest too," she said, finally lifting her cup.

"He's mentioned it, but I doubt he's ready to move on it."

"Well, he's got a location picked out in the Fifth, not too far from here. He hasn't asked you for money lately, has he?"

Heat flared around my neck. "Why's he still harping on that? He knows I can't draw on any money without my grandmother's consent until I'm twenty-five." Jesus, I'd have to set him straight, I told myself, as I tore the wrapping off the petit mint in my saucer (complimentary in expensive cafés).

"Actually, he hasn't said a word about your financial situation. In fact, he hasn't mentioned you much at all lately." That said, Sasha began to stare out the window.

How was I supposed to respond? Again, Kevin's "Don't be a stranger" echoed in the back of my mind.

"I haven't heard from him since the day we went to Versailles," I told her, with as much nonchalance in my voice as I could inject. "And I've been too busy to think about him or call him," I added, and then popped the chocolate mint into my mouth.

She studied me, the keenness back in her eyes. "He's also been tied up."

Who the hell cares? I wanted to say. "Sounds like you know him better than I do," I said, instead. "Why ask me whether he's responsible?"

Sasha resumed her distant gaze, right past my shoulder. "I probably do know him better at this point...I'm pregnant." Her voice remained flat and her eyes didn't move.

"What?" I said.

Finally, she acknowledged me. With a weak smile, she turned up her palms and dropped them in her lap. "Anyway, you shouldn't be surprised if he doesn't call you for a while."

Heat began stealing up my neck again. "I take it he knows he's going to be a father..."

She nodded. "I've only known for about two weeks, myself."

"How did you find out for sure?"

"Take-home pharmacy test."

"Wow, France is pretty advanced."

Sasha shrugged.

I scanned the chic room. All these self-styled Catherine Deneuves and Alain Delons, with Bulgari watches and Christian Dior suits...I wondered how many of them had availed themselves of take-home pregnancy tests. No doubt most of them were too sophisticated to have gotten into such a mess in the first place. Unlike Kevin. He was closing the chapter on me. That's why he hadn't called.

Sasha pregnant. The magnitude of it made me shudder—better her than me, thank God. I thought of Kevin again. *I* meant to be the one to sever our ties. For a moment I felt a fire of jealousy over his ability to be in control.

"Sasha Smythe," I said. "Some kind of ring that has!"

The dreaminess in Sasha's eyes dried up. "Who said anything about marriage? I haven't told anyone besides you two. I don't even want this kid!"

"Sorry," I said. All I had aimed to do was take some of the tension out of the situation—bring back that ironic smile so typical of her. "Listen—"

"Wait!" she said, and reached for my hand. "I'm sorry, Haley, I'm a little touchy these days."

"Sure," I said, feeling bad about the joke. "I understand." I also realized Kevin probably felt as helpless as Sasha over their plight.

When I considered her again, it seemed a forlorn, fearful look had entered her eyes. She pushed her cup and saucer away. "Let's go to Harry's Bar for a drink. Coffee's just not cutting it. Okay?"

We could have ordered something stiff right there at the Flore, but Sasha's pleading tone and pitiful expression worried me. She seemed so lost and needy, so not-herself, I couldn't deny her the comfort of that American joint Harry's.

On the metro she stood silent, barely hanging onto the long silver bar. She let the train jostle her like a rag doll as it sped through the tunnels, jerking us around every corner. She wouldn't brace herself. She didn't seem to want to fight the forward momentum as we charged towards the Opera, the quarter Harry's called home. Both of us stared straight ahead, as expressionless as the rest of the commuters, like still, impassive fish in a luminous aquarium hurtling through the dark.

Harry's didn't do much to cheer Sasha up. Not the bar's fault—warm, wood-paneled, with lively chatter bouncing about the place in both English and French. Sasha told me she didn't know what she would do about her condition, and then put an end to all conversation coming close to the subject. I didn't want to force the matter so I ended up enlightening her about Luc and Thierry and how we had met. That procured a chuckle at least—a spark of envy too when I described our road trips. I stopped short of mentioning our stay at Thierry's grandparents' flat. I knew she would blab it all to Kevin, and even though I didn't give a damn about his opinions in general, I still didn't want him to get some perverted idea about the three of us. He had his secrets and I had mine. Only now I knew one of his.

I wanted to keep Sasha buoyed, so I figured why not reveal my preoccupation with George, the phony Greek. He had been at the back of my mind off and on at the Flore, since the café sat practically next door to the Deux Magots. I told her about his seeking me out there, his emotional display the first time I met him, how he pretended to be Greek but was probably Iranian, and of his mysterious visit to the Alliance Française.

"I'd really like to investigate this guy," I said.

"You're not serious?" she asked, and then drained the last of her martini with much more satisfaction than she had sipped her coffee at the Flore.

"Well...I'd just like to learn who he really is and why he's interested in me enough to look me up at school."

Sasha narrowed her eyes and cocked her head. "Do you think that's wise, considering he's already deceived you and acted creepy?"

A touch of embarrassment kept me from answering, and I appreciated the boisterous laughter in the bar that covered my silence.

Sasha leaned in. "Haley, when you told Kevin and me about going for coffee with the little Jew you ran into on the street, I laughed and supported you. When you left after Kevin jumped all over you, I defended you and told him he was out of line." She shook her head. "Now I can see his point. Why do you want to pursue shady types like that?"

I finished my Negroni and pushed my glass aside. The last sip of cocktail had magically erased my embarrassment. I dismissed Sasha's question with a shrug and said, "I'm not going to do anything imprudent, maybe just confront him if I see him again. Just a thought." I stopped there and sat back. I decided not to reveal my whim of going to the Poseidon restaurant and having another peek in the window.

She studied me in her feline way. A smile twitched at the corners of her mouth. "I'm not sure I believe you. You're hard to read sometimes."

Just as well, I thought. I would share nothing more of this with Sasha who had turned out to be as narrow-minded as Kevin. They did, in fact, deserve each other.

With Luc back at work and managing a new cinema, Thierry and I spent a few afternoons together exploring the city. "If you want to be an expert on Paris," he told me, one of those days Luc was on day shift, "you have to know where the important people live and work." That comment excited me, and when he suggested we sweep the city to locate the pulses of Paris's power, I could barely keep my enthusiasm reigned in, in order to appear cool and contained the way Thierry acted most of the time. This outing promised an immersion into the history and grandeur of Paris, something that impassioned me and that Thierry knew a lot about. He and I were a practically a pair of new shoes in this respect, barely broken in, but already synchronized in step and stride, ready to achieve plenty of mileage.

The tour started in the Fourth arrondissement in front of the most important building concerning the running of Paris: Hôtel de Ville, City Hall, headquarters of Paris mayor, Jacques Chirac. Thierry didn't know I had already spotted and fallen in love with Hôtel de Ville, and that it rivaled the Conciergerie for my affections. I loved its beige façade aged golden with time; its niches that held scores of statued heroes and classical columns and arches that seemed as light and graceful as ballerinas, uplifting the spirit of countless eras. I told this to Thierry, as if it were the first time I had noticed the structure, so as not to spoil his tour. As we stood across the street away from the traffic in front the building, I raved that it was the most magnificent municipal structure ever.

"Quite possible," he replied, "but it's also had its dark moments. Do you know who met his downfall in this building?"

"Nope," I said, "you're the expert here."

That made Thierry hesitate. He frowned, and I wondered if he feared sounding like a know-it-all, after the time Luc had mocked him for knowing the name of Charlemagne's horse.

"Go on," I said.

"Have you heard of Robespierre?" he asked. "Leader of the Terror during the French Revolution?"

"Sure. Prissy, puritanical type, right?"

That lit him up, and Thierry launched into his story, all in French, to my delight. "When his enemies in the government went after him, Robespierre took refuge here, in the Hôtel de Ville. He barricaded himself in, but they sent forces to storm the building. He didn't want to be taken alive, so he took a pistol and tried to shoot himself in the head. But the shot fell short, and the ball ripped through his jaw, leaving half of it hanging, barely attached. They took him away, got his jaw bandaged together, and prepared him for execution because they wanted him alive for the humiliation of the guillotine." Thierry paused to smile at my queasy, incredulous look. Then he swept on.

"They loaded Robespierre into a wagon, hands tied behind his back, and drove him to the guillotine. Everyone knew where he was headed, so crowds lined up to shout at him, throw garbage at him and such. Finally, on the scaffold, the executioner strapped him down on the plank. But before he put Robespierre's head in place under the blade, he grabbed the rag holding his jaw together and ripped it off. Up until that moment they say Robespierre remained stoic during the whole ordeal—from his botched suicide attempt to the pain he endured when the doctor pulled a couple teeth and tied up his jaw. But when that rag was ripped off his face, tearing away pieces of flesh, they say he let out a scream that shocked even the habitués of the guillotine—those were the group of Parisians who reserved their seats for every execution, which was every day during that year."

Another break for me to digest my squeamishness. Actually, I was more fascinated than anything. I adored learning this type of history, the kind that textbooks neglected.

I smiled, and Thierry said, "So then the executioner shoved his head into place, neck under the blade. The drummers began their roll while the crowd screamed for blood. He loosened the rope, and the blade dropped with a thud. Execution accomplished. Painless, according to Dr. Guillotin who invented the method."

"*Painless*. Wow!

"*Eh, oui.*"

Thierry grinned and we charged on, crossing the Seine to the Left Bank. We made our way into the Seventh arrondissement, past the sculpted-stone Hôtel Matignon, once an elegant private residence.

"Now," said Thierry, "our prime minister Raymond Barre lives there."

The route led us on to Invalides, known to tourists as Napoleon's tomb. I had already visited the enormous shrine to the emperor and his gargantuan coffin, so we passed up going in.

Still, I asked, "Why such a giant coffin?"

Thierry shrugged, hands in his pockets as he walked. "Actually, there are six coffins within the big one, with him in the smallest. The big one you see is marble and porphyry. It probably conveys the image that Napoleon was bigger than life—that he transcends time."

The intellectual exchange excited me, along with the brain power Thierry projected. I pictured the little emperor within. "Or it could be *overcompensating*," I said. "Showcasing an exaggerated power and virility in proportion to the physical man."

Thierry slowed his pace and lit a cigarette. He blew the first stream of smoke out of the corner of his mouth and looked at me. "In life, Napoleon liked to display his virility. When you went to Invalides, did you go downstairs where Napoleon is sculpted as a Roman Emperor?"

"Yes, I wondered about that."

"Well, the toga makes him look more important and powerful in more ways than one."

"How?"

Thierry slowed his stroll even more. He sent another stream of smoke up-ward and then glanced at me. "Like a Scotsman in his kilt."

I didn't understand and hated to admit it.

When I didn't respond, he continued. "You know what a Scot *doesn't* wear under his kilt?"

"...Ohhh!"

"Right, well, they say the Romans didn't wear underwear under their togas either."

I grinned and Thierry reciprocated. No one in the city could make history more interesting. And best of all, I had processed his entire discourse in French, which he had stuck to from the beginning of our walk. By the time we reached the Alexandre III bridge, my mind felt like a combustible engine, pistons cranking out competency and fluency in French.

"The most elegant bridge in Paris," Thierry said of the Pont Alexandre III. Look at all the sculpture."

As we crossed the bridge leading to the Right Bank, I saw lions, dolphins, cherubs, and old-fashioned lampposts embellishing the bridge's expanse. The dynamic sculptures emitted the kind of movement and energy I could feel in my evolving mind.

When we reached the Right Bank, Thierry said he had one more residence to show me. "The most powerful man in France lives there," he said.

We crossed the Champs-Elysées and headed to avenue Marigny where Thierry pointed right. "Behind the wrought-iron enclosure and the high hedg-es is the Elysée Palace, residence of the President of the French Republic— Valéry Giscard-d'Estaing, otherwise known as the *mec* with the launch codes to France's nuclear arsenal."

I might as well have been trying to spot the planet Neptune. The whole complex was fortressed with a high, black-iron railing whose top prongs reminded me of gilded spear tips. Beyond it, all I could see were trees *à gogo*, a catchy French word for "galore" I loved using.

Thierry looked at his watch. Almost time to meet Luc at the cinema he now managed on the Champs-Elysées. We looped around to take in ritzy rue du Faubourg Saint-Honoré where Thierry wanted to check out the latest luxury cars parked in front of boutiques such as Chanel, Hermès, and Dior.

No Fords or FIATS here. Thierry stopped to admire a yellow Ferrari, while my eyes fixed on a charcoal Aston Martin on the other side of the street.

We approached the sculpted, polished-wood storefront of Hermès, and Thierry halted. "Like to go inside?"

To do what? I thought. I wore bell-bottom corduroys and a pullover sweater. That in itself stopped me. Plus, my recent experience in a boutique close to this neighborhood still hovered in my mind. My eyes had locked on a pair of leather boots in the window of a little shop between the Opéra and the Madeleine church. Of course I couldn't afford them, but their shiny buckles made me long to see them up close, so I entered. After a curt "bonjour" the saleslady surveyed me, starting with my wind-blown hair, on to my worn purse, and finally down to my blue-suede shoes, one tip of which was scuffed. Her crinkled look of skepticism stiffened into a frown as she asked if she could assist me. I guess I just wanted to assure her that I admired the store's taste and lifted one of the shiny, buckled pair of boots off a shelf. "Don't touch the merchandise—you'll ruin the display!" You'd think I planned to drag it through the mud, the way she erupted. I felt like I'd been caught under the giant spotlights of a prison-camp yard. The shame, the embarrassment seared me to the core, and I couldn't excuse myself and retreat fast enough.

Now, Thierry proposed I flounce into the kind of boutique where Grace Kelly probably shopped, and where my finances wouldn't permit me to buy a handkerchief. I marveled at the cool he kept regarding these exclusive stores, when he was wearing jeans and tennis shoes, and one half of his collar stuck out of his sweater.

"Not today," I answered. "I'd still like to see the inside of Luc's new cinema."

The excuse rang natural enough, and when we arrived Luc didn't mask his excitement at giving me a tour of the vintage, 1930s Normandie. The Salle Prestige must have contained five hundred seats set on plush carpeting, surrounded by ribbed wood paneling on rounded walls. It was the biggest, most glamorous movie theater I had ever seen.

With Luc's shift over, he drove us to the Pub Saint-Germain for a drink where we snuggled into a dark moleskin booth. I settled in my seat next to Thierry and let him take the lead in describing our afternoon to Luc across the table.

"We started at Hôtel de Ville, then we went over to the Matignon and Invalides, past Palais Bourbon—"

"Whew," Luc whistled, cutting Thierry off. Hand out, he sliced the air downward, fingers pointed at the table in gesture signifying, *enough!* "Were you trying to bore Haley to death?" he asked.

"Not at all!" I said. "I enjoyed it and learned a lot."

Luc's eyes darted from me to Thierry and back. "So, Professor Kérouac gave you a walking lecture."

"He didn't lecture and it wasn't boring in the least," I said.

Thierry lit a cigarette and cast a mocking smile at Luc. Then he blew smoke in his face.

Since Luc was also smoking, I didn't know what to expect. A cigarette dangled from his lips, and next thing I knew, he lowered his hand and flipped off Thierry French fashion—left arm up and flexed, right hand slapping the bicep. I tensed up like a newly-tightened guitar string.

Then, of all things, Luc started blowing smoke rings: one, two, three, four. And Thierry had to keep up: five, six. Luc fired two more, exhaling a stream of smoke straight through the center of the second ring. I sat back and observed the immature contest. Then I asked myself: what did these two say and do when I wasn't around? More precisely, what did they say about me?

3: Paname

I treasured my cassette player more than anything in my hotel room. I had use of a little bathroom, a small armoire, and a desk and chair, but I didn't own them. My cassette player, and the tapes I bought, belonged to me and made my months-long hotel experience more like apartment life. Many times I even had meals in my room. Bread, cheese, fruit, nuts; as long as I didn't set up a hot plate and cook, Madani didn't mind.

I slipped in a Serge Gainsbourg cassette and listened to "La saison des pluies"—"The Rainy Season." Serge sings of leaden skies and an increasingly hostile climate, and I found he was spot on. With the advent of October came days of drizzle, like ice needles pricking my neck where my pea coat left gaps. Winter had begun sharpening its teeth.

"La saison des pluies" plucked notes deep inside me. An electric guitar, bass, and Serge's vocal formed the simple, elegant ballad. It reflected Paris in 1979, spare and spacious, particularly in October when the tourists dispersed and I had the beige-and-grey city to myself. Jazzy and subtle, the strumming of minor notes in the song suggested the pattering, melancholy rain itself—especially on lonely afternoons when I had no date with Luc and Thierry, and when I thought about Sasha and Kevin. Two weeks had passed since I'd seen Sasha, and Kevin still hadn't surfaced either in person or by phone. To my bemusement, I kind of missed them.

My stack of French music cassettes kept rising on my desk like plastic building blocks. One day, I happened onto the music department in BHV (Bazar de l'Hôtel de Ville), my economical department store across from City Hall. As I clicked back one cassette after another, I delighted in the cheap prices that beat every other store I knew in Paris. Suddenly, I stopped at a cassette with a close-up photo. None other than Melina Mercouri grinned at me, the Greek actress and stepmother to American-in-Paris singer, Joe Dassin. I flipped the cassette over and saw that she sang in French as well. I turned back to the cover and scrutinized the close-up. The smile was infectious and the price too good to pass up.

Melina's French, on the other hand, challenged my brain. Just like all French music, it was a crap shoot. I could listen to one song and comprehend three-quarters of it. I'd play another by the same artist and only glean three or four words. Why did music in a foreign language present such a tantalizing mystery?

These "mystery lyrics" threw up a cognitive roadblock, and it drove me mad when I really liked a song and couldn't understand it. Like Melina's "Paname." Paname is a nickname for Paris, and the song's melody pierced my soul. So why couldn't I understand all the words? Melina adored Paris—*that* I could grasp from her low, intimate tone. Vibes and a French accordion wove in and out in a 1960s style that produced pure magic. The vibes struck me as bouncing balls of light. They warmed my soul and buffered the sadness of encroaching darkness on these cold autumn evenings. I would listen to a phrase of "Paname," rewind and listen again, each time getting maybe another word or two. Not enough—I had to know all of this song.

And I knew who could help me. Thierry and I had planned to go to a movie while Luc was on shift at the Normandie. I figured we would have time to decipher my song, see the film, and meet Luc afterward.

Now, where could we work? I balked at inviting Thierry up to my room with Madani at the front desk. He was a Muslim, and I didn't know how he would react to that kind of Western boldness. I stood at my window that late afternoon, watching dusk envelop my little street and the art nouveau-styled Samaritaine at the end of the block. Then an idea hit me. I left my room, hit the stairs, and hurried down.

When I entered the lobby, I greeted Madani, scrutinized him for a couple of seconds, and began. "I was wondering...I have this project I'm working on. Translating songs from French to English."

"Bravo," he said. "Always studying."

"The problem is...I can't figure out a couple of songs and I'd like my friend Thierry to help me. You know Thierry..."

"*Bien sûr.*"

"Well, if you wouldn't mind...if it wouldn't bother anyone, tomorrow evening I could bring my cassette player down here to the breakfast room, and Thierry and I could work." I noticed Madani's dark brow furrow, and added, "I'd keep the sound really low."

"Hmm. I'd like to oblige you," he said, "but the music might be distract-ing— "

"Oh, I wouldn't want to disturb anybody..."

"Wait," he said, still frowning. "I don't want to appear indelicate...but per-haps you and your friend could work in your room." A splotch of red instantly tinged his olive complexion. "Pardon me, that was impolite..."

"No, no! You're right. It's the only way. Thierry's a gentleman, there'd be no problem. Thanks for the idea!" I said with a big grin, and whisked out of the room. My powers of manipulation amazed me.

The next evening found me sitting at my desk at the controls of my cassette player, hitting play and rewind. Since there was only one chair, Thierry sat on the edge of my twin bed.

"Stunning woman," he said of Melina Mercouri. "Driven out of her country by the fascists because she clamored for freedom."

"Exiled," I said. "Just like her husband who was forced out of the United States by McCarthy. How long was she banished from Greece?"

"Until about 1974, I think."

George, the dubious Greek, popped into my mind. I considered bringing him up but decided against it, remembering Thierry had mocked him in the Deux Magots.

Instead I asked him, "Is your family left wing?"

"About half and half. My mother's a teacher and tends to be—you'll have to meet her. My father navigates more towards the center."

"What about Luc?"

He shrugged. "Center-right, probably." Thierry leaned toward me. "Now, which song do you need help with?"

"It's called 'Paname,' a nickname for Paris, right?"

"Yeah, but don't ask me why. I have no idea."

Lo and behold! I had stumped the living encyclopedia. Still, Thierry filled in the lyrics I couldn't get, and the full impact of the song charged me with a desire that pulsated in the pit of me.

"Paname," Thierry translated slowly, "it's your eyes, your skin that I want to... to make love to. The right way...with the know-how of a gigolo."

I didn't stop him. Didn't insist that I knew how to translate; that I needed him only to clarify the words in French. He had hesitated, translated *baiser* as "make love," when I knew full well it was at least as vulgar as "screw." I didn't correct him. The French word sounded less coarse, more romantic and perhaps required a gentler English equivalent.

When we finished the song, for some seconds we studied each other. Thierry's olivine skin complemented his dark eyes, which searched my face but gave nothing away. He hadn't moved from his perch on my bed the whole time, and then suddenly he leaned forward and reached for the cassette player. His hand slid across the machine and brushed mine, which clung to the controls. His fingers alighted on mine and I felt the same *frisson*, the shiver of thrill that "Paname" had stirred in me. Then, a wave of laughter drifted down the hall, and I withdrew my hand and broke my gaze to glance at the closed door.

"I was going to rewind it," Thierry said in a thick voice, "so we can hear it again."

I looked at my watch, fearful my eyes might reveal something I wasn't sure I wanted to feel. "I guess we'd better leave or we'll miss the movie," I said.

Slowly, Thierry nodded.

We hardly uttered two words the entire metro ride down line One. We sat side by side without even our shoulders touching. If Thierry hadn't reminded me of our stop, I might have traversed the entire line, past the Etoile, right out of Paris. My two friends kept flashing in my mind: Luc, Thierry, Luc, Thierry, their individual charms alternating like singers Joe Dassin and Serge Gainsbourg.

I thought of Luc's assertiveness, his bouncy positive way, his quickness at keeping me entertained. I had stamped Thierry an introvert in comparison. Until this evening. Had he meant to touch my hand? I didn't know. Nor did I know which of my friends I liked better. I finally reminded myself to keep my urges confined to the city or risk ruining the equilibrium of our three-way friendship. When we surfaced at the Franklin Roosevelt stop on the Champs-Elysées, spikes of cold air slapped my face. Luc worked a few blocks up and across the street. The sidewalk seemed an emotional tightrope until I turned my thoughts to the movie to come.

American Graffiti, another film that had slipped by me in the States. Thierry had already seen it.

"Are you sure you want to watch it again?" I asked him, not exactly enthusiastic about revisiting the 1960s youth Americana.

"Definitely," he said, voice and demeanor back to normal. "I can't believe you missed it in America."

We sat slouched in semidarkness, our heads resting on the back of our chairs in typical movie posture. All of a sudden, a woman started screeching. Up we shot and twisted around. The woman, an usher, was verbally lashing a man about her lack of tip.

"Why do you think I work here?" she asked, loud enough for the whole cinema to hear. "Do you think it's a hobby? How do you think I pay the bills?" If that wasn't enough, she shoved her open hand under the man's nose and slapped it twice with her flashlight.

He didn't answer.

"You always tip them." Thierry said, as we turned around and sunk back in our seats. "A franc—half a franc if you're really tight. It's the only money they earn since the cinema doesn't pay them."

That was new cultural information. I didn't always see ushers in the cinemas. No one had appeared to show Thierry and me to our seats. On the other hand, I recalled uncomfortably, the odd time I had seen one of these enterprising women, I produced no tip. My face started heating up as if I were next in the usher's sights.

Later, over pizza, we told Luc about the incident.

"That's going too far!" he said. "She's out of her mind."

"Maybe," Thierry said. "She probably got exasperated by one tight wad after another."

"Do you think humiliating people will make her tips roll in? *Quelle oie!*"

Luc's slang for a dumb, empty-headed girl didn't please Thierry.

"That's extreme," he told him. "You know she doesn't earn a cent working there. What's she supposed to do when one jerk after another refuses to cough up a lousy half franc?"

I leaped in. "She did call the manager over."

Luc groaned. "And what did he do?"

"Started explaining the ushers' situation," said Thierry. "How all they earn is their tips. Then the lights went out and the sound came on and that's all we could hear."

Luc considered Thierry with a sour smile and then sighed. "I'm for ushers getting a salary, but hysterical scenes like that only run customers off. Thanks to her insane behavior, she'll earn even less. Not to mention the position she put the manager in. I mean what's he supposed to do?"

Thierry shrugged and that ended the discussion. I felt sympathy for both the usher and the patron. The *mec* might have been an unsuspecting foreigner like me. Thank God I had learned this new tipping practice before a similar fiasco could befall me.

One did anyway, and in one of my favorite restaurants. The Drugstore Matignon constituted one of three restaurants in a fabulous chain. Each housed a pharmacy, bookseller, record stand, and an eatery, all under one roof. I loved the Drugstore Matignon for its menu and its floor-to-ceiling picture windows from which I could gaze out onto the sidewalk. If needed, the restrooms and telephones could be found upstairs where the *dame pipi* manned the floor. I wondered whether the amusing term describing this type of woman's job had been coined out of affection or mockery. Whichever, the *dames pipi* seemed practically an institution all over France, and butting heads with one of these ladies who surveilled the restrooms could net nothing but trouble.

The *dame pipi* at the Drugstore Matignon appeared on top of things. With the air of an eagle alert for prey, she sat knitting in the vestibule of the restrooms where the ladies' and the gents' rooms diverged. Whenever a customer exited the W. C. her sharp eyes would dart up from her spectacles to verify the person had plunked a half franc in the saucer on her counter. The contributions ensured the smooth running of the restrooms, in theory.

One day I popped up to Madame's floor to call Luc. I made straight for the pay phone on the wall without setting one foot in the direction of the ladies' room. After I hung up I headed back to the stairs, and had almost gained them when a shrill *"Excusez-moi, Mademoiselle"* reached my ears. I slowed a little and then continued on my way without turning; no one had business with me here.

"Mademoiselle!" I heard again. This time I stopped and turned to face *Madame Pipi*.

Her glasses hung next to her chest and her raptor-like frown focused on me. "You must leave something, Mademoiselle," she said in a sing-song voice.

"What?" I said. "All I did was use the phone."

"No, no, no, no—right here!" she said, stabbing the air above the white saucer, speckled with silver coins.

I squinted and shook my head. "But I didn't go to the restroom."

"Ici!" she ordered, and pointed to the saucer again.

I stood there chewing my bottom lip. Madame must have mistaken me for someone leaving the lady's room. I closed my eyes for a second to better assemble my French. "But, you see, I never went near the restroom. I made my call and—"

Nothing doing. She stood up and launched into a scolding that sounded like speed-typing, half of which I couldn't understand. To boot, a cluster of W.C.-goers had gathered to watch. Oh là là, that sufficed. I dug out a franc—a whole franc since my nervous fingers couldn't find a fifty centime piece! I flung it in the saucer and flew downstairs, wanting to cover my ears.

That day I realized that as much as my French had improved—Thierry even spoke to me in French most of the time—I still faced a steep climb before I would feel confident enough to argue with a French person dealing with the public. Let alone find a job that could lead to a career.

The tiff didn't put me off my Drugstore Matignon, though. I just avoided the upstairs until I figured *Madame Pipi* had forgotten me. I had to eat, and the Drugstore made an excellent dish that didn't drain my pocketbook.

The dollar was in free-fall by now, and anxiety filled me each time I went to the bank to cash Gram's monthly money orders. I had scoured the city for the institution with the best exchange rates, and finally flushed out an Arab bank on the Champs-Elysées that sometimes offered a centime more per dollar; it wasn't much, but I felt better just gaining that little edge.

Food tasted even better since icy air had sunk its teeth into Paris, *and*, now that I had less money. I never appreciated the flavor of food as much as when I was forced to deliberate whether I could afford it. I didn't want to hit Gram up for more money, because she had already agreed to shell out more for my new hotel (she liked to keep me in hotels with concierges, rather than think of me entirely on my own in an independent flat). So I stuck with dishes like my *piperade* omelet at the Drugstore, which bulged with tomatoes and sautéed red peppers. I didn't let a trickle of it go to waste and consumed at least five pieces of bread to soak up the tangy sauce. Thank God for the French tradition of serving limitless portions of bread, since I had already been forced to cut meat from my diet.

That meant saying good-bye to my favorite restaurant, the Assiette au Boeuf. It served a cut of sirloin in a savory sauce that made my stomach rumble just thinking about it—especially now that I couldn't afford it. The beef's rich sauce had first strayed onto my fries by chance, and the explosive flavor made me an addict—until now. I also adored the Assiette au Boeuf's signature dessert, *charlotte aux noisettes*. Those ladyfingers layered with crème anglaise and chopped hazelnuts excited me as much as a sale in Lido Musique. Alas, both the former and the latter had spiraled out of my budget. Gram constantly preached not to scrimp on food. "Haley, you've got to keep meat on those bones!" All my life she had hammered me with that cliché, and if she knew I was skipping meat...and lunch...

I didn't dare suggest dropping a class at the Alliance Française to economize. Gram would order me home, for sure. Anyway, she would never know about my sacrificing meat for the occasional cheap music cassette at BHV, and replacing solid protein with omelets, *galettes* (peasant crêpes stuffed with cheese and potatoes), pizza, and bread and cheese in my room.

Plus, apples *à gogo*, a stash of which I kept on my desk. Propped on sidewalk fruit stands, apples incarnated late autumn in Paris. So did roasted chestnuts for sale on street corners and leaves piled on abandoned café chairs. By November, straggler-leaves, stressed with cold, still clung to the trees. Bruised and withered, they hung on their limbs like rags on a frail hobo.

I hadn't seen Luc and Thierry for about ten days. Thierry had been investigating a job with Air France, and Luc and his family had taken a trip south to visit relatives in Nevers. So when the three of us finally made a date, I wanted to caper about like a young colt. Part of the thrill was the latest rabbit they had pulled out of their hat: tea in the café of the Grand Mosque of Paris, a destination I could never have predicted.

There we were again, the simpatico trio in the Lancia, cruising the Fifth arrondissement for a parking place. Bingo, right next to the white-washed, domed mosque we spied an abandoned spot—the perfect prey, which happened to also be in the sights of a car in front of us. The Renault sedan had just eased past the space and sat poised to back in, brake lights on, right blinker flashing. Too bad for them, with Luc at the wheel in the jungle of cutthroat Paris parking. The driver of the Renault probably hadn't shifted into reverse before Luc gunned his orange missile and cut in nose first. No one got the upper hand on Luc. Still, I thought smugly, I did rattle him one day when I turned right on a red light while driving his car. Evidently, that's illegal in France.

Out he stepped in his grey suit and long, matching-wool overcoat. Luc dressed for success, especially now that he managed the Normandie. Thierry stuck to sweaters and jeans or corduroys for the most part. This day he wore dark-green cords and a black pullover; maybe to look dressier for the mosque.

The Grand Mosque imposed no dress code on Luc and Thierry. A different standard applied to me, on the other hand, since the mosque served Paris's vast Muslim community.

"We're not allowed in the mosque proper," Thierry had told me beforehand. "Just in the tearoom. And you should wear a longish skirt or trousers."

I didn't own a skirt longer than mid-thigh, so I settled on something dark that covered most of me. The November weather featured grey skies and cold winds, and my navy-blue wool trousers and pea coat suited me fine.

We crowded cozily around our little table, three bell-bottomed Westerners sipping sweet, steaming mint tea. I let the hot glass warm my hands and watched our server glide back and forth through the Moorish archways of the room. His thin frame spared plenty of long white robe to swish behind him. He wore a short, cylindrical white hat as well, and the way he bowed to people, eyes half-closed, transported me to Casablanca.

"I read the Egyptians are in charge of the mosque now," said Thierry, laid-back as usual, his wide collar protruding unevenly from his sweater.

"They seem to be doing a good job," Luc said.

"They'd be even nicer if they let us check out the mosque," I said, using English as a cover for the comment. "I know you can visit the famous mosque in Istanbul."

"This is a working mosque," said Thierry, continuing in English, "the most important in Europe. It's not a tourist sight like Istanbul."

I started to follow up and then halted. Nearby patrons seemed to direct odd stares and murmurs toward us. Two mustached men in business suits actually nodded at us.

Luc noticed too. "This is the first time I've been gawked at here."

"I think they're staring at me," I said.

Thierry's eyes narrowed. "They're staring at all of us. I'd suspect their Muslim sensibilities—two men out with a girl—but there's a young couple two tables down and no one's bothering them."

Luc shook his head. "Something's up. That old grandpa with the beard is trying to eavesdrop on us. See him leaning this way?"

Thierry sat up straight. "Speak English, Luc. They won't catch as much."

The tactic didn't help. People fixated us all the more. Even our white-robed server slipped a discreet peek in our direction—at me, I thought.

When I got home, Madani took the trouble to come out from behind his counter—a strange gesture.

"How went your tea?" he asked, frowning.

"Delicious. We left early, though. People kept staring at us and whisper-ing..."

"Of course, you haven't heard the news."

"What news?"

Madani drew a breath: "Iranian students have taken over the American embassy in Tehran."

After almost six months in Paris, my French rolled out with hardly a hitch. I couldn't remember the last time someone had flung, "Are you American?" at me. Not that people didn't suspect by my accent. I just rarely hesitated long enough for them to insert the question.

Now this reversal! Thanks to the plight of the hostages, anyone I conversed with at length managed to force in: "Are you from the States? So sorry about your countrymen in Tehran!" I appreciated their concern, but it made me feel like I had just arrived in France and was starting all over again. They even reminded me of the people who used to commiserate over my being an or-phan.

I read up on the hostage situation, of course. I delved into *Le Monde*, *The Times of London*, and *The New York Herald Tribune* for the American point of view. Other than keep myself informed, what could I do? I felt sorry for the hostages, but I just wanted to be left alone with *my* Paris.

That would not happen.

For one, Sasha started harassing me. Shortly after the November 4th inci-dent, she left a message for me with Madani. I called her back from the Poste, Téléphone, Télégraphe in rue du Louvre, two blocks from my hotel. That particular PTT office suited my phoning needs best, since booths on the street required the feeding of tokens into the phone as time ticked away. At the PTT, I could make my call tranquilly and then pay for it based on the time and distance of the communication.

I got comfortably seated in my booth and rang Sasha, expecting to hear all about Kevin and her, and their "problem."

Not even close.

"Come to the American rally," she sprung on me, after barely asking how I was. "It's at Place de la République. There'll be hundreds of people demon-strating against Iran."

I sagged a little. "No thanks, I'm trying to blend in here. I've gotten to the point where people on the street take me for Parisian and ask me directions—"

"Christ, Haley, Kevin supports America more than you! Anyway, I was hoping you could bring along your two French friends for a show of solidarity."

I shot straight up in the phone booth. "Why would they want to get involved in American politics?"

"It's not about politics," she said. "It's about the Iranians breaking international law. And maybe if I met them, I could gauge their interest for myself."

"Listen," I said firmly. "In the first place I do support America. I just don't want to march around with a sign making a spectacle. In the second place...I can't see Kevin going ecstatic about me bringing two French guys along...but if you'd really like to meet Luc and Thierry, fine. The three of us *do* speak French together..."

Sasha let a couple of seconds elapse. Then she spewed a stream of sarcasm. "Are you finished? I'm not ignorant of the language, you know, and I didn't say Kevin was coming to the rally. He's not my shadow. Especially now."

I sat back down. "What do you mean, *now*?"

"Let's just say he needs testing."

This was too oblique for me, and I told Sasha I'd have to think about the American rally. When I exited the PTT my head was reeling. A gust of cold air slapped my face and I was thankful for it. I needed to be on my feet, walking with a clear head in order to deal with this tangle. Never mind Sasha's little games with Kevin. Even parading about at the American rally would be preferable to introducing her to Luc and Thierry. The nuances of our trio confused and challenged me enough. Throwing Sasha into the equation with her raving patriotism...well, I found it unthinkable. Still, to keep her at bay, I had agreed to inform Luc and Thierry of the rally. That would buy me time to figure something out.

It turned out I didn't have to mention the rally to Luc at all. Of all people, his mother brought it up out of the blue at their home in Montrouge, where I had been invited for yet another meal.

"Do you know anyone going to that American rally this weekend, Haley?" Madame Perri asked at dinner.

After my initial surprise I tried to look blank. "Umm..."

Luc perked up. "There's a rally this weekend?"

"For the American hostages in Iran," answered Monsieur Perri, voice calm and sedate.

"Right," I said, before anyone might suspect disloyalty to my compatriots. "At Place de la République."

"Shouldn't you go?" Luc asked me.

Before I could decide what to say, Jeanne's sweet voice drifted across the table. "Luc, why don't *you* accompany Haley?" With that question Luc's sister sealed my fate. "Course, I'll go." Luc eyed me. "We'll go together."

"Good idea!" said Madame Perri.

"Shouldn't you verify whether Haley plans to attend the rally in the first place?" Again, the soft, rational voice of Monsieur Perri. We exchanged brief smiles. Then I looked around at the other Perri eyes focused on me.

"Sure, I'll be going," I said, verging on that tight voice people in the movies use when they've just been stabbed or shot.

"Luc," said Madame Perri, "why don't you bring Thierry too."

"Oh, I doubt he'll go, *Maman*," said Jeanne, in that high French sing-song voice.

Jeanne treated me decently, it seemed. Truth was, I really didn't know what she thought of me, given the ambiguous way she expressed herself. I wondered what she meant about Thierry.

Madame Perri asked, "Why wouldn't Thierry go?"

Luc shrugged. "It's not his style. He's not into that kind of thing."

"And he's too far to the left," Jeanne added.

"Not necessarily," Luc said.

"Oh yes. I'll bet he hates anything that suggests nationalism."

"It's not a question of nationalism—"

I would have liked to take part in the siblings' duel, but I had my work cut out just following the fast French, like arrows zinging back and forth.

"America needs Kissinger back in government," said Madame Perri. "He would know how to deal with Iran."

"I'm sure you're right, my dear," said her husband. "Still, we shouldn't harp on politics. It's bad for the digestion."

As much as the Kissinger comment intrigued me, I realized Monsieur Perri was charmingly correct. I gazed around the table and my eyes fastened on Jeanne. Because of her I would have to go to that blasted rally. With Luc willing to escort me I was cornered. An intentional maneuver on her part?

I studied her and then cast an idea. "Jeanne, you should come to the rally with us."

Watching her squirm in an awkward pause almost made up for the inconvenience she had caused me.

"...I'll try...have to check my calendar ...I'll let you know."

I almost laughed out loud.

Back in my hotel room, feet on my bed, I reflected on Sasha, the original culprit in this American rally mess. She owed me for this one. Would she do me a similar favor? I'd probably never know.

Furthermore, it was irrelevant. In a heartbeat the dreaded weekend arrived and I had a rally to attend.

Its location took me to Place de la République, an enormous square on the Right Bank bordering the north of the Marais. A looming black statue of liberty dominates the rectangular Place and makes it the ideal venue for the champions of freedom and justice. In this case, the demand for the release of the American embassy workers in Tehran.

The square teemed with waves of humanity. Bodies jockeyed for position and hopped up and down to get a better look at something or someone else in the continuous sea of people. Signs bobbed above heads, banners unraveled fifteen feet wide, and music thundered from loudspeakers.

Luc and I (minus Jeanne who conveniently had something important to study) had taken the metro. It wouldn't have been wise to leave our pet, the Lancia, on the street with a demonstration going on. Still, a problem presented itself. Multiple metro exits funneled onto the immense square, so that finding Sasha seemed impossible in the swelling crowd of French, Americans, and other nationalities.

I yelled against the noise. "I can't see to the end of this square with all the people."

Luc yelled back. "Too bad your friend didn't give you a landmark where we could find her."

Too bad...or a silver lining? We could flee this chaos right now, I figured, and head down to the Marais for a cup of steaming café au lait in a warm café. Mid November and it was cold as the core of winter. Luc's shin-length wool coat and my woolen pea coat provided leaky shields at best, for they couldn't plug the damp drafts of icy wind whistling up our legs and down our necks.

Yet, the words *steadfast*, *dependable*, even *patriotic* kept badgering me. I told Sasha we would be here and we could still run into her. Plus, if four-star-hotel Sasha could bear this paralyzing cold and see the rally through, so could I. Assuming she, herself, hadn't cut out. The thought made my cheeks burn. Unfortunately, the little spate of fury did little to heat up the rest of me.

So, collars up, Luc and I hustled about the square looking for Americans. Hunting for signs in English didn't help since almost all banners and signs displayed English text, including those borne by Germans and Italians. And as we forged through the crowds, I noted that not every sign's slogan supported

America. CIA, SHOW YOURSELVES! and YANKEES PAY FOR OUSTING MOSSADEQ! were embarrassing examples of placards shouldered by Middle Eastern types. So we followed some "good" signs that happened to lead us to a thicket of young people hoisting American flags as well as signs. One youth waved a large sign in big, red-block letters: KIDNAPPERS = CRIMINALS. It was Sasha, without Kevin.

"We're lucky we found you," I said, after introducing her to Luc.

"We've been moving around," she answered in a hoarse voice. Enthusiasm barely shone through her flagging facial features, turned red and stiff with the cold.

Luc used his English. "Have you encountered some adversity?"

That made Sasha's smile loosen up nicely. "No, not really. People are pretty supportive."

"We've spotted several anti-American signs," I said.

"Yeah, but no one's said anything to us. Most people are on our side." She swiveled back to Luc." Too bad your friend couldn't make it..."

Luc cast what I sensed as an apologetic smile at Sasha—and a little shrug.

Then as fast as she had focused on Luc, she swung back to me and shoved her sign into my hands. "Here, Haley, you can take a turn."

It took me a bit to recover from having a big piece of splintery wood foisted on me, but I noticed Sasha turn her smile back on Luc.

With a little laugh, I said, "Wait a minute, I didn't come here to parade around with a sign..."

"Then why did you come?" On the surface it seemed an innocent enough question, but Sasha's earnest eyes and wide smile didn't fool me. She was posturing for Luc and embarrassing me. Again she shifted her smile to him.

"I came to lend my support," I said testily. "Strength in numbers."

What a mistake. My stupid cliché did nothing but invite retaliation.

"Sometimes you've gotta put your money where your mouth is," said Sasha.

"I can carry the sign." Sasha and I swung toward Luc who stood there with a mild, neutral smile. Sometimes I forgot how much English he understood.

"Never mind," I said, glaring at Sasha. "I'll hold it for a while."

"Right," said Sasha, still eyeing Luc. "You and I can go fetch some flags. Would you mind bearing the Stars and Stripes, Luc?" And off she trotted.

I wondered whether she even heard Luc's "Not at all," as he trailed after her toward a group of fellow demonstrators. I almost hated them both.

But I didn't have time to dwell on it. What happened next came like an ava-
lanche. I was still gazing in Sasha and Luc's direction, when I heard a voice
bark English in a foreign accent. "The criminals are the CIA, idiot!"

I turned to face a dark-haired man whose mustache and beard framed a
nasty sneer.

"What are you talking about?" I asked.

"Your sign, airhead!"

His insult, textured with rolled r's, made me wince. I couldn't remember
what the damn sign said, so I had to rotate it casually to see KIDNAPPERS =
CRIMINALS.

The *mec* produced an ironic smile. For a second it softened the severeness
suggested by his dark facial hair, and I could tell he wasn't much older than
me. Then he yelled, "Your sign makes our students criminals, when they are
patriots! *You* are the criminals—your American government!"

The barrier between us hardened again. "Listen," I said. "The embassy is a
piece of the U. S. on foreign soil. Your *students* had no right to invade it."

"Spies! That is what is in your embassies. CIA criminals, hiding there to spy
on us!"

"Who says?"

"We Iranians." His black eyes intensified and I noticed his right hand had
balled into a fist. "We have lived with CIA interfering in our affairs for forty
years. They destroyed our democracy—"

I cut him off. "*We*? You weren't even born then."

Probably not a bright thing to say. The bearded jerk had been edging steadily toward me. Soon I would be able to feel and not just see his breath. Yet I
refused to give ground, although he had moved close enough to strike me.
Then he started pointing. If anything provoked a temper in me, it was someone pointing in my face.

"You are an American fool!" he said, stabbing the air in front of my nose. "A
foolish woman! You should not be let out of your house."

That was it. Down came my sign on his finger.

"Get out of my face!" I said, watching him alternately examine his finger
and glower at me. By now the burdensome sign had become my ally. I held my
weapon in front of me and rotated it like a battle-ax. He lurched, and I
thought he was going to try to wrench it out of my hands. Then I saw a hand
grasp his shoulder from behind. He spun around and started talking in what
had to be Iranian...to a person I recognized. A person I knew.

The exchange calmed him a bit.

Then the other man spoke to me in English. "You had better stop; someone said the police are headed this way."

The Iranian spat a final invective at me, which I couldn't understand, and took off.

After that it was just me and George. George, the fake Greek.

Who I found out, after we started chatting, was not really a phony.

"My mother is Greek, from Crete, that is how I received the name George."

"But you were speaking Iranian..."

"We were speaking Farsi, the language of Iran. It is also the language of western Afghanistan where my father is from. George lowered his dark eyes and then raised them a fraction. I shifted my weight and smiled uncomfortably, continuing to give my sign little quarter turns.

"Thanks for intervening," I told him. I held up my sign. "Who knows what I might've done to him with this?"

"He should not have assaulted you with his words."

"Something else would've been more appropriate?"

George's dark brows creased.

"Just kidding," I said, feeling jittery.

"It is not a day to joke. Things are not all what they seem. Not on the American or the Iranian side."

I knew there was more to this crisis. When I saw the sign about Mossadeq being ousted by the Yankees, I remembered some articles I had read in the papers. This mess merited further investigation.

"Still, an embassy's an embassy," I said. "If its personnel's safety can't be guaranteed, there's no future for international relations."

George's sad eyes were smudged with dark circles. He nodded and started to speak. Then his voice shrank. Luc and Sasha had finally reappeared, each clutching the staff of an American flag. Luc's rested on his shoulder.

"More reinforcements?" Sasha said. "Just as I'm ready to fold with this cold."

"This is George, a Greek acquaintance of mine. Luc and he have already met."

Luc extended his hand. "I remember, at the Deux Magots," he said in an even tone.

George gave his hand a quick shake and stepped back. "I must leave."

A couple of coughs and some scraping of shoes filled an uncomfortable silence.

"Well, thanks for coming," Sasha said.

"I'll see you around, George," I decided to say, after all that had happened. "I'm still haunting the cafés around the Alliance Française." I thought about rephrasing that idiom since George might not have understood it, but it was too late. The crowd had already absorbed him.

The three of us decided to leave as well. We ditched the signs, crowds, and cold in order to find a quiet, toasty café. Luc suggested the historical, elegant Café de la Paix across from the Opera.

Sasha delighted in the proposal, and as we hopped down the steps to the metro, she whispered something to me I hadn't thought of for a while. "Funny, you and Luc look alike."

I considered him as we walked through the gleaming, white-tiled metro tunnel. Through Luc I experienced everything that was Paris. Luc equaled Paris. A Paris where America had disappeared off the map, except for irritating reminders like the American rally.

Café de la Paix, Luc informed us, had served the likes of Oscar Wilde and other turn-of-the-century celebrities. As we sat waiting for our beverages, I started to ask him about the other famous people.

Instead, he changed the subject. "You seem friendly with that Greek *mec*, or whatever he is..."

Sasha chimed in. "Isn't he the Iranian guy you told me about? The one who broke down crying in public?"

Christ, I had to put a stop to this. "He didn't *break down*, and now I know he really is Greek."

Luc wouldn't let it go. "*Faut te méfier de ce mec*," he said to me in a low voice.

"Why should I beware of him?" I answered back. "He was at the rally, wasn't he?"

"What I meant," Luc said, "was any man who cries in public can't be very solid. And we don't know why he was at the rally..."

"Yeah, whose side is he on?" asked Sasha.

"...Ours, of course. He even defended me against an Iranian jerk who hassled me over the sign." That was the last I said about George. He had implied that much more lurked beneath this American embassy business, but I didn't want to go into the nuances of America's dealings with Iran with Luc and Sasha. They seemed to be rooted in black and white territory, or at least Sasha was. Yet she did have a legitimate question when she asked whose side George was on. He did nod his head in agreement about the sanctity of an embassy...but he didn't come right out and condemn the Iranians either...

At any rate, when our drinks came I steered the discussion back to the sterile, mindless subject of the Café de la Paix celebrities. Iran, I would save for my personal pursuit.

I read all I could about the grey terrain of Iran and the hostages. In the French and English-language newspapers I gleaned some interesting motives for the seemingly insane actions of the Iranian students. Until 1979, I read, the Shah had been the British and Americans' dependable man in the Middle East. From 1941, he permitted those Western powers to make Iran their political and economic base, and a convenient symbiotic relationship developed: what was good for American (and British) capitalism, mainly cheap oil, benefited the Shah as well. Then came the early 1950s, when democratic forces in the country rallied for a prime minister, and a certain Professor Mohammed Mossadeq stepped forward to fill those shoes.

He posed no threat to America until he decided to nationalize oil production. Then the U. S. and Britain closed ranks and plotted his overthrow, with the CIA engineering the coup. They discredited Mossadeq and forced him out. Hence, the YANKEES PAY FOR OUSTING MOSSADEQ! sign I saw in Place de la République. Things settled back into the status quo for some twenty years. Until the rise of the Ayatollah Khomeini. If the CIA's image-busting machine had portrayed Mossadeq as sickly and effete, Khomeini proved the opposite. The Shah had played the ruthless dictator and had to flee, finally ending up in the U. S. for state-of-the-art medical treatment for his cancer. That made the charismatic Khomeini and his disciples rip their hair out with rage.

Fine, all that was understandable. But the religious fanaticism and the savage attack on our embassy? I decided to call Thierry and pick his brain.

He puffed casually on his cigarette, adding to the vapory quality of the small café off avenue Foch. Thierry had chosen it for our afternoon rendezvous. An old-fashioned atmosphere enveloped the place, the way a droopy old fedora and sagging overcoat embrace an old man. Curvy, outdated wooden chairs and tables crowded the interior, condensation fogged up the windows, and a pale-yellow light filtered a blanket of smoke floating around ghost-like. The barman and I were the only individuals in the room not puffing on something. Nevertheless, I liked it. I had fallen into Paris circa 1930, half expecting a fellow expat to slink in, clad in hat and trench coat à la Humphrey Bogart.

Thierry stubbed out his Marlboro and began to offer his take on the American-Iranian entanglement. "The Iranians say CIA spies were trafficking in the embassy."

"Yes, I've heard that," I said "But I've read that all embassies are crawling with intelligence agents." By now I figured that was common knowledge.

"Spies," said Thierry, "are a given in Russia and Western countries—the Cold War and all. James Bond, George Smiley—"

"Mrs. Peel, The Man from U.N.C.L.E.," I added, and we started trading comic anecdotes involving our favorite secret agents.

"I'd like a shoe-phone, like Maxwell Smart's," said Thierry.

"Yuck—I can't imagine putting the sole of a wingtip that's been all over the city streets to my face! I'll take Emma Peel's repertoire: Beretta, leather jump suit, karate moves."

"That's a girl for you!" Thierry laughed, and I joined him.

Then we got back to business. "Muslims," said Thierry, "can be awfully touchy, compared to us Westerners. A lot of them don't trust us because they think we're immoral infidels. Whereas with the Russians and us, it's just spy versus spy."

I almost brought up *Mad Magazine,* thinking Thierry might have read it, but I decided to keep the discussion serious. "I'm not surprised the Iranians distrust Americans, but they don't have to take people hostage. They could've just severed relations with us."

Thierry nodded and lit another cigarette. "Death to America, the great Satan, does seem kind of extreme."

"They see James Bond and Emma Peel lurking behind every pillar."

Thierry started laughing again. "James Bond and Emma Peel shredding documents in between kissing and getting it on behind the Xerox machine!"

"Sounds fun to me!"

"I'd give it a go!"

Little by little we wound the laughs down. Our eyes locked and a nervous tingling stirred at the base of my abdomen, similar to what I felt the time we found ourselves alone in my room.

I forced myself to blink and return to the matter at hand. "Seriously, is the whole CIA coup business what kept you away from the American rally?"

Thierry looked away. "Nah. I don't like rallies, period. People act like automatons, stamping about and chanting stupid slogans in unison."

"Exactly what I think."

Thierry's smile returned, though his dark eyes had shifted from laughing to sober. He cleared his voice, a nice baritone. "You know, I'm glad you called me. I've got something to propose to you...What would you think about you and me doing some translating? English to French, French to English. I know someone who would pay us, and together we could do some good work."

I tried not to gasp. "I'd love it!"

"And how about coming to my house for dinner sometime?"

Of course I accepted. When we exited the café into the swelling darkness, a shot of adrenaline coursed through me. I pulled up my coat collar and we headed up avenue Foch to the Arc de Triomphe. We were going to climb to the top.

We took the passageway that conducted us under the pounding traffic of the Etoile, and when we emerged next to the arc, Thierry said, "When we get up there, you're going to see why this square's called the Etoile."

The cold's grip on me weakened with each flight of steep, stone stairs. By the time we reached the top of the Arc de Triomphe, I wanted to fling off my pea coat. Then a gust of wind slapped me, pricking my face with icy arrows. I yanked up my collar again and we started walking the circumference of the terrace.

I looked over the perimeter's wall. Below, twelve wide avenues, including the Champs-Elysées, radiated splendidly from the gigantic roundabout: the Etoile—the Star.

Rivers of light streamed up and down the Champs-Elysées, the intensity and speed of which followed the ebb and flow of traffic. Now, at rush-hour, lights gushed at certain points and caked up elsewhere. I watched the cars in the Arc de Triomphe's immense cobblestoned roundabout. With no painted stripes delineating lanes, harried, hurried drivers made their own paths, racing around the Etoile with sparking lights. In and out and around one another they zigzagged, passing at the fastest speeds possible. Rush-hour lights engulfed every spoke-like avenue leading off the roundabout, and the Etoile blazed like a true star in the nocturnal heaven that was Paris.

The gelid blasts of wind had calmed, and I started to feel the blood circulate in my face again. I looked across the Champs-Elysées toward the dormer windows of Paris's roofs. Lights blinked on there too.

Roofs of Paris. How many films had featured chase scenes on them? How many secluded rendezvous had they hosted? How many songs were dedicated to them?

Thierry had waltzed me into another dimension of Paris. I took his arm and squeezed it. But when I felt his hand cross over to graze mine, I thought of Luc and let go. Plus now, Thierry and I had a job to do.

4: In the Shadow of the Eiffel Tower

Around 11:00 p. m. I thought an electric cattle prod had zapped my brain. I shook myself and finally focused on the phone buzzing next to my pillow. An urgent call for me, Madani informed me after I picked up. I shot down to the lobby in my robe to take it. After that, I hurried back to my room, threw on my clothes, and within about fifteen minutes I was metroing to the Seventh arrondissement.

As the train lurched around a corner, my thoughts flashed on Madani, faithfully at his post behind the hotel desk. He looked alarmed when I told him not to expect me back the rest of the night.

I exited the metro and noticed the Eiffel Tower glowering in the dark. Its only light was a communication signal on top, but tonight I likened it to a cyclops' sinister eye.

Kevin answered my knock, which dealt me a jarring surprise since Sasha was the one who'd phoned me. He brushed my cheek with a kiss and swept me into Sasha's hotel room, arm around my shoulder. "Grateful you could make it, Haley. Come on, she's over here."

Sasha sat snuggled in bed, curled up next to the lamp with a copy of *Paris Match* magazine. She cut a glum, dark figure in that big bed, with only the night-table lamp on in the immense room. Her dark hair hung longer than I had last seen it and it looked flat and oily. Nothing in the room seemed amiss. Only Sasha's matted coiffure and swollen-red eyes indicated all was not well. I expected her to at least look pale or peaked, or too weak to sit up. Instead, as soon as she saw me, she smiled and slapped the bed with her magazine.

"Haley, come sit by me. Such a dear friend to rush over so late."

"Well"—I scanned the bed quickly and sat down—"I thought you were in trouble."

"I am...sort of." Her eyes started to glisten. She glanced at Kevin who stood at the foot of the bed with his arms crossed, and then she turned toward her night table, shaking her head.

Before he spoke, I thought I glimpsed a flash of impatience in Kevin's eyes. "Sasha lost the baby, Haley."

I turned back to Sasha's sharp profile. She wouldn't stop staring at the lamp on her night table.

"I know," I said, looking back at Kevin. "She told me over the phone. Did you call a doctor or something? It doesn't seem like someone just lost a baby here."

Kevin dropped his arms. "Didn't you tell Haley you miscarried two weeks ago?"

Sasha's answer came in a murmur. "I neglected that detail."

"Why?" I asked her.

She finally faced me, eyes dull as faded-brown marbles. "...Because that was the least of it."

Kevin turned his back to us. He sighed and rubbed the back of his neck.

Sasha went on a little louder, "It was nothing too hard to endure. Plus," she said with a slight smirk, "Kevin stuck around to help with the messy part."

He turned to me. "I'm sorry, Haley, I wasn't here when she called you earlier. I could have set things straight." That said, Kevin excused himself, walked to the bathroom and shut the door.

I frowned at Sasha. "You didn't go to the hospital or anything?"

"Nope," she answered, her plucky tone back. "It was a homemade job. I can't imagine ending up in a French hospital with something like that."

"You think miscarriages don't happen here?"

"That's not—"

"If you don't trust French care, there's always the *chichi* American hospital in Neuilly," I said, barely hiding my sarcasm.

She let out a dry laugh. "I'll remember that next time."

I peered into her puffy eyes. They were not laughing. "So you've pretty much healed, then?"

"*Healed*, that's a good one!"

"I mean, you don't look too sick..."

"Oh, my body's recovering all right. A little bleeding still. That's all."

Kevin had opened the bathroom door a crack and then shut it again.

Sasha nodded in his direction. "He's still nervous about that part. He was scared shitless when it happened. Blood everywhere. You'd think someone was murdered here. The Paris Chainsaw Massacre!" When she didn't even get a smile out of me, she turned serious. "Really, Haley, he was good about helping me to bed, running back and forth to the pharmacy. Kevin was the one I half expected to call you, what with his dim French. Yet he and his language rose to the occasion—my knight in shining armor, armed with loads of Kotex!" She was back in full form, unleashed on stage.

I was not in the mood for it. She could ham it up to some other audience! "So, *physically* you're all right," I said, and started to check my watch to see if I could still make the last metro home.

"*Physically*," she repeated, and her eyes darkened. "I'll tell you straight away: pain and blood are like kindergarten compared to *this*—this aftermath..."

She finished the fragment in a whisper, just as Kevin ventured out of his refuge. "Let's all have a drink," she said, as soon as he reached us.

Her smile looked fake and cold, and her invitation effectively put a damper on the discussion I imagined was the motive for getting me over there. Either that, or she just couldn't face being alone. We hadn't dented the surface of her problem, and my watch confirmed it was too late to catch public transport home. I had no money for a taxi either.

Kevin encouraged me to have that drink and went straight to Sasha's mini fridge for the preparations. Sasha insisted I spend the night, and by the time we had sloshed down a couple of scotch and sodas, I knew I had no choice. A regular slumber party it turned out to be, with me on the sofa-bed (yes, the deluxe room even had one of those) and Kevin with Sasha in that king-size bed, enough space between them to play Ping-Pong. Christ, what a bust!

I woke the next morning with gritty eyes and a pasty mouth. All night I had rolled around like a log in water—trying to get comfortable, listening to Kevin's intermittent snores and Sasha's high-pitched sleep-sighs. How the hell could *they* sleep so solidly, given the situation?

I probably should have stayed for a four-star-hotel breakfast. God knows my stomach would have appreciated it. But I couldn't take any more of Sasha's moody, phony crap. So, after gulping down a café au lait delivered by room service, I dashed out of there.

Outside, I squinted against the anemic sunlight. Thank God for Luc and Thierry, I told myself as I headed toward the metro station. The triangle fit me perfectly. I just had to make sure it stayed that way—nice and balanced. In the train on the way back to the Lux, I reflected on doing translations with Thierry. A job in Paris: what could be better?

Two jobs...perhaps.

The amazing prospect started with a peculiar visit. The visitor had first come to the Lux the morning I was still at Sasha's and had left a message for me at the desk. A gentleman representing an American organization, Madani had informed me. He would be back the next morning.

Ten o'clock the next day, Sunday, I sat waiting for him in the lobby, question marks spinning in my brain like a mobile.

Finally, the glass door swung open, and in stepped a portly old guy (he looked at least fifty), uniformed in suit, tie, and overcoat. He flashed a badge at me before he shook my hand and introduced himself as Frank Jenkins, FBI. Before I could say anything besides "Oh?" he suggested we take a walk to speak in private.

When we left the Lux, he turned right, and led me to the end of rue du Roule where it met a narrow, long relic of a lane called rue Saint-Honoré. The street wasn't unfamiliar to me. In fact, I used to buy my fruit from a vendor there, back when I could afford it. I followed Mister Jenkins as he turned right again and jay-walked across the street. There, we entered a café with a chipped and peeling façade—a secluded locale by virtue of its sheer unattractiveness.

We got seated and Mister Jenkins ordered a cognac. So much for abstinence on the job. In France that rule didn't apply, anyway. With his red and veiny complexion, I imagined Jenkins didn't give a hoot about drinking on the job wherever he worked. As for me, at ten o'clock in the morning all I craved was another cup of coffee, which I let go cold given my state of nervousness and curiosity. I barely noticed my surroundings, save a pinball machine with a young teenage boy grinding away at it. My eyes did little but search Mister Jenkins.

Who, after raising his glass in a toast, said, "I believe you frequent the Alliance Française, Miss Morgan?"

I stiffened. "Yes," I said, perhaps a little too loudly. In the back of my mind I remembered reading about foreign youth residency in France being tied to student status."

"Don't cut class too often, do you?" He said that in a chummy manner, the way one states something that should be true and then winks to the contrary. Mister Jenkins didn't wink, but I detected something cheerfully conspiratorial in his voice and eyes.

"No, I don't," I said with conviction.

"Good, you can't overvalue education, languages included."

He took another sip of his cognac and breathed a tranquil *ahhh*. "You're dying to find out how I know your business here, aren't you?" he asked, continuing to smile.

I nodded grudgingly. Of course I wanted to know! On the other hand, I refused to act like a tail-wagging dog who barks for satisfaction.

A hearty laugh erupted from him, as if he had read my mind. "It's no big secret, Miss Morgan. We've been following a friend of yours."

I bit my lower lip to avoid looking surprised.

"Which one? you're asking yourself. Not your two French buddies. They're your steady company, I believe."

I continued to chew my lip, not wanting to give Mister Jenkins the satisfaction of a confirmation. Shock, resentfulness, fascination—that's what he provoked in me. I wanted him to get to the point and tell me why the hell he had invaded my life.

He did, with smugness. "It's your friend George Abdi who concerns us."

I must have blinked five times before I answered. "Friend? I barely know him."

"Then how would you describe your relationship?"

I shrugged, trying to mask the awe I felt about his knowledge of me. "He's an acquaintance I met in a café. We've run into each other from time to time. But you obviously know that."

"Hmm." Jenkins frowned. "He knows some Iranians here. Speaks their language. Father's from Afghanistan."

"Mother's from Greece," I said, to show I knew something he might not.

"Right." He downed his remaining cognac and expelled another sigh of contentment. Then he sat up straighter and pulled down the cuffs of his jacket. "Miss Morgan, George Abdi is an unknown quantity. We'd like to know how deep he's in with a certain Iranian element here in Paris. Young men who know the people who made up Khomeini's entourage when he lived in Paris. Did you know Khomeini once lived in exile here?"

"Yes, but I didn't know George was involved with his people..."

He chuckled. "Understandable. But remember, we're not talking about association with Khomeini. George Abdi knows certain Iranians who in their turn know the Khomeini entourage. A bit of a leap, I know. Still, it's of interest to us."

I finally detached my eyes from Jenkins and glanced around the café. The boy in the corner was still banging at the pinball machine. On the other side of the room sat an old lady sipping tea. Neither could possibly hear our conversation.

I eyed Jenkins again. "What does this business have to do with me?"

"Exactly the purpose of my visit. We would like your help."

I must have appeared taken aback, for he quickly said, "Nothing dangerous, don't worry."

"I'm not worried," I said, and sighed with impatience.

Jenkins cleared his throat. "I just want to put you at ease..."

For a few seconds I stared at him. Cognac in the morning, loose tie. He even smoked his cigarette down to the nub. I wondered from what shabby armoire the FBI had plucked this agent.

"The Bureau would be grateful to you, Miss Morgan, if you could frequent George Abdi—socially. Meet him in cafés, and so forth. Then pass on to me whatever you cull from your conversations." His eyes darted around the room before he continued. "Of course we would compensate you monetarily."

I fully admit that as much as Mister Jenkins irritated me, I saw dollar signs and adventure dancing around him.

"What information would I look for?" I asked.

"Good," he said, nodding and smiling. Then the smile vanished. "I'll brief you and prepare you with a list of questions we'd like you to ask Mister Abdi. The first list will be casual stuff. When we meet again, you'll be debriefed, and I'll give you a new list with more personal questions relating to the company George keeps. A set of questions to follow will zero in on the target associations. Of course you'll have leeway to navigate the situation yourself. You're a college graduate and a history major, with experience of the world here in Paris."

My insides balked. Debriefing, graduating sets of questions, navigating on my own...my stomach went cold. What experience did I really have? None. Plus, the fact that this *mec* knew about my history degree gave me the creeps. Where did he draw the line at snooping?

"Listen," I said, feeling my face heat up. "I don't know whether this is for me..."

"No problem," he said, and shrugged. He pulled a card from his jacket pocket and set it on the table in front of me. "Think it over and give me a call." He cocked his head and lifted an eyebrow. "By the way, we'll start you with twenty dollars a session with George. Your pay will rise commensurately with the value of information you report to us."

Mister Jenkins tossed twenty francs on the table and rose without waiting for change. "Keep our little talk to yourself," he said casually, and I watched his smooth gait as he slipped out of the café onto the sidewalk. He didn't move badly for an overweight boozer.

Like a pagan god descending onto the stage of a Greek play—that's how Jenkins' visit struck me. Still, as much as his intriguing proposal tempted me, I planned to start a job with Thierry. One that didn't involve reporting to an old alcoholic. And yet, the money...twenty dollars minimum just for a casual chat with George. I would only have to look him up at the Poseidon where he worked for his uncle...an Afghan. Jenkins had said George associated with Iranians. Whose side did he really support? First, I decided to get things going with Thierry. Later, I would see about Jenkins.

A job in Paris. The mere thought of it amounted to an early Christmas present in the approaching winter.

Shadows lengthened as the sun stole away earlier and earlier each afternoon. One day it left behind a golden treasure ablaze over a vast swath of clouds and sky. The rareness of such a sunset almost brought me to tears. As the sun sank and twilight rose, a chill nipped at my memory: of home, of Gram, of a train's horn sounding in the distance. Of a cold afternoon when I was about four and accompanied Gram as she collected house-to-house for the heart fund. When we got home, she made me a caressing cup of hot chocolate whose warmth radiated throughout me, all the way to my aching red ears. Now that I look back on it, to my heart as well.

In Paris, all I had to return to was a hotel room. Still, I clung to the cold city. I continued to admire those venerable limestone buildings, all the more noticeable through naked trees whose branches formed random sketches across a pale-grey sky.

Sure, I missed my grandmother. Of course, she wanted to see me. So much, she insisted on buying me a ticket home for the holidays. She proposed the plan as I sat in the rue du Louvre PTT where I made my monthly calls home.

I declined the offer. I didn't want to abandon my friends, my cafés, my cinemas, in short, everything that had become my Paris. Plus, now I had my work. That's what I played up to Gram. How could I leave when I had a job?

The timing just wasn't right, I told her, and that tabled going home at Christmas for the time being.

I already knew Thierry's general coordinates: southwest Paris, Fourteenth arrondissement—a vague geographical indication that finally came into focus when he invited me to dinner at his home. He picked me up and ferried me across the Seine to a classic limestone building with flowery balconies. Yes, he drove me, in the car I didn't know he possessed.

"I never bother taking it when we're with Luc. His car's a lot more fun."

So I wasn't the only one who felt eclipsed by Luc. I deemed Thierry's white Peugeot sedan a fine vehicle and told him so.

"If you want to know the truth," he said, as we reached the fourth floor, "I'd rather have the car you owned before you came to Paris. I mean a 1965 Mustang—you shouldn't have sold it, Haley. Or at least sold it to me!"

Thierry unlocked the door. And I entered what I could only describe as a residential Shakespeare and Company.

I never saw as many books in a house in all my life. The living room alone had at least ten shelves worth. Warm wooden shelves that complemented the hardwood floor. And the books didn't stop there. Shelves aching with heavy, hardback volumes continued down the halls, multiplying from floor to ceiling in every room of the house. Books on each region of France, on practically every country in the world, every literary genre. Volumes on science, history, politics.

Thierry's mother gave me the tour of the place, after which we settled in the living room. "Who's the collector?" I asked.

"My husband. He's the bibliophile. He collects books. I just read them and teach from them." Madame Kérouac tilted her head. "And you're studying French, Haley? You speak it quite well."

I smiled and deflected the praise. "Thierry told me you teach French in a lycée, similar to an American high school, but different..."

"A little more far-reaching. You basically have to prepare yourself for university or a career in your lycée years."

"Not a bad idea," I said. "I know plenty of Americans who don't have any idea what to do when they get out of high school."

"Not everyone leaving lycée does either," said Thierry, slouching next to me on the comfortably-broken-in, burgundy-leather couch.

"Thierry's still debating whether to pursue a career with Air France," Madame Kérouac said. "Even though he'd be a shoo-in with his knowledge of English and German."

"I didn't know you speak German too," I said to him.

A subtle smile creased Thierry's mouth. "There are many things one can do with languages."

I had started to relax and was thinking about a response, when I heard a key click in the front-door lock. The door swung open, and in stepped a middle-aged man with blue eyes, fair skin, and thinning, wispy blond hair. Back to my feet I rose, to be introduced to Thierry's father. He and Thierry stood facing each other, which led me to conclude how much Thierry resembled his mother. She and Thierry shared dark-brown hair, dark, impassive eyes, and an olive complexion. In an armchair with curved legs and dark-purple velvet cushions, she sat smiling. The smile made her look young, almost like Thierry's sister. Monsieur Kérouac, the Breton, looked the northerner. Paris teemed with contrast and variety, from people to homes. I thought of Luc's modern, carpeted, gadget-filled house and wondered at the world of difference from this home, warmed with wood, leather and books.

"What do you like to read, Haley?" Monsieur Kérouac asked me, once we got resettled with hors d'oeuvres and aperitifs.

I finished a sip of my Kir Royal and set it on a coaster on the coffee table, while I mentally reviewed my reading interests.

"Actually, I'll read most anything..." I paused long enough to enjoy Monsieur Kérouac's smile of appreciation. "I like European history. I love the classics. And spy novels."

Thierry grinned at me. "James Bond, Emma Peel!"

Monsieur Kérouac cleared his throat. "Perhaps Haley enjoys more mature, realistic works depicting espionage. John Le Carré, for instance."

I must have revealed a shadow of puzzlement, for Thierry came to my rescue. "The Spy who Came in from the Cold," he said.

"I've heard of it," I answered immediately, having remembered the movie starring Richard Burton.

"Very realistic portrait of the spy business," said Monsieur Kérouac. "I've got it if you'd like to borrow it."

I was wondering if he had the book in French or English when Madame Kérouac called us to table.

The French rarely begin dining before eight o'clock, and with guests they never finish a meal in under about three hours. So it was no surprise that we were still chatting on at eleven p. m. What I didn't expect at that hour was for Thierry to make a major announcement.

"*Papa,* I'd like you to hear a proposal," he started. Then he proceeded to break the news of our translating collaboration. After introducing the general idea of the venture, he added, "I've already got contacts. Monsieur Garnier, who's procured books for you, says he can get material for Haley and me to translate from French to English and vice versa. He glanced at me. "Together, we'll make masterpieces!" He stopped for a breath.

I sat frozen. I had barely met his parents and Thierry was springing our project on them. So far, Monsieur and Madame Kérouac showed no reaction.

"We're the perfect team, Haley and I," said Thierry. "We both have a good command of each other's languages, and between us, French and English are native languages, so we'll do a brilliant job."

Monsieur Kérouac took a sip of his *digestif,* all the while his eyes on Thierry.

His mother finally broke the tension. "Would you be translating mostly English texts to French?" she asked, a spark in her eyes.

Thierry leaned over the leftover bits of Brie on his plate. "Yes, but as I said, also French to English."

I said nothing. I was too nervous to even touch food or drink.

When Monsieur Kérouac spoke, I tensed up again. I noticed a sharp glint in his blue eyes. "And you're suggesting this enterprise could substitute a career with Air France?"

Monsieur Kérouac was an airline man himself, a French representative for British Airways in Paris. I held my breath for Thierry's reply.

It came in a cracked voice from the flushed face of a boy. "I'd like to try, *Papa.*" Then he cleared his throat and sat back. "For a while, anyway. If I get it, the Air France job won't be available until January or later."

"Which is right around the corner," said his mother. I couldn't tell whether her brief smile was one of compassion or condescension.

Monsieur Kérouac drew himself up and folded his arms. "Well, do what you can from now until January. Then we'll review the situation. It's late now, and you should get Haley home."

I could finally breathe. Monsieur Kérouac had relented. He and Madame accompanied me to the door and wished me a warm good night. On the way back to the Lux, Thierry talked non-stop about what a prospect we had. I agreed, but when I reached my hotel room and crawled into bed, I thought back on what Monsieur had actually said—in particular about "reviewing the situation." He said *we'll* review the situation, and I questioned whether he meant that he and Madame Kérouac would have to assess Thierry's progress and then make some kind of decision. After all, they still supported him. But what about me? Monsieur Kérouac didn't even mention my part in the scheme of things.

It didn't merit losing sleep over. No, my worries lay elsewhere—with my grandmother. She had the power over my purse strings. At the end of November, when I again attempted to put her off about coming home for the holidays, she announced she was flying to Paris to spend Christmas with me. Probably to check up on me and review *my* situation, because I could sense waning enthusiasm about my continuing on in Paris.

"Gram," I said, standing up in my booth in the PTT, "translating is my education paying off. My partner Thierry is a scholar. He knows, French, English, German, Latin and Greek. We couldn't make a better team."

A pause ensued. Gram never rushed to words, unlike me. Sometimes, like now, I found it unnerving. "I understand everything you've said," she replied, in an even voice. Not low, not high—just level and solid. "My point is, the dollar is buying less and less. I've been following the currency exchange and I'm concerned you're barely getting by."

"That's why this job's come at a perfect time. Not that I'm having a tough time with money...I mean, I only spend on the basics. My translating income will just be a handy supplement—a hedge against the dollar."

"...And your studies? I won't stand for school taking a back seat."

I sat down and allowed myself a silent sigh. Gram was on the verge of capitulating. "That'll never happen, Gram. I'm as committed to education as you. In fact, the translating will only sharpen my French—give me practical experience of a professional kind. Someday this could even be my career." Wow, I was proud of myself! No one could have argued my case better, and with only a couple of fibs.

"Well," Gram said, "I'll see for myself when I get there."

Fine. Thierry had carte blanche to work into January. Once I had totally convinced Gram of the wisdom of my enterprise, I would have the rest of the year and the following school term to produce results.

Thierry turned twenty at the beginning of December, two months after Luc had left his teens. At that time he received what he said was his greatest present—an actual book to translate. Up until then, we had only translated a few technical manuals. Now, Monsieur Garnier presented us with an actual book, a short memoir to translate from English to French. A test, to be sure. If we effected a satisfactory job, by the publisher's standards, there could be steady work. And the book? Some obscure memoir nobody ever heard of, called *Cold War Chronicles*. Probably a sleeping pill, I thought, but nevertheless a debut for us.

It was a beginning worth celebrating along with Thierry's birthday. Luc offered to treat us. Magnanimous Luc. He seemed happy about Thierry's and my collaboration. He chose a Russian restaurant off the Champs-Elysées for our party, and that wasn't all.

He asked if Sasha could join us. A foursome, he said, would be fun, didn't I think?

How could I refuse?

To avoid stuffing two people in the coffin-sized rear seat of the Lancia, Luc and Thierry pulled up in front of the Lux in Thierry's Peugeot. We shuttled over the Seine to fetch Sasha and then crossed the river again, where we ended up in the glamorous Eighth arrondissement. Sasha preened in the front next to Thierry while Luc directed the show from the back seat next to me.

Act One: a cocktail at the Safari Club on avenue Matignon. The place had the aura of an English gentleman's club. Sedate, tranquil, with paintings of big-game hunting on the walls, and furniture upholstered in zebra and leopard skins. I glanced uneasily at the pictures and observed plenty of violent wild animals. I felt no discomfort...because I was surrounded by people, I assumed. The art terrors hadn't visited me in months. With any luck, I had outgrown them.

We all ordered gin and tonics, just like Englishmen. The Safari Club was in Paris, though, so the service of the gin and tonics was...peculiar, let's say. As soon as the waiter brought the drinks, Sasha weighed in.

"That's different," she said, examining the four uncapped mini-bottles of Schweppes next to four slim glasses. At their bottoms, a jigger of gin sat sloshed over two token ice cubes.

"You mix your own," said Luc, leaning toward her. "Permit me?" With a flourish, he raised a Schweppes from the table as if he were executing a commercial for the beverage. He poured until he received the nod from Sasha. Then he turned to me and repeated the gesture.

"What about me?" Thierry asked, feigned innocence dancing in his eyes.

Luc slapped his bicep with a solid *bras d'honneur.*

Sasha giggled. "Do you think they could bring us more ice, to do the gin and tonics justice?"

Americans and their stupid ice addiction, I complained to myself.

Luc wasn't at all put out. His fingers flew into the air and motioned the waiter over. When the little bowl of ice landed on our table, Sasha fished out three more cubes with the tongs. Then Luc helped himself, no doubt to put Sasha at ease. Gracious Luc. Normally, I loved that quality in him. This evening, not as much.

All of a sudden, Thierry joined in—to act American, I figured. Two tiny cubes remained, and all eyes had lighted on me. Jeez, was I the anomaly in Paris now? I shrugged and popped the lone pair into my glass.

I thought we would move on after our drink. Instead, Luc ordered a second round replete with extra ice. This second departure from French culture shocked me. One aperitif was standard in France. Ice and booze flowing without a bite of dinner, the night was gearing up cock-eyed.

Once we did leave, we had a short walk up the sidewalk to our Russian restaurant.

"I love your last name," said Sasha to Thierry. "Any connection to Jack Kerouac?"

"Well...we're kind of distant cousins," he said.

"Far out!" Sasha said. "You remind me of a Beat-Generation poet, or something like that."

I watched Thierry's smile broaden. "Kerouac did live in Paris too. Before my time, unfortunately, or I might have met him."

Oh, brother! I really wanted to set Sasha straight on that score, but I noticed a furtive look from Thierry and stifled the urge.

As we continued up the sidewalk, coats pulled tight, Sasha sidled up to me. She zipped her short mink jacket up higher and whispered, "I love your friends. Luc's technique is really suave. And Thierry's so cool and laid-back, with such good English. Not that I mind speaking French for Luc, he's so considerate."

"So, have you dumped Kevin?" I asked coolly.

As we passed under a street lamp she winked at me, and her eyes flashed like a cat's caught in headlights. I waited for her answer, but Luc and Thierry closed in and herded us to the door and into the restaurant.

Act Two: Candlelight glowed in a grotto-like locale. The owner, a short, middle-aged lady, said she came from Saint Petersburg—that's what she called it, instead of Leningrad. She lent a gypsy air to the place, her dark, highly-teased hair and heavy black mascara contrasting pale skin. Madame Marushka, I nicknamed her, and pictured her with a deck of tarot cards and a crystal ball on the bar behind which she surveilled her establishment. Tables crowded the room, so as I pulled out my chair, I took care not to bang the diner behind me.

Then the vodka arrived, waves of flavors whose names I can't remember, save the lemon and pepper varieties. I loved the lemon and hated the pepper. The others must have gone up in fumes, taking most of my memory with them.

The next day I had to squint, and squeeze my grey matter to attempt patching the evening together. I felt like Joe Dassin singing "Tellement bu, tellement fumé" ("Drank so much, Smoked so much"). Weird, because I could swear I heard the song at some point in the evening. I do remember the clever way they served the umpteen glasses of vodka, in little test-tube type glasses nestled in stylish containers of crushed ice. I remember the borsch, but not much else about the menu. I also recall the four of us jabbering and laughing, louder and louder as the night unfolded and the alcohol gushed, and that my chair kept slamming my neighbor's. And smoking. I did that too. "Madame Marushka" conversed exuberantly with Luc and Thierry, throwing in flamboyant gestures. Then at one point, voices from another table rose up—to complain about us. All I know for certain is the icy lemon vodka slid down smooth and fast.

When the hour came to leave, I remember I had a hard time standing up. Numbness and tingling traveled through me from head to toe. Not only my foot, but my whole body had gone to sleep.

I swayed like a boat in a squall all the way to the car, leaning on Luc, on Thierry, on whoever was close. I refused to put on my coat (who said it was cold in December?), but all three of them forced it on me. They packed me into the back seat of Thierry's Peugeot and I went right to sleep.

Act Three: I woke up the next day in my bed. My eyes started to focus around the room and found none other than Sasha, asleep at my desk. I squeezed my eyes shut and then opened them wide. Yep, that was her dark-brown mane straying onto her folded arms on which rested her sleeping face. She looked like a teenager in school unable to fight nodding off, whose head has nowhere to go but down on her desk. I shook my head and attempted to get out of bed. Every cliché describing a hangover fit me: the hammering headache; the aching bones; tipping off balance when I finally mustered the strength to rise. My mouth was so parched and pasty, it felt glued shut. My throat burned and my bladder verged on bursting, so I pushed on to the bathroom.

After making my way through the preliminaries, I grasped the sink with one hand and ran the water. Then I gazed into the mirror...and gasped at what stared back at me. Glaring-red splotches covered my face and neck. The appalling sight shook me more than all my other hangover symptoms combined; this one I had never seen in a movie. I filled a glass with water and guzzled it, in hopes of clearing my thoughts. No use: the alien polka-dots frightened me as much as ever. I plodded out of the bathroom, flopped back on the bed, and gripped my forehead. "What's happened to me?!" I said aloud.

"You mean, *what did you do to yourself.*" Slowly, Sasha's head rose from her folded arms. She plunged her hands in her hair, groaned and stretched.

"How did you end up here?" I asked her in wonder.

"Don't tell me you don't remember," she said. She turned sideways toward me and rested an arm vertically on the desk to prop up her chin. Dark circles loomed below her eyes. When I didn't answer, she emitted a sigh and gave a slow shake of her head. "It took all three of us to haul you up here. I almost asked your concierge to help."

"Madani?" I said, alarmed. "He owns the place...and he saw me like this?"

"Who do you think let us into the hotel so late?"

"Right," I murmured. "Does he know I passed out?"

Sasha stood up and stretched again. "We told him you were sick, and that I was staying over to take care of you."

"Oh...If I was out, how come you had to take care of me?"

Hands on her hips, she stared at me with wide eyes. "Are you kidding? You weren't just *out*, you were blue by the time we got you up here. Luc didn't want to leave you. Neither did Thierry, I imagine, he just didn't say it. He's not the extrovert Luc is."

As if I didn't know that. You'd think Sasha had known Thierry and Luc back before The Flood. Still, there she was, my blowhard, egocentric friend sitting at my desk.

"So you slept here all night?" I asked her.

"Yeah, I had to monitor your breathing off and on."

I started to open my mouth, but I didn't know what to say so I closed it.

"You probably feel like hell," she said, adding a little grin.

"To tell you the truth, I'm more concerned about these spots all over my face."

"Alcohol poisoning," she said. "I've seen it before. Seriously, Haley, you were slinging back the vodka like no tomorrow. And smoking. I never saw you do that before."

"*Lemon vodka*," I said, feeling my stomach lurch. "I wanna throw up just picturing it. Hey, how did you carry off all that booze so well?"

"Simple, I don't like vodka. I sipped a couple types, then stuck to Vittel. I guess you don't remember that either."

My frown was confirmation. "Sorry you had to sleep sitting up like that," I said, embarrassed about my dinky twin bed.

"No big deal." She yawned. "I could use some coffee, though. First, I'm going to borrow your shower. *Ick*, I'll have to put these clothes back on."

"Go ahead, then I'll treat you to café au lait and croissants."

Madani had terminated breakfast service hours ago, and, frankly, I couldn't really cozy to the idea of food. Still, I wanted to do something for Sasha, so I suggested we head out to a café in my neighborhood. I'd hoped to skirt Madani's attention as we crossed the lobby, but I was dreaming.

"You're still not well..." he said from behind the counter, dark brow furrowed.

"It's nothing," I said, pointing to my spots. "I must've had an allergic reaction to something."

I didn't think Madani, a Muslim, knew anything about alcohol poisoning. Still, I wasn't sure he'd bought the allergy business.

It took a couple of days to get rid of my red splotches. As much as I was happy to see them go, another departure was in the making. That one did not please me.

Sasha had finished her semester in Paris and now prepared to leave before Christmas. She had booked a flight on Pan Am and was wrapping things up before heading back to Manhattan and to a career. I figured she aspired to be head chef in a fancy restaurant like Tavern on the Green, or something. But no, she said she intended to open her own restaurant with some partner or another and her parents' financial backing. Of course, she would want to be her own boss.

Clothes and cosmetics littered her king-size bed, and I lay stretched out on the far side, watching her pack. "Tell me the story about how you almost ran down Jackie Onassis again," I asked. Strange, my wanting to reminisce about that stuff; how when we first met, she bowled Kevin and me over with her scandalous stories of Jackie O and the Kennedy kids. Truth was, I didn't want her to go. Her story-telling had grown on me with the passage of time and all that had transpired, especially now that she was leaving.

"Well," she started, already eliciting a grin from me. "She must've just slid open the latch on the bathroom-stall door, and I was busting to get in. So I shoved the door right in her face. I almost knocked her right back on the can."

The image sent me into a nostalgic laugh fest. "She even told your mom, right?" I asked, still laughing.

"Better believe it. She marched me right to her office and told her what a rude kid she had."

I regained my composure. "Did Jackie O really use the word *kid*?"

For an instant Sasha frowned. "No, I think she said *child*."

"You could've told her what druggies she had for kids," I said, enjoying the fantasy, for I still suspected Sasha's tales of Studio 54 cried exaggeration. But I didn't care. I just loved laughing and imagining the whole crazy scene again.

Sasha replied, "She probably wouldn't have believed me, plus I'm not a narc."

I sat up Indian style. "Do you think people will believe it when you tell them how we got robbed in the woods at Versailles?"

She placed a blow dryer in her suitcase and then smirked at me. "That one, I think I'll skip. Why broadcast what naïve idiots we were?"

I shrugged. "How could we know those guards were phonies? They did have knives." As I recalled, Sasha had been the one who freaked at those big hunting blades. The one who lost her cool. If she ever did tell that story, I reflected, she'd probably embroider it to her advantage.

Earlier, she had given me the address and phone number of her residence on Manhattan's Upper East Side.

"You've got to look me up if you come to New York," she reminded me. "And stay with me—that's an order."

I intended to follow it...someday. For the time being, I would stay put in the city that fit me well and felt so familiar I might have lived there in another lifetime.

Sasha had invited Kevin to visit her in New York too. That made me feel good, and I couldn't resist voicing a little curiosity. "So you guys managed to work through that little problem you had?"

Sasha's eyes dulled. She walked around the other side of her hard Samsonite suitcase, whose lid screened her, and stooped to busy herself. "More or less," I heard her mumble.

When she finally shut the suitcase, her bubbliness had returned. "I can't wait to eat some good cheesecake when I get home, in a proper Jewish deli. I don't know if I'll do that first or go ice skating at Rockefeller Plaza! If you visit in winter, we'll do both."

I let the whole Kevin business drop. Maybe she had never planned to confide in me that night. She might have just wanted my company. All I knew was I missed Sasha already, and she hadn't even left.

Thierry and I would have to rush the translating job gifted to us. We owed the finished French manuscript of *Cold War Chronicles* to Monsieur Garnier before Christmas, and it had to be a stellar work. Our financial venture depended on it. We decided to work at Thierry's house, in his mother's little office, so we could spread out dictionaries and notebooks and avail ourselves of his mother's typewriter.

We started poring over the text. Since we had to translate from English to French, Thierry and I had agreed he would do most of the handwriting while I filled in gaps, explained idioms, and verified the translation's correctness.

We hadn't finished two pages before we halted. Nothing rang cold about these *Chronicles*. Only hot scandals about communist Russia. We eyed each other, and then I resumed reading aloud while Thierry wrote. Again we stopped, and Thierry put down his pencil to join me in the reading. Being a faster reader in English, I flipped the pages before Thierry could catch up.

"Slow down, Haley, I'm not getting everything."

"Sorry," I said. "I wanted to read about her shopping spree in the communist-elite store."

"We should each read this thing on our own before we start translating it," said Thierry. "It's nothing like the manuals we've been doing."

"Okay, you read it first," I said, hoping I didn't sound begrudging.

"It's short. I won't take long."

"Just read it," I said. "Don't take notes or anything until I've read it too. Otherwise, we'll miss the deadline."

Turned out, I was too impatient for Thierry to finish and hand the book over to me. Apart from my great curiosity about the subject matter, I didn't want to risk delivering a late translation. So I set out on an expedition that took me to every English bookstore I knew of in Paris, looking for my own copy. I went to Brentano's on avenue de l'Opéra, supposedly the oldest bookstore specializing in English-language books in the city, but they didn't have it. I checked Galignani and WHSmith's on rue de Rivoli, with no luck. I even braved my ambivalence and headed across to the Left Bank to Shakespeare and Company. Half of me wanted to see Kevin and the other half still felt weird about him and Sasha. In the end it didn't matter because he was off work. I couldn't believe my luck, though, when the English girl on duty flushed out a ratty, dog-eared paperback copy of the elusive *Cold War Chronicles* from a dusty stack in a corner.

How could a little, unassuming memoir about the Cold War ignite such enthusiasm in Thierry and me? From page one, the title belied its contents. All the Cold War had to do with the book was to lend it a timeframe and douse it with irony. Nothing even implied the West versus communism. Just the opposite. The memoir exposed the outrages of de facto Soviet *capitalism* from the first-person view of a high-class Moscow prostitute. This voluptuous comrade, called Katya, earned her living as a call girl and escort. And from there, she made her way, bed to bed, from the shadows of the Russian mafia to the loftiest levels of the politburo.

I read *Cold War Chronicles* in one afternoon and an evening. I started it in a café, only to snap the book shut after about five pages, so I could rush back to my hotel room and laugh out loud at the antics of the call girl from Moscow. In the bosom of full-blown communism, I couldn't believe the materialistic haul she made: minks from Russian mobsters, a new car from a Kremlin big shot (no wait-list for her), jewels from her foreign business clients—oh là là! Good thing she had spirited her racy chronicles to Britain where she had somehow managed to immigrate. In Russia the high mucky mucks would have packed her off to a gulag for exposing all that dirty laundry. Not, however, without confiscating every ounce of her loot and pocketing it.

I roared at the way she described her clients: "In bed, Italian men are really timid rabbits," she wrote. Boy, did that blast a stereotype! "If you expect a Swiss guy to be more than a cool codfish," she said, "you may have to wait for the Second Coming when the Alpine glaciers melt with fire." And Russian men: "If you wait long enough for them to sober up, they might just hit the mark, instead of your belly button."

English slang *à gogo* salted the work, which sent Thierry into ecstasy over the linguistic ammunition he amassed, as we hammered out our translation each afternoon at his house in Montparnasse. Thierry hand-wrote the first drafts in French with my collaboration, and then I typed them. I didn't type fast, since I had barely paid attention in my high-school typing class, but at least I didn't hunt and peck like Thierry. That style would have kept us milling away through the Epiphany. Instead, our finished product, *Chroniques de la guerre froide*, rolled out of the typewriter a week before Christmas.

Thierry just had time to pack for his family trip to Creuse, in central France where his mother's relatives lived. A lovely holiday plan in principal, but worrisome to me.

"What if they call about the *Chronicles* and offer us more work?" I asked him, in the time we had for a quick coffee.

"Trust me, no one will call. They won't get back to us until after January 6th. Everyone in France shuts down for the holidays." Thierry finished his espresso and grinned at me. "Relax, you work in France now. We're not so uptight here about business."

"Oh," I said with a nervous sigh. "I hope my grandmother understands these cultural differences. She wanted to meet my business partner."

"And she won't stay until after New Year's?"

"Nope. Two weeks is her limit. After that, she'll be on the plane, and I suspect she'll try to take me with her."

Thierry's eyes widened. "She can't make you go back, can she?"

"I hope not."

When my grandmother traveled, which wasn't often, she went all out. She arrived in Paris before Christmas with a plan. Through a travel agent she had booked a room in a four-star hotel where we would both reside while she stayed in the city. Left Bank, Seventh arrondissement, flags flying on the building, by coincidence it was the same hotel next to the Eiffel Tower that had housed Sasha for some five months. Luc dismissed the district as old-fashioned, and I had found the quarter completely tourist-saturated when Sasha lived there.

It wasn't my Paris, but I could put up with it for a few days, since my grandmother's plans extended beyond Paris and beyond France—all the way to England, in fact, where she had organized Christmas for us. Grandmother Morgan, as much an Anglophile as I a Francophile, had traveled to Britain in the Fifties with my grandfather, Lloyd Morgan, to find their roots. Born Emma Thorn, her ancestors hailed from northern England. My grandfather's heritage, like his name, was solid Welsh. Sad, that Grandfather Morgan died of a heart attack in the early 1960s. As much as he and Gram loved Britain, they might have bought a little cottage in England or Wales as a sort of second home. My grandmother didn't like traveling on her own. She always said she worried too much about her rental properties to go anywhere. I knew she just didn't want to venture out solo.

With me in Paris, Gram Morgan had reacquired her wanderlust. She intended to check up on me first and foremost. No illusions about that. Now she could make merry, as well, in jolly old England.

Fine and dandy. I welcomed a trip abroad. With Thierry abandoning Paris before Christmas, Luc and his family leaving on holiday soon after, Sasha gone for good, and Kevin a virtual ghost, I looked forward to Gram's company. Now, if only I could restore her enthusiasm for my continuing endeavors in Paris.

Four days before Christmas, early in the afternoon, Gram landed at Charles de Gaulle airport. I had planned on taking the RER train to the airport to meet her, but Luc nixed that. Returning on the metro with the luggage would be a nightmare, he'd said, and taxi drivers equaled highway robbers. We would fetch Gram in the Lancia. Just as well, I decided. That way she could meet at least one of my friends.

While waiting for Luc in my hotel room, I tinkered with an idea...passing him off as Thierry. Crazy as it sounds, it actually made sense. I would give Gram the whole spiel about our translating business again, and, forewarned, Luc masquerading as Thierry could help me reinforce the venture. Profit dangled in front of us, I would re-emphasize to Gram, and the work would put to use everything I had learned in college French and here in Paris. All the money she had invested in my education could bear significant fruit. Luc gave the impression of a born businessman, with his suit and tie and outgoing air. He could inspire confidence in anybody and continued to amaze me with yet another career climb. He had netted a position selling telex equipment starting in January, to the tune of roughly 2000 dollars a month. A dream salary at twenty years old. Anyway, the Luc-for-Thierry caper wouldn't be entirely dishonest. All the facts about my translating business were true—one hundred percent. The one tiny, misleading detail regarding Luc impersonating Thierry didn't amount to a hill of beans. What did it matter?

Something, obviously, because I caved like a coward. I couldn't bring myself to ask Luc to collaborate. I would have to get a hell of a lot gutsier, I told myself, if I wanted to succeed in business the way he did.

Gram, dressed in a matching-tweed skirt and jacket, looked the same as I'd last seen her in Reno, only maybe a little gaunt and whiter of hair. I gave her a warm hug, and after we picked up her luggage, I made sure she sat in the seat of honor next to Luc on the drive back to Paris. May wonders never cease, he didn't exceed the speed limit by more than about fifteen kilometers per hour! Thank God, because I wanted her to trust Luc, and the way he burned the orange bullet's rubber when he had his mother in the car...

One day, for example, I sat in the back while Luc chauffeured Madame Perri. I don't remember our destination on that carnival ride, but after G-force-like accelerations, runaway-elevator stops, and speeds of eighty-some kilometers an hour in the heart of Paris, Madame Perri shot into hysterics.

"*Doucement, Luc! Doucement! Arrête—je descends et je prends un taxi!*" With Madame shrieking, "Slow down, Luc, or I'll get out and take a taxi!" I had to bite my knuckles not to laugh.

No doubt he was showing off for me in front of his mother. With Gram Morgan, he acted the quintessential French gentleman. After we dropped off Gram's luggage in the hotel, he took us to lunch at the Assiette au Boeuf on the Champs-Elysées. Months ago I had renounced my favorite restaurant for lack of funds. Now I could enjoy the bliss of savoring its succulent steak and sauce again!

In the Assiette au Boeuf, the three of us sat down to a classic-French Sunday lunch: white tablecloths, shiny floors, leafy décor. Back months ago, when I was alone in the City of Light, observing this kind of family outing made me envious, and left me with the *cafard*. These days, I felt as cheerful as any other family appeared around me.

Following my lead, Gram dipped her cotton-light fries in the rich beef sauce. "I'm glad to see you're eating well, Haley," she said. "Still, you look thin."

I limited myself to a polite smile. Not much escaped Gram.

Nor did it Luc, who had targeted our waiter. Friendly and solicitous, the blond, thirtyish *mec* made small talk with me every time he stopped at our table. I guess he was trying to impress a young lady out on the town with her grandmother. He didn't waste a glance on Luc or Gram, and by the time he brought our *Charlotte aux noisettes* for dessert, Luc had had enough.

"Voilà," the waiter said, as he placed our dishes in front of us—mine first. He smiled at me and lowered his voice. "Some extra sprinkles of hazelnut for Mademoiselle." Next, he set Gram's plate down. It wasn't until after he'd deposited Luc's that he got a response.

"Is chatting up customers part of your service?" Luc asked him.

"*Pardon?*" our waiter answered, and flicked a few strands of hair off his brow.

"And you deliver *Mademoiselle's* plate before Madame's? Is that how you were taught—to place a young woman's dish before her elder's?"

The unfortunate *mec* turned red as a poppy. "*Excusez-moi,*" he mumbled, and peeled off without looking at Gram or me.

I figured I owed Gram a rough translation. "Luc just reminded the waiter he had a job to do."

"Good for Luc," she said. "Such a rude fellow, jabbering in French to you and ignoring us."

Gram's first brush with public Paris hadn't measured up quite the way I would have wished. Still, Luc had scored points. After our now-sheepish waiter dropped off the bill, Luc snatched it and pulled out his wallet to pay.

Gram wouldn't allow it. "Let me have that check, Luc. Age trumps gallantry."

Why hadn't I introduced him as Thierry after all?

With Gram's largesse I bought first-class metro tickets to ferry us about town—the only time in my life. I couldn't have Gram luxuriating in a four-star hotel and then shuttling about Paris in cramped trains, on hard wooden seats.

Speaking of first class, our hotel room near the Eiffel Tower contained every luxury Sasha's had: refrigerator, television, a safe, plus a telephone that communicated directly with the outside. Last but not least, came the perk that I suspected Gram shelled out the fat francs for: a postcard view of the Eiffel Tower.

That monument, as well as the rest of high-profile Paris, Gram had already seen when she and my grandfather traveled to Europe in the Fifties. So, before embarking for Christmas in England, I revealed the best of *my* Paris to her. I introduced her to my favorite shops, restaurants, and cafés, figuring it fit with her goal of investigating my life.

Gram was a lightweight in the liquor department. She claimed tipsiness by just having a wine cork waved under her nose. Yet, she insisted on trying everything I liked. During lunch in a brasserie, I ordered us a couple of smooth, rich Belgian beers. I drained mine steadily throughout the meal, savoring the thought I could order anything I desired and not have to pay for it. Gram took tiny sips of hers, and halfway through the meal her glass remained almost full. She said she couldn't finish it and commenced pouring some into my glass. I held up my hand—enough!—but she merely waited until I looked the other way. When I turned back, I found my glass topped off. Grey-haired Gram could really be a kick on a trip.

She liked ethnic food, so I took her to the food bazaar near Place Saint-Michel. The little maze had mutated over the months. Summer hawkers had gone into hibernation and doors stood shuttered against the cold. Suspended, were the wafting food fragrances that had swirled under my nose during the summer. Yet, with Greek, Arab, Vietnamese, and even a French restaurant tossed in the mix, we could have been buried in the burden of choice.

I, however, had a little idea tucked away. Ever since George had appeared out of nowhere at the American rally, I couldn't get him out of my head. Along with him, floated the image of Mister Jenkins of the FBI. The mystery of the duo haunted me, like two faces of the same tarot card. I had informed no one of Mister Jenkins' visit, and that weighed on me even more. Now, I reckoned the time and circumstances to be perfect for a visit to George. What could be more innocent with my grandmother as cover? I told Gram I had met a waiter in one of the restaurants and steered her right to the Poseidon.

Mandolin music trilled, just as it did in most Greek eateries in Paris, even those run by Afghans. We entered, and I spied George stacking menus on a counter next to the cash register. I observed his slouch, his gloomy expression, and then a look of alarm when he lifted his head and spotted us. He recovered quickly, though, and reassumed his typical laconic air as he greeted us and led us to one of his tables. Master of tight lips, the sad kid from Crete nevertheless demonstrated great politeness toward Gram. I introduced him to her and he pulled out her chair. He then explained the specials, directing his speech toward her and barely noticing me. I didn't mind. It was nice to see the opposite of Gram's first experience in a Paris restaurant.

My eyes wandered around the room and over to the cash register where I noticed an older man with salt and pepper hair. I thought I recognized him from that sunny day in September at the Deux Magots, when Luc, Thierry, and I were lodged at Thierry's grandparents' flat.

"George, is that your uncle?" I asked.

"Yes..." He drew the word out in a high pitch, while his dark eyes darted around the restaurant. I waited to hear more, but he strode off to fetch us some bread. God forbid, that even in the remotest corner of the hexagon that is France a table might get caught without bread.

"Overly-serious boy," said Gram. "You can go from one extreme to the other here."

"Hmm," I said, distracted. I had focused back on George's uncle. Another waiter had paused to chat with him in that exotic language George had identified as Afghan Farsi. I could have sworn the waiter nodded toward us.

George slid the bread onto our table.

"Thanks," I said with a cheery smile. "You know, George, we're not in any hurry. It's Christmas. Tis the season to eat, drink, and while away the time!"

George's dark brow contracted. Then it relaxed and he muttered, "Right."

"Anyway, for us it is," I said. "I guess you have to wait a week or so for Orthodox Christmas..."

His shoulders tensed. The tone of his answer seemed neutral, non-committal. "Yes...I have to keep moving, Haley. We are, how do you say, à court de serveurs tonight."

"Shorthanded," I translated.

He wrote down our order, placed the slip of paper under the sheet of generic-white paper that covered our tablecloth, and whisked off.

"They may be shorthanded," Gram said, "but the present help seems overly interested in us."

One other waiter roamed the restaurant besides George, plus Mister Abdi, which made me wonder how they could feel short-staffed in a small place like the Poseidon. A total of only ten tables filled the restaurant. George, revved up like a Maserati, put the other waiter to shame. Moreover, Gram was right. The second waiter and George's uncle kept eyeing us on the sly. Just like teatime in the Grand Mosque...

I couldn't keep my suspicions to myself. "Gram, you know when I told George that it's Christmas for us, and that he'd have to wait if he's Greek Orthodox? He never responded. He circled around it and took off."

"He was in a hurry. What does it matter, anyway?"

"It doesn't...It's just that he's a mix—mother Greek, father and uncle Afghans." I nodded toward George's uncle manning the cash register. "They speak the same language they do in Iran."

"Iran?" Gram's faded-blue eyes sharpened. "That's why they're staring at us. They still have our people hostage—"

"*They're* not Iranians, Gram, they're Afghans. I'm wondering, though, whether George is a Muslim..."

"I hope not," Gram said.

I observed her frown and tense jaw. Most Americans I now ran into in Paris reacted this way to the topic of Iran and Islam: suspicious, defensive, resentful. I didn't pursue the subject of George with Gram, and, of course, I kept quiet about Mister Jenkins.

Three days before Gram's and my departure for London, Luc and I treated her to a tour of the Marais, where we showed her the Jewish community and a couple of houses claimed to be the oldest buildings in Paris. Half-timbered, faded, gnawed at the bases, they clung decrepitly to their fifteenth-century foundations. Paris's arthritic bones, I mused, as we strolled up to rue des Francs Bourgeois, one of the main thoroughfares of the Marais.

I had planned to show Gram the prettiest feature on the busy street, but as we turned into rue des Francs Bourgeois, I was stymied by an eyesore. Before I could point out the fancy little turret I liked, I had to explain a police paddy wagon left in the middle of the street. A *panier à salade*, to use Luc's slang. Why it sat alone in the middle of rue des Francs Bourgeois was anyone's guess. Luc said it wouldn't last long in that state. Indeed, we had barely started to move on when we heard banging on metal. We turned to see two teenage boys pitching stones at it.

After they cleared off, Luc said in English, "The destiny of police vehicles abandoned in Paris." He added a chuckle, but when Gram frowned, he cleared his throat.

I thought we could continue on, but the stoning of the paddy wagon turned out to be just a warm-up. A trio of swarthy young men now arrived from a cross street. They carried three signs—*MORT AUX FLICS, MORT AU CIA, ALLAH AKBAR*—and chanted their lines. Why here in the Marais, I didn't know. At any rate, plenty of passersby joined us to watch.

"What do those signs say?" Gram asked.

"Nothing. Stupid things," Luc told her in English before I could speak.

I didn't relish translating DEATH TO THE COPS, DEATH TO THE CIA, and ALLAH IS GREATEST. The paddy wagon was bad enough, and I didn't need this rot muddying Gram's view of Paris.

But Gram wouldn't let go. She squinted. "Something about the CIA—'death' it looks like. And the Muslim word for God. Iranians tormenting us here too?"

"No!" I said. Immediately I lowered my voice. "It's just some lunatic fringe. You get them in every big city. If anything, people support the hostages here."

"If you say so," Gram replied, with little conviction in her tone.

I found myself clenching my teeth.

"Let's continue," said Luc. "We have still much to see before you leave. Don't worry, those guys are just *voyous*. How do you say that, Haley?"

"Louts." That sounded better than hoodlums or hooligans.

Gram made no comment, and we finally made our way down the street. I didn't even notice my little turret. Instead, I pondered. The demonstration brought back the American rally and my encounter with that Iranian jerk whom George had calmed down. What *was* George doing at the rally? According to Mister Jenkins, he ran with a crowd with ties to Khomeini's entourage. And he acted like he didn't know when Orthodox Christmas started. So, perhaps he was a Muslim...

The next day, embarrassment continued to stalk me. Gram and I had ensconced ourselves in an elegant tea and pastry room across from the Louvre, next door to my little Gothic church, Saint-Germain l'Auxerrois. If we just hadn't lingered so long, nursing our hot tea, nibbling those delicious mini-muffin-like *financiers*, enjoying the classical decor of the salon...we wouldn't have crossed paths with him. Shortly after he sat down, a man with voluminous curly-blond hair and luminous blue eyes latched onto my gaze. An inane smile danced in his eyes and wouldn't leave me. Each time I stole a glance at him, the smile swelled.

"Let's get going," I said, hoping Gram hadn't noticed him. "I want you to see my hotel and meet Madani while it's still daylight."

The corners of Gram's mouth went down. "How long has that jackass been staring at you?"

I dismissed her observation. "Not long. He's just a goof."

We walked out, across the sand in front of the lacy Auxerrois, and headed toward rue de Rivoli, the direction of my Lux Hotel. I shivered in my pea coat and hunched my shoulders against the cold. I raised my face toward the pallid sky, trying to absorb a stray ray or two of sun. I rotated my head left...and stiffened. There he was: big eyes, big hair, big silly smile beaming at me from across the street as he strolled parallel to us on the sand in front of the Louvre. Fortunately, I had Gram on the other side of me. I quickened my gait, only to relent to keep even with Gram and block her view. At the corner of rue de l'Amiral de Coligny and rue de Rivoli he was still with us, like gum stuck to my shoe. Surely he would get bored and leave off when we turned right.

Nothing doing. Gram and I crossed the street and turned right. As did Bubble Eyes, still grinning like a caiman.

This type of behavior didn't surprise me in Paris. One night, I was trotting home late, when I came face to face with this African-looking guy. I made my mistake, I suppose, by looking him in the eyes. Instead of walking on by, he swiveled and started following me. From Place de la Concorde all the way back to my hotel he dogged me, right to the door where finally he backed off, and that was the last of him.

Now, an encore, with Gram evaluating my life in Paris—just as I prepared to introduce her to Madani and show her how well he had lodged and looked after me. One more block and we would be turning onto rue du Roule and pulling into the Lux. The street was so short and narrow, even the presence of a busload of sightseers wouldn't mask this *mec*.

Closing in on the Ciseaux d'Argent, a corner shop on my street. Time to turn left. Done. A few paces down rue du Roule I threw a casual glance back. Hallelujah—he had disappeared!

Gram spoke without looking at me. "Is your young man still following us?"

Merde! I complained to myself and then drew myself up confidently. "Nope, he's loped off," I said, as if referring to a stray dog.

"Good," said Gram. "It'll be nice to get you away from here for a week."

Throughout the entire train ride up to Boulogne on the English Channel, I brooded and watched the brown winter landscape file by. I feared my grandmother planned to quash my life in Paris. Things couldn't get any worse after Bubble Eyes, I had hoped. Then, that very evening after I'd shaken him off, we happened to land in a taxi with a dishonest driver. He tried taking us the long way back to our hotel, so I ordered him to halt and let us out so we could take the metro the rest of the way home. And if that weren't enough, the day before we left for London some jerk of a waiter attempted to over-charge us for lunch. I called for the manager and he adjusted the bill. On my own, no one tried to cheat me. By speaking English like a couple of tourists, Gram and I invited predators.

The curious thing about Gram is she didn't recite the litany of incidents; didn't throw them in my face, not even the stoning of the paddy wagon and the vociferous Muslims. She had to be saving them up, I assumed. Mentally collecting them to spring on me when her purpose required them. Meanwhile, all I could do was wait and watch.

I continued to brood when we embarked on our ferry. As soon as we hit the high waves of the English Channel, though, everything fled my mind, chased out by a violent onset of seasickness. I couldn't even stand, let alone explore the shops onboard. Gram felt fine and could have accomplished all the exploring for both of us, except she claimed to be tired.

My fate was to sit dead still and stare straight ahead. I couldn't even move my eyes without a flood of nausea threatening to eject the contents of my stomach. Gram sat next to me, tranquilly sipping a cup of tea she had bought at the refreshments bar. "The waves aren't big at all," she said. I found that hard to believe and impossible to verify, since I couldn't even turn my head to look at her while she talked to me. I only managed to smile weakly at the seat in front of me and envy Gram's constitution.

Once on dry land, my nausea subsided and we boarded a train (I, still a little wobbly) that took us to Victoria Station in London. From there, we taxied to the Kensington Hilton in London's West End and settled into our room and base for our holiday. Gram continued her silence on the subject of my life in Paris, but it stopped troubling me when London began to swallow me up.

Gram became the guide in London. Her itinerary—pub lunches, a play at the Phoenix Theatre, a tour of the Tower of London with its jewels and weapons, a visit to the houses of Parliament and Westminster Abbey, plus a side trip to Stratford-on-Avon—more than monopolized my mind. Cab drivers called me "Luv," and I didn't even wince when a desk clerk said, "Haley! Like our Hayley Mills." In fact, I enjoyed it.

Gram bought me a new coat for Christmas, a long, camel's hair variety, and I gave her a bottle of Hermès eau de toilette, which even at the Samaritaine cost me almost the last of my cash.

"You've got to have a warmer coat," Gram said about the camel's hair. I suspected she had grown sick of seeing me day after day in my pea coat. Whatever her main motive, I appreciated the gesture. With the British pound grinding the dollar into the gutter, Gram was spending a fortune. Plus, she gave her all every day in order for us not to miss anything. Then, in the evening after dinner, she retreated to bed exhausted. I looked on the bright side: she didn't do badly for a lady in her late sixties.

I never let on about my money problems, and she made no further comments about the martyred dollar or me not being able to keep up financially in Paris. "I'm getting old, and I don't know if I'll be around for another trip like this," she said one day, after she had splurged and bought me a new portable radio-cassette player with dual cassette capability. I knew she had to be exaggerating about "her last trip." Gram just didn't like leaving home by herself.

The Christmas coat came in handy, but she knew I had longed for a cassette player to record from cassette to cassette and make music compilations. After watching me halt in front of every electronics window we passed, she finally steered me into one and bought me my Christmas toy. I felt like a little kid again.

Still, I felt bad about not being able to contribute any money. Too bad Monsieur Garnier was waiting until after the holidays to pay Thierry and me for *Cold War Chronicles*. About all I could afford to buy myself in London was a candy bar every now and then. Not that Gram would have let me pay for any of the major expenses, but I would have liked to offer.

At the end of our trip, Gram gave me her leftover pounds and I bought a Rod Stewart tape, the one with "Da Ya Think I'm Sexy?" I chose it to christen my new player, because the tune reminded me of my early days in Paris when I was still taking baby steps. I guess I had come a little ways.

I waited until Gram busied herself in the bathroom to put the album on, so I could savor the song alone. Rock didn't please Gram, and I wouldn't have dreamed of sharing "Da Ya Think I'm Sexy?" with her. Plus, I needed a moment of privacy to review my situation. To take stock. I stretched out on my bed, feet up, with my head and shoulders propped against the headboard. After a week in England, I still had no idea where I stood with Gram in terms of my future in Paris. By now I knew time had run out for her to arrange my immediate transfer home. Yet she still hadn't given me the go-ahead to stay on for another entire semester. And I was afraid to ask her.

Three days later, I found myself in the same position: lying on my bed, resting against the headboard—this time, in the shadow of the Eiffel Tower. Christmas week had come and gone: go, go, eat, eat, hardly time to think. Then the return to Paris and to our hotel. Gram's last day of vacation had arrived, and now I watched her pack. Before she left for home Gram had counted on visiting my school, but when we returned to Paris, we found the Alliance Française shuttered until after January sixth. By not taking her there first I had blundered badly, and I continued to scold myself as I watched her place her things carefully in her suitcase. School—solid and serious—constituted the one thing my grandmother believed in unwaveringly.

Gram swung by our room's elegant desk and lifted some papers from it. "Is this the book you translated?"

I leaned over to see what she had uncovered. "Yeah," I answered, and sat up straight. "It's the one I'm getting paid for after the holidays. Then more work will follow."

She picked up my copy of *Cold War Chronicles* and sat at the richly-carved, curvy-legged desk. I observed her for a moment and then turned an eye to the television so as not to appear nosy. I couldn't concentrate, though, so I looked back at her and waited as she read.

After skimming it, she finally turned the book over and put it down. Then she faced me. "You mean to tell me people are paying you for translating this?"

The comment disconcerted me. I smiled and shrugged. "It's a true story. And a revelation about communism."

"It shows Russia's worse than I thought. And this Katya!"

I swung my legs off the bed and sat up straight, for an impulse to argue vigorously had seized me. Then, I stopped myself. I relaxed my hands and looked her in the eye with my most sober expression. "It's a very marketable work that'll earn the publisher a lot of money."

Gram's glare slowly melted and a subtle smile took its place. I could have sworn her pale-blue eyes even emitted a twinkle.

"I've always known you were a bright, capable child," she said. "Last week, you kept them from over-charging us in the restaurant and stopped that cab driver from taking us God-knows-where." She glanced at *Cold War Chronicles*. "I'm sure you did a fine job translating this, and I don't think many people will get the best of you." Her eyes turned sharp again. "Are you signed up for school next semester?"

Her speech had stunned me, but I think I managed to smile at her. "Of course!"

"Good. Because it's important to finish what you've started. And don't forget: education is the reason you're doing good work."

Relief washed over me and I let my shoulders relax. "You know, Gram, I could get myself an apartment here. Save you some money..."

"Oh no. I'd like you to stay put at Mister Madani's. I approve of the way he holds down the fort."

I smiled to myself at the implications.

"I'd like you to call me every two weeks from now on," she said. "And I'll expect reports on your business pursuit."

I agreed whole-heartedly. Gram's concession amounted to nothing less than a new lease on life. I vowed to make my best of it.

With Luc and Thierry absent from Paris, Gram and I hired a taxi to the airport where I saw her off and then caught the RER train back to town. During the forty-five minute return, a strange hollowness stole into me, gliding with me back to Paris and over to the Eiffel Tower hotel where I had to stay until January. By error, Madani had booked someone into my room in the Lux until after New Year's, and not one other room was available. He had given me the bad news while my grandmother was still in Paris, so, at Gram's expense, I would be stuck in our Eiffel Tower hotel room until mine came vacant at the Lux. That seemed to calm a fretting Madani who said he looked forward to welcoming me back into the fold in January of 1980. I wished it could be sooner.

After I arrived at my four-star hotel, I had nothing to do but lounge in a cushiony armchair. I tried imagining what Luc and Thierry might be up to, but I couldn't stop reflecting on my fun with Gram "the tour guide" in London, and her assessment of me that followed. I stood and started wandering around the big room. I walked past the fancy desk and my eyes lighted on *Cold War Chronicles*, lying the way Gram had left it—spine up and flattened. I picked it up to read where she had left off. Katya had just earned a bundle through a threesome involving a politico and a fellow working girl. Poor Gram, no wonder she had flared indignant. Obviously, she couldn't quite wrap her mind around unconventional sex. Yet, without too much trouble, she had digested DEATH TO THE CIA, the pelting of the paddy wagon, and leering Bubble Eyes. Not bad for a sixty-eight-year old. And of course, there remained her assessment of me.

I slid Rod Stewart back into my brand-new cassette player and sat down again. Gram popped back into my mind. This time I pictured her filling my glass with her beer. She had continued that comical behavior in London. I started to laugh out loud...only for a couple of seconds. Because then I began to cry—just like a baby. Maybe it was the vacuum of vacation, or that I just missed Gram and hadn't told her. Either way, I felt like an empty shell.

The *coup de cafard*, the blow of blues, that hit me in the Eiffel Tower hotel continued to plague me. Having a television helped. I got engaged in some French shows, and the American programs dubbed in French amused and fascinated me. Translating American shows for French TV, that's what Thierry and I needed to break into.

I finished the last Orangina in my fridge, so I decided to go shopping now that I had Gram's remaining francs and her money order for January. Before I left the room, I gathered up all my laundry to drop off at the hotel desk. Might as well reap what I could from the colossal tomb I inhabited.

Escaping the hotel, despite the arctic air outdoors, made me feel better. I hugged my long camel's hair coat, which offered twice the warmth of my old pea coat, and squinted against the cold. I didn't want to buy more Orangina until right before returning to the hotel, so I pondered what else to do. It didn't take long for a brilliant idea to strike me: Shakespeare and Company. I had given Gram the tour of that phenomenon of a bookstore before we left for London, but an employee had told me Kevin too was on holiday and wouldn't be back until after Christmas. It was about time he and I caught up.

After hiking across the entire Seventh arrondissement and part of the Sixth, with my hands in my pockets, I got tired of the cold. Well, not exactly—I couldn't wait to see Kevin. From my purse I extracted my *Plan de Paris par Arrondissements*, a bible for anyone living in Paris. The brownish-maroon, vinyl-covered book contained maps of each arrondissement, replete with metro and bus information—basically the whole city dissected page by page. With a quick glance, I found my metro route: Mabillon to Maubert-Mutualité, a straight shot on Line Ten.

The store hadn't lost an iota of its charm now that the sidewalk books had been reeled in for the winter and the creaking, drafty doors were kept approximately closed against the elements. I entered and found Kevin, layered in a shirt and wool pullover, studying a shelf of books on the ground floor of the chilly shop. I tiptoed up behind him and tickled him in the ribs. "Boo!"

He whipped around. "Bloody hell—it's none other than Hayley Mills!" His feigned surprise instantly turned to laughter. "Where the hell have you been?"

"What about you? I was in here before Christmas and they told me you'd taken off somewhere."

"England—home for the holidays. Well, Christmas anyway."

"England—that's exactly where I've been," I said proudly.

"You're joking? Where in England?"

The small talk pitter-pattered on as we went out for a coffee break, which turned into making a date for the evening and me inviting my old chum for a drink at my hotel. Why waste all that space, when I could actually *entertain* there?

Kevin said he would be bringing my Christmas present. That threw me into a tizzy and granted me barely the afternoon to find something for him, without a shadow of an idea.

Jostling shoulders with invading tourist hordes normally annoyed the heck out of me. Nevertheless, I started out browsing rue de Rivoli next to the Louvre. It was a tourist trap for sure, but the street's arcaded bazaar of shops offered a slew of choices. Plus, I just felt like being around lots of people.

After glancing into a variety of windows, I chose to enter a little boutique stuffed with inventory. Trinkets, such as miniature Eiffel Towers, abounded. Scaled-down copies of museum statues crowded glass shelves. I actually liked the sleek little discus thrower and the fierce Roman charioteer, but the proportions of the mini Michelangelo David looked positively grotesque.

Bins bulged with small, rectangular prints of Louvre and Jeu de Paume masterpieces, printed on something canvas-like and stapled to wood backings. Monet and Renoir reproductions dominated, considering tourists went gaga over the impressionists. Flush with Gram's francs, I decided to expand my after-the-fact Christmas shopping to include presents for Luc and Thierry. Not here, though. These chachkas (another one of Sasha's expressions) belonged on American mantelpieces.

I started to make for the door, but couldn't get there fast enough. A young clerk swooped down on me and shoved a Monet print under my nose. "This is from the Jeu de Paume, Mademoiselle," he said, long dark hair obscuring part of his eye. "You know, Paris's impressionist museum? Look, it's on canvas."

I managed to avoid a smirk. "They're copies of works from the Jeu de Paume."

"*Oui, d'accord,*" he said, "but they're good." Then he attacked my other flank. "Take a look at these Greek statuettes." He pointed to a glass shelf next to the window, right above the discus throwers. "Check out the Venus de Milo—*real marble.*"

I couldn't resist a skeptical frown. Still, I thrived on the banter and unleashed my colloquial French to distinguish myself from the tourists. "Listen, the *mecs* I have to buy for are Parisian, so if—"

"Mademoiselle, you should have said so!" With a jerk of his head, he flung his hair back and shot me a complicit grin. "Please, come to the back."

I followed his beckoning index finger, my frown intact. And there, draped on some racks, hung the payoff—winter scarves.

The *mec* probably noticed my eyes brighten. "Look at this one. Very attractive in red and blue, with *Paris* written stylishly on it."

My frown returned.

"Oh, right, you're buying for Parisians." He waved his hand toward a group of plaid scarves. "Take a look at these."

One hundred percent acrylic, I read on a label. Not wool, but ever so soft and about five dollars apiece. The colorful plaids could cheer the atmosphere of these interminably leaden days, I thought, so I bought three, and the enthusiastic clerk gift-wrapped them.

There it shone, a pretty little gold package finished with green ribbon, displayed on one of the tables of my four-star room. On another table stood two small bottles, one of Martini and Rossi sweet vermouth and another of gin. I had picked them up at the end of my outing, along with the almost-forgotten Orangina. Tonic, a hotel standard, already waited in the fridge. All that remained was to soften the lights for my guest.

"Happy Christmas!" As he came through the door, Kevin kissed me on both cheeks and handed me a moderate-sized, red-wrapped box. As soon as I relieved him of his coat, I gave him his gift, and we sat down with drinks. When I was a child, I couldn't wait to tear into my presents. Now, a grown-up, I wanted Kevin to unwrap his gift first to see whether my purchase had been a hit. Evidently, Kevin felt the same.

"You go first," he said.

"No, you go."

Back and forth, until we both plunged in.

Kevin reached his surprise in about two seconds. He grinned and slung the scarf around his neck.

I, on the other hand, unwrapped one box, only to discover another within. The second one dismantled, I plucked out an even smaller package. "What did you do, get me Russian nesting boxes?"

"Just keep going," Kevin said.

He smiled subtly and took a swig of his gin and tonic. I sighed and pulled open the third box, in which I finally found a cassette of French music. Serge Gainsbourg—Kevin had obviously taken good time to search this out for me.

"You're a genius, a mind reader! Seriously, how did you know I like Gainsbourg?"

"Haley, you know I didn't know anything of the kind."

"You just guessed?"

"Well, this is a special album. Gainsbourg sings duets with Jane Birkin. Have you heard of her?"

I shook my head.

"She's like us. A foreigner—English in her case—who came to Paris to build a career in music. She got in with Gainsbourg and now she's made her life here. Even has a child with him."

The old envy began to mount in me. I sipped my Martini rouge and said begrudgingly, "I bet her French is fabulous."

"You'll find out when we play the album."

I went to the desk to retrieve my new machine, brought it to the table between our chairs, and inserted the cassette.

We settled back and Kevin gave me a serious look. "The first song, sung by Serge and Jane, is really special, a groundbreaker in 1969."

I pushed play, and soon a few notes of electric guitar rose. An organ followed. Then Jane Birkin's breathy voice whispered, "*Je t'aime, je t'aime, oh oui, je t'aime!*"

Serge Gainsbourg whispered back, "*Moi, non plus.*"

The contradiction jarred me. Jane had said, "*I love you, I love you, oh yes, I love you!*" And Serge had replied, "*Me neither.*"

I listened on, intrigued, as Serge sang, "*Je vais et je viens, entre tes reins, et je me retiens...*"

Wow! *I come and go between your loins, and I hold back.* "When did this come out?" I asked.

"1969—historical. The BBC banned it, the pope complained." Nostalgia floated in Kevin's eyes. "I was just seventeen."

At the song's climax, Jane moaned and Serge repeated, "*Je vais et je viens, entre tes reins, et je me re—*"

"*Non! Maintenant, viens!*" said Jane. *No! Come, now!* The song then drifted into completion, with Jane's heavy breathing and moaning slowly fading out.

I nodded my head. "Ten years later it still packs a punch." I hit rewind. "Let's hear it again."

Kevin smiled at my appreciation, but before we got to the middle of the song, I started to giggle.

"What's so funny?" he asked.

"Serge, saying he's *like the wave, irresolute!*"

"Rather poetic, I'd say."

I mocked more of the song, waving my hands for effect and translating, "*Physical love is without issue!*"

Kevin's expression turned sour. "All right, maybe it is a little corny, but imagine in 1969—"

"Sorry," I said. "I didn't mean to be rude. I do like it. Thanks, really." I finished my vermouth. "I'm getting hungry."

Kevin's warm smile reappeared. We stood, and he looped his scarf another turn around his neck. We fetched our coats, he draped an arm around my shoulder, and we struck out to find dinner in a neighborhood restaurant.

When we finished, he wanted to come back to my room. "Shall we have a nightcap and finish listening to Serge and Jane?"

It sure beat hanging out alone. Another advantage to a big four-star hotel: with all the comings and goings, no concierge cares who accompanies you to your room.

We settled back in our same chairs next to the cassette player and I restarted the tape. The rest of the album played out with Serge continuing to demonstrate he was an iconoclast. Not a bad addition to my collection.

When the cassette stopped, Kevin stood up and hit rewind. Fascinating, the things that can weave through your head in the time it takes to rewind a tape. The recorder hummed while I observed Kevin's freckled hand dangling over the play button. Contemplating his skin conjured visions of his and Sasha's tattoos and the disco where Sasha had first appeared. I wondered how they had said goodbye. In the restaurant the only thing he would say about her was that he'd received her Christmas card. She'd sent me one too. Basically, I knew nothing more than before. Then my arguments with Kevin invaded my thoughts, the last of which had ended up leading to my finely-balanced friendship with Luc and Thierry. Thierry. He sure acted cavalier about our translating business. Maybe he could afford to, but I had Gram on my back.

A "click" halted the wheels in my head. Kevin pressed play and reached over to squeeze my fingers just as the guitar started. When the organ began, he pulled me to my feet.

"*Je t'aime, oui, je t'aime!*"

"*Moi non plus.*"

Kevin kissed me.

"*Oh, mon amour...*"

"*Comme la vague, irrésolu.*"

I started giggling again. I felt like a nerd, but I couldn't help it. "I'm sorry," I said, almost hiccupping. "It's a neat song, but I just can't get romantic over it."

Kevin sighed. "Haley..." Then he smiled and shook his head. Finally, he let my hand go. "Listen, Monday there's going to be a giant New Year's Eve party at the Winston Churchill. Call me, if you'd like to come. I'll know the time by Sunday."

I gave a neutral nod. "I'll see." And that ended our evening. I ushered Kevin out and sauntered back in. I sat on my bed and stared at the empty room. Serge's song echoed in my mind. *Comme la vague, irrésolu*. When it came to love, I felt like a wave myself, vague and irresolute. *L'amour physique est sans issue*: Physical love is without issue.

I clasped my face, fingers forming a catcher's mask, and a rush of sadness hit me again. Maybe I would go to the party, I told myself, running my hands through my hair—if nothing better came up.

The Serge Gainsbourg album continued to fascinate me. One afternoon before the holiday, I started analyzing Jane Birkin's voice. She didn't even try to disguise her English accent. Her voice came off weak and playful—sex kittenish. And with that she had achieved fame and fortune in France. *Christ*, how hard could it be to moan and whisper, *Je t'aime, oui, je t'aime*? I could do it! "*Merde!*" I said aloud, and stood up and punched "stop."

I turned on the TV, landed on a talk show, and made myself sit down and watch. Television had turned into a kind of schooling while I waited out vacation from the Alliance Française. I found it the best exercise in listening comprehension I had ever encountered. It presented a rocky challenge when I tried to keep pace with fast regional speech. Unlike in person, no one slows down for you on television.

Interestingly enough, today's talk show offered an exception. Guest Charlotte Rampling did talk pretty slowly. Not for my benefit, though, but because she was an Anglophone, like me. An expatriate actress from England, she spoke French only a touch faster than me and with a good accent. I had seen her in *Un taxi mauve* in one of the hole-in-the-wall cinemas in the Fifth. She had a hypnotic set of blue eyes, like crystals flashing rays of mystery, and I learned in the interview she had a knack for playing the bad girl and the emotionally dangerous woman. The interviewer suggested she had played the naughty girl in real life as well, living with two men in the Sixties—at the same time. "A ménage à trois?" asked the interviewer. Her response: "Not in the way you think. I loved them both." A mysterious answer to go with her enigmatic eyes. Still, that took courage in the Sixties. Now she had settled down and married French musician Jean-Michel Jarre. Think of how much French she knew as a result of her experiences—colloquial, slang, intimate…

A wave of envy rushed over me. Jane Birkin, Charlotte Rampling, Joe Dassin; their French skills left mine in the dust.

My mind leaped to Thierry. When the hell would he come home? What if our contact, Monsieur Garnier, had tried to get a hold of him with another book? In a flurry of nerves, I extinguished the television and turned on my cassette player's radio.

Thierry had turned me on to FIP—France Inter Paris—an eclectic station that was now firing out big band. "Temptation," to be precise. I owned the Artie Shaw album as part of my father's musical legacy. Who knows why, but through his music I could sort of relate to my father, David Morgan. I fancied that "Temptation" communicated a shade of his personality—fun-loving and passionate, like the song. He also loved opera and classical music, so he must have been a bit cerebral too...or soulful.

"Temptation" pleased me so much on my new-and-improved machine that when the telephone rang, I yanked it up impatiently.

"*Allô!*" I said, and then leaped to my feet. "Hold on, I'm turning the music down."

It was Luc, back from Nice and full of propositions. What plans had I for New Year's Eve? Did I want to go to dinner and toast in the New Year? I had to calm myself to keep my *yes!* from sounding like I was being rescued from the Sahara Desert. Luc had tracked me to the Eiffel Tower hotel through Madani, who had also sent a message reminding me that my room in the Lux awaited me on January 2.

December 31, 1979: only two days before my return home to the Right Bank; one day from starting a new year and a new decade. I celebrated by donning the outfit Gram had bought me in England to wear on Christmas: knee-length, grey wool skirt, red cashmere sweater, and tall, black-leather boots.

When Luc arrived, I swung on my long camel's hair coat and felt as elegant as he looked in his grey overcoat. He tossed his original scarf on the bed and wound my Christmas scarf around his neck. Arm in arm, we stepped out for our nine o'clock dinner reservation.

Luc spared nothing on the spread. Aperitifs. Hors d'oeuvres. An intermezzo of apple sorbet accented with Calvados. Veal Normandy flanked with baked apples and au gratin potatoes. Crème brûlée to punctuate the feast, and Pouilly Fuissé to highlight the whole and tie it together like a Christmas package. Unlike the Russian calamity, I remembered every morsel.

Back in my hotel room, we readied ourselves to toast in the New Year with the bottle of Tattinger I'd bought.

Luc examined the cassettes on the desk while I set the hotel's champagne glasses on the table. He also had gotten me music for Christmas—two cassettes. "We need a soundtrack for this evening," he said.

"We should play the ones you got me."

"I see you have another Gainsbourg tape. With Jane Birkin. May I put it on?"

"All right, but I want to hear yours after."

Click. Here it came: guitar warm-up, organ flowing in, hard breathing. Then, "*Je t'aime, je t'aime, oui, je t'aime!*"

"*Moi non plus.*"

My mouth twitched, but I didn't laugh this time. "Do you remember when this song came out?" I asked.

Luc grinned. "Of course! 1969. My mother complained every time she heard it, which made it even more intriguing."

We smiled at each other from the same chairs Kevin and I had sat in.

"Then Jeanne bought the 45 and *Maman* threw a fit. She said, *You're not playing that in this house!*"

"So what did Jeanne do?" I asked.

"She listened to it in her room with the door shut. Wouldn't even let me in."

Wa-da-ya know? Jeanne had a passionate side.

When the album ended, I reached for the cassettes Luc had brought me. "Let's hear yours now."

Midnight closed in when Françoise Hardy belted "Ce soir," from Luc's album. We had stood and started slow-dancing to the song whose refrain went, "*J'ai envie de lui plaire...*" Six months ago, I might have translated to myself: *I feel like pleasing him.* By now, I skipped that step. I could think in French, and this song radiated right to the core of me. The base of my abdomen quivered and my inner thighs felt weak. The lead guitar mounted slow, even, and strong, pumping waves of desire through me. The lyrics faded away. Midnight struck. We stopped, clinked glasses, sipped, and kissed.

On the lips this time.

5: Hallucinogène

I stretched my legs under the covers. The first time with a Frenchman. Who knew what I had expected? No complaints, it's just that with all that talk about French lovers, Latin lovers, oozing passion, steeped in savoir-faire...not that Luc lacked passion. Still, people everywhere tout the French in the romance department, with lovers kissing on the street (not nearly as often as the stereotype suggests) and men making passes in cafés—more often than people expect. Then I remembered *Cold War Chronicles* and Katya's comment about Frenchmen: their bark is ferocious, but their bite...less. And yet, Luc was only twenty. Compared to Kevin, for example, who had eight years on him. The Englishman could teach the Frenchman technique, no doubt, but Luc ignited my emotions as well as my body.

A trickle of sunlight infiltrated the crack in the drapes, and I considered the back of his head while he slept. At twenty years old he had two managerial positions under his belt, and he would start a $2000-a-month telex-vending job after the holidays.

I sighed. At twenty-two, I had begun to appreciate a job for the first time in my life. Translating became the most important commitment I had embraced since college.

I folded back my blankets, careful not to uncover Luc, and sat up. Sensations of both joy and anxiety took hold of me. I had learned just before New Year's that Thierry would return at the weekend. About time! I pictured Monsieur Garnier telephoning futilely with a translation to propose while Thierry dawdled in Creuse and I lingered in bed.

I peeked around at Luc's face, and the idea we had started a potential relationship sprinkled oil on the flames already igniting my nerves. Wherever Luc and I were headed, Thierry should not find out.

We spent New Year's Day eating and hanging around the hotel room, like a couple of Romans lounging on couches, dropping grapes into their mouths.

No choice, with everything closed for the holiday. We amused ourselves by ordering breakfast to the room just like in the movies, where a knock arrives and a white-jacketed waiter wheels in a table covered with white linen and laden with orange juice, coffee, and whatever else your heart desires—in our case, piles of croissants and baguettes accompanied by baby jars of jelly. Oh, and of course we had linen napkins and real-silver cutlery. I would have to purge my mind of this luxury by the next day when I would return to the Lux and Madani's basic, no-nonsense breakfast: one croissant and French bread, paper napkins, and a steel knife in whose dim reflection you couldn't see yourself. Perfectly adequate.

Around one in the afternoon, we ventured out for some frosty air. I chuckled at the little dogs on leashes enveloped in winter sweaters, merrily trotting down the sidewalk. One poodle sported a red sweater, perhaps a Christmas present like my red cashmere.

1980 rang novel and alien. Just pronouncing the date felt science-fictionish, Orwellian. I tried to spot something indicative of the New Year besides newspaper headlines, but everything appeared the same as the day before. That included the tall, curved trestle that was my neighbor and symbol of Paris. I silently saluted it. Tomorrow we would part company and I would return to my old neighborhood. In the meantime, why not continue enjoying the four-star hotel Gram was paying for?

After a casual lunch in a brasserie, we returned to the room, satiated with food and fresh air. We flopped on the big bed we had created by pushing the two smaller ones together. Our bodies soldered, I felt my spirits float to the ceiling like a balloon. Too bad they didn't stay there. Once we exhausted love making, Luc turned on the television and I watched the night descend behind the hotel's sheer curtains. For some reason the rising shadows at four in the afternoon reminded me of an accordion playing melancholy notes. Even with Luc resting against the headboard next to me, I couldn't shake a sensation of hollowness.

The next day, January 2, Luc helped me haul my stuff back to the Lux. The return to home and familiarity helped fill me up, especially since Madani had a homecoming surprise for me: an invitation for the following evening to dine with him and his wife and children where they lived in the north of Paris.

"Chaban will look after things here," he told me the next day, before we started the drive up the hill toward Montmartre. Madani's younger brother manned the desk at the Lux from time to time, though mostly he helped with breakfast. Chaban's skin shone the shade of a dark, unpolished copper, and his glowing eyes matched his glistening black curly hair. He looked much more North African than Madani.

I figured that dinner in the home of an Algerian family had to be an exotic, but probably conservative event. I chose to wear my new Christmas outfit, whose grey skirt reached my knees and could even pass in the Grand Mosque's tea salon.

What awaited me in this Muslim household? Madani's mystery wife had never made an appearance at the Lux when I loafed around the lobby, so all I knew was her name, Fatima. Would she greet me with veiled hair and shy, self-effacing dark eyes that barely emitted a smile before darting to the floor? Would she even converse with us? What had Madani told his wife about me? That I was a freewheeling American who went out with three different *mecs*? With any luck, he had played up my serious side—the student-translator whose grandmother came to Paris periodically to check on her.

As soon as we stepped into the Madani home, Fatima wished me Happy New Year with a double-cheeked kiss. Snug bellbottoms and a form-fitting red satin shirt silhouetted her slim figure. Her long dark hair flipped up at the ends, giving her the bouncy allure of a movie star. No veil, no harem décor in the home, just European furniture, television, and stereo—so much for my conjectures! I reckoned Fatima was in her mid thirties, a tad younger than Madani, and her skin had an olive hue, like her husband's and their two sons'.

When the boys came into the room, I had to look twice. When had I last seen Malik and Karim that they'd changed so much? I remembered them as little boys, scribbling their homework in the breakfast room in between asking me about American super heroes. Malik favored Batman, while Karim touted the superiority of Superman, master of every power. Their preferences reflected their ages, I recall thinking at the time. Malik, the older, probably identified with a more complicated, somber hero, rather than with the ever-upbeat, but boring Man of Steel. I'd told them I preferred Spiderman, because I loved the idea of swinging from building to building.

Months must have passed since those days. Taller and more filled out, they seemed to have stretched into adolescence. Malik had shed the skin of the funny little boy with over-sized spectacle frames and now verged on my height, close to five foot ten. He poured into the room like a long drink of water. Karim had turned stocky, baby fat gone from everywhere but his round face.

As for Malik, I sensed he had left something else behind: a kind of vague innocence I couldn't put my finger on.

Couscous and its sauces showcased the dining room table. When it came to delving into the traditional North-African fare, though, we did it Western style.

Fatima explained. "Coming from Algiers, we've long since taken to French furniture and silverware."

"Rural Algerians still sit on their carpets and use communal bowls and so forth," Madani said.

"And eat with their fingers!" said a grinning Karim.

Malik expressed a subtle smile. "I still like to eat that way."

Fatima eyed him. "You never eat that way, Malik."

"Yes, I do, when we visit people in Algeria."

"Country people," Madani reminded him.

I estimated Malik at about thirteen years old, and figured this was the beginning of true teenage contrariness.

Apart from the couscous, I didn't gauge any particular Algerian flavor to the evening. Madani even treated me to wine. "Algerian, 20% alcohol," he said, tapping the label-less bottle of black wine.

I nodded my head. "I didn't know they made wine that strong."

"They do in North Africa. All that hot sun renders our wine hardy and aggressive. When you taste it, you'll understand what I mean."

He poured the inky brew to fill half of my short stemless glass.

I took a sip and my reaction reflected a stunned palate. "It's almost like vermouth...no, not that sweet—much better." Still, I couldn't imagine drinking a beverage that potent with daily meals. "Have they always made wine in Algeria?"

Madani smiled. "For a long time. And no one has appreciated it more than the French. That's saying something, as you must already know. Our wine," he said with a chuckle, "was probably the thing the French regretted most about pulling out of Algeria."

Even Fatima let loose a little laugh, which pleased me since Madani had been doing most of the talking. The boys remained silent, engrossed in eating.

Until Malik swallowed and spoke up. "The French should've taken all the wine with them and the people never should've made any more."

I didn't know which surprised me more, the assertion or the grave tone in which Malik delivered it. His serious eyes shifted from his father to me.

Fatima gave a nervous laugh. "What kind of nonsense is this, Malik?"

He whipped his attention to his mother. "It's not nonsense. The stuff is horrid!"

"Don't pay attention to him," Madani said, with his own dismissive laugh. "Once, he wanted a sip of this wine and I gave him one. Just a drop on his tongue, and you should have heard him bellow!"

Malik fixated his father. "It wasn't just the taste, *Papa*. You know it's a bad drink."

"Malik, you're being disrespectful to your father," said Fatima, without a hint of humor.

"Oh, let him be," said Madani. "He's only repeating tales he hears in the neighborhood."

Malik's sharp frown through black-framed glasses made him look even older to me now. "It's not a tale," he said coolly. "It's what the Prophet says, isn't it?"

A silence as cold as an underground cave followed. Madani and Fatima stared at Malik. Karim peeked at Madani. Malik diverted his eyes to his plate, though not before glancing at me. The split-second look was not friendly.

"The Prophet also tells you to honor your parents and their judgment." Madani's granite words landed hard and heavy. "Mohammed was concerned with drunkards, not with people like us."

Malik did not raise his eyes, much less counter his father. And that closed the Algerian wine discussion.

I thought.

"Can I taste the wine, *Papa*?" asked Karim. I couldn't remember whether he was one or two years younger than Malik, but his eyes still bulged like a child's. Malik glared at his brother, and Karim smirked back at him. "Really, *Papa*, I'd like to try it!"

"Don't be a moron!" Malik said with disgust. "It's a sin."

"Malik, that's enough!" said Madani. "Karim, you're too young. Look how that one sip of wine long ago has made your brother act ever since."

Fatima supported her husband. "Both of you get back to your dinner. Haley will think we're the rudest household in Paris."

"I wouldn't think that," I said, hoping to smooth ruffles. I avoided Malik's eyes and concentrated on Karim. "But your mother's right. We should get back to this fantastic zesty food, or we'll be the ones who are rude."

Fatima turned to me with an expression of gratefulness and relief. "Try this one, Haley, if you like spicy flavors."

"And drink wine with it!" Madani said, ignoring a glowering Malik.

All that fuss over some red wine. Evidently Madani didn't serve his special reserve every day. I represented his occasion to celebrate, and I had to go and stumble onto Islamic sensibilities—those of a kid! And yet not quite a kid, for Malik reminded me of that disrespectful Iranian at the American rally who had called me a stupid woman. The boy acted almost as obnoxiously. I wondered how my old acquaintance George might fit in. More like rational Madani, or closer to fanatical Malik? I thought of Mister Jenkins, the FBI agent. If I were to accept his proposal of "studying" George, perhaps I could find out. At any rate, I couldn't understand why in Paris, stage of the secular French Revolution and capital of a modern, secular republic, this religious extremism kept popping up.

Luc and I had become sort of a couple. Not long after, his parents invited me on an outing to Place des Vosges in the east Marais.

The Place mutates into a different animal in winter. So many chestnut and lime trees thicket the square's center that for about six months out of the year you can't see from one side to the other. The jungle of leaves even obscures the English-style architecture. Then winter arrives, and naked trees reveal all the buildings ringing the Place, each façade striped with red bricks broken by staggered hyphens of limestone.

I toured the square on foot with the Perris as shards of sunshine pierced the pall of the January sky. Minus the leaves, I could even make out King Louis XIII astride his horse atop a towering plinth.

We stopped in front of the statue. "The king meant more to the people before the Revolution," Madame Perri said, "when this square was called Place Royale."

"The Revolutionaries wanted to rub out everything called "royal," said Luc, a glint of pride in his eyes. "Thierry's not the only one who knows history."

I smiled to myself. "Why did they rename it Place des Vosges?" I asked.

Jeanne interjected before Luc could demonstrate more knowledge. "The Vosges was the French department that sent a volunteer army to battle back the Prussians from Paris."

Luc edged back in. "But now the Place is more famous as the location of Victor Hugo's house." He pointed to the building where the titanic author of *Les Misérables* once lived.

"Then there's the statue of Louis XIII," said Jeanne. "The original was torn down during the Revolution."

"And now it's back?" I asked, my hand forming a visor against the sun so I could gaze at the king. I shifted my regard back to Luc and Jeanne.

Luc frowned.

Jeanne cast him a wry smile and waited a couple seconds before replying, "They rebuilt it after Napoleon, when the monarchy was restored."

"It shows how things actually revolve in the course of a revolution." That astute comment came from Monsieur Perri. "First they tear down the king's statue, and then it returns along with the monarchy itself."

"Of course, Paris went through another revolution in the 1800s." Luc had rejoined the game, chest puffed out.

"One of several," Jeanne said.

The whole family was a fountain spraying jets of history. When I started counting all the revolutions, uprisings, and protests throughout its past, including the 1968 student riots, I concluded Paris had to be a breeding ground for these things, a magnet for protesters and revolutionaries the world wide. Witness the American rally and the fact that the Ayatollah Khomeini had even holed up in exile here. Who knew what else lurked in the shadows?

My first Perri family outing had shaped up so nicely, I wondered how much they all knew about Luc and me. After our two-day romp in the Eiffel Tower hotel, we had retired to simple dating. With me back in the Lux and Luc living at home, occasions for deep romance dwindled to practically zero.

Then Thierry called with news of a new translation from our furnisher, Monsieur Garnier. Garnier had no complaints about *Chroniques de la guerre froide*; indeed, he paid us adequately. Now he proposed the translation of *L'Islamisme*, written by a French woman.

Thierry briefed me on the translation while we indulged in tea and *financiers* in my *salon du thé* next to the Auxerrois. "This time Garnier wants us to go from French to English for some market or another. With the American hostage situation ongoing, he says the interest in Islam is strong."

"Great, I'm ready!" This would be our first project in English, and the potential for taking the role as lead translator jazzed me. Tragic about the hostages, but if work resulted from their situation, I wouldn't complain.

"Good," Thierry said, "because I think this translation will be another type of test. If we convince Garnier of our expertise in French to English, we'll be in solidly."

I took a bite of my *financier*, savoring it and the prospect of our next job. Things had finally started to turn around. I just needed to preserve the Luc-

Haley-Thierry triangle, as beloved to me as Paris itself. I wondered whether Luc felt half as strongly about our three-way friendship. If so, he would keep his lips buttoned about our separate relationship. I debated asking him about it, just to see where he stood, but decided to let well enough alone. We all had our hands full with challenging new jobs: Luc with his telex-machine sales, and Thierry and I with *L'Islamisme*.

I also needed to keep Gram content to subsidize me. Who knew if and when I would be able to support myself translating. I had promised to call her every two weeks, and I decided not to let that slip.

"I've got a new book to translate," I immediately told her from my booth in the PTT."

"That's good." She exhaled a little sigh that seemed to echo weariness.

"Do you feel all right, Gram?"

"I'm just tired. The dollar's not doing so well, as you must know, and I'm a little strapped for cash at the moment..."

Amazing she had waited this long to complain about the whipped dollar. I snatched the opportunity. "Gram, I can look for an apartment, no problem, and— "

"Haley dear, I'd rather you stay at Mister Madani's."

I stood up, exasperated at being at her mercy. "Why? Don't you trust me with my own place?"

"It's not that. I feel you're safer at the Lux, that's all. With all this international unrest and hostility towards Americans—"

"You mean the Iranian situation," I said brusquely. "I've told you, no one hassles me. They're on our side here. Gram, I live with Muslims! Madani's a Muslim and he even invited me to dinner in his home with his wife and kids. Muslims are like that in Paris."

"That's why I feel secure with you staying in his hotel."

"But if money's a problem..."

"I'm not going to lie to you. It's becoming a problem with fuel costs. And I've had to order quite a few repairs on the rental properties. Worst comes to worst, you may have to come home before your year is up."

I rubbed my forehead with my free hand. Before my year was up— *unthinkable*. "Gram, I've got my work now. Books are coming in steadily because we've done such a good job. I could be completely supporting myself, so—"

She chuckled before I could finish. "Supporting yourself. I have a hard time imagining that with the kind of translating you've been doing."

Gram's sarcasm made me burn, and I fought against revealing a defensive and desperate tone. "You've only seen the first book. This second work on Islam is serious stuff. Really timely matter that's in demand..."

A lump in my throat threatened to undercut my voice, and I couldn't afford that—couldn't reveal weakness. The days of little Haley plunked in Gram's lap at the age of two were over. Gram had to perceive me as strong and vigorous, in charge of my life. I could grant her no excuse to take Paris away from me.

I made my voice firm. "We could draw money from my trust."

"No, Haley," she said with another sigh. "Just keep working hard. And please stay on at the Lux. You can ease an old lady's mind in that way, can't you?"

She sounded so weary that I decided not to push it. Plus, I felt short-winded, like I'd been holding my breath for an hour. After I hung up, I collapsed back down on my seat.

Our new translation project must have eased the Kérouacs' concern about Thierry. Madame Kérouac, the French teacher, acted flattered when we consulted her for advice from time to time, and since we worked at the Kérouacs' every afternoon, I crossed paths with her often. She was keen on architectural design, which led to a particular affinity: our shared fascination with Paris's myriad balcony designs. She longed to conduct her own study of the creative art and write a book on it complete with pictures. "Someday," she emphasized, "when I have time."

Thierry and I each had a copy of *L'Islamisme*. Tooled with texts, dictionaries, and an English Thesaurus Thierry had given me for Christmas, we approached our task like scholarly pros. The confidence I felt made my next call home to Gram an occasion to vaunt success. I have to admit, though, as I entered the PTT, I couched an ulterior motive. School and homework crowded my mornings, as well as some of my early afternoons and evenings. All those passive hours piddled away at the Alliance Française I should have been devoting to my work. I told Gram so, though not in those exact words.

"This translation we're doing on Islam is really long, Gram. Much longer than our first work, and school's getting in the way."

Silence.

It was true. When I got home from Thierry's, I would edit and refine what we had written that afternoon. Then, before I got sleepy, I would start on the next passage. For at least two weeks I pushed myself at that pace, until I began to skip classes again.

I threw out a line to test Gram. "Maybe I should cut my hours down at the Alliance Française..."

"...Do you see more work on the horizon?"

"Not yet, but we didn't see this book coming either. We got it because we did a good job on the last one."

"Hmm," she murmured. "Try to stick it out at least until the end of the semester. School can only help you in your work. Besides, we've already paid for the term."

"Gram—"

"Credentials do matter, Haley. You might as well accumulate them while you're there. You'll be twenty-three this month and I'd like to see you as well prepared for life as possible."

Obviously, I had to agree, and that ended the discussion.

As well prepared for life as possible, I repeated to myself as I left the PTT. I had no practical skills to speak of. I could type acceptably, despite the "D" I received in the subject on one of my report cards. Of course, I possessed my degree in European history, and plenty of French. But that was it. I would turn twenty-three in the bizarre, Big-Brother decade of 1980, and time and the future marched on. I refused to be left in the dust, and reckoned I could only meet the challenge by pushing my own agenda. Even if it meant skipping school when necessary.

On my birthday, January 12, I received a golden gift. Luc and Thierry invited me to dinner. The trio hung together—sometimes, I think, due to my sheer will.

Our restaurant, A la Claire Fontaine, was located on rue de Richelieu, in the epicenter of Right-Bank Paris. I entered first and noticed an elegant, intimate atmosphere that I deemed perfect for a memorable birthday dinner.

Then my satisfied smile creased. Immediately to my right, behind the bar, lay an enormous pig's snout on a stainless-steel salami slicer. Large as a human head, it had nostrils three times the size of bowling-ball holes. No matter how French I felt, I had to admit that culture shock remained alive and kicking in me. Granted, the pig's snout represented an extreme example of cultural conflict, and yet certain "regular" French foods continued to create roadblocks to my otherwise adventurous palate. I recoiled from sweetbreads and *boudin*, nixed kidneys and anything from the nether regions. Any food made with animal organs stopped me cold.

Luc ordered *Alouette* and Thierry called for a side order of *andouillette*. Compared to roasted larks stuffed with goose liver and sausage produced from pig intestines, my rabbit with white-wine-mustard sauce seemed boring—yet brave, perhaps, for an American. I did feel good about that. *And* about the fact we were all three together again.

Toward the end of dinner, I couldn't resist a quick consultation with Thierry on *L'Islamisme*. From my first reading of it, the last line of our book's introduction had me antsy to argue, and I wanted to mention it to get Luc's input as well.

"According to the author," I said, "Muslims are assured the rule of the universe and predestined for Paradise, where they will find the delights of this world in abundance. What do you two think of that?"

Luc spoke up first. "It's probably to motivate their believers."

"Maybe," I said. "But it shows they're light in the spirituality department. 'Delights of this world in abundance' doesn't sound very spiritual—more vulgar, I'd say. Presumptuous too, when it comes to being *predestined* for Paradise and the rule of the universe."

"*Ouais*," said Thierry. "It's a relatively young religion, immature—"

"Enough shop talk," Luc said. "It's time for Haley's presents." I saw a look of impatience in his eyes, a nervousness, or something.

On evenings like this I wished I had Gram's four-star hotel at my disposal. I could have invited my friends for an after-dinner drink and opened my presents in privacy, instead of in front of the whole restaurant.

Both Luc and Thierry reached for the boxes they had set on the table when we arrived. Luc was faster, though. "Happy Birthday!" he said, and handed me a narrow, shallow package wrapped in shiny silver paper.

I carefully removed the paper, opened the box, and discovered black leather gloves. I tried one on, enveloping my hand in soft, warm fur. "My hands'll never be cold again. Thanks, Luc!"

"They're Italian leather," he said, with a bit of pride in his smile.

"Happy Birthday, Haley." Thierry's voice was even, and his dark eyes emitted a barely perceptible twinkle, almost a wink as he handed me his present.

I pulled off the blue paper and lifted the lid: a silk scarf with oranges and dark reds running through it. I removed the glove and slid the scarf sensuously through my fingers and said, "It's beautiful, thank you!"

I placed both presents in my lap. I felt cornered. Wrapping paper littered the table and Luc and Thierry watched me intently. I wondered if they were mentally judging which gift I liked more. "Shall we go for a quick walk through the Louvre gardens before it gets freezing?"

Luc shrugged. "Sure. The usual crew probably won't be soliciting in this cold. Wouldn't want to stumble into them."

"The Louvre gardens too?" I asked in disbelief.

"The Bois de Boulogne, the Bois de Vincennes, the Louvre," said Thierry, in reference to hooker hangouts.

Luc gave an impatient sigh. "Haley knows about the two Bois."

Yes, I knew about the two woodsy parks at night, but I didn't like Luc reminding Thierry so rudely.

As we stepped into the night I thought about putting on my gloves, but decided against it and placed them in my purse with my scarf. Better not to emphasize one gift over another. Instead, I inserted myself between my friends and took their arms. Not three paces later it started to rain. We retreated to Luc's Lancia where a piece of paper lay sponging up water under his windshield wiper.

He swore softly. "*Nom de Dieu, un autre!*" Another damn parking ticket. He shoved it in his pocket and we ducked into the car.

"Not disposing of this one?" I asked.

"They're cracking down," he said.

I missed the bravado-filled Luc who ripped up tickets with impunity, and I hated to see a little rain and a ticket shut us down. "It's my fault again. You always get tickets when you're doing something for me. I'll pay it this time."

"Forget it. I've only got one umbrella in the car..."

"Haley, don't even suggest we all share an umbrella," said Thierry from the back seat.

I glanced at him and then turned to Luc behind the wheel. I didn't want to let either of them go. Who knew when we would get to splurge like this again? "How about letting me take us for a drive?"

It was my birthday and Luc obliged. Thierry voiced no objection.

Thierry always said that Paris felt more like Paris in the rain. For me it wasn't the rain so much as Paris's characteristic overcast skies. And yet, some kind of light always managed to reflect from Paris the Prism, piercing the grey with a positive note...masking a troubled situation.

Tonight the rain reflected an impression, almost a hallucination that dazzled me behind the wheel. As I cut over to boulevard Saint-Germain on the

Left Bank, FIP radio oozed a slow, syncopated jazz beat. The smooth saxophone and bass complemented the steady, cautious flow of traffic down the
rain-drenched boulevard. The sax's deep, ominous-sounding notes magnified
the atmosphere of a slick dark night full of risk.

Then a sonorous trumpet sounded, just as I was struck by splashes of light
dancing on the shiny-black asphalt: shimmering strips of white headlights and
red taillights; brush strokes of modern painting swishing before my eyes. I
kept cruising, driving anywhere I could find bright lights darting like quicksil-
ver to the trumpet's wails. My eyes devoured the spectacle until the strain of
staring made them ache. I directed the car back to the Right Bank, but the jazz
kept me in its clutches, like a siren. *What was this mysterious, sinister music?*

Luc told me. "*Ascenseur pour l'échafaud*, by Miles Davis."

Thierry translated in a pedantic tone. "The soundtrack to *Lift to the Gallows*. A Louis Malle film—"

"Starring Jeanne Moreau—"

"Who falls in love with a man who murders her husband. He then gets
stuck in the elevator, hence *Lift to the Gallows*."

In the dark, Thierry and Luc's exchange came across like a race of words,
with Thierry finishing almost breathless. To avoid setting off another round of
competition I said, "brilliant jazz," and that was it.

Then the red sheen from the stoplight turned green, the traffic picked up
pace, and a different number clicked in. "Another cut from the album," said
Luc.

A busy, muted trumpet, accompanied by rapid drum brushes and bass
picking, rushed from the speakers. I hit the gas hard and sent the Lancia
gliding in and out of traffic like a dolphin weaving through schools of fish, ever
upwards and eager to break out of the water and breathe.

"You've gotten a lot better since the last time I saw you drive," said Thierry.
He didn't know about my one-on-one practice with Luc.

"You'd better slow down here," Luc said, as I approached my street. "The
cops like to lie in wait between the Hôtel de Ville and the Louvre."

I coasted up to the Lux and cut the ignition. All three of us exited the car,
and I dished out double-cheeked kisses to my friends. I would have loved to
clasp them both in a group hug, but Luc and Thierry would have found that
beyond silly. When Luc settled into the driver's seat he found 100 francs.

"Hey, what's this?" he said, before I could slip into the Lux.

"Keep it," I said, and darted through the door before he could counter me. Gasoline was expensive. So were traffic tickets. And friendship was the dearest.

Finding people in Paris can be easy if you've spotted them in a café. Even if you've only seen them there once, chances favor them making a repeat visit. My café near the Alliance Française served as a pit stop to recharge myself with French espresso and dash out a quick homework assignment before peeling off to Thierry's for translation. Even though homework now ceased to be a bother, I still called the café mine.

That's where George Abdi found me two days after my birthday dinner. He said he had just happened to stroll by and catch sight of me through the picture window. After he sat down and ordered a coffee, I asked him about the coincidence.

"George, did you plan to stop by here today?"

It appeared he hadn't slept in weeks. Behind his wire-rimmed frames, deep dark circles looked like bruises under his bloodshot eyes. Nevertheless, a shy smile trickled out. "I was looking for you, actually. I wanted to explain about that evening you came to the restaurant with your grandmother…Is she well?"

"She's fine, thanks, back home in America." I waited.

In the meantime, the waiter swept by to drop off George's coffee.

"Good," he finally said, as he dropped cubes of sugar into his demitasse. His brow crinkled as he stirred his coffee, and then it relaxed. "Listen, Haley, I was busy that night…and, well, you know my uncle and the rest of the personnel at the Poseidon are Afghans…"

"Uhuh…"

He took a sip of coffee. "I'm sorry they were paying so much attention to you and I was not."

The wording of that apology made me smile to myself. "Why did we interest them so much? The hostages in Iran?"

"…Yes." George shifted in his chair. "You see, they are Muslims in the restaurant…"

"Shiite Muslims, like the Iranians?"

"Yes, but they are not fanatics. They welcome business from all people. They felt curiosity about you…that is all." His last words trailed off as if someone lowered the volume of a radio.

I felt bad for him and turned up a smile. "I guess I can understand that. Are you Muslim?"

He perked up from his slouch and aimed a frown at me. "I choose my own way." He slid a hand through his short dark hair, revealing its oiliness. "I believe in the good qualities of the religions of my father and of my mother." His voice had risen higher. He spoke British English, but his nervousness caused his Greek accent to thicken.

"Sure, that makes sense," I said. I almost asked him whether his Greek mother had baptized him Orthodox, since George was a Christian name. I sensed a defensive aura, though, and with work waiting for me at Thierry's, I didn't have enough time to deal with it.

I checked my watch. "Sorry," I said, and started to collect my things. "I've got to go."

George finished the last of his coffee. "Do you still go out with that *French man* I have seen you with two times?"

My eyes and hands froze. "...Sometimes." I avoided his sunken stare by filling my canvas bag with my newspaper and Pariscope. "Luc's a friend." Finally, I faced him. "Maybe we'll have coffee again sometime."

That's how I left George, a suggestion floating in the air, and he catching it with a silent nod. Granted, I wasn't exactly forthcoming about Luc, but George might have written me off if I had told him the truth about our relationship. The *mec* George intrigued me like a sphinx, and I didn't want to chase him off. Besides, Mister Jenkins kept visiting my thoughts: twenty dollars just for a simple conversation with George. I could have earned it through this last chat with him. So I would keep George tethered on this strange intangible wavelength we seemed to share.

God knows, Luc would never understand my interest in George, so I would hold my tongue on that score as well. The rows with Kevin over my casual encounters flashed through my mind. Could people ever really understand each other?

I asked myself the same question about Luc's sister, Jeanne. One Sunday Luc had invited me to a movie with the two of them. Just Luc, Jeanne, and I— minus Thierry. Jeanne had flitted about me like a butterfly, chitchatting, laughing, showing intense interest in what I had to say. She always graced Paris in nylons and a dress or skirt, even for a movie. The whole Perri family emitted vibes of success, which made them ever-so appealing: *Papa*, the electrical engineer, Luc, the ascending entrepreneur, Jeanne aspiring to law, and *Maman*, conductor of their home par excellence. Sometimes I felt dwarfed in their presence. They radiated class and ambition and still demonstrated kindness and generosity—even Jeanne now.

Our outing to the cinema hadn't been the end. Shortly after, she invited me for a tête-à-tête, just the two of us. I suggested the *salon du thé* next to the Auxerrois. What better place to plumb a personality? Perhaps we would come to a meeting of minds.

I could transform tea into a tool in this type of situation. The pot and other trappings constantly provided something to do with the hands, unlike a simple French coffee consisting of about five sips. Or three sips—*très serré*—the way Thierry ordered it, and how I had learned to love it.

My one-on-one with Jeanne required a longer refreshment, one that could be replenished over an hour's time or so. One that could fill pauses and buy time.

"I approve of your choice of tea room," she said, admiring the marble tabletops and gilded crown molding of my neighborhood *salon du thé*. Today she wore a dress and blazer, while I sat in my wool bellbottoms.

I smiled my appreciation. "I enjoyed the film we saw last weekend."

"So did I. Do you prefer French or English-language films?"

I felt relaxed. My tongue had loosened nicely, and it nimbly embraced those challenging French vowels with the finesse of a classical guitarist. "French, most of the time. Thierry likes English movies, but fortunately Luc's the opposite."

"Ah, you're getting to know my brother better and better."

I couldn't tell whether that suited her or not. But certainly, I realized, Luc had to be the object of her visit, and I needed to prepare myself for it.

She sipped her tea, sitting back in her chair with her cup and saucer held close to her chest. "Do you spend a lot of time with Thierry too?"

"Sure, we work together."

"I mean outside of work."

"Usually it's Luc, Thierry, and me."

"Right, the Three Musketeers!" Her fingers made a flourish in the air with an invisible rapier. Cute gesture, except I wondered whether she was mocking me with her accompanying wry smile.

I straightened my posture. "More tea?" She nodded and I poured.

Then her tone turned earnest. "I admire your dedication, learning French and our way of life...What do you plan to do with your knowledge and skills?"

I chewed my bite of *financier* very slowly. After swallowing, I answered, "I'd like to continue living and working here for a while, to really perfect my French, and all."

"What would you be doing if you were back in America?"

"Hmm, good question." I dabbed my mouth with my napkin. "It's all so big in the States, overwhelming even..."

"Lots of freedom ..." she said, almost wistfully.

I decided not to let her maneuver me into saying things were better in America. "There's plenty of freedom here too," I pointed out.

A smile creased one corner of her mouth. "Especially for you. You have much more freedom than I had at your age."

I hadn't seen that coming. I poured myself more tea and mashed the lemon in my cup with my spoon. Then I sat back and tried to look relaxed. "I never noticed any lack of freedom in your family. Luc—"

"Yes, well, Luc's a man."

I leaned in for a slow sip and sat back again. "Looks like you're doing what you want. Law school *is* your choice, isn't it?"

"Yes, it'll make a good career," she said with a placid smile.

"Are you happy studying law?"

Maintaining her serene smile, Jeanne added more milk to her tea and stirred it. "I'm happy, though I've never had the luxury of spending a year away to experiment and try different things."

Like me, you mean.

"Luc's had more leeway to 'find himself,' as you Americans put it, although he's always had a job ever since he left school."

Unlike me.

"And Thierry?" I said, in order to steer the subject away from me.

"He's more like you—doing his own thing."

Touché.

She sipped her tea with a reflective expression. "Don't misunderstand me, there's nothing wrong with the freedom you have. You're lucky. Lucky, you were born when and where you were. Americans have always enjoyed more freedom and leeway than other people."

Freedom *and* leeway. From where had she plucked that idea? American TV, I suspected.

"But you're your own woman now," I said. Jeez, she wasn't any older than Kevin. She had her whole life ahead of her.

The wry smile returned. "I've also got two parents I don't want to disappoint. They have expectations of me. And of Luc. We're a very united family."

"*Mazel tov*," I said in a low voice. I could feel my face heating up.

"Pardon?"

"Nothing. It's Yiddish for *good for you*." Sasha would have been amused.

I couldn't tell whether Jeanne understood my sarcasm, because she simply gave me a neutral look. "Luc is very fond of you, Haley, and understandably so. Don't disappoint him, however."

"I wouldn't think of it." I considered my reply sufficiently even-toned, and I had nothing left to add. So I told her I had to go.

On the sidewalk across from the Louvre, Jeanne flashed a generous smile and pinned a two-cheeked kiss on me. "*A plus tard!*"

'See you later!' is what she said, but I found the tone a little too enthusiastic given our discussion. I watched her head up the sidewalk and disappear down the stairs into the metro. What had all that meant? *Don't disappoint Luc*, or the consequences could be dire? The Perri family will come after you armed with fraternal love? I couldn't tell. When it came to figuring out Jeanne Perri, I was back where I started. I had deduced a couple of things, though. She was discontent with her lot and envious of me. I guess I should have taken the latter as a compliment. And I did somewhat, though Jeanne's implication of *"we, the Perris*, versus *you, the spoiled American,"* left me with the sting of a hornet.

I lived only blocks from my two favorite buildings in Paris. Hôtel de Ville, Paris's City Hall, loomed a few mini blocks east of me. And a brief stroll down to the river brought me face to face with my beloved Conciergerie, a fortress floating in the middle of the Seine. Oddly enough, I hadn't noticed either of those stunning structures lately. All I did was commute from home to school (when I wasn't skipping) to Thierry's and back home again. The only break from that routine consisted of evening dates with Luc when I had time.

Months ago, I had always taken time to purchase mineral water and fresh fruit at a little grocery store behind the Lux on rue Saint-Honoré. The oranges and apples in their bowl on my desk had livened my room with a little mound of color and aroma. I cut those purchases when the dollar sank another franc. Now, coarse, rusty-tasting tap water had to meet my drinking needs. I didn't dare ask Gram for more money.

When forced to buy necessities, I either jaunted down to BHV across from Hôtel de Ville or to Samaritaine in view of the Conciergerie. Even then, I barely acknowledged my two prize buildings.

One morning, as I walked to the metro station across from the Louvre, a young English woman stopped me to ask how to get to the Conciergerie. A sudden pride welled up in me; I almost felt she had inquired about a child of mine.

"Walk down to the river and turn left," I told her, indicating the street between the Louvre and Saint-Germain L'Auxerrois. "You'll see it on the island...wait, follow me, I'll show you."

Affection choked me when I pointed out the three medieval towers of the first building in Paris I had fallen in love with. Why I felt so sentimental at that particular moment, I didn't know. Maybe it had to do with playing tour guide, because I felt a prick of envy toward my anonymous companion. There she was, just getting acquainted with Paris, learning to love El Dorado on the Water. I saw the enthusiasm blaze in her eyes as she gazed at my first love, the Conciergerie. I sensed the excitement of discovery in her voice as she said, "It's stunning!" The surprise and thrill of 'the first time.' I ached to feel that way again: to take a time machine back six months and fall in love all over again. After she walked on, I stared at the Conciergerie until my teeth started to knock and my eyes to water. Then I hurried on my way, cold and pressed for time.

L'Islamisme counted about 170 pages. Already, the introduction made me frown. Islam, claimed the female French author, was misunderstood by the West. Well, we would have to see about that.

Next, came a profile of Mohammed and his revelation. At only twenty years old, he married a rich, widowed aristocrat named Khadidja. She was a powerful entrepreneur who ran her own caravan business for which Mohammed had already been working. He had married the boss, who happened to be twice his age. He held great respect for her, the author emphasized, and as long as Khadidja lived, Mohammed would take no other wife.

Interesting.

"Do you think he felt repressed?" I asked Thierry, "considering his situation in the Arab world?"

Thierry looked up from the notes on his mother's desk where we worked. "He couldn't have felt very macho," he said with a thoughtful air.

We scrutinized the next paragraph. Forty-year-old Mohammed, undergoing some kind of retreat in a cave, received a visit from the angel Gabriel who declared him henceforth Allah's prophet. From then on, he traveled around, claiming to be God's spokesman, and like many others who have threatened the status quo, he found himself persecuted and run out of town. He tried courting the Jews and proposed they join forces to fight the pagans. Nothing doing. They shunned and mocked him.

I raised my pencil. "No wonder Muslims have it in for the Jews."

Thierry read on. "In fact, here it says they believe Jews and Christians have twisted the words of Abraham, Moses, and Jesus."

"Do you think Mohammed denounced the Jews' version of scripture after they rejected him?"

"I don't know, let's stick to the text so we can finish this section."

When Mohammed's wife Khadidja died, the prophet seemed to go into what I could only figure was a mid-life crisis.

"Let me get this straight," I said, and started translating into English: "In order to obtain the most enticing girls, Mohammed covers himself with a divine revelation, which gives him permission to marry Zainab, the wife of his adoptive son Zaid (Zaid must've loved that!). The Prophet would end up having no fewer than nine wives, or close to twenty according to some traditions. This license, going against the Koran, which allowed for only four wives and actually recommended monogamy, was a privilege accorded very specially to Mohammed."

I took a breather, and Thierry picked up the translation:

"He wasn't tender towards the wives who ceased to please him. But, attention to those who would take them over: it is not...licit to marry the wives of Mohammed after him, in the regard of Allah, an immense sin."

"Not bad," I said, although deep down I enjoyed a slight pleasure in being able to correct Thierry's English. "Let's polish that now. Instead of *attention*, we'll write: '*beware* to those who would take them in. It is illicit in Allah's eyes to marry the wives cast off by Mohammed—an immense sin.' After I finished, I made a little joke. "If Mohammed wouldn't have them, no one could!"

Thierry smiled subtly. "Right, let's move on."

The next day we transcribed Mohammed's battles, his command of jihads (according to the author, an obligation for Muslims) against polytheists and Jews, and finally we reached present-day Islam and the great confrontation with the West.

Nothing in the Koran, we learned, even resembled the principle "Render unto Caesar what is Caesar's." Everything, theoretically, belonged to God. No distinction between the sacred and the profane. No separation of church and state.

"A mentality that leads straight to theocracy," I said. "Like Iran under Khomeini, with the mullahs—"

"Listen," said Thierry, "I know you're worried about the hostages, but this is 1980, not the 600s."

I put down my pencil. "A lot of countries still follow the Koran and cut off people's hands for theft and stone women for adultery—"

"I know, but those are backward countries."

"Not very comforting for women," I said. "And what about *excision*? African immigrants bring that practice straight to France."

The term *excision* meant female genital mutilation, and it made the hair on my neck stand stiff. It was a custom practiced among Muslims in Africa, Yemen, Palestine, and God knew where else. To render a woman completely passive in the act of procreation, the author explained, though the Koran itself made no mention of it.

"It's so twisted and barbaric, it blows my mind!"

"Right," Thierry said, red-faced. "Let's move on."

My outrage didn't end there. Allah preferred certain of his creation more than others, our female French author pointed out. Men, of course. According to Mohammed, they have authority to cloister women, collect them as concubines in addition to their wives, arrange their marriages, divorce them unilaterally and keep the children.

I slammed my book shut. "Christ! This is diabolical!"

Thierry sighed. "Calm down, Haley, we're just the translators."

He was right. If I didn't get a grip on myself, we would never complete this job.

"I've told you," he said, "Muslims aren't like that here. Women don't even wear the veil in Paris. And look how Madani treats you. With the utmost respect as far as I've noticed. No, we don't have radical Muslims in Paris."

True. Madani could never have advocated what I'd just read. I only had to observe how his one-and-only wife dressed and acted. Still, Thierry had not been present at Place de la République in November.

"You didn't witness the rudeness of those Iranians at the American rally," I said.

Thierry turned philosophical. "Islam's a relatively young religion. Their mentality is where ours was during the Middle Ages. They just need time to catch up."

"A medieval mentality with modern means to repress people," I said bleakly.

I wasn't convinced at all that the backward moron at the rally wanted to "catch up." He had called me a foolish woman who shouldn't be let out of her house. So, I should be collected and cloistered by some jerk like him? A dangerous element weaved through Islam despite these modern times. I wanted to pursue the topic, but I let Thierry off the hook. No use preaching to the choir and we did need to stick to work. On the other hand, I did know one available person...George could prove useful in more than one way.

In the meantime, call it a manner of shoring up Western culture, I went to mass at Saint-Germain l'Auxerrois. We Morgans belonged to a category of Church-on-Christmas-and-Easter Catholics, along with weddings and funerals. My grandmother attended mass more often after my grandfather died, but from the time I became a teenager I always had better plans.

In Paris I went to church with a purpose, and it felt good. I entered Saint-Germain l'Auxerrois for the first time since summer. A breath of fear actually brushed the back of my neck as I crossed the threshold. With all the art in the church, I dreaded Stendhal's syndrome might rear its ugly head again. Instead, the opposite took place. The airy, high, vaulted ceilings and luminous stained-glass windows filled me with a sensation of lightness and wonder. All in all, I felt serene and content. I would have to visit my neighborly Auxerrois more often.

At the beginning of February, Luc made his latest conquest, the acquisition of an apartment in the Marais: Right Bank, Fourth arrondissement, rue des Archives, about twelve blocks east of the Lux. French blocks made that distance shorter, since some were only a quarter of the length of an American block. The district ran high in rent, though. Luc paid 500 dollars a month for one bedroom, a sole bath, a tiny kitchen, and a sitting room. Still, he could afford it on his 2000-dollar-a-month salary selling telex equipment. Compared to what I shelled out in the Lux—600 dollars a month, and I still had to buy lunch and dinner—the deal looked damn good.

It certainly changed our dating configuration. I spent almost every evening at rue des Archives. Cooking dinner together, watching a little TV, making love—the whole dance was a novelty I couldn't get over. Playing house, that's what we indulged in. Luc would drive me home about eleven o'clock, and you'd think I would be able to sleep like a child saturated with play on a hot sunny day.

Instead, money gnawed at my nerves.

I had pared down my dinner expenses by sharing food shopping with Luc. Yet, even though Thierry and I had put the final polish on what we christened *Islam—an Exposé*, Monsieur Garnier hadn't come through with a new translation. Translating revenue constituted my spending money based on Gram's financial downsizing. The income had to cover everything except hotel and food. Not just movie and music money, but essentials like shampoo and toothpaste. I never said a word about it to Luc, fearing he would want to pay for all our food and entertainment, and I couldn't tolerate that. Why become financially hostage to yet another person? I had already accepted a trip to Mont-Saint-Michel, his treat, and I didn't want to get in any deeper.

I craved freedom, and not just from Gram's financial vise. At night, before drifting off to sleep, I would conjure up visions of myself thriving in Paris on my own, be-bopping down rue de Rivoli in my own MG, furnishing my own flat. I wished I had Luc's luck, the way he charged ahead like his Lancia, roaring to success after success, winning race after race.

Islam continued its grip on my thoughts as well. Although Thierry and I had finished *L'Islamisme,* I hadn't buttoned up the debate. I needed an interlocutor, and I knew whom to choose. But first, I wanted to make a phone call.

I waited for Frank Jenkins in the same café on rue Saint-Honoré where we had conducted our initial meeting. Events had overwhelmed me then, so I hadn't noticed much about the place. This time I got there early and took time to examine the locale. The pinball machine still stood in the corner, though no one played it. I didn't know whether I liked that or not. The device could be annoying to talk over, but at least the noise covered the words of conversation. Outside, snowflakes floated to the ground like feathers, so light they melted on the sidewalk. The winter scene made the café's interior cozy, despite the drabness of the décor. I couldn't tell whether the walls were faded or merely stained yellow from years of cigarette smoke. No picture or poster livened them. Besides me, only three other individuals made up the clientele. A middle-aged woman sipped what looked like a café-crème. An older man sat reading a newspaper, an empty espresso cup next to him. A younger man stood at the bar, one elbow on the counter. I wished he would place both elbows there. Instead, he stayed positioned to keep an eye on the room while he chatted with the barman. I sat as far away as I could from everyone.

I had already finished one coffee when Mister Jenkins entered from the street. He walked straight to me without meeting my eyes and removed his coat and hat. He folded the navy-blue overcoat over the back of his chair and dropped his black fedora on the table.

"Stand up and greet me like a French person," he said in a low voice.

I frowned, and then stood and shook hands with him, the way the French always do with people they're not on intimate enough terms to kiss. Then we sat down and Jenkins ordered a Calvados.

I got down to business. "I know on the phone you told me this would be easy, but if I approach George directly, he might think I *like* him."

"Why? Don't you like him?" When I started to explain, Jenkins interrupted me with a chuckle. "Just kidding. I don't want you to run after him like you're in love, Haley. Do you mind if I call you *Haley*?" he asked me with that florid smile of his.

I shrugged. "Go ahead."

"You can call me Frank. Interesting, we both have Welsh last names—Jenkins and Morgan."

I didn't respond to that. I didn't even know "Jenkins" was Welsh, and I wasn't going to call him "Frank." It would have made us almost chummy, and I felt grubby enough already. Here I sat rubbing shoulders with Jenkins the alcoholic who started on apple liqueur at eleven o'clock in the morning. God knew what the rest of his workday was like.

He took a sip and smacked his lips. "Just like Maigret. Know who Jules Maigret is?"

"Sure—the famous French police *commissaire*. I've read a couple of the novels."

"Maigret always takes time out for a Calvados. The French definitely know how to live. Boy, am I going to miss Paris when they deploy me back to the States. You're lucky your grandmother's letting you live here indefinitely."

"My grandmother?" I felt as if he'd kicked my chair off balance. "What does she have to do with anything?"

This time he actually did wink. "We check out anyone who works for us. Freelancers included."

"How did you—"

"Can't give away tricks of the trade, kid. Don't worry, she has no idea about us, so you can relax and enjoy your time here."

Why did he mention my grandmother? Was Jenkins trying to put me off? I steeled myself and went at him. "You obviously know who my friends are, my grandmother...but what do you really know about me? Why do you even trust me with this mission? I mean, what if I tell George about you?"

Jenkins shook his head. "We might lose out on some useful information, that's all. You're our only bait for George, but then again you may come up with nothing of value to us. It's a crapshoot either way, and it's not as if we're talking high stakes. He flicked me a sympathetic smile. "Sorry, no top-secret mission." With that, he tossed back the rest of his Calvados.

I wanted to tell him to shove the whole thing. Come on, Haley, speak up, I coaxed myself. Tell him! But I didn't, and Jenkins evidently took that for an *okay*. He launched into my instructions, and I just sat and listened, intrigued in spite of myself.

Before he got too far, I asked, "I get twenty dollars for meeting with him, regardless of what kind of information I get?"

"Right—a win-win for you."

Jenkins told me to wait a few days before seeking out George. He produced a list of questions for me to memorize covering George's interests in Paris, particularly what he liked doing with his friends.

"You'll only address these items during your first contact. Are we straight? You got everything?"

"Yeah," I said.

"Good."

After Jenkins left, I stared out the window at everything and nothing. It seemed the FBI knew more than I did about George's company. It would take many meetings to get him to open up to the point I could glean more than Jenkins already knew. I had told him so, but Jenkins didn't seem concerned with time.

Luc and I cruised out of Paris early Saturday morning, course charted for Mont-Saint-Michel. The drive immediately began to sweep a few clouds from my sky, although there remained the murkiness of hiding our getaway from Thierry. I would've loved it if all three of us could have made the jaunt north, just like old times, but that type of thinking proved more and more unrealistic. I didn't know whether Luc had told Thierry about our trip, so I just concentrated on preserving the status quo.

With Thierry, I had resorted to evasiveness. We met every weekday, and only occasionally did we see each other on the weekend, which made it easy to divert discussion away from weekend plans with vague, "I-don't-know-for-sure" kind of talk. I had already practiced plenty of verbal wriggling with Gram and it never bothered me. Being evasive with Thierry, on the other hand, stressed me because I didn't know what, if anything, Luc had already told him. The whole thing made me feel slippery and dishonest, and before we had been on the road half an hour, I felt compelled to ask Luc what he had told Thierry about us.

Once we had engaged a nice straight stretch of road, I got started. "Did you happen to talk to Thierry before we left?"

"When? This week?"

"Recently, before today."

"*Ouais*," he said lazily, eyes stapled to the road.

"Does he know we're going away for the weekend?"

This time there was a pause, which Luc filled by shifting gears to slip past a truck. "It didn't come up," he said.

"What didn't come up?" I said, determined to sort things out once and for all. "The weekend or our trip?"

"Neither. The weekend didn't come up, so neither did the trip."

"Would you have told him if it had?"

Back into the right lane we breezed. Luc continued his steady stare. "I don't know. Maybe, if it happened to be relevant."

I didn't let go. "I think it definitely qualifies as relevant. Do you think he knows about us?"

Luc's eyes didn't move. "He might. I haven't told him because it's not really his business."

I gazed at the grey sky, the grey road, back at Luc in his grey overcoat, and pushed on. "He's our friend. I'd say he's got an interest."

"...Thierry's not stupid. If he's interested, he'll figure it out." Luc shot me a quick glance. "Unless *you* want to tell him."

"Sounds like you value our three-way friendship too." I said, heartened.

He let out a little laugh and reached over to ruffle my hair. "Thierry and I have been friends almost ten years. We'll be fine."

Luc skirting the issue didn't surprise me. Why would he talk to Thierry about something as emotional as an affair, when he had never expressed his feelings even to me about our relationship? Frankly, I couldn't blame him. Neither of us, since hooking up romantically, had murmured those dodgy words, "I love you." As for our mutual friend, Thierry? Well, easy for Luc to take his good buddy for granted, but it didn't reassure my place in the scheme of things. I sighed to myself. With Paris almost an hour behind us, I decided to shelve the matter.

I rummaged through Luc's glove box and found Françoise Hardy's album, *J'écoute de la musique saoule.* As soon as I slid it into the cassette player and the title song started, Luc recovered his chattiness.

"Do you understand the double meaning of this song?" he asked.

I translated the cassette cover. "I listen to music drunk."

"Ah, but *saoule* in French also sounds like 'soul,' as in soul music."

"Soool music," I mimicked. "I listen to music drunk, or I listen to soul music. Same sound in French."

"Bravo! You know, your grammar is good. Now you just need to work a little on your accent to sound more Parisian.

I appreciated the compliment, but the follow-up irritated me. For seven months I had tried my hardest to copy Luc and Thierry's speech, and it still wasn't good enough. I called on the gods of patience and perseverance, and mentally changed the subject. I examined Françoise Hardy's cover photo. Stringy hair parted down the middle, a clump of bang hanging over the corner of one eye. She looked hung-over, in sync with the title.

In the meantime, the next song spiraled from the speakers and caught me unawares. I couldn't catch all the words to "Hallucinogène," but the mercurial melody and dreamy electronic arrangement mesmerized me. In my imagination, Luc and I turned into ancient travelers, voyaging through the grey winter countryside of primitive Normandy. Gliding through the mist, we searched for a treasure, a prize—the Holy Grail, or something. Whatever its essence, I imagined it hovering out of reach. A mirage, a hallucination, it floated in and out of the wispy clouds.

Then something real emerged from the mist and reared before us: a mount on which reigned a medieval village. The stone community seemed to spring from the rocky hill, its steep roofs losing their caps in a layer of fog. The former abbey of Mont-Saint-Michel looked positively Merlinesque.

"It's fabulous!" I said.

"In summer it's a tourist magnet," said Luc. "In winter it has more of a medieval feel."

The land surrounding the Mount stretched flat and wet. No marvel there, since not far off lay the English Channel. An asphalt causeway linked dry land to the Mount. Not so in the past, when the tides governed the comings and goings of men.

"Tricky business back then," Luc said. "If you lost track of time up there, you needed a fast-galloping horse to get back to the mainland before the tide flowed in and stranded you."

"Stranded on an island," I said.

This ancient village should have swept me away, considering my fascination with history. Narrow, sinewy paths climbed through it, and at the highest point of the Mount soared a spire, atop which stood a statue of the archangel Michael. Clad in armor, he pierced the clouds above the former abbey. The setting alone should have kept me in its grips, while the restaurants, specializing in steaming scallops, should have stolen a couple of my other senses.

Yet every time I began to enjoy myself, I sank inside as soon as the experience passed. Our night in a hotel near the Mount was no exception. As soon as Luc fell asleep, Thierry appeared in the void. Thierry, my friend. Thierry, essential to my career. And my ruminations didn't end there. As soon as I managed to shake off the image of Thierry, Mister Jenkins materialized in my head.

It must have been about one o'clock when I again turned over and observed Luc's dark silhouette. Lucky Luc, lost in the comatose sleep of a little boy. He had warned me about George both times we'd run into my sphinx-like acquaintance. I never told Luc about my other café encounters with George, let alone discuss Jenkins with him. Heck, I didn't even tell him about my tea with his sister.

Thierry had written George off as laughable after meeting him in the Deux Magots. I wouldn't be informing him about Jenkins either. For one thing, he might think I needed more money; that our translating jobs didn't cut it.

I even pictured Kevin's potential reaction to the George-Jenkins business. I knew precisely what he would say: "went and got yourself mixed up with a couple of shady blokes. I warned ya, ya twit!"

Maybe they all were right. It didn't matter. I wanted to crack George and get paid on top of it. I thought about the City of Easy Encounters and smiled in the dark. Life wouldn't be nearly as fascinating in Paris if I had nestled into a comfort zone and stuck to it.

I couldn't fall asleep, so I made every character I had met in Paris parade through my mind. The little red-haired Orthodox Jew with the bouncing curls I collided with in the Marais that led to the most savory cup of coffee I had tasted. The middle-aged lecher who pounced on me in Montparnasse and revealed the four Hemingway cafés. The enthusiastic old lady who pointed out the uniqueness of the Tour Saint-Jacques. Dear Professor Bertalot who found me my priceless Lux Hotel...I could use his advice about now, I thought, as I started to nod off...too bad I hadn't seen him in ages...always loved his red tie and shiny cufflinks. Who else in the parade...lots more people...eyes getting heavy...show's over.

I woke with a start. My travel alarm clock read three o'clock, and George and Jenkins had intruded on my slumber. I dreamt I had gone to the movies with them. Absurdly, the two of them had invited me. When we returned to the Lux—they were staying there too!—and I had snuggled into bed, a series of knocks startled me. On the other side of the door, a soft voice pleaded to be let in. Through the door I could see George mouthing words that turned into groans. Jenkins stood behind him and clawed at his shoulders like a raptor with real talons and sharp, severe eyes. Then I woke up. My eyes burned with fatigue.

The dream did not arrive out of nowhere. Real events had somehow woven their way into my sleep. Two other characters in my parade of Paris personalities hadn't made their appearance before sleep claimed me. So they had barged into my dreams disguised as George and Jenkins, almost as if to say, "How dare you leave us out!" They were a couple of wild Albanians in their late twenties who had sojourned at the Lux the month before. Both worked as journalists in the reclusive communist country, and they craved a nice saturation of the senses in El Dorado on the Water.

Intrigued, I accepted their offer of a movie and dinner and watched them act like two spirited boys unleashed from a strict boarding school. In a way they reminded me of free-wheeling Katya, the Russian call girl, because they too made a farce of the Cold War. Even their contrasting looks fascinated me. One was a tall rail with fair curly hair, while his pal and colleague had dark hair, a dark complexion, and stood short and stocky as a tree trunk. The blond penned the stories for their newspaper, his partner snapped the photos, and both exuded as much spastic energy as a couple of teenagers at Coney Island.

I figured a light supper would be in order, since our movie didn't finish until ten o'clock. But these nominal communists on the lam demanded a banquet. They raided the dinner and drinks menu as if they'd never sampled French cuisine in their lives. They ordered four courses, with two wines, plus aperitifs at the beginning and cognac to finish. Then we took the metro home, filed past a vigilant Madani, and closed ourselves in our respective rooms. I couldn't have been asleep long when light tapping at the door woke me.

"Haley, are you awake?"

I shook myself into focus. "What? What's going on?"

A whispering voice floated in. "Haley, it's Enver. I'd like to talk to you. Open, please."

I punched on my nightlight and squinted at my alarm clock. Enver, the tall blond writer of the Albanian duo was at my door. I sat up. "At two in the morning?" I said.

"I have something important of which to talk to you."

"Tell me tomorrow morning." By now I was awake as an owl, and my voice started escalating.

"There's no time. We leave at dawn. Please, Haley, open the door!"

"Go back to bed!"

"I would love to go to bed—with you! I'm crazy for you!"

Had he gone mad? If pleading weren't enough, Enver now started rapping on the door. I decided to take a stand of silence and turn off my light. After about fifteen minutes, it paid off. No more pleas. No more knuckles. Only a subtle rustling.

I peered at the door. Something small and flat inched underneath it. I slipped out of bed and crept towards a square piece of paper, barely illuminated by the strip of light from the hall.

"Haley, are you still awake?"

I froze in the darkness.

"I'm leaving now, but please read my note."

I must have waited half an hour before I turned on my light. Then I unfolded the paper and read a silly love letter written in big, cursive, broken English. From where I sat in bed, I flung it into the trash.

My mind returned to the present and my hotel room with Luc. I pondered how I could have led on that Albanian nut. What power did I not know I had? Then I focused on George and Jenkins. Why the freakish dream? I turned over in bed with my back to Luc. The job Jenkins dangled before me smacked of baseness. Snitching. No doubt he would whitewash it with patriotism. I could help the hostage situation, couldn't I? Strange, he hadn't made that pitch to me. Did he know I needed money? It didn't matter; I would dabble in this business for a while. Just a few rendezvous, some conversation. Oh, and if I could help the American hostages, better yet.

When I got back to Paris I began my strategy. Jenkins had recommended regular visits to Place Saint-Michel and the cafés and restaurants around the Poseidon. I would be bound to intercept George that way, and it wouldn't look like I was running after him.

Logical advice, but strangely ineffective. For days I tried it. I had quit going to school, and before heading to Thierry's for translation, I trod every path leading to the Poseidon. I frequented all the cafés in the neighborhood, as well as the crêperie. I tried different hours on the weekend, working around Luc so he wouldn't suspect my secret. Who knew why I never ran into George? Or why a supreme irony transpired.

I had just set foot on the Pont Neuf one drizzly Saturday morning, poised to cross my favorite bridge over the Seine on my way to Place Saint-Michel. The wind started swirling, and I soon found myself assailed by rain droplets that felt like icy bullets fired from invisible machine guns. I made my umbrella a shaky shield against the gust-driven spray and trudged on, anxiety over an anticipated call from Jenkins rivaling the wind. So far I had obtained nothing and feared I would have to approach George directly at the Poseidon. Right after that thought, the umbrella almost flew out of my hands. A gust had snagged it and a tug-of-war started. I held my ground as the umbrella shook and almost danced out of my hands. When the wind gave a final thrust, my umbrella turned inside out. I stared at it in disbelief, sliding the catch up and down repeatedly while rain stung my face. Nothing doing. My wobbly shield now amounted to a limp corset of bent bones. *Merde*! I said aloud and pitched it in the Seine, not giving a damn who saw me.

The rain kept lashing me and left me no choice but to hustle back to the Samaritaine to replace my fallen umbrella. With all the coffees and crêpes I had been forced to consume around Place Saint-Michel as part of my "mission," I could ill afford the expense. Still, the rain wouldn't relent and neither would my shrinking window of time. I hurried into the Samaritaine, if nothing else feeling relieved to at least be sheltered.

Once I reached the umbrellas, however, I again swore out loud. *Nom de Dieu!* Same lot from which I had purchased the beige piece of rubbish now floating down the Seine. Even the same colors—beige, blue, and grey.

"Are you in difficulty, Mademoiselle?"

I whipped around at the intrusive English. "George!" I said, gaping as if I faced an apparition. "What are you doing in these parts?"

His hair dripped like mine, and his glasses bore smudges where he undoubtedly had wiped them of rain. Yet, to my satisfaction, he had made a joke, calling me *mademoiselle*, and he posted a bright smile.

"The same as you," he said, and pointed at the umbrella rack.

I smiled back, marveling at my strange luck. "The wind took mine and mangled it. I hate this weather!" *Keep talking*, I told myself—put him at ease.

He shook his head. "Maddening it is, this weather."

"I bet it's different in Crete. None of this pelting rain every other day."

"That is certain," he said with a nostalgic look.

"Tell me about it, about Greece..."

"Not here," he said. "Better to sit down."

"I know the perfect place for this kind of day," I said, "and it's right around the corner. You see, I live in the neighborhood."

I didn't care about having to settle on the exact brand of umbrella that had already failed me. I had achieved a first successful step and I felt almost giddy about it. George bought a grey umbrella and I bought a blue one, and with confidence I proceeded to lead us out of the Samaritaine and over to the *salon du thé* next to the Auxerrois.

"These *financiers* are quite good," George said, before he swallowed his bite. "I'm glad to know about them."

I flashed my most enthusiastic smile. "Fascinating history: they were originally created in a pâtisserie next to the Bourse—the stock exchange. That's how they got the name *financiers*. So, anyway, tell me about Crete. It's got to be warmer than Paris in February."

He nodded and swallowed another mouthful. "Not only warmer, it can be hot. We eat outdoors many times in winter. And the air is dry." He gave a weak smile and sighed. "I miss it."

"I can relate. The air in my hometown, Reno, is really dry. It could be zero centigrade, and if you've got a thick coat on, the cold just bounces off."

"Do you miss your town?"

I paused for a moment. "Sometimes. I miss my grandmother and a couple friends. Who do you miss in Crete?"

"My parents...and my sister." His eyes went glassy for a moment and it made him look more weary than usual.

I leaned over our little marble table. "I didn't know you had a sister."

George paused to sip his tea. "She's younger, only twenty years old."

"What's her name?"

"Rania."

"Pretty," I said. "A Greek name?"

"No, it's Muslim. My father insisted that."

All right, I thought. Maybe we're getting somewhere. "Which religion does she prefer?"

He shifted his weight. "...She sees herself as Greek. Only Greek. She wants people to call her Eleni, her second name, which is Greek."

I sat back and crossed my legs. "How do you feel about that?" Like a psychologist, all I needed was pen and tablet.

He shrugged. "She is extreme. But she can do what she wishes."

I wondered if he remembered passing *himself* off as "just Greek" the first time we met. "Is there discrimination in Greece against Muslims?" I asked.

"Yes, and Rania agrees. She wants nothing to do with Muslims. She is as bad as the Greek Christians."

And you? I wanted to ask, but thought it prudent to hold off personal questions for the time being. Instead, I said, "That must make a mess in your family."

His laugh rang sarcastic. "You should see my father; he is always angry with her."

"Because she rejects Islam?"

"Because she wants extreme freedom, even more than a Greek woman." Quite disdainful, George's tone. He didn't approve of his sister any more than his father did.

That pissed me off. Eleni dared desire the freedom of not only a Greek woman, but probably of an American woman—like me. I wanted to confront George with it. Fling all the crap I had learned about the Koran and the inferiority of women in his face. Dare him to defend the outrages. I chewed the inside of my cheek and finally decided not to risk turning him off and losing him.

To get back on track I shifted tactics. "You were saying you missed your friends. Who do you hang out with here, Greeks? Afghans?"

For a second he squinted. "Both. I get along with both groups. Who do you...hang out...?"

I laughed. "*Hang out with.* It's American slang."

This answer would be tricky. I popped my last piece of *financier* into my mouth, patted my lips with my napkin, swallowed, and finally resumed. "There was my good pal Sasha, the girl you met at the rally, but she left for the States before Christmas. It's been a little lonely without her."

"Was she your only friend here?"

"Well, I do some translating and spend a lot of time with my colleague. You met him at the Deux Magots, the dark one."

"The other French man," George said in a flat tone. In his continuing habit, he pronounced *French* and *man* as if two separate words. "You work with him?"

I nodded.

George's eyes saddened, as if he was disappointed. I started to regret my revelations about Thierry, and then he said, "Well, if you are lonely, you may call on me. The talk is good."

Relief washed over me, followed by a soft warmness that filled me. Then the feeling mutated to embarrassment—this mission wasn't meant to make me feel soft or warm. I produced a casual smile. "Thanks, you can call on me too," I said as blandly as possible.

A flicker of enthusiasm animated his dark eyes. "Do you still visit the café near your school?"

"I'm not in school at the moment...had to take a break with work. Now I mainly hit the cafés around here, near my hotel on rue du Roule."

He smiled. "Then we may likely see each other again."

When George left for work, I breathed a plentiful sigh of satisfaction. I had completed my first task. What was more, I had left George Abdi with a means of contacting me.

Timing: one of the world's maddening mysteries, right up there with coincidences, and luck, and fate. In this case Monsieur Garnier played the role of providence's puppeteer and finally granted Thierry and me a new translation. He presented us with *Backpacking through America's Monuments,* and he wanted all 200 pages translated into French by the end of March. Inwardly, I smiled at the irony of it. Now I had two jobs.

From day one I predicted this new translation would hold none of the fascination and stimulation of either *Cold War Chronicles* or *L'Islamisme*. Not for me, anyway. Sure, pictures of the Grand Canyon, Zion, and Bryce Canyon jumped off the pages. The text, on the other hand, could have cured my insomnia in Mont-Saint-Michel.

Thierry raved about it. "I can't believe you haven't been to these places," he said, when we first received the book. "You practically live next door to them!"

I held back a bored sigh. "What can I say, my passions lie here."

"Lucky for me."

I wondered what he meant by that. Did he refer to our friendship as well as to our translating partnership? I hoped so. Did he harbor suspicions about Luc and me? If he did, he was master of the mask...or, he didn't care. Each day I went to Thierry's home, I basked in hospitality. I felt embraced by the home's warm wood. The floors, the furniture, the shelves stuffed with books, caressed my spirit the way my fur-lined gloves hugged my hands.

Luc's apartment, on the other hand, flashed style and modernity: tile floors, glass tables, state-of-the-art stereo and videocassette recorder. I enjoyed the electronic toys, no doubt about it. Warmth, though, I felt only with Luc next to me on the over-stuffed couch...

Or in bed.

I lay on my side, while Luc rested on his back. My arm lingered on his chest.

His hand grazed my leg, and out of the blue he said, "Why don't you move in with me?"

In my post-climactic dream state, my mind empty as clouds, his words blindsided me. I took the time to turn onto my back, feeling the need to disengage before answering. Finally, I said, "I've never thought about it."

"We're together now," he said, "and we could both save money. You wouldn't have to pay Madani 3000 francs a month. The rent here's only 2500..." Typical of Luc, always figuring the financial side of things.

"It *could* make sense..." I said, and then lapsed silent while my mind buzzed with the novel idea.

Luc tickled the inside of my thigh. "What are you thinking about?"

"...Just that I've never lived with a guy. And if I did, my grandmother would cut me off financially." Thierry's view would enter the equation too, but I didn't mention that.

"*Ouais*," Luc said, propping himself on an elbow. "My parents are old-fashioned too. They like you a lot, but I know they'd rather see us married than living together."

Married. That stung me. Christ, how had things accelerated this fast? I turned back on my side so I could study Luc's silhouette in the dark.

"I like having you with me like this," he said, and stroked my hip with his fine-boned fingers. "I like it very much..."

I caught his fingers and laced them in mine. "So do I. Don't worry, I don't plan on going anywhere. It's just that..."

"You don't want to upset your grandmother."

"That's pretty much the situation. You're not disappointed, are you?"

He freed his fingers. "Not really. As I said, the two of us living together would be hard for my parents too. But I'll do it, if you change your mind." He rolled over onto me. "Now, let's make a little 'nightcap,' as you say in English. You're not getting away from me this early!"

For a couple of days I couldn't stop thinking about Luc's proposition. The potential of upsetting my cherished triangle scared me. For without Luc *and* Thierry, my Paris would be unrecognizable.

Then again, "my Paris" had already started to assume a new dimension. The time had arrived to move on George again. When I called Mister Jenkins about the chance meeting in the Samaritaine, I could practically feel his pats on my back.

"Couldn't have occurred more fortuitously, kid. You seized the opportunity and started working your way into his personal life."

My confidence swelled. "What if I take the initiative now and look him up directly?"

"Excellent. He said he liked talking to you, so go ahead and invite him out for coffee. Keep moving forward. Remember, twenty dollars minimum every contact with him."

We hung up. Everything was aligning in my favor. I had two sources of income now…So why did Jenkins always leave a bad taste in my mouth? *Working my way into George's personal life.* Did he have to make it sound so invasive and sleazy? From day one I had wanted to figure out George, and I would take the money because I needed it. No need to rub in the fact that the two were connected.

My first move was to cancel an afternoon session with Thierry. About a week after the initial meeting with George, I told Thierry I had to take care of some business at the Alliance Française and couldn't make work until the next day. The lie didn't make me feel good, but at least I could arrive at the Poseidon around three when business slackened. It didn't take much to lure George out for a chat. In fact, the normally sad kid from Crete radiated a bold smile. His hair looked thicker, as if he had just washed it, and his glasses were smudge-free. The dark circles under his eyes persisted, but the whites shone clear of red. All in all, he bore a fresh shine.

I told him I'd just finished a Greek sandwich in the neighborhood and had a hankering for coffee. We chose a café and I continued small talk while I finished my espresso. Then I commenced my approach. A different one this time.

With deliberation I placed my cup in the indentation of its saucer and met George's eyes. "You know, I'm curious. After our last conversation, I've wondered if your father and his family consider you Muslim..." Of course a silence followed, a typical George-pause that tempted me to check my watch to see how many seconds he would let pass.

Then I received a shrug and a frown. "I suppose they do. Not because I go to the mosque. But I don't go to the Greek Church either."

"The Afghans view you as Muslim, though..."

For a moment he eyed me with curiosity, if not suspicion, which made me fear I was moving too fast. Then he said, "They say if your father is Muslim, you are Muslim, so to them I probably am. To them everyone should be Muslim."

Just as I had figured. "Thanks," I said, "I wanted to confirm something I'd read. In this guide to Islam I translated, they say everyone is born Muslim. No need for baptism or anything. Unless parents make their children Christians or Jews, or whatever, they're Muslim. So if your mother never had you baptized Greek Orthodox..."

"My father would never have given that permission."

"Of course not!" My enthusiasm for the topic began to get the best of me and I started babbling. "From what I read, if a Muslim man marries a Christian, Islam demands their children be raised Muslim—"

George leaned over the table. He got as close to me as he did that very first day we met, when I thought he would breathe fire at me. His voice was stone-solemn and his right hand formed a fist. "In my case, I choose my own way."

Then he sat back, and his eyes softened to reflect their characteristic sadness. "My father took me to a mosque when we visited Afghanistan. But in Crete, in my town, there are no mosques." He frowned at the table. "The Greeks do not like Islam. This is not fair, is it?"

His eyes rose, and I didn't know what to say. I couldn't tell George that I actually understood the Greek attitude. That I would hardly welcome mosques mushrooming in my hometown of Reno either—not after all I had learned about Islam. But what about the good people like Madani and probably George's family? All those Muslims who believed in peace and charity, not in the literal meaning of jihad? I had to grant them credit. "No, it's not necessarily fair. But there are some problems with Islam," I said with delicacy, "that alarm people…"

George shifted forward again. "How do you know about Islam's problems, that book you read?"

"Read and translated. I do have some background."

I caught a flash of amusement in his eyes. "After reading one book?"

"Listen, I don't claim to be an expert on Islam, but what I've read about the Koran would be hard to counter. Check for yourself. Ask me a question or whatever…" *Merde!* I complained to myself. I had put myself on the defense when I was supposed to be steering the conversation.

As for George, he had settled back again and was gazing out the window. Perhaps he didn't want to play verbal chess either. I observed the sidewalk through the glass panels that slid open in summer so patrons could inhale the sounds and smells of life on the street. At this time of year pedestrians hustled by, huddled in their overcoats, heads butting an obnoxious wind. I wondered what kind of prickly matters absorbed their minds.

Finally, George turned a casual look on me, breaking a silence I found rather comfortable. "Do you get paid for translating?"

"Yeah, it's a job I've had for almost two months." I felt confident and relaxed again.

"This book about the Koran, is your first work?"

"Actually it's my second major job. The first book was on…communism."

George tilted his head and raised his eyebrows, as if communism represented a truly serious subject. That pleased me, until a feeling of fraud crept into me about using communism as a cover for the true content of *Cold War Chronicles*. I wanted to come off at least halfway honest, so I refashioned my answer. "I mean it's a book on the Cold War…taking place in Russia."

"No doubt interesting," he said, "but your book on the Koran…"

"An exposé on Islam, written by a French woman."

"French woman?" His olive-black eyes turned mocking. "Excuse me, but is she an authority on Islam?"

"Enough to be part of a team that writes on the major religions of the world. Do you have a problem with that?"

"No problem. I just wonder…"

"What?"

He shrugged. "If a French person can understand Islam. Most are Catholics, I believe."

"The author's not Catholic, she's a convert to Islam and she writes about your situation, about Muslim fathers and Christian mothers." That, I hoped, would get us back onto personal issues so I could move things forward.

"What does she say about a woman's place in Islam?" George asked, before I could follow up.

I sensed a trap. If I answered, "appalling," it would imply the author was insane to convert in the first place (something I actually believed). On the other hand, if I suggested she deemed it fine, George might think I agreed with her.

I watched him as he fiddled with his coffee cup and saucer. Then I replied, "It is what it is. What do you think?"

George sighed. I saw weariness weighing in his eyes. "It is a complex problem. No simple answer you can find in books."

I wanted to pin him down, but he claimed he had to get back to work, and I figured I had derailed my mission questions enough for one day. When we separated, I left a casual, "see you around," to linger in the air.

Before running its course, February gifted Paris a glimpse of spring, a few days of blue skies and temperatures shy of face-numbing and bone-chilling.

One of those golden-blue days, Madame Perri invited me to see the Monet museum—just the two of us. After Luc had let the word "marriage" escape, I wondered how much his mother knew about us. Could she be viewing me as a potential daughter-in-law? I found this unsettling, and it wasn't the only unknown quantity facing me. I had to deal with entering a new museum as well.

I stepped into the Monet museum with the hope no painting would rattle me. As long as I stuck with the other visitors I could be reasonably sure I'd be all right. I had no intention of following the crowds like a sheep, though, and I purposely wandered into a room by myself just to test myself.

Waves of vibrant color surrounded me. I held my breath, squinted, and took a step forward. No quickening of my pulse. No constriction in my chest. No shortness of breath. Nothing flew off its canvas at me, so I relaxed my eyes. Light emanated from the pastel colors and tranquil impressionist landscapes. I breathed out and began to revel in beauty, relief and satisfaction—no problem with this art. Granted, Monet's impressionism and Delacroix's emotionally violent style stood poles apart, but I couldn't help feeling that Stendhal's

Syndrome may have melted into a memory of something I wasn't sure had ever existed.

When we left the museum, my positive mood accompanied me. Neither Madame Perri nor I wanted to waste this azure day on a bus or in the metro, so we strolled down the sun-soaked sidewalk.

I smiled at the sun's warmth. "I can't tell you how much I enjoyed that museum, Madame."

"Call me Marie, dear. You're practically one of the family."

My gait slowed. What did she mean by that?

"I can never get enough of the Impressionists," she went on. "In the dead of winter, they give hope that spring will return."

"I about lost hope in spring until these blue skies appeared," I said, resuming my pace.

"Don't let the weather get you down, dear. Try to keep busy. How's your work coming along with Thierry?"

"We're on our third book, about hiking through America's natural monuments."

"Thierry must adore that. He's always longed for the wide-open spaces of America." Madame gave a little laugh. "When he was about twelve, he told us he wanted to go off to the wilderness and live in a log cabin. '"

I almost started laughing. "Cute," I said instead. Thierry and I certainly longed for opposite lifestyles.

"He was crazy about that film where Robert Redford lives in the wild, builds a cabin and gets around on snowshoes..."

Loses his mind and goes on a killing spree, I finished to myself. "*Jeremiah Johnson*," I said.

"That's it. Then there's Luc, my city boy. Always will be, I imagine."

"One reason we get along so well."

"That you do." She reached over and patted my shoulder.

What to make of that gesture?

Right before we went our separate ways, Madame Perri changed the subject. "What do you think about the next election in America?"

I hardly expected that either. "Well, I haven't thought about it much so far..."

"I think Reagan would be good for the United States. He projects strength, and if he brings Kissinger in, maybe he could put an end to this Iranian mess."

Politics was the last thing I wanted to discuss, especially with someone I felt deferential to. So I didn't tell Madame that I considered Reagan an inveterate actor; that it wasn't President Carter's fault America had botched its Iran policy thirty years ago, nor was it his doing the Iranian clergy and students had gone barking mad. I avoided all that and told her I wasn't quite up on things, but that I thought Kissinger was fine. Anyway, I had George for my discussions of Iran.

I slogged through *Backpacking through America's Monuments.* All those glossy photos belied a tedious text. Geography, geology, history bogged me down before we could even get to campsites, recreational activities, and tours. Thierry had enrolled in a morning Spanish class, so we could only work together afternoons. On my own I devoted mornings to the translation, since many evenings I spent at Luc's. Weekends, I barely had time to do laundry and go out with Luc.

In other words, I busied myself with everything short of savoring Paris. I couldn't remember when I had last treated myself to one of those long, solitary walks that enabled me to commune with the city. I would have to remedy that, I told myself.

Sometimes Thierry would invite me to lunch or dinner at his house, and one Sunday he proposed a surprise meal. "Don't eat breakfast," he had warned. So I didn't, and my stomach rumbled in protest until he showed up at 10:30 in his white Peugeot sedan. Destination: the Hilton Hotel.

"Why are we here at this time of the day?" I asked him, as we rolled into a parking place. Jazz couldn't be the answer, not in the morning, and no one in Paris ate lunch until twelve. As for breakfast, I'd missed that boat. By now, if even one single croissant or brioche lingered anywhere in the city, it would be rubbery enough to play sports with.

I shared the thought with Thierry who said, "You're completely off base." His impassive brown eyes gave nothing away as we trailed through the expansive Hilton lobby. Then we entered a restaurant, and a familiarity flooded me as if I had run into a childhood friend. Thierry ushered me into an American-style coffee shop that served brunch.

"How did you come up with this place?" I marveled.

"I rooted it out after I got back from Michigan. The pancakes are excellent."

Hunger had its claws in me, and for a moment the nostalgia of home nipped at me as well. "Then bring on the pancakes!"

I submersed mine in butter and syrup. Thierry did the same and then further suffocated his with eggs.

"Never gotten over American breakfasts," he said, between bulging bites. "I love it all: waffles, *French toast*—that's a good one! Unfortunately, there's nothing like that in French cooking."

"Fried eggs, scrambled eggs," I added.

"*Ouais*. Everything except American coffee."

We drank that anyway, just to experience the ritual of refill after refill, something that never occurs in the France of the French.

"If you lived in the States," I said, "would you eat this stuff every morning?"

"Yeah, I'd scramble my eggs, butter my toast nice and heavy—"

"All in your little log cabin perched over the Grand Canyon!"

Thierry's eyes flickered curiosity. "That is a kind of dream of mine," he said. "Only I'd want to be far from the tourists. Montana might be better."

"Big Sky country."

"Why do they call it that?"

"Because, like Nevada, the sky's a vault of never-ending blue. Probably sunsets to die for too: gold, pink, purple, red. That's what they're like in Reno at least."

"Haley, when you're back home, I'm coming to visit you!"

"You'd be welcome."

After about an hour, I didn't know how I had ever in the past gotten used to enormous breakfasts. It felt like the brunch left a deposit of rocks in my belly. Thierry suggested a walk. I just wanted to beach myself.

"Come on, all you need is a good *digestif*," he said, and steered me out of the Hilton, into a café in the neighborhood. "I think *Génépi* should work," he said, as we settled in front of the café window.

I stared out at the traffic on the sidewalk, devoid of energy and ambition, as if excessive gravity weighed me down. Then guilt swooped in, and I questioned whether I would ever accomplish anything meaningful at all in Paris. When the liqueur arrived, I took a long sip, expecting something stiff and sobering to punch me awake. Instead, a bouquet of strong, sweet herbs blossomed on my tongue. Immediately it began liquidating the boulder in my stomach.

"I'm feeling better. What is this stuff?"

Thierry looked pleased. "A distillation of herbs from the Alps. Works wonders after a heavy meal."

I felt physically lighter and returned my gaze to the window. Another whitewashed Paris day. The sky looked brushed with a boring coat of smooth white paint. I hated to admit it, but after all that talk of big blue skies I itched to scrap Paris for somewhere sunny.

I looked at Thierry. "Where in France would you most likely find blue skies right now?"

"Hmm...Corsica's a good bet. Or somewhere else on the Mediterranean. Nice, Cannes, Marseille. Why?"

"A dry, sunny getaway sounds good to me."

"All of the places I named fill that requirement."

I sat up straight. "Which one's easiest to get to? Not Corsica, I know."

"By plane they're all easy. By train...Of course driving offers the most freedom. I'd choose Nice and Cannes. They're prettier than Marseille."

I stared past Thierry's shoulder. "A lot more alluring too, from what I know." My spine started to tingle just thinking about Cannes with its palm-dotted coast and famous film festival...

"Do you need a break from work?" Thierry asked.

"No, I'm okay. I'm in the mood for sun, that's all. Sun and sea..."

"I could go for that myself." He rubbed the shadow of dark beard on his square jaw, a strong jaw that complemented his overall huskiness. "We could go together...take my car..."

Our eyes met and my pulse started to thump. "Let's make a plan," I said. Then I blinked. "Should we invite Luc?"

Thierry hesitated for a moment, but his eyes revealed nothing. "If Luc comes, we'll have to travel on a weekend. I was thinking we two would go during the week and take our work with us."

A heavenly plan: a chunk of work in the morning, broken by a walk in the sun along the beach, followed by lunch on a terrace...a little more work...then off for a drive...dinner...

"Do you want Luc to come with us?" Thierry asked, yanking me from my dream-vacation.

Honestly, I didn't know. Luc didn't have a lot of patience when Thierry and I discussed work. How would he react to being left on his own while we worked on *Backpacking through America's Monuments*? If this was to be a working trip, it should take place during the week...when Luc couldn't go.

Then something struck me. "Luc was just in Nice at Christmas—he probably wouldn't want to go back so soon."

Thierry aimed a serious, level look at me. "With you going, I'd say, he would."

"Because..."

"Listen, Haley, the two of you aren't a state secret."

That was all he said about Luc and me, but my tongue found itself in a knot all the same. What had happened to those simple, carefree days filled with the ecstasy of the three of us? I still held my two friends close, but our places had changed on the game board.

"The hell with it," I finally said. "Let's go find the sun—the midweek sun!"

6: Once Upon a Time, the Three of Us

Of course it didn't prove that easy. My heady confidence lasted as long as I bummed about the afternoon with Thierry. As soon as I closed the door of my hotel room, it bottomed out. When and how would I break this bright idea to Luc? Would he be jealous? Did he even know Thierry had caught on to us?

I sat at my desk, tapping my foot in a nervous rhythm until I decided I would tell Luc that Thierry knew...when I found the timing convenient. Then I closed the door on the entanglement and tried to delve back into *Backpacking through America's Monuments*.

My phone buzzed. A visitor downstairs, reported Madani. I slammed my book shut and skipped out the door. A distraction was just what I needed.

When I swung open the lobby door, only one observation struck me: he had taken the bait. He had found me.

I lied. "George, what a surprise!"

His eyes glowed and his teeth gleamed whiter than I had remembered. My sphinx was revealing some emotion. I recalled that day in the Dôme when his eyes glistened with what had seemed tears—sudden and silent—and a sensation of weakness floated like a feather in the pit of my stomach. Get over the guilt, I told myself, as George chattered on. Too late to turn back. Don't want to go back. He invited me to tea next to the Auxerrois.

"I have not been able to stop thinking of these *financiers*," he said, after swallowing a bite of muffin. "They are so delicious, I wanted to come back."

I showed a smile of approval. "You made a good choice. I never turn down a chance to come here."

He picked up his napkin and dusted the crumbs off his fingers. "I must tell you, Haley, I also came to see if you were all right. I mean, if you were still...lonely..."

My chest tightened. "That's awfully considerate." His concern shocked me, but I swallowed the grit in my conscience and went on. "I'm glad you came because I didn't have anything to do the rest of the afternoon but work. Inappropriate for a Sunday, don't you think?"

"That is what my mother would say," he answered, and savored another bite.

"Not your father, though. Sunday is just an ordinary day for Muslims, isn't it?"

His smile came slowly, along with a tilt of the head. "Yes, but you must know that from the book you translated."

"...Right." I paused. Better to ease into things. "That book on Islam's made me do a lot of thinking. About the hostages in Iran, for example. It's not easy discussing it with Americans and other Westerners." After registering George's quizzical look, I continued. "Americans and Europeans can't get past the hostage part and dig into the complexities, if you know what I mean."

George sat back and seemed to study me through his nicely-polished lenses. "Yes, I have experienced narrow heads...how do you say...?"

"Narrow-mindedness? Me too," I said after he nodded. "Take my friend Sasha. She coaxed me into that American rally when she had no background, no idea about how this mess in Iran got started, and why the Iranian clerics and students mistrust Americans."

"There is very good reason for them not to trust the Americans."

"I know, I've read up on it!"

"Have you read about how the Americans used Iran for its oil?"

"Oh yes!" I said.

"And when the Iranian people wanted a democracy and not a Shah, the American CIA stopped them..."

"Exactly. They drove out Prime Minister Mossadeq and propped the Shah back up."

That knowledge appeared to impress George. "You are different from many Americans. You know a lot for..."

I chuckled. "...For an American? For a woman?"

He started to blush and gave me a sheepish smile. "The problem is that there are many Americans who do not understand this history. Not only Americans, French people too."

"It's got to be frustrating. But you must have friends here in Paris who show solidarity."

"Not Americans. Except you..."

Was I his friend now? I brushed off a pinch of guilt and smiled. "How about the Afghans in Paris, are they supportive?"

George shrugged. "For the most part."

"Do you have any Iranian friends?" There, I finally got it out. Under the table I crossed my fingers.

"I know some here..."

I leaned in on my elbows. "Well, if they're upset with America I can understand."

"You don't think the Iranian students are criminals?"

"What?"

"The sign in your hands at the rally..."

"Oh!" I said. "Sasha shoved that thing at me before I could read it. I had no intention of carrying it."

George shifted forward and smiled. "You did appear uncomfortable that day. But you defended yourself against...that rough fellow." For some reason his eyes assumed that glassy look of his—the sphinx expression.

"Yeah, I did hold my own," I said, wondering what had caused the change.

Then he focused back on me. "Haley, there *are* some criminals in Tehran. They use the problems with America, the history, to be rough. But most of the students only protest to have their rights. To have the government they want and to make America give back the Shah."

I shook my head. "What good would it do to return the Shah now? He's probably dying of cancer."

"It doesn't matter, the students and the clerics want him to face the people and his crimes."

"Do you think he'd get a fair trial?" When George didn't answer, I swept the air with my hands. "Regardless, innocent Americans shouldn't be kept hostage."

Both arms on the table, he leaned closer. "Not all are innocent. Some are CIA. But you are right, the innocent people should be free."

"Hard to figure out the innocent from the guilty..."

"Yes—that is the difficult part!"

Suddenly he sat back and went silent, as if losing steam. I retreated into my own thoughts. I had neglected my mission to follow up on his Iranian friends. Our discussion of the Shah flowed so naturally, I'd let myself get carried away. How to get back on the rails and maneuver him into talking about individual Iranians? I looked out the window and observed the inky night that had sneaked up on me. So had hunger, despite the swamp of pancakes, syrup, and bacon I'd devoured earlier. One of those nice mixed salads with beets and corn at the Opera Drugstore sounded perfect. I checked George. He seemed to be examining the peacock feathers fanned out in a tall vase on the floor in a corner of the salon.

"Haley, I fear I must go," he suddenly said, his typical sad smile back.

"Me too," I conceded. "I should get back to work."

He wagged his finger at me. "Remember, no work on Sunday!" Then he grinned.

It pleased me when he ventured into humor, and I laughed. "Thanks for coming by. I can always use a distraction from work!"

We exited the salon and parted ways, I to the Opera district for my salad. Before descending into the metro, I turned back to glance at George as he melted into the vapory blackness of Haussmann's city. Despite our individual preoccupations, we had remained in vague agreement on issues as slippery and shifting as the cold, misty air that enveloped us.

That evening I called Mister Jenkins. He praised me and promised forty dollars for the rendezvous in the tearoom. That raised my total to sixty. Now he wanted a meeting.

The next day I set out for another of Jenkins' tucked-away cafés. The muddy Monday sky couldn't decide whether to rain or not, and that seemed to poison my mood. I almost felt guilty about accepting the earnings for which I had worked so hard. Each time I scanned the ambiguous sky, I felt like its ballooning-grey billows sucked job satisfaction right out of me. God, I needed that Mediterranean sunshine, a big push broom of it to sweep away the murkiness that threatened my peace of mind.

Funny thing, once I settled into the café my ambivalence dried up. For starters, the Left-Bank locale turned out to be cheerful, unlike Jenkins' former haunts. Its windows gleamed, posters of tropical beaches adorned the walls, and its customers consisted of animated young people, as opposed to old men with their noses in newspapers.

Jenkins himself even seemed changed. He didn't express any of his winking, backslapping ways. *That* Jenkins appeared to be on hold, substituted by a sober, pensive *mec* who took moderate sips of his Calvados.

"You're homing in," he said, bloodshot eyes sharp and darting. "Soon we'll learn about George's friends."

"Well, that's just the thing," I said. "I'm not sure they're up to anything bad." I cleared my throat. "My feeling is they're serious people who don't really want the American hostages hurt. Even in Tehran, I understand, they'd give up the hostages if we gave back the Shah."

Jenkins stared at me. "Sounds like you're reciting George's view," he said without sarcasm. "Listen, we know his friends support the Khomeini government, which would just as soon jail the hostages, throw away the key, and shut off oil indefinitely." He clasped his hands together under his chin and continued to look earnestly at me. "Think about it. Khomeini's a religious dictator whose entourage is manipulating George and his pals. So just keep fishing, kid. If his buddies are in touch with the students in Tehran, I'd like to know what they're planning or advocating. If they're truly well-meaning then I'll be the first to congratulate you."

The lecture rang reasonable.

Jenkins pinched his chin. "One other thing. Try to find out about his Afghan friends. We're interested in them too."

My shoulders sagged. "What should I look for there?"

"Ask how they feel about Khomeini as opposed to the communist government in Kabul."

"Khomeini couldn't rule Afghanistan..."

"No, but George may have friends who come from western Afghanistan where they share ethnicity and language with the Iranians. I'd like to know their take on this."

Dubious Iranians, rogue Afghans, the ratcheting-up of this business made me feel I deserved my money. And, thank God, Jenkins paid me in francs. I left the café with 260 of them, about sixty dollars, and as I headed out to explore the discount music in Joseph Gibert, a brilliant thought seized my mind. I could actually afford the sun, sea, and palm trees I so needed. Then I turned my reflections to Luc and how to break the news of my vacation in Nice without him.

I decided to start tinkering with this piece of potential ordnance that evening after dinner. Whatever the outcome, I didn't want our appetites ruined—I knew my French priorities! I set a Joe Dassin album on Luc's expensive turntable for some background music, and we started doing the dishes. Then I began to loosen a nut.

"It'd be nice to get away for a couple of days," I said, as I dried the plates Luc handed me.

He continued scrubbing and rinsing. "We just got back from Mont-Saint-Michel."

"And I loved it. But this weather's got me down—I feel the need to go somewhere sunny."

Luc placed the last dripping glass on the counter. "I don't know if I can get away."

I dried the glass and then started twisting and stretching my towel. "You don't have to worry about that. I'd have no problem going alone. I sort of have my sights set on Nice or Cannes, for the sunshine and dry Mediterranean air."

No comment came from Luc as he rinsed the sink.

I slung the towel over my shoulder and went on. "I even mentioned it to Thierry. It's that *Backpacking* translation that's got me longing for a dry, sunny place. Just for a couple of days."

Silence continued as Luc wiped down the counter.

I pulled the towel off my shoulder and gave it a twirl. "Thing is, Thierry wants to go somewhere sunny too, so he offered to drive me down to Nice. We'd have to work there to keep our deadline." Whew, what a spiel! I took a silent breath through my nose and waited for Luc to face me.

Finally, he laid his dishrag down, leaned back against the counter, and looked at me with his arms folded. "Thierry wants to go too?" he asked, brow slightly creased.

"Well, he likes the idea of sunshine, and we really do need to keep working..."

"Hmm..." he said, which made me hold my breath again. Then he shrugged. "Might as well go."

I stiffened with astonishment. "You think it's a good idea, then? I mean, the probability of sunshine down there..."

Luc added a little smile. "Better than here."

I couldn't hold back. Next thing I knew my arms encircled his neck and my lips crushed his. As we wound our way out of the kitchen, Joe Dassin's voice boomed from the stereo. He sang about the "Promised Land," always out of reach. A place only to glimpse from afar, or in a dream. When we finally waken from that dream, right before the end, we pass on.

An unsettling song. What did the *Promised Land* mean, anyway? Perfect place, perfect friends, perfect happiness? And if you don't achieve it, then what? I shook it out of my head, and in its place I remembered I hadn't informed Luc that Thierry had caught on to us.

Paris to Nice by car makes for an all-day excursion, one that presents a pageant of terrains. The contrast between the north and south of France struck me as the difference between two families. I lived in the lush, verdant north—the rich family. By the time we reached Provence, the brilliant-green fields and dark, rich pines had dried up, and arid, grey-green mountains and hills greeted us—the poor relations, I thought.

Until we descended upon the Mediterranean, and what I had perceived from the freeway as impoverished countryside turned into a splendor I never expected to witness in full-fledged winter. Palm trees, I had expected. But the olive groves and thin, tapering parasol pines whose tops arched up and out like umbrellas surprised and charmed me. I saw roofs of cheery-red terra cotta and flowers blooming everywhere. Petunias, geraniums, and pastel-petaled oleanders flourished at a time of year when their relations in the North had long passed on. I started to seriously envy this branch of the French family.

The whole colorful scene sat under a limpid-blue sky, a few shades lighter than its complement, the sea. When I stepped out of the car in Nice, I felt a caress of sea air so mild that I chucked my camel's hair coat in the backseat and set off exploring Eden in a blazer. God, maybe this was the Promised Land.

"You'll even love the coffee here," Thierry said, as we headed toward an outdoor café. "It's more Italian. Nice's phonebook is full of Italian surnames, like Costa, Rossi, Brunetti."

"And Perri," I replied. "Luc's roots. He said since we're close to the Italian border, we should drive over and have a look."

Thierry's impassive eyes revealed a spark of surprise. "Luc made recommendations for our trip?"

"Yeah, it amazed me too."

I thought about Luc at home in Paris. If he had joined us, he would be running the show, rushing us from place to place. With Thierry I could relax. Indulge my senses and enjoy the scenery. On the way to the café, we crossed through Old Nice by the waterfront. Some of the streets defied the name, their paved paths so narrow, dwellers on both sides could have an intimate gossip from their balconies. On wider streets, people lounged at sidewalk cafés, the better to absorb the southern February sun, and luxury cars lined the thoroughfares.

We followed suit and nestled into an outdoor café facing the water where bougainvillea climbed the wall next to us. As I sipped my coffee, I looked out at the sea. I knew the ancient Greeks had founded Nice, and I pictured Poseidon's waves rocking all the way back to Africa. Then I turned toward the hulking Maritime Alps and imagined Zeus transforming ancient Titans into mountains, when the parricidal young god usurped power. I shared the fantasy with Thierry, and with his background in classical literature he took the metaphor and spun it.

"Then, with such beautiful sea, coast, and mountains to rule over, Zeus made Helios shine on the realm 360 days a year. Like in Reno," he added with a grin.

I picked up the thread. "And he favored and spoiled the mortals who lived here, showering them with warm, dry air, bestowing vineyards and olive trees for two of the most important staples of life—"

"Wine and olive oil," Thierry quickly said.

I nodded, and forced an inconvenient thought out of my mind: Luc would have found this conversation boring. Then I resumed. "They fished and ate figs, grapes, olives, and dates..."

"And built temples to Poseidon and Zeus. To Aphrodite also, for love and fertility."

Like Zeus's children, Thierry and I spoiled ourselves. We indulged in pasta and seafood for dinner, after which we returned to our hotel facing the sea. And to our separate rooms.

The next morning we decided to postpone work until afternoon, because we wanted to visit one of the most famous places on the coast. We drove west to Cannes, the town that blossomed each spring with movie stars during the film festival. We took tea in the swanky Ritz Carlton and then drove to Antibes to walk the lofty ramparts of the old city walls.

After finally meandering back to Nice, Thierry and I still didn't feel like settling down to work. So we strolled the rocky beach to continue enjoying the cool, salty air.

When we finally went to my room to bang out a page of *Backpacking*, the sun had begun to set. I watched it from my window and couldn't help alluding to the classics again. "Look, Apollo in his chariot driving the sun into the sea." There, it sizzled, sending off swaths of gold, red, and purple flame to engulf the sky. The palm trees on the Promenade des Anglais were reduced to shadows, like burnt sticks with black feathers brushing against the sky's fading colors.

Thierry stood beside me.

"See?" I said. "These are the colors you see day in and out in the Far West."

He squeezed my shoulders. An awkward feeling came over me, but I turned and managed a smile. So did Thierry. Then he lowered his hands and we went to dinner.

The next morning, I thought the gods had decided to punish us for slacking off with only one page of translation. That stunning sky of the day before began to drizzle rain. So much for Eden. We couldn't face staying cooped up, so we chose to drive to Italy for the day.

On the way, we stopped in Monte Carlo, home of another famous Anglophone and compatriot of mine. This American girl had landed on the scene before my birth, and her French had to be damn good after twenty-some years of residence. Grace Kelly enjoyed the best of all worlds, a palace in Monte Carlo, elegant digs in Paris. The princess of Monaco could bask in Mediterranean sunshine, jet to Paris whenever she missed El Dorado on the Water, or fly to America if she got homesick. And yet, I didn't envy Princess Grace. She was too old, for one thing. Plus, I didn't like the idea of marrying into a life in France. I wanted to achieve my own success.

The rain now formed a steady curtain of water slapping our windshield. Thierry and I persevered, climbing the winding roads of Monaco's hills to get a grey view of the bay below. Then we descended, and I really felt the hairpin switchbacks. Hardly a guardrail in sight and the road so narrow, some tracts had room for only one car. The route reminded me of a long, treacherous serpent, all the more dangerous in the slippery, blinding rain. I looked out my side window and saw sheer drop-offs with no barrier between me and hundreds of feet of dizzying air. I gave a silent gasp and faced forward.

Thierry never batted an eye throughout the drive and made no comment when we finally reached the two-lane coastal road. Just another normal French driving experience for him, I figured. A few kilometers later we reached the Italian border. A guard flagged us down just long enough to nod at my passport and Thierry's identity card and wave us on our way.

Flowers, palms, and parasol pines continued across the border to San Remo. So, unfortunately, did the rain. Not in warped sheets as before, but like steady piano notes, obliging us to dodge puddles and hide under our umbrellas once we left the car—a second new umbrella, in my case, one I was forced to buy in Nice.

I joked about leaving my new navy-blue one in Paris. "It's not supposed to rain in paradise."

"It *is* February," said Thierry, as we hopped over another puddle.

Finally we ducked into a café on the famous Via Aurelia where Thierry couldn't resist launching into a history lesson. "This super-highway dates back to ancient Roman times. We could basically drive the whole coast of the western Mediterranean, all the way to Spain, without veering off this road."

I was just keen on being in a new country. "What's the coffee like here?"

I found out when something I had never seen before landed on our table. This coffee came with a creamy crest, and though it rose to only a quarter of the cup, it was the richest, smoothest brew I had ever tasted.

"I could drink two of these," I said, with an urge to lick the cup.

"*Cameriere!*" Thierry called out. "Two more, please."

Sitôt dit, sitôt fait, il ne l'a pas raté: no sooner said than done, the way Thierry jumped on my wish. The French words flew into my head from "Quand on a du feu," the first song I had heard by Joe Dassin. "When you've got a light," Joe sings, the possibilities are yours for the pickings. Just strike that match at the right moment, and you could meet the love of your life...

That is, if it's meant to be. I had struck a match when I acted on my stolen purse some seven months ago, and now I counted Thierry and Luc as my close friends. Was that Luck or Fate? And why could I still not be sure whether I was in love with Luc?

Ruminations like this channeled thoughts of my parents. They had barely surpassed my age when Fate wiped them out in that accident. Or was it Chance? If assigned to Chance, the importance of the accident in the immenseness of the universe amounted to a single hair falling from someone's head. If one blamed Fate, who else was slated to die young? Why did God, or the universe, or whatever the hell operated out there even bother?

I looked out the window and wished it would stop raining. Fortunately, Thierry started talking about Italian food, and dinner. None of my interests escaped his competency. I couldn't imagine a better traveling companion.

At dinner in a trattoria, our discussions multiplied, accompanied by all the courses traditional to Italian dining. With wine lubricating my tongue, next thing I knew I had leaked the secret of George and Mister Jenkins.

"Wow, you've really become a spy," Thierry said in a voice so low I could barely distinguish it above the clanging and clattering magnified by the restaurant's tile floors.

"Not for love of country," I said. "I'd just like to figure this guy out. He's got both the Western World and Islam tugging at him."

"Or he likes both cultures and can't choose." Thierry produced a little smirk. "Personally, I don't think he acts very Greek."

"He's from Crete," I said, and sipped more of my Limoncello digestive.

Thierry blew smoke from the side of his mouth and shook his head. "It's not that. He doesn't have the air of a Westerner. His Afghan father must be the main influence on him."

I leaned in. "You came to that conclusion after seeing him for two minutes five months ago?"

Thierry smiled and moved forward so that we almost touched noses. He lowered his voice again. "I'm perceptive. I'm your John Steed, Mrs. Peel, so keep me informed."

That sent a thrill up my spine.

By the time we hit the road, the rain had finally grown sick of itself and ceased. Thierry drove, thank goodness, for a warm vibration teased my head.

We babbled all the way back to Nice, mixing French and English like a schizophrenic salad. Man, what a crazy concoction! The conversation continued all the way up to my hotel room door, where eventually it started to wind down with a series of "okays" and "bon, alors." Then we initiated the double-cheeked good-night kiss...and ended up banging foreheads. We mumbled a couple of "pardons," but didn't try the gesture again. We held fast to each other's arms and then relaxed into a hug. Thierry's lips grazed my neck. A chill rippled down my back. In a spasm I pulled him closer, closed my eyes, and let myself sway rhythmically against him.

"You know," I murmured, "in The Avengers John Steed never seduces Mrs. Peel."

He kissed my neck. "Right now I feel more like James Bond."

I sought his lips without meeting his eyes. I fumbled with my key and opened my door to let us in. Then I quit thinking and gave way to the throbbing electricity under my skin.

A barrage of light and noise woke me. Thierry had risen, turned on the desk light, and started rattling the pile of cassettes on the desk next to my player. I shoved my pillow up enough to prop my head against the headboard without emerging from the covers, and squinted at him and my mechanical companion. We had brought it along to provide a little background music while we pumped out work, but in two days we had translated exactly one page of Backpacking through America's Monuments. Guilt initiated a two-pronged attack.

Thierry glanced at me. "Sorry, I couldn't sleep. Mind if I play my Simon and Garfunkel low?"

"Why not—it's only one in the morning."

I didn't mean to sound sarcastic, but Thierry must have taken it that way because his face reddened. "I didn't know you'd dozed off..."

"Go ahead," I said. "I wasn't sleeping very soundly."

Thierry slid in Simon and Garfunkel and slipped back into bed. He rubbed my shoulder. For a moment I studied him. I pulled one hand from the blankets and fingered the dark hair on his chest. Thierry trailed Luc in age by two months, but he exceeded him in bulk, and beard too. With Thierry I felt I had made love with a mature man.

The song "America" played like a travelogue in the background. Thierry squeezed my arm. I wondered what part I represented in his fantasy—in his dream of living in a log cabin in the Far West. I pushed the image out the revolving door of my mind and let in a different fantasy: Luc, Thierry and I, all living together in one jolly household, like Charlotte Rampling with her lovers in the Sixties.

Neither of us asked about the other's musings, and Thierry said, "We should try to get some sleep, since we have to leave in the morning."

At the end of the song, Thierry returned to his room. I didn't sleep more than about an hour the rest of the night. I couldn't stop wondering why, despite pricks of guilt, I didn't regret sleeping with Thierry. Shouldn't I have been in love with Luc? I just couldn't tell. Charlotte Rampling claimed to have been in love with both men she lived with. Couldn't I profess the same with at least one of my friends?

The next morning over breakfast, I settled down to reality.

"You know," I told Thierry, while busying myself with bread and jam, "we can't continue what happened last night."

Thierry finished a slow sip of café au lait and placed his cup in its saucer. His eyes met mine with a kind of grimness. "I know. I don't fancy sneaking around."

"Right. Imagine trying to get around Madani, or your mom. We'd have to act like we were in a sitcom."

My humor didn't change Thierry's expression. "That's irrelevant. Luc has first dibs on you."

His bluntness clipped my tongue. Then a wry smile appeared on his face. "Someday, though, I'm going to Nevada, and I'm going to track you down."

Back in Paris, I forced my thoughts elsewhere. I had to review my notes covering my last meeting with George and then strike again. The *Avengers* fantasy and the idea of a newfound confidant in Thierry excited me. Monday morning I decided to move on George at the Poseidon. This time I was determined to make significant progress.

The Poseidon hadn't opened at 10:00 a. m. , but I spied George inside setting tables. I waited for him to turn and waved. That probably seemed aggressive, given the Muslim culture no doubt percolating in the Poseidon, yet I didn't care. I watched as George spoke to his uncle. At one point the old guy turned and eyed me sharply, but I just backed away from the window and waited. Finally, George walked out the door.

We barely said hello when he gave me a peck on each cheek. Christ, we were friends now! I didn't know whether that would prove good or bad, so I focused on the task at hand. "I was over getting stationary at Joseph Gibert," I told him, "and thought I'd stop by..."

George looked at his watch. "I only have about half an hour."

"There's a great crêperie around the corner," I said, referring to a place I had learned to appreciate from the time I was forced to stake out George.

Today, my appreciation of the restaurant reached a new level. When we got settled and my crêpes *à la crème des marrons* arrived, I spread the warm, creamy chestnut sauce over the skin-thin crêpe and sighed to myself. Finally I could order such delights and afford to pay for them.

Then I got down to business. "Where do you and your friends go for snacks?"

George prepared his own crêpe with Nutella and answered without looking up. "...That depends on which friends."

"I don't know," I said, before taking my first bite. "What about your Afghan friends?"

George folded his crêpe and cut into it. Soft Nutella oozed out. "They like Iranian food. It is similar to the food on the Afghan side of the border."

"Do you like it? Sorry if I seem nosy, but the exotic always interests me."

George swallowed his bite and smiled. "Not at all. I do like it. I have got used to that food on our trips to visit my father's family."

I savored my last mouthful of thick, smooth, semi-sweet chestnut sauce and let the flavor echo on my tongue. George ordered coffee for both of us, mine short and *serré*. By now, he knew my style, and this intimacy emboldened me to take the next step.

"By the way," I said, after the coffee arrived, "I wanted to ask you...I got curious last time we talked...Do you have any Iranian fr—" I stopped. "I mean, do you know any Iranians who support the Khomeini government?"

George's gaze dropped to his cup. It didn't surprise me, and during the interval I examined his short, matted hair and the delicate skin under his eyes that looked bruised from lack of sleep. *What's your move, George? Do I have to start bringing a chess timer?*

As if he had ESP, his eyes popped up. Then they started darting around the restaurant. "It is as I told you," he began slowly, eyes returning to me. "The Iranians whom I know, they would support to give up all the hostages, if America gave back the Shah."

"Do any of them actively support Khomeini?"

He gave a half smile and placed his crossed arms on the table. "Yes, Haley. Because it is their government now, not America's."

A point Jenkins had made flashed through my mind. *Their* government—in a religious dictatorship?

I kept the contradiction to myself and moved on. "Do your friends plan on going back to Iran to get involved? I mean, it's sort of one's civic duty in a democracy."

"They might go. But for now their affairs are here."

A shot of electricity coursed up my spine. My opportunity had arrived. I tried to look nonchalant. "What are they doing here?"

George frowned and sipped his glass of water. "...They raise money and support for Iran, things like that."

I had extracted George's answer so effortlessly, I wanted to grin. But there was no time for inner gloating, and I pushed on. "Money from the international community here in Paris?"

George sat back and shot me a condescending smile. "Many people believe that Iran has the right to govern itself."

No shit! I said to myself. Did he deem me an ignorant American girl again? I calmed myself. "Of course it does. Every country should have that right. So the money must go to the Khomeini government, then..."

George's frown returned and he shifted in his chair. Again, I caught him surveying the restaurant. "I don't know if all the money goes to Khomeini," he said slowly. "But I know they would like him to free the innocent hostages. The students are working on that, I can guarantee you."

If he viewed me an ignorant girl, I could label him naïve. About that, Jenkins was right. And why did George have to stall before answering me? Unless he sought out someone as he scanned the room...I gasped inside. Jesus, could Jenkins still be shadowing me...and George have recognized him? No, no, I reassured myself, if George knew about Jenkins he wouldn't be talking to me.

I recovered my cool and ploughed on. "I wonder if mostly Arabs and other Muslims contribute to Iran?"

George seemed to relax as well. He removed his glasses and started polishing them with his paper napkin. The wire frames, I thought, jazzed him up with a note of modernity.

"Most money," he said, "comes from Shiite Arabs. They want to see Iran standing alone."

You mean, I wanted to say, they intend to usurp America's place and start their own meddling. I resisted the political argument, however, and concentrated on what remained for me to ask, such as names. Who were these friends who solicited donations for Iran? The problem was, I didn't know how to ask the question without coming off too transparent and provoking suspicion.

"What kind of music do you like?"

I blinked at George. He had used my silence to change the subject. Actually, I was grateful for the diversion. "Jazz, French music and other stuff..."

"Do you like British rock and roll?"

"Sure—the Beatles, the Dave Clark Five..."

"They are fine," George said, "but I prefer the Animals. They sing with more of the soul." His eyes reflected something melancholy or sensitive.

"I know what you mean," I said, and thought of the song that went, *It's my life and I'll do what I want; it's my mind and I'll think what I want.* The spirit certainly suited George.

"Eric Burdon sings of struggle," he said, "and...I don't know how to explain in English..."

"Of the disadvantaged in society—the misfits," I said. "I like his music too." And I wasn't lying just to keep George on my side. The melodies and themes of Eric Burdon and the Animals appealed to something kindred in me as well. For the first time I felt an authentic meeting of the minds with George.

"Exactly," he replied, with the most warm, earnest look I had ever seen in his eyes. Then he lowered them, and I wondered what he was thinking. When he looked up, he gazed around the room again before focusing back on me. "I must return to work."

"Of course. I've probably kept you too long. I'll pay," I said, and reached over the table for the bill.

George extended his hand, palm down. "No."

"But I invited you," I said.

He scooped up the bill and stood. "I cannot feel right that way," he said, as he pulled out his wallet.

I sighed, and remembered him acting similarly the first time we met. The subsequent two meetings, *he* had suggested we go to a café, and so I'd let him pay. That's the way it is in France. Whoever invites, usually treats. George, on the other hand, insisted on playing the traditional *old mec*. It bugged me, but I had to accept it if I was to get anywhere in this mission.

We parted with kisses on the cheeks again, and as I headed toward the metro, a couple of things began to preoccupy me. Apart from the who-what-when-where questions Jenkins required me to ask, I wanted to know *why*. Why had George masked his Middle-Eastern heritage when I first met him, only to appear at the American rally in the midst of a nest of Iranians? And why had he so readily disclosed his friendship with Iranians who funneled money to Khomeini? I couldn't ask him for risk of blowing my mission, and, to tell the truth, I kind of feared digging that deeply into George's personality, even though he now acted like my friend. Which presented another challenge: how to keep this friendship superficial?

Mister Jenkins sent his congratulations over the phone. He promised me fifty dollars, after which he promptly told me to leave off George for a while. "Lay low now and let the dust settle. Don't mention Iran or Afghanistan, or any of his friends if you happen to run into him. Don't start anything up until I give you the go ahead. From now on, I'll assign my assistant to contact you at the Lux, following which you'll call me. From a phone booth, of course."

"Like I always do."

"Right, but avoid the PTT and use the street booths. Your fifty dollars will come in the mail."

When I told Thierry about Jenkins' latest instructions, curiosity shone is his usually impassive eyes. I was thankful for his role as my confidant, especially now that I had experienced success, only to be followed by Jenkins suspending my activities. We agreed the FBI intended to act on my information in some way, but how? And why had they now reined me in?

Spring had arrived with longer days in its train. Although winter refused to loosen its jaws completely, the sun trailed longer and helped to melt the vice-grip on the land and city. When I left Thierry's house that afternoon, I saw daylight stretching ahead of me like a promise, and I finally decided to indulge in a long walk. Just like the old summer days when I had spent entire after-noons scouring the city.

I strolled east on boulevard du Montparnasse, for once my hands free of the fur-lined leather gloves Luc had given me for my birthday. I passed the Hem-ingway cafés, which I hadn't noticed in months, and slowed in front of the Rotonde where I'd first taken George long ago in some kind of age of inno-cence. Who could have predicted the suite of events? Chance, Fate, Provi-dence?

I shook my head and couldn't decide whether to turn right or left where boulevard du Montparnasse becomes boulevard de Port Royal. Right, led to the Observatoire. The observatory's dome reminded me of a crystal-ball thrust into a pale, pessimistic sky, and I wondered what lay in the invisible stars.

I decided not to turn at all, and continued toward a route I had never charted on foot. Within a few blocks, rue Saint-Jacques appeared on my left. Too bad I couldn't see far enough down to spot the friendly green dome of the Sorbonne. The familiar beacon had welcomed me home from many a wander-ing when I lived on rue des Ecoles in that wacky hotel where the same key fit every lock.

Those early days in Paris hovered in my mind like a ghost. I worried about nothing back then. I glided from one week to the next as in a dream, intoxicat-ed with El Dorado on the Water. I thought about Kevin and Sasha. I had lost contact with them and felt bad about it. Though I didn't want to resurrect our trio again, I still missed them. It doesn't make sense, I know, but that's how I felt.

How had my former life vanished so quickly? As I walked down boulevard de Port Royal, I grasped at the memories, and realized that one event had led to another and that the past and the present were as connected as macramé. I had constructed a new reality in Paris with the building blocks of the past. It lacked the carefree cavorting of my days with Luc and Thierry, and Kevin and Sasha, but maybe I had replaced all that with my newfound productivity—the money-earning kind. So why did everything still feel hollow and disjointed?

I longed to relive moments in the past I could only recreate in my mind. Luc tearing up parking tickets, their confetti raining down like laughter. Thierry and Luc jumping on their beds in the hotel in Tours. Our joy, our exuberance, equally divided into three. Yes, my mind could recreate these moments almost flawlessly, like frozen frames. But the snapshots had already begun to fade. Certainly, no one could take them away from me. Nor, however, could I touch them, feel with my hands that they had indeed been real. I wanted to hook Luc's and Thierry's arms again, feel their warmth with me in the middle. Who knew if I would ever do that again?

By now I had reached avenue des Gobelins. I flashed on an autumn day on the street when Luc and I had waltzed alone down to Place d'Italie to view the enormous bronze lions. Thierry had been absent, busy preparing for interviews and employment with Air France. More moments with Luc and fewer with Thierry could have planted the seed that sowed the end of our equal-sided triangle. Did Fate grant Luc and me the opportunity to germinate a relationship, or was it Chance? Now I had slept with both of my friends and didn't know which I should prefer more. As the sun began to melt away, I only knew I needed them both.

With daylight at a premium, I checked my *Plan de Paris par Arrondissement* and cut left toward the Seine while the pale, veiled-white sun still lingered. After zigzagging across the Fifth arrondissement, through the tangle of little Latin-Quarter lanes, I couldn't resist stopping at my favorite tiny park on rue des Ecoles. I chose a bench where I could contemplate the stately, cream-grey Sorbonne in the dusk. In summer, tree branches laden with green framed the view of the venerable university. Today, it stood etched with the lacy designs of winter branches. I swept Luc and Thierry from my thoughts, and for the first time on the whole walk I concentrated on the beauty of Paris. With the Sorbonne in front of me and the Cluny Museum behind, I felt sandwiched in timelessness. The Sorbonne boasted solid medieval roots while the Cluny rested on Roman ruins. They had existed long before me and would probably remain well after my last days had slipped through my fingers. Then a new day would break, and Paris would belong to someone else.

The end of March approached in a dash to finish the *Backpacking* translation. I avoided the Poseidon as Jenkins had instructed, but I suspected that wouldn't stop George from looking me up. Not long after my conversation with Jenkins, in fact, he showed up in the Lux lobby and invited me to the café Deux Ma-gots. I considered ways of putting him off, and yet I really didn't want to. I figured a quick coffee couldn't hurt as long as I avoided discussing Iran.

George shifted around in our brass-trimmed booth, making the leather creak. His eyes jumped from me to his little silver coffee pot and back. Typical George-like stalling, I thought. After I made some small talk, he finally spoke up. "I must admit, Haley...I have also felt loneliness lately."

I observed him while his eyes lay trained on the table again. Glasses clear, hair glossy, he didn't look bad if I discounted his bloodshot eyes. "Aren't your uncle and cousin good company?" I asked.

"My uncle is old. And my cousin is getting married soon. You are better company than him, anyway."

He had washed his hair and shined his glasses, maybe just to meet me. And he preferred my company. *How much did he like me*? Suddenly, all words dried on my lips and I didn't know what to talk about. Then I remembered he had a sister who rejected her Muslim name and went by Eleni. I smiled and asked, "What's your sister Eleni like? Does she look like you?"

I received a sad smile and a pause. What else from George? "Her skin is like mine," he finally said, "but her hair and eyes are light, like our mother. Like you..."

I cleared my throat and skimmed a response off the top of my head. "Sounds exotic...didn't you once say she wants more freedom?"

"You remember," he answered, seeming impressed.

"Does she date or anything?"

That provoked a grimace and another George-pause. "I would like if that was all..."

"But...?"

George expelled something between a sigh and a groan. Again he shifted his weight in the booth. "She dates many men, that is the trouble."

All right, I thought—something completely neutral to talk about and equally intriguing. I leaned forward, elbows on the table, chin on my fists. "You're worried, huh?"

This time he didn't avoid my eyes. "Haley, she is very young. She goes with those men to anger my father. She understands nothing."

I nodded, and decided to offer some advice from the young, female perspective. "Your father shouldn't get upset. Psychologically, it probably makes her act worse."

George shook his head. "You don't understand. My father comes from Afghanistan. There, they would kill her for this behavior."

My chin came off my hands. "*Kill* her—are they psycho?"

"*Psycho*? What does this mean?"

"Insane!"

George stiffened. His face tensed and his black eyes flashed. "Not insane," he said in a deliberate tone. Then he smirked at me, as if I were an ignoramus or something. "In Afghan villages that is how young people are controlled. My father handles my sister much more soft."

I felt the urge to laugh, but I didn't want to offend him.

He sighed again. "She is supposed to be at university studying languages, but she quit. She wants to come to Paris." He shook his head. "My father will not allow money for that."

"Couldn't she work here, like you?"

"My uncle will not support that idea."

More macho discrimination. "How do you feel about it?" I asked.

"It doesn't matter," he said, avoiding my eyes.

Typical. He refused to give me a straight answer. Barbarism in Afghanistan, liberalism in Paris, no wonder George's psyche seemed polarized.

"Haley," he suddenly said, squinting out the window, "do you mind if we walk a bit?"

"...No, I guess not."

He continued scanning the street. What interested him out there? Jenkins jumped into my head again. "Do you see someone you know?"

"No," he said, and finally returned his gaze to me. "Well...I thought I saw a fellow who taps on my nerves."

That made me smile. George was mixing up his French and English, and he thought he had spotted some guy who got on his nerves. Not Jenkins. Again, I reminded myself that George could not know Jenkins; that all of Jenkins' initial spying on me had made me plain paranoid.

George paid our bill and we left the Deux Magots for a stroll west on boulevard Saint-Germain. Curious, this guy who supposedly was such a nuisance. Usually, irritating people don't watch you from afar; they invade your space every chance they get.

I shrugged to myself and returned to pursuing George's views on double standards. "What do you think about me living alone in Paris?"

The usual hesitation ensued, which I found amusing by now, and I waited.

"...You are a student and you have work here."

"Your sister could work here."

"You don't act like her." For a shaved second he eyed me, and yet he didn't add, *Do you?* No, George was too polite for that. Or nervous. He glanced behind us. "I think that fellow is following me."

"Why?"

"...He wants to borrow money, no doubt. And he will not ask in front of you."

"Then go deal with him," I said, annoyed. "I've got to get to work anyway."

"I'm sorry," he said. Then, without the usual double-cheeked kiss denoting friendship, he turned and strode off.

I watched his back as he wove in and out of the foot traffic. His bluntness astonished me, and it didn't take me long to change my mind about my duties. I wanted to know more about this mysterious *mec* who hounded George, so I waited a couple of seconds and then began tailing him. I followed him back to the Deux Magots where he hooked left and headed down rue Bonaparte. When he looped into rue l'Abbaye, I risked him spotting me in the long, quiet, deserted stretch. And yet, for some reason he didn't look back. Instead of trying to avoid some guy soliciting money, George seemed to be the seeker. He turned left into Place Furstenberg, and still not a soul appeared. Here, at least, I wasn't left out in the open. I could hide behind corners of the tiny, circular Place marked by lampposts and buildings with shuttered windows. The scene felt eerie, though, and I wondered if anyone observed us through the slats of the shutters.

George slowed, as if deliberating. I waited and watched. Then he quickened his pace and I followed. We wound around rue Cardinale, a street so narrow you could spit across it, and immediately butted into rue Jacob. George still gave no indication he knew I was following him, and whoever he had in his sights evidently kept well ahead.

I continued to track him until we reached rue de Seine, where he halted and faced a busy street. Pedestrians swarmed like ants. He looked in one direction and then the other. Perhaps the *mec* looking for a loan had gotten away. Ironic.

Finally, he stuffed his hands in his pockets and turned right. Head down, he walked back toward boulevard Saint-Germain. I slipped into the stream of people around him, my eyes fixed on his short black hair shaved at the back. He now appeared decisive and directed his steps toward metro station Odéon. Right before his descent, however, he stopped and turned around. Jesus, that made me jump back into the crowd and trample someone's shoes. "*Merde!*" I heard, which I ignored, keeping my eyes on George in hopes his sweeping gaze hadn't snagged me. I seemed to be safe, for he resumed his direction and headed down the steps underground.

I slowly backtracked. Expelling a deep breath, I walked over to Danton's plinth and sat on its base beneath the skeletal winter trees. What the hell was George playing at?

That night at Luc's, the question still absorbed me. I had to deliberately shake George out of my head when Luc asked, "Which city do you prefer, Nice or Paris?"

I frowned. By now I had told him all about the trip to Nice with Thierry—well, almost all—and had put the city behind me. We had discussed the merits of north versus the south, yet for some reason Luc continued to rave about southern France.

"By March," he said, "it's really nice down there. The buds are out on the trees..."

I went on to remind him that Nice's charms lay mainly in the outdoors, and that it rained on the Côte d'Azur just like in every other place, only that I definitely preferred foul weather in Paris. For even in the darkest Paris weather, you could count on an army of cafés, cinemas, museums, and every other distinction of a metropolis, including raving lunatics and the odd stalker.

"You can't beat this city," I said, as we lounged on the couch, television humming in the background.

Luc considered me with a curious expression. "Maybe...but there are things a lot more important than big-city stuff."

"Oh?"

"Work, for instance. The quality of your job can be loads more important than the city you do it in."

"I guess," I said. For me, Paris equaled my work, but I followed his reasoning anyway. "What job would be worth leaving Paris for?"

"Something with career advancement, more money, greater prestige..."

I looked at Luc as if he were an alien. "*Mince*! You should move to New York and work on Madison Avenue! Why are you in such a hurry to get to the top?"

He shrugged and picked a piece of lint off my sweater. "It's what I want, and I don't like standing still."

I studied the individual who seven months before I had fancied my twin. The green eyes we shared, in Luc now seemed tinged with greenback. As I sat there pondering him, even the dull drone of the television reminded me of how little we had in common.

"Well," I said, "maybe you'll reach the top right here."

He looked down at his folded hands. "That's just it. I've had a job offer."

"In Nice?" I asked.

"No, in Lyon. But it's a lot farther south than Paris." His eyes rose to meet mine, earnest and serious. "It's not as big as Paris, but the firm is offering me a better position and a bigger sales sector. More money too." He searched my eyes for feedback.

I didn't want to give him any, but I still had to ask. "When would you have to start?"

"In May, maybe as soon as April. I don't know yet."

I shook my head. "This job must be worth Paris and your family and..." I sagged back against the fat cushions of the couch. "Wasn't it Henri of Navarre, future king of France, who said, 'Paris is worth a mass?' He changed religions for Paris!"

"To be king," said Luc. Then he stroked my hair. "I was hoping you'd come with me."

I tried to relax and release the tension in my jaw.

"Listen," he said. "If you're worried about your grandmother cutting you off, my salary could support us both."

I shook my head. I did not want to be kept by anyone. "That's not the point..."

"Do you want to get married?"

For a second I closed my eyes. "Do you realize neither one of us has ever said the words *I love you*? Let alone talked about marriage."

"So who will say it first?"

I emitted a nervous laugh. Luc gave me an ironic smile. Then he filled the standoff with a kiss.

I sighed and pulled back. "So we'll cross one bridge at a time, all right?"

He nodded, and we resumed our embrace.

Thierry and I ripped through the remaining pages of *Backpacking through America's Monuments* and met our end-of-March deadline. I could still feel the decompression when I finally got myself over to the PTT and called Gram.

"Sorry I'm late with my call," I told her immediately. "Every two weeks isn't doable. I can't phone you any earlier than three in the afternoon here, and I'm usually working then."

"Haley, you know you can call me any time of the day."

"Before six in the morning? I'd wake you up."

"I'm always awake by four. Now, what's your next translation project?"

I rubbed my forehead. "I don't know yet. Thierry's bringing our manuscript to Mister Garnier and hopefully he'll come back with another book...How are you doing?"

"Keeping my head above water. It's tiring at my age."

I didn't pay too much attention to that because I had seen her in action in England. She got tired in the evening, which had to be normal for her age. I didn't mention money either. I knew Gram had her financial worries, but truthfully, I didn't want to go into them. I figured as long as she didn't bring them up, things remained more or less status quo. Plus, I had Jenkins' money to fill the hole—over one hundred dollars' worth now.

"Just keep working as hard as you can," said Gram. "No matter what, always give a job your best and approach it with honesty. Remember, there's dignity in all work."

A queasiness filled me, a kind of mental nausea. Jesus, if Gram knew how I was using George...

"How's school?" she asked.

I had to stifle a sigh and offer her the blandest lie possible. "Nothing new there. It's still too time-consuming. I don't get much sleep..."

"Now I don't want you jeopardizing your health..."

I kept my tone of voice neutral. "Right."

"Are you getting run down?"

"You could say so...I just got over a cold." Now that was bold-faced.

Gram gave me one of her maddening pauses. I swear she reminded me of George in that. "You could suspend your earlier class," she finally said. "I don't want to see you sleep-deprived."

I diverted my eyes from the phone's base. I wished I could distance myself from the receiver as well; remove myself as far as possible from my lie's destination. I stared out the window of my booth. "That would help, since lots of nights I work late in my room."

"All right. But keep up your grades in the second class."

"Of course, Gram."

I pushed out of the PTT against a nasty wind. As I butted the gusts, I cursed them and winter, and everything else that put me out of sorts. If only spring could entrench itself, it would surely boost my morale.

April did usher in those coveted higher temperatures. Unfortunately, on the first warm morning, I woke up feeling my head weighed fifty pounds. At first, I wrote it off to lack of sleep. Nothing that couldn't be cured with a few cups of strong French coffee. Instead, breakfast finished, it felt like someone had started pounding my head with a hammer. That afternoon, as I rested on my bed, it seemed the same miscreant was stabbing a pencil in my ear. By evening, the torture had migrated to my throat. When I swallowed, I felt something like a mini, medieval mace lodged next to my left tonsil. I wanted to scream "mercy," but instead made my way down the stairs to the Lux lobby, gripping the banister for support. I had to call Luc to cancel our evening.

"How are you going to eat?" he asked.

"I don't want to eat. I'll just drink a little water to keep my throat moist. I could use some lozenges...and some aspirin for my headache..."

"I'll bring them over."

When Luc knocked at my door, he was juggling pharmacy items, a pot of soup, a packaged block of gruyere, and a baguette under his arm. I asked how he managed to get his knuckles to the door.

"I used my shoe."

"I didn't want you to bring all this," I said, half in dismay. "You'll get my germs."

"I'm not worried about it," he said as he barged in.

I no sooner shut the door than I heard another knock. Madani this time who swept in with a tray topped with a pot of tea and the dishes and utensils we needed to consume the feast I didn't want. After Madani left, I soothed my throat with soup and tea and then sent Luc home with the leftovers and many thanks.

I managed to sleep from nine until midnight. That was when the little villain in my throat changed tactics. As if the spiked mace hadn't sufficed, he had now set a fire that raged from my throat to the roof of my mouth. Every time I swallowed, I woke with the searing pain of a hot poker in my gullet that almost made me faint. So I sat up with the light on to avoid falling asleep and swallowing dry. I sloshed my throat with water and sucked on lozenges, which seemed to keep part of the pain at bay.

Until the lozenges backfired and I almost choked to death on one while dozing off. God, I wished Gram was there with one of her medicinal concoctions, even though I didn't deserve her care after having lied about still going to school and catching a cold. This real illness just might be instant karma, I thought.

I staggered through the night, and in the morning my eyes looked like two smoldering coals sinking into black holes. Other than a little visit to the bathroom, I hunkered down in bed, skipped breakfast and slumbered off and on all morning. Until another knock woke me. I pulled my robe on and opened the door a slit, just enough to see who it was and send the intruder away.

Instead, I sighed and smiled at Thierry who stood there with a pot he said was *choucroûte,* of all things.

"How did you know I was sick?" I asked, making the entrance a bigger crack.

"Luc called me this morning before I left for my Spanish class. Madani said I could warm this up downstairs if you feel like eating."

"Thanks," I said, feeling as slimy and vulnerable as a newborn baby. As soon as he went downstairs, I shot into the bathroom.

My little demon had carried out pogroms throughout my body. My limbs and torso felt like a building had collapsed on them. The warm shower, and then my new layer of clothes, seemed to slap raw nerves. Rushing to beat Thierry's return left me exhausted. At least the little miscreant had spared me nausea. I was hungry. When I opened the door, Madani followed Thierry in with a second tray of dishes and cutlery, more tea, and some bread left over from the breakfast service.

And yet, as well-intentioned as my friends proved to be, their attention brought home one clear message: I needed a place of my own where I could store food and medicine, and where I could barricade myself, if necessary, and slop around all day in my pajamas.

After Thierry left, my nasty companion kept me unpleasant company the rest of the day. But I slept quite a lot again, and when Luc arrived in the evening, bearing Vietnamese take-out, most of the fire had died down in my throat.

Then night came, and cold trepidation crept into me as I put out the light. A lone soldier, I dreaded a surprise assault by the enemy right after I had fallen asleep. I feared flamethrowers to my throat, tanks running over my body, and God knew what else.

Instead, the cunning warrior again swung his mace, this time at my right tonsil. The pain tunneled into my ear. Crushed with fatigue, I slept in spite of it, and the next morning I came down to breakfast.

When I finally got out the next day, I felt like a chick emerging from an egg, craving fresh air and a good stretching of its legs. After his morning Spanish class, Thierry and I took a turn around one of the biggest pieces of green space in Paris, where I had yet to set foot since my arrival in the summer of 1979.

Père Lachaise, the most celebrated cemetery in France, lay on one of the city's seven hills.

"Nothing like touring a cemetery to make you feel alive and well," I said, inhaling the caress of spring air as we walked through the gates. My eyes made their initial sweep of the cobbled grounds, consisting of endless tall, mature trees and stone tombs. "*Mince*, this place is as big as a town."

"You'll recognize the names of some of the residents because lots of celebrities are buried here. Chopin, for example."

"Chopin," I said. "Early nineteenth century. Romantic period."

We struck up one of the tortuous, cobblestoned paths just wide enough to accommodate a hearse.

"Héloïse and Abélard?" Thierry said, as if quizzing me.

"Twelfth-century lovers, condemned because Abélard was Héloïse's tutor."

"They're here together, united in a mausoleum."

"How old is this cemetery?"

"It goes back to the early 1800s; that's when Héloïse and Abélard were transferred here. How about Oscar Wilde?"

"Turn-of-the-century Irish writer. *Picture of Dorian Grey*."

"Marcel Proust?"

"Uh...French writer, early 1900s, but I haven't read his work."

"Hmm," said Thierry. "What about Géricault?"

"Oooh...French painter...let's see, which century...?ï

"Good enough. And Colette?"

"Uuuh...you got me."

"One of the most important French women writers of this century. One more, then I'll stop." Thierry aimed a studious frown at me. "Mind you, this one's difficult, so concentrate hard."

I frowned back, steeled for the challenge.

"Jim Morrison."

I had to close my mouth. "You're kidding! I knew he died in Paris..."

Thierry produced a smug grin. "His grave's one of the most famous. Come on, I can find it."

He grabbed my hand and we took off. We snaked along the cobblestones flanked by rough, timeworn tombs, many sculpted like little houses. And I thought: why take my hand, and not my arm? Hands are more personal, more intimate than hooking arms. An arm is more friendly...brotherly.

Every stone tomb we passed displayed a name unknown to me. I didn't recognize anyone. Thierry had let my hand go, and we continued hiking high and low. We followed one narrow, serpentine path after another, hunting for the elusive leader of The Doors.

"Not everybody here is famous," he said, "and there are so many tombs..."

It seemed we were the only ones exploring the place, until we encountered a group of people milling around a grave.

Thierry pointed. "That's it!"

James Douglas Morrison lay in the ground, occupying a little plot covered with white gravel. Only a small stone marked his resting place, unlike most of the residents of Père Lachaise, sheltered by roofs, or even elaborate mausoleums. I wondered whether Jim had felt at home in Paris before he died and who had chosen to bury him here. Didn't anyone care about him in the U.S.? He became an expat later in life than I had, and not for long. No envy there.

Père Lachaise had the magnitude of at least a village, and everyone's domicile, and all the cobblestoned streets, lay under a canopy of green shade. The green shone light and tender. Delicate, budding spring leaves appeared barely born. Barely reborn, defying the death and decay of the necropolis. After my illness, I counted myself among those leaves and longed to get my life going again.

I waited for two calls once I got well. I desperately needed one from Thierry with news of a new translation we could sink our ink into. Monsieur Garnier had assured us something would come our way. But when? Jenkins owed me the second call. Almost two weeks had passed since we'd talked on the phone, and I itched to resume tapping George for information.

Jenkins finally did call. This time he set the rendezvous off rue Saint-Honoré, back in the recesses of the Bourse du Commerce. To get there I had to follow a cold, shaded street called rue Sauval. Its sidewalks weren't even wide enough to walk on, and the lane was so narrow the sun couldn't pierce it with even a fraction of a ray. When I approached the Bourse, a small circular structure with a dome, I started circling it, per Jenkins' instructions. Only I couldn't see around it and almost got hit by an oncoming Mini. I leaped back and practically had to flatten myself against the Bourse's wall. Why did Jenkins have me navigating this rat-maze?

The route eventually channeled me alongside the huge church called Saint-Eustache, whose rose window I could see from the Lux. Jenkins had said if I reached the church, I would have gone too far. So I retraced my steps back to rue du Jour and finally found the hole in the wall where we were supposed to meet. The café sat in such a way that we could see anyone coming from three directions, though not even a stray cat showed itself on the street.

Here, in this rustic little establishment furnished with long, coarse pine tables and naked beams suspended from the ceiling, Jenkins laid into me.

"What the hell were you doing out in public with George last week?" he asked, the moment I sat down.

I stared at him. The realization that he had indeed been following me hit me like an anvil. The waiter arrived and took my espresso order. After he left, I protested. "It wasn't my idea. George came to see me at the Lux."

"Then you should've told him you were busy and sent him away."

Jenkins' face shone redder than usual and he was slinging back cognac, the lush.

His whole attitude made me bristle, and I continued to defend myself. "I avoided the topics you said...but why were you following me in the first place?"

"Never mind. I told you to steer clear of George until I gave you the signal."

My face burned with indignation. "That's not what you told me," I said, feeling a tremor in my voice. "You said if I happened to run into him, not to bring up Iran or Afghanistan or his friends."

Jenkins didn't yell. He kept his voice even, in control, with just a hint of menace, like the low tones of a bass saxophone. "Well, I thought you'd have more common sense and understand that *lay low* means *lay low*."

As soon as he said that, I remembered Jenkins' exact words the last time we met: *Leave off George.* My mind smarted so intensely, spillover occurred and I could feel my ears singe with embarrassment. I glanced at a group of three men lunching at a table near ours and hoped none of them had noticed my discomfort. Laborers in blue work-trousers with multiple pockets and loops for tools, they chatted at their long table while they drank red wine. The bottle was larger than the usual 750 milliliters and it had no label. They gobbled up bread and *steak frites* and showed no interest in us, thank goodness.

"I'm sorry," I finally said. "I thought if we only talked about family...the weather..."

Jenkins sighed and rubbed his chin, a stubbly one today. "Forget it. Just avoid George from now on. And whatever you do, never follow him again."

A touch of doubt tinged with nausea hit me. "Have you ever met George?"

Jenkins took a last drag and crushed his filterless cigarette butt, his fingers grazing the base of the ashtray. "No, why?"

I lifted my shoulders. "I just wondered whether he might've recognized you out and about."

"Not a chance. Anything else?"

I tried to ignore his smirk. "So you'll let me know whether I need to follow up?"

"Right."

That sounded vague. Jenkins took a swig of cognac and sniffed sharply, as if testing the air. His eyes narrowed to cobalt slits and mechanically scanned street and sidewalk out the window. He had hardly looked at me the whole meeting.

Boisterous laughter rose from the laborers across from us, and I envied their carefree comradery. I turned back to Jenkins. "Do you think you'll want names of George's friends?"

"Maybe." With one hand he rubbed his face, the way men do when they want to clear their thoughts, unlike women who worry about smearing their makeup. He finally aimed his narrow blue eyes at me. "I want you to keep the lowest profile you can, Haley, and wait for my orders. Don't screw around, or you'll get me shipped straight back to Washington." He gave a dry laugh. "Just kidding."

I didn't answer him. I just looked down at the knotty-pine table and chewed the inside of my cheek.

When I raised my eyes, Jenkins was pulling a white envelope from his jacket. "Do you understand?"

I nodded.

"Here," he said, sliding the envelope to me. "Pay the bill and keep the remainder as a token of the Bureau's ongoing appreciation." With that, he pushed away from the table and stood up. He swung on his trench coat and walked out the door, collar up, head down.

I watched him round the corner before I picked up the envelope. I sighed at it before opening it and plucking out the bundle of bills. After I had settled with the waiter, almost 200 francs remained—over fifty dollars with the greenback's relentless erosion.

I frowned at the money before returning it to the envelope. I didn't like the idea of not seeing George. To tell the truth, not only did I find him interesting, I actually identified with him a little. We had both ended up solitary foreigners trying to make it abroad, and now that Luc prepared to relocate, the feeling hit home even harder. George and I both had family worries, though my frustrations with Gram paled compared to the drama playing out with his father and sister. I didn't know what I would do if George popped into the Lux again. Certainly, I could make excuses, but I didn't want to have to lie repeatedly.

Again, I watched the workers in blue. They had finished their bottle of wine and laughter now tumbled from them. One, an older *mec* with a grey mustache, delivered a couple of good-natured slaps to the cheek of a curly-haired kid about my age who sat next to him. The third guy reached over the table, snatched the older *mec's* cigarette, and lit his own with it. How I longed for this type of everyday comradery.

I stuffed my envelope in my purse, left the café, and wandered east. I mean, really wandered. I had no idea what to do with my time. No work at Thierry's awaited me. George was off limits, and I had this cash that I hadn't even earned bulging in my purse. Just picturing Jenkins disturbed me. The whole situation made me feel *mal dans ma peau*—uncomfortable in my skin.

I swung right and landed square in front of the giant space called the Trou des Halles. Until a few years before, an enormous market about seven blocks long and four wide filled the area. Then, around the same time they started sandblasting Paris's buildings, the city decreed the immense, unruly market full of comestibles and animals unhygienic. Rats scurried through the lanes of the market. So they shut down the whole operation, bulldozed the terrain, and had now started to build a shopping area. Still, they hadn't eliminated all the rats. I had just had coffee with one.

I meandered east into the Fourth arrondissement where I ran upon Beaubourg. I gave the gargantuan blue building a sour look. To say it clashed with the architectural scheme of Paris screamed understatement. Okay, this Sixties museum of modern art, known officially as the Pompidou Center, could have been more avant-garde than the Guggenheim, but to me it looked like a tumor gone wild. All of its guts, consisting of pipes and metal framing, spilled onto the outside. It was a building turned inside out with all sorts of crazy metal shapes jutting from it. Thierry had told me the architect designed it to look exactly that way. I couldn't see Beaubourg fitting in anywhere, not even in New York.

Today, however, the big blue blight fit my mood. Between Jenkins' bizarre attitude, Luc moving to Lyon, and the dearth of translation work, I felt turned inside out myself. Finally, I shook my head and turned back toward rue de Rivoli. Once I got there, I would have a nice, self-pampering gaze at one of the true jewels of Paris: the Hôtel de Ville.

Arms folded, I stood across the street from the palatial city hall and watched traffic race in front of it. I wondered why I actually had to force myself to notice my second favorite building in Paris. In my daily comings and goings I looked right through it, just as I did the Conciergerie. The problem with living in Paris, I confirmed bitterly, is you gradually stop seeing it. The beauty around you becomes as banal as your kitchen.

I faced east again and resumed my walk, all the way to Place de la Bastille. A column in the middle of the square remained the only testimony that the infamous prison ever existed. I didn't know why I had come this far, except out of hope the walk would order my thoughts. Help me decide what to do about Luc and Thierry, George and Jenkins…

Anxiety nagged me. I wanted to do something, so I descended into the Bastille station and hopped on the metro. It took me back to Hôtel de Ville, the closest station to rue des Archives. I had to backtrack on foot a couple of streets, but it didn't matter. The way I had it timed, I would drop in on Luc right after he got home from work.

I punched the button to Luc's interphone and he buzzed me in. By the time I reached his floor, he already had the door open.

"I didn't know we had a date tonight," he said, as he let me into the flat.

"We don't. I was in the neighborhood." I also knew the time had arrived.

It was too early for dinner, so we made tea and sat on the over-stuffed couch.

"Have you heard anything definite about Lyon?" I asked him.

His eyes shifted to the glass coffee table. "Yesterday. They told me they'd like me to move by the end of the month."

My heart plummeted. "I was hoping for May."

"*Ouais*," he said a little too casually, and offered a helpless smile.

After a bleak silence I finally spoke. "I can't follow you to Lyon."

Luc tilted his head, eyes wide and clear. "I don't expect you to." With that, he picked up the TV remote and started surfing between France 1, 2, and 3. "By the way, I do love you."

I stared at his profile as he continued zapping the television. I felt queasy. "I love you too, but I don't want to move." I wondered whether I had said it too late to be convincing. On the other hand, Luc's avowal didn't sound particularly sincere, considering his eyes never left the television.

Finally, he turned to me. "So it's Paris or nothing?"

I chewed my bottom lip. "I don't know…I have work here…I'm not ready to…"

I looked at my teacup.

Luc must have felt sorry for me. He gathered up my hands and smiled. "I'm going down to Lyon to look into a couple of apartments. You can come with me; see where I'll be living at least..."

I nodded and squeezed his hands. Then we turned back to France 2.

The prospect of exploring a new city excited me in the way some people get turned on by climbing a new mountain. I wanted to live my whole life on the move, discovering new architectures, cafés, cultures. With Paris as a base, I fancied wandering all over Europe, exploring all sorts of cities, never really settling anywhere.

So I went south with Luc. I wanted to scrutinize Lyon for myself and see what he had renounced Paris for.

The temperature in Lyon registered several degrees warmer than Paris. Perfectly normal, Luc pointed out, and one good reason to move there. Sunshine, blue skies, and Lyon's red terra cotta roofs combined to cheer me up, as long as I banned Luc's actual move from my mind and pretended we were simply tourists.

Lyon kind of seduced me, in fact. On one of its hills reigned the ruins of an ancient Roman theater. Luc and I hiked the grassy grounds, past crumbling blocks of classical stone. I breathed in the immensity of time, and my mood continued to lighten, as if every tourist step held the real reason for our visit to Lyon at bay.

Then the present slapped me. Luc and I finally had to return to the modern city where the two apartments awaited his perusal. There, he narrowed his choice of flats down to one, and my spirits crashed. I would lose him in two weeks. Sure, we babbled about paying each other visits. In the pit of me, though, where my most common sense resided, I knew that wouldn't suffice. Life grew branches, sprouted buds and leaves wherever a human planted his flag. In addition to his new job, Luc would find new friends and relationships. The gravity of that reality sunk me, and the last night in our hotel I couldn't face making love. For love had morphed back into stark sex—if it had ever been much else.

For once I even felt down about returning to Paris. Luc and I remained mostly silent on the drive back, minus a few utterances.

"Do you want to drive?" he asked me.

"No, not tonight."

"So, Lyon's not a bad place to live..."

"It's a fine city. You'll have a great career there. What'll you do with your apartment in Paris?"

"I don't know. It's up to my father."

I knew Monsieur Perri had bought the flat, so I asked, "Would he take me on as his tenant?"

Luc drew on his cigarette, the red glow expanding in the dark before a rush of smoke muted it. "I don't know why not. So now you're ready to leave the Lux?"

I detected a mixture of surprise and irony in the tone of that question, and answered, "I've been ready ever since my bout of flu."

He emitted a short, dry laugh. "I'll mention it to him."

Then we each retreated into the private corners of our minds. Until the myriad lights of Paris's suburbs—the *banlieue*—blossomed on the night horizon. We should have whisked through and engaged the boulevard Périphérique straight into Paris. Instead, Luc wanted to stop for cigarettes in one of the little communities.

"I want to get them before things close," he said, as he pulled up in front of a bar-tabac in an urban neighborhood I had never seen. "And it's easier to park here."

"Go ahead. I'll wait."

He barely got one leg out of the car when the sound of an explosion rent the darkness.

"What the hell?" I blurted.

"Something blew up," said Luc, one shoe still resting on the car's edge.

I opened my door and leaned out. "Where?"

"Around the block, I think."

"Let's go see," I said.

Luc hesitated, looking out into the darkness warily. Then he ducked back in the Lancia and we slinked around the corner.

What we beheld was nothing short of an inferno. Fire was devouring a huge truck parked next to the curb.

Luc practically spat his comment. "Probably kids. That's what some do in *banlieues* like this. They torch a vehicle and wait for the firemen. When they arrive, they start stoning them. One time, I read, they used guns."

"Jesus!" I said, gaping at the red and orange flames that swayed up and clawed the sky. I had never seen such a conflagration. Not in person, that is...but somewhere else. An unsettling sensation of déjà vu filled me. I *had* witnessed this scene before...or something like it.

"Stay here. I'm going to a phone booth and call it in to the operator," Luc said, and slammed the door.

I barely heard him. Mesmerized, I opened my door and stepped out. The air, warmed by the fire's furnace-effect, felt vaguely good. I marveled at the flames that painted the night—red and orange flung violently onto a black canvas. No sooner had I made the observation, than a familiar uneasiness began to creep into the pit of my stomach. Cool sweat pearled my hairline. At first I assigned the discomfort to the fire's heat. Until my insides started to writhe. I stepped back behind the car, for the flames seemed to bounce off the night at me. They burned my eyes with the brightness of malignant scarlet, contrasting the black sky. I shrank inside and shaded my eyes. And yet, I forced myself to watch. I wanted to remember where I had seen these flames before. I placed my hands on the roof of the car and pushed. Everything inside me contracted, fought, pulled. My breath came short. It was the art terrors of the Delacroix museum all over again.

"You shouldn't be out here!"

I jumped, and then stared gratefully at Luc.

"I called the operator and she's checking to see if the fire department's been notified."

Sirens began howling in the distance.

"The delinquents who started this probably called the firemen themselves. Come on. They could attack us too if we hang around."

As Luc pulled the Lancia out into the street and steered it away from the fire, I turned to stare out the back window—dumbfounded.

Back at the Lux, I tucked myself into my warm, secure bed. Every time I closed my eyes, though, I saw red flames licking my eyelids. I twisted in my sheets and told myself that the disturbing museum paintings I had endured in the past were much preferable to the live show I had just witnessed. *A live show.* Yes, the spectacle had something to do with my déjà vu. Curiosity calmed me, and I concentrated on the burning truck. But the effort only intensified my fatigue, and the clawing red flames slipped from my mind's grasp only to curl higher into the enveloping darkness...

I woke with a gasp from a dream. A jungle was on fire...or some kind of woods. Trees dripped flames. Fire engulfed everything, so that I couldn't distinguish night from day. People ran, scantily dressed, fleeing in panic, screaming...

I turned on my light and sat up, my eyes wincing against the brightness. I leaned back against my headboard and breathed deeply. These dream images had followed in the wake of the burning truck. I squinted and rubbed my temples. Somehow, they *were* the burning truck. I just couldn't understand the connection. Except...

A movie popped into my head. I had already seen the jungle on fire in some film. A long time ago, before I should have been old enough to remember such things. My first memory, perhaps. I massaged my scalp. Where could I have seen it? The drive-in...the only place to take a small child? I sighed and slid back down in bed on my back. Better to change the subject of my thoughts, since this movie business was going nowhere. I reflected on the burning truck again. *Mince*, violence like that taking place in a suburb of Paris. I shook my head, and little by little dozed back off.

The next day about six a. m. U. S. time (three p. m. in Paris), I entered the PTT in rue du Louvre and called my grandmother.

"Are you all right, Haley? You just called last week..."

I stood in the booth, fingering the phone's cord. "Perfect, Gram. I just wanted to ask you something...a strange question: do you remember seeing a movie where fire engulfs an entire jungle, or woods of some kind? At the drive-in probably, when I was about two or three."

"...I have no idea. What's so important about a movie?"

Disappointed, I sat down. "Nothing, just a dream I had about a forest on fire. I could swear I saw it before at the movies..."

"How long ago?"

"I don't know...at least twenty years ago."

"That would be 1959 or 1960...amazing memory you have. Why is it worth calling about?"

Too long and complicated. I would give Gram the abbreviated version.

"No big deal. I saw a burning truck last night and it gave me this weird déjà vu, like I'd seen it or known about it before. The dream followed, with the woods or jungle burning, and I knew a movie was involved..."

"A burning truck," Gram stated. I waited for her to continue. No response.

I went on. "Right, a truck caught on fire. Does that sound familiar?"

"You know...a truck caused your parents' car accident."

I softened my voice. "Luckily I was staying with you." I didn't like going into that story. Gram always got pensive while I felt awkward. "Are you okay?" I asked, after her pause lasted a little too long.

"I'm fine. That burning truck you mentioned...I couldn't help thinking about your mother and father..." She lowered her voice. "I never told you that when their car went off the road, it caught fire."

I stood up. "I thought the car just rolled and they died on impact. It caught fire?"

Gram either sighed or cleared her throat; a crackling noise over the wire made it difficult to tell. "I didn't want to tell you when you were little. Too traumatic. When you got older, you never asked about the details... easier to avoid the subject."

"That's what *I've* always tried to do, Gram—avoid the subject, for you."

"Well..."

What was she thinking? If I could only see her, I thought.

"At any rate, about this movie business..." she said.

No. One thing at a time. "Did you ever mention the fire around me when I was little?"

"With the family, I suppose, right after it happened. Certainly not after you became old enough to understand."

How in the hell does an adult know what a two-year-old does or doesn't understand? I probably *had* understood something.

I shook my head. "That doesn't explain the dream, and the movie quality it had."

Gram let out an indignant sigh. "I was trying to tell you when you interrupted me. Sometime after the accident, your grandfather and I did take you with us to see *Green Mansions* at the drive-in. The movie does have a scene where the jungle burns down. Haley, this call is going to cost you a fortune."

"Huh? Oh, right." In a daze, I said, "I'll go for now. Thanks for solving the mystery."

We said our good-byes and rang off.

I left the PTT stunned and quite a few francs lighter. How could I have stored memories like that for twenty years and never know they lurked deep inside? The Delacroix paintings and my old dinosaur book had presented the first clues, but nothing came to fruition until the burning truck and dream. I now understood the phenomenon, but why did I still shiver when I pictured the red and orange-skinned dinosaurs with their red eyes glowing against the dark jungle?

I should have enjoyed a certain satisfaction in the solving of a mystery like that. Only now I shuddered to think of that burning car. Had my parents died before the car burst into flames? God, I hoped so. I just couldn't accept the idea of David and Carolynn Morgan burning to death; that their remains lay there roasting. No—some passersby or motorists must have stopped to pull them out, I told myself, as I drifted down the sidewalk, looking right through everyone who crossed my path. That had to be what happened. Oddly, I felt my eyes tearing up. My vision started to blur and I ploughed into a lady. She took one look at me, and the irritation in her eyes turned to surprise. I rushed on and gained the Lux. Madani, in discussion with a group of guests, handed me my key without turning to look. I climbed the stairs and closed myself in my room. There, I sat on my bed and continued to marvel at the tears that wouldn't stop flowing down my cheeks. Little by little, I slipped further down onto my bed until I finally embraced my pillow, hugging it the way I wished I could have done David and Carolynn, my dad and mom.

7: *On s'en va* (We move on)

When Luc moved out, I avoided falling into a funk again by reminding myself of the positive in the situation. Monsieur Perri had decided it would be easier to let me take over the rue des Archives apartment than to screen renters. I now had a place of my own and could save over a hundred dollars a month. I settled into the flat, furnished with all the essentials, minus the TV, VCR, and stereo Luc had taken south with him. No matter: I had my radio-cassette player and music and books to fill the gaps. Almost all of them.

Madani made me promise to visit the Lux every now and then, and I agreed, with an ulterior motive: Gram believed I still lived there. She couldn't call the Lux since nobody spoke English there, but I would check the hotel three or four days a week for mail, Madani having agreed to let me continue using it as my address. The plan would require the occasional bout of verbal manipulation on the phone with Gram, but how hard could that be, considering my professional manipulation of George?

George. I hadn't heard a peep from him, and Jenkins hadn't shown himself since our last covert meeting. After the scolding he gave me, I almost didn't care. I just wanted a signal about resuming contact with George.

A quick peek in the window of the Poseidon couldn't hurt...only to see if he was working. And if Jenkins continued to poke his nose around? This time I would surely spot the bastard. Unless he had someone else tailing me...no, not round the clock; that would waste resources. And whether to call Jenkins, I deliberated, to inform him of my move out of the Lux...

The problem was I had too much time on my hands. Fortunately, it didn't last long, for Monsieur Garnier finally came through with a new translation for Thierry and me: a simple guide to Paris—*Guide de Paris*—to be translated into English. A job perfectly tailored to me.

Nothing could prove easier, I thought. Instead, Thierry and I had a tiff right off the bat about the title. He wanted *Paris Guide*. I insisted on *Guide to Paris*.

Honestly, I wasn't sure who was right; I simply pushed my gut instinct. All guidebooks in English read, "Guide to" something. "Paris Guide?" I didn't think so.

Thierry persisted, as we sat over coffee. "The beauty of *Paris Guide* is the double meaning. You've got a guide to the city, a book. And a city, *Paris*, who's your personal guide, like a companion."

I kept politely silent.

"You don't understand?"

"I get it. No one else will, though." I sighed. "People want something clear and simple to help sort out a busy, confusing city. They're not looking for poetry, they want an uncomplicated road map."

"It's just a title, Haley," replied Thierry, with an edge to his voice. "But go ahead, write it your way."

I insisted on common sense in English and typed, *A Guide to Paris*. Deep down, I felt pedantic.

My living room in rue des Archives felt like what I imagined a Buddhist meditation hall to be—sweepingly empty, save a couch and a chair Monsieur Perri had provided. Tile floors made its echo all the more sterile. At least at the Lux, my tiny room's carpet warmed the place. I could flip off my shoes and pad around in my bare feet. The frigid tile in the Perri apartment made my toes curl. Instead of reveling in my new independence, I felt a tad disappointed. I knew the problem lay inside me. Luc had left and I had a hole to fill.

I would have liked to help fill it with more work from Jenkins. Yet with May underway, Jenkins still refused to surface. I left a message with his secretary, or whoever the hell the impersonal woman answering the phone was. Now I started to suspect he had sprouted wings and deserted our precious Paris.

At least I began settling into my new neighborhood. My street in the Marais held the old, medieval-looking structure called the Paris Archives. Its turret jutted high over the sidewalk and served as a new beacon to welcome me home.

Rue des Archives lay only a few blocks from the Lux, so I didn't really miss my old neighborhood per se. Now that spring had arrived, it was the Latin Quarter that started seducing me again. Its concentration of outdoor vendors surpassed every other quarter I knew in the city, and the relentless proliferation of bookstores and record shops especially delighted me now that I had more disposable income. Granted, the extra hundred dollars a month that I saved in rent came from Gram's pocketbook. What could I do, though, without giving away my move from the Lux and setting her to worrying?

One morning, I set off across the river to roam around the Latin Quarter, no particular agenda, just to celebrate a day of dazzling sunshine. It reminded me of a rich relative home from a long winter's absence, and I wanted to partake in the largesse. I hit boulevard Saint-Michel where thick plane trees flanked both sides of the street, and the May warmth had fleshed out their leaves into giants' hands.

I noticed that people had begun to slow their pace compared to how they hustled down the sidewalks in winter. They browsed and chatted. I started shuffling through the big coffee-table books and paperbacks idling on sidewalk stands and tables. I reveled in the art books, histories of Paris, detective novels, and classics that surrounded me. Finally, I bought a second-hand copy of a Maigret novel. The time for prospecting was back!

I took a turn through Joseph Gibert and thought of my student days. I had bought all my books and school supplies there, and again I loved making the store's old, scuffed hardwood floors creak as I re-explored the place. Its musty, old-book odor made me nostalgic for the Alliance Française and Professor Bertalot. With my extra income, I couldn't rule out a return to school...maybe just one class. With Thierry wrapped up in his Spanish course, we never started work before one o'clock.

Tingling with nervous energy, I left the Boul Mich and headed down to Place Saint-Michel. The statue of Michael the archangel stood vigilant in its huge stone niche at the bottom of the street. Arms wide, wings spread menacingly like a black cape, the bronze angel stood atop a defeated Satan—no quarter for the enemy.

I sprang on. Heck, I thought, why not grab a Greek sandwich to-go in the little maze?

The restaurant hawkers had returned en force, as seasonal as committed birds come home from the south. I stopped at the open, side window of a Greek restaurant where a huge hot gyros about the size of an elephant's thigh rotated. I ordered my sandwich, and the cook sliced off some strips of meat, slapped them between two halves of French bread, and tossed in some tomatoes and onions. Joy humming in my pulse, I paid and walked away with my wrapped sandwich. After all the months of paralyzing cold, I could eat and amble at the same time.

I didn't leave the Place, however. To come clean, I had another motive for being there. I didn't care if Jenkins had five agents tracking me, I was determined to check up on George. Why not, with Jenkins vanishing like a ghost whenever it suited him? A quick look in the Poseidon's window couldn't hurt anybody.

It turned out to be a long look, for George was nowhere in sight. His uncle, on the other hand, remained faithful to his cash register. I glanced around the tiny lane whose shadows persisted due to its sheer narrowness. People trickled by, some pausing to pore over the exotic foods in the window cases. No one looked suspicious. So I slipped into the Poseidon and introduced myself.

Mister Abdi shook my hand with the weakest grip I had ever felt, and when I asked about George he shot me a dark frown. "George has had an accident."

"Accident?"

He lifted a thick, black eyebrow. "Not to worry, he is home from the hospital."

"...Can he have visitors?"

Mister Abdi held his frown on me and tilted his head.

I cleared my throat. "Maybe you could just tell him Haley stopped by. I'll come again to ask how he's doing."

I waited two days before I returned to the Poseidon, hoping to find out what had happened to George.

This time when I entered, Mr. Abdi's eyes lit up. "You are Haley..."

I breathed relief. "Yes, George's friend. How's he doing?"

"He is better. He said he would welcome your visit. At our home in boulevard Raspail."

George's building didn't have an elevator, so I took the stairs two at a time. Almost breathless, I reached the third floor and rang the bell. The door opened, and a middle-aged lady faced me in a beige linen skirt and matching top with big buttons—George's aunt, I presumed.

"I'm Haley Morgan, George's friend," I said, boosting my voice with perkiness.

The slim woman looked surprised, and after uttering a nervous *bonjour*, she asked how I had gotten into the building without pressing the Abdi apartment buzzer. I told her I'd followed a tenant in, and her expression registered a little less worry. She smiled faintly. "Yes, George's friend. My husband called to say we should expect you today. Come in. George is resting on the couch in the sitting room."

I followed Mrs. Abdi into a room with polished parquet floors and oriental rugs. There, I found George lounging on a dark-blue velvet sofa. I had never seen him dressed so casually, and in jeans and a white undershirt he cut an incongruous figure against the regal-looking blue velvet. His face was mottled with bruises and crusted-over cuts shadowed by beard stubble. He wore no glasses. I don't know which of these observations threw me the most. When George sat up straight and called out my name, I swallowed my shock and approached. I sat in a matching velvet armchair and waited for his aunt to leave us.

When she finally closed the living-room door to go make tea, I let fly my questions. "What in the world happened to you?"

George managed a wincing smile, tribute to the cuts around his mouth. He reached for his glasses. "It isn't that bad," he said, as he carefully set the wire frames around his nose. "It doesn't hurt much anymore..."

"I'm glad, but the *accident*," I said. "How did it happen?"

His hand swept the air dismissively. "...Some rough guys beat me up."

He looked as if he had flown through a car's windshield.

I shook my head in wonder. "Why?"

George held his side and grimaced as he shifted on the sofa. "I don't know...they stole my wallet."

"Where did it happen?"

"Downstairs. At night, by the trash cans..."

"And some guys just jumped you?"

"Yes, as I was bringing out some trash."

All that carnage for a wallet? He couldn't even move without obvious pain. Something didn't ring kosher, and the way they had ripped up his face seemed overkill for pickpockets. That's exactly what most thefts on the streets of Paris amounted to—subtle pick pocketing. And the garbage...must've been a big item. Otherwise, you simply tossed your trash down the chute on the landing on your floor.

"What did the police say?" I asked.

George shook his head and waved his hand again. "A waste of time that the doctors called them."

"Do they have any ideas?"

"...No."

I frowned. An anomaly then. Mysteries orbited this *mec* non-stop. "So did they hurt more than your face for you to end up in the hospital?"

He stroked his side. "They broke two of my ribs; that is what hurts the most. My face is nothing—it only looks bad."

George's nauseated expression of pain and his bruised and scabby face made me queasy. Still, it didn't square. Pickpockets smashing ribs, too? No, they would snatch your money and get the hell out of there—not linger around pummeling you. Maybe I had watched too many crime shows, but this beating seemed personal. I wondered whether the police thought so too, but for some reason George refused to admit it.

The door to the hallway swung open and in stepped Mrs. Abdi with a tray of tea. When I turned back to George, he had his index finger pressed to his lips. So, I wasn't the only one suspicious about this bizarre beating.

Mrs. Abdi set her tray with its tea paraphernalia on the dark-wood coffee table. The subtle contraction of worry hadn't left her face, although she managed a slight smile and graciously invited me to partake in the tea. I did so wholeheartedly, calculating it would give me more time to dig the truth out of my friend. I counted two cups and saucers. Good. Mrs. Abdi planned to leave us alone. She filled our cups, offered me milk and sugar, and added both to George's tea. George thanked her and didn't say another word until she left the room.

Then he grunted. "Good, she is rendering me mad. I am looking forward to going back to work in the Poseidon."

"Can you get around with broken ribs?"

"More and more everyday. I shall be back to work next weekend." Delicately, he engaged his lacerated lips with his cup and took a sip of tea.

I ignored my tea. "Have the police followed up?"

George puffed out a sigh. "They are irritating. I told them in the hospital that I have no more information, but they have come here too."

"What do they want?"

Again, he waved his hand in annoyance. "Oh...more description of those guys...I have already told them everything."

My tea had gone lukewarm, so I guzzled it down and poured myself a second cup. "The police always think you're forgetting some detail that could help them." I fixed George square in the eyes. "Some people leave details out intentionally..."

He blushed through his cover of cuts and bruises, but remained silent.

I radiated my warmest smile. "Come on, George, you can tell me. I'm not the cops or your relatives...I can keep a secret." Truth was, I had my own partial-theory, and I now felt confident to express it. "Does this have something to do with our last meeting, when that guy was following you?"

George expelled a bitter sigh, full of grit and tinged with desperation. He glanced at the door to the hall and lowered his voice. "It does."

"The guy wanting to borrow money...Why would he—?"

George shook his head. "He didn't want to borrow money. He followed me to see who I was meeting..."

My stomach went weak and my face hot. "Me? I don't understand..."

"Haley, the Iranians I know, they are no longer my friends. They don't trust me. They think if I am talking to an American, I don't support them. They don't trust any Americans. I'm sorry...I believed them to be better men."

An icy-white blanket enveloped me. It shrouded me in a sensation of being stranded in the Arctic. That's what Jenkins had done—abandoned me in an affair that had spun out of control.

I whispered. "So they beat you because of me..."

"They are ignoble. Fortunately, another tenant arrived at the trash area and they ran off like dogs."

The icy blanket weaved into the core of me, wrapping around my vital organs. I could barely breathe. And when I thought of all the things I couldn't tell George, the Arctic inside me became all the more bleak.

"You'd better watch your step, Haley," said Thierry when I told him what happened to George. "If those Iranians find out you're working for the FBI..."

Thierry and I had started working some days at my place. We rented an electric typewriter and now executed much of our translation on the kitchen table in rue des Archives. It was just a plain wooden table with four matching chairs, but it worked fine. I didn't want anything more elaborate in terms of furniture, because other than translating and sleeping, I spent little time in the apartment.

"I'm not working for the FBI any longer," I said, as I inserted a piece of paper into our machine.

Thierry stopped arranging the books on the table and considered me. "The Iranians don't know that."

"Who says they know anything about the FBI in the first place?"

Thierry folded his hands on the table and gave me a look that argued reason. "Either way, you should stay away from George so they don't have a motive to find out."

What did he take me for? Of course, I wouldn't give the Iranians reason to discover my true business—or, to punish George again. "Don't worry, I've already decided to give George a wide berth," I said, barely containing my impatience. Naturally, I knew he was right. I just didn't want him thinking I lacked the same skills of judgment he had.

After we finished and Thierry left, I sat in an over-stuffed armchair in my sitting room and reflected on him and my new living situation. The space I had gained in my new flat was a luxury I didn't like filling alone. I actually preferred making the commute to the Fourteenth arrondissement to work in Thierry's warm library of a home where Madame Kérouac often crowned my afternoon with an invitation to dinner. Thierry preferred working at my apartment. Sometimes he wanted to stay late, but I didn't feel like being tempted to start something. Not so soon after Luc had left, and with anxiety clawing me about George and Jenkins.

The swelling emptiness of my flat made me shrink at times. I had Luc's former couch and armchair, the glass tables, bed, armoire, and kitchen table and cabinets, all courtesy of Monsieur Perri. It sounded like a lot, listing them, but the sum only averaged about two pieces of furniture per room.

The hollowness of the rooms forced me to think more, and the lack of distractions led me to ruminate about George, Jenkins, Luc, Thierry, and my failure to resolve those situations. I couldn't stand that for long, so usually I would get up and leave—go for a walk, stop in a café to read the paper, or drop in on Madani at the Lux. If only I knew how to replace "thinking" with meditation, like a Buddhist monk. Sit on a mat in the lotus position and chant "om," until eventually I achieved mental peace and perceived the true reality of things. On the other hand, who says enlightenment is always pleasant?

When I lived at the Lux I had next to nothing, and yet my three pieces of furniture crowded my quarters. I saw Madani at least twice a day and I could always hop down to the lobby in the evening to join the TV watchers.

I blamed Jenkins for most of my tension and discontent. Why he had used me to prolong his stay in Paris, when the FBI didn't officially work outside the U. S., continued to evade me. So one day, I paid a visit to the library and found out that the Bureau did indeed send its agents to foreign countries in special cases (as consultants, for example), although only for brief periods of time.

From the library I went to a phone booth and rang Jenkins' number again. This time I steeled myself to tell his associate to go to hell, if she repeated one more time that he wasn't in. I gripped the receiver as if poised to club someone. The *someone* who answered turned out to be Jenkins himself, which made me scramble to prioritize my questions.

"I've been trying to get you for a week," I said coolly, my jaw still tense.

"Sorry, things have been cooking. Hey!" he said, his voice suddenly sounding like a muffled blur. "Get that telex off, pronto!" Then his voice came into focus again. "Barely have time to breathe in this business!"

"Me neither," I replied, determined not to be deflected. "Do you know what happened to George?"

"...No."

Where the hell had the know-it-all been? "George got beaten up by his so-called Iranian friends. He ended up in the hospital, all for talking to me."

"Do they know you worked for me?"

"I don't think so," I said. Christ, couldn't Jenkins at least ask if George was all right? "If they knew," I continued, "they would've said something to George, right?"

"Hmm..." he answered. Not a word of reassurance. "Well, I guess that's the end of your stint with the FBI, kid."

Frustration made my face, ears, and scalp burn. That's all he had to say? As I searched for a reply, a recording interrupted our communication, and a woman's automated voice warned me my phone time was running out. *"Merde,"* I said. My hand shaking, I gathered up three more tokens and fed them into the slot.

With the line secure again, I heard Jenkins chuckle. "I thought you were about to shut me down!"

I lashed out. "Don't you even care how George is?"

"Haley, if his condition was grave, you would've told me. Give me some credit for being an FBI agent."

"Who shouldn't even be working outside the U.S..." There, I'd gotten it out.

He laughed and said, "Star pupil of your high school civics class, no doubt? There are exceptions to that rule."

"And in your case?"

"Can't discuss Bureau business, you know that. Anyway, it no longer matters. I'll be packing my bags before long. Too bad all good things come to an end."

All good things come to an end? I wanted to reach down the telephone and yank him by the collar. Ask him: don't you give a damn about anything except being a bonvivant in Paris? You just kick aside your collateral damage and move on?

"You, on the other hand, kiddo, better keep your head down. I'd drop George for good if I were you. Can't be too sure how much his Iranian friends know."

"I've already figured that out for myself."

That reply left me with a slice of satisfaction after I hung up. At least Jenkins and I could agree on something. I would stay away from George. I would not set foot anywhere near Place Saint-Michel, much less the Poseidon. If George concluded I had lost interest in him, so be it. It was for his own good. And mine.

That decision proved the easy part. The hard part came inevitably. A couple of weeks after my conversation with Jenkins, George called and left a message at the Lux. When I called him back, he said he wanted to meet me, which set off an excruciating dilemma. What could I invent and reinvent to keep putting him off? Would I have to tell him we were through as friends? Right after he received a beating because of me, and he still had the courage to want to see me? He obviously didn't worry about another pummeling...

So I had agreed to meet him. I chose a café in an ancient trickle of a street in the Marais. In my pocket I would bring a decent lie. I would inform George I had got involved with Thierry. That way he would have the option of dropping me himself. If not, I would call it quits.

When Thierry came to my flat to work, I told him only part of the story: that I would meet George to end things.

During a break from our *Guide to Paris* translation, he decided to weigh in. "I think Jenkins is right. I wouldn't see George at all, if I were you."

I shook my head. "Am I supposed to tell him to shove off over the phone?"

"Not so rudely, but yes."

"I can't dismiss him like that. He's sensitive..."

"I know. He might start crying."

I frowned at Thierry's crooked smile and again cursed myself for having told him, Luc, Kevin, and anyone else about George's weak moment those many months ago.

"Sorry," he said, shrugging. "I only want you to be safe. You shouldn't have gone to his house in the first place. Now you can tell him you simply don't want to be put in danger."

Charging over to George's had been an impulsive act. Now I had decided to be more cautious by choosing a tiny cubbyhole café for our meeting in the Marais. As for danger, no need to wax paranoid.

"There's no evidence the Iranians connect me to Jenkins," I said. "They hate George seeing me because I'm American—that's all. Anyway, he's already split with those guys."

Thierry had been fiddling with the pages of his dictionary and now slapped the book shut. "Why do you insist on meeting this *mec* at all?"

How to explain my friendship with George? Mere companionship as lonely expats made our relationship superficial. On the other hand, my drive to understand the mystery of his part-Western, part-Muslim mentality made it philosophical as well. He loved Eric Burdon and the Animals for all their soul, and like me, he insisted on exploring his own way through the grand bazaar of Paris. None of it, though, did I wish to share with Thierry.

I leveled my look, evened my voice, and said, "I don't want to keep seeing him. I want to end it—on my terms."

The terms played out in a hole-in-the-wall café in the Marais, on a narrow street you could practically hop over. When George arrived, I was already there, hidden in the back away from sliding picture windows. Almost a year had passed since my arrival in Paris, and if anyone had suggested seeking a viewless table back in June of 1979, I would have said, "Go find yourself a McDonalds, you idiot!" How things had changed.

We ordered coffee, and George launched into his latest news. "I have cut myself from those Iranian wretches," he said. His face had lightened-up. The residual blemishes from the beating could even have blended into that down-and-out air that tended to float around him like an anti-halo.

Only today, the hangdog look was absent. This afternoon his black eyes glowed, and he reminded me of a little kid on tiptoes, busting to relate an event.

He leaned over our little round table on both arms. "I am sticking with the Afghans now. They are more noble men."

"Noble?" I said. "Sounds kind of old-fashioned." George's quaint expressions once amused me. Now, I could only think of how to extricate myself from a dead-end association.

George cast me a slight frown. "I mean these men have a noble cause they are fighting for. And they don't hate Americans." His smile swelled back. "That's why I called you."

Jeez, what now? I decided to let George prattle on, since my only game plan consisted of lying about Thierry and me, and I felt no hurry to start. "What about the Afghans?"

George's eyes reminded me of burning coals again, just like the first day I met him, practically an eternity ago. "Haley, I know some Afghan men here in Paris who are preparing to return to Afghanistan and fight the communist government."

"What...?"

"Mujahideen! That is their work."

"Mujahideen...aren't they—"

"Holy warriors, yes! Young Afghan men from all over the country, including my father's region, are joining the cause. From all over the world they are returning to the homeland to fight the Communists."

"Fight the Soviet-backed government?" I asked, my mind sifting through memories of newspaper articles.

"Right! The Soviet invaders and their Afghan slaves will be removed, just like the Shah in Iran."

I must have raised an eyebrow or something, because George rushed to explain.

"Haley, this time the Americans are welcome. They are helping the Mujahideen, arming them and everything. And I can tell you, these fighters are their own men. They will not take orders from anyone when Afghanistan is free!" George finished his sprint just short of breathlessness, his right hand in a fist.

I scanned the quiet little café. Still only one other customer besides us sipping coffee—an old guy with his nose in a newspaper. The barman eyed us as he emptied his dishwasher.

"Let's keep our voices down," I said. "What's holy war got to do with this?"

George cleared his throat. "Did you not learn of the term in your book on Islam?"

"Of course, but why *holy* war? Once they topple the Communists, then what?"

George sat back, and his smile turned smug. "Finally, a government formed of Afghans and their values."

"Religious values, by chance? A Muslim government?"

"Not necessarily. Holy war is a struggle against evil, a struggle to return the country to its rightful owners."

Boy, would I have loved to have Jenkins here. Good ol' America, backing Muslim holy warriors in Afghanistan, when an Islamic government continued to burn us next door in Iran. Having translated *L'Islamisme* and *Cold War Chronicles*, I concluded we would be better off with the Communists in control in Afghanistan. Under their skin flowed green blood, just like ours—capitalist green. I regretted not being able to fling this Afghanistan farce in Jenkins' face. Instead, I had George to set straight, and he had started tapping the table impatiently.

He threw up his hands. "Don't you see, Haley? America is finally doing the right thing. By supporting the Mujahideen, America is showing Iran and the world that it is not a selfish country. There is no oil in Afghanistan. America is backing the Mujahideen because it is the right thing to do."

I shook my head. "America isn't backing the Mujahideen out of nobleness. They're supporting them to drive Soviet interests out of Afghanistan. Trust me, this is part of the great American crusade to rid the world of communism. It's been my government's goal for as long as I've been alive. I wonder what they'll do if a religious regime takes the Communists' place."

"No worries. The Mujahideen are capitalists."

I smiled and shrugged. "I hope you don't want to run off and join the holy warriors, George."

He laughed and cupped his hand over mine, holding it a little too long for my comfort. "I only admire them at this time."

When he released my hand, I slid my cup and saucer to the side of the table. George's enthusiasm fascinated me; I almost envied it, but I didn't want to hear any more about this Mujahideen nonsense. I wanted to leave, maybe find my own cause to get interested in. By now I had no idea of how to segue into the artifice about Thierry and me, so I simply told him I had to go.

"We could go for a walk..." he said.

I shook my head. "Did you forget you were recently beaten to a pulp?"

"Haley, I have broken completely with those guys."

"I don't want to take any chances." His mouth opened, but I cut him off. "We should exit the café separately."

"That is silly," he said with a laugh.

"You leave first. Just humor me."

He gave me the kind of smile that made me feel he was holding my hand again. It remained on his lips when I showed no reaction, but sadness entered his eyes. He nodded and rose.

I waited to be reasonably sure he had gotten out the door and down the sidewalk. Then I pushed away from the table. What a bust, I thought. Not only had I failed to sever ties with George, I might have led him on, letting him practically hold my hand. As I passed the bar, I slapped myself mentally for not putting my plan to work. I stopped to look out the open windows before I made my exit. Nothing struck me as suspicious, until I saw a car pass the café going too fast for the tiny street. I heard brakes screech and the torturous sound of metal scraping metal, or something equally hard. The car revved up and took off again.

I rushed out the café's open door and looked right. The sight I beheld defied belief...George, rolled up in a ball on the sidewalk. I ran to him. Passersby began to crouch around him, and I pushed them away so I could kneel beside him.

"*Appelez une ambulance!*" I cried. "What happened, George?"

He moved his lips, but no sound came forth. His eyes remained closed.

"*Une ambulance!*" I repeated. I wanted to pound the sidewalk with my fists.

"We *have* called an ambulance, Mademoiselle," I heard.

I wanted to jump out of my skin. *To do something!* So I ran back to the café to check for myself. Indeed, an ambulance had been called and the police as well. I sprinted back to George and sat down next to him. His limbs had uncurled a bit from their crumpled-up-paper state, and he looked more relaxed now. He still lay on his side, but his eyes had opened a crack and his mouth hung open.

A woman who had knelt beside me started taking his pulse. Her worried eyes made me try his other wrist. Then I felt his neck, to no avail because my own heart hammered so hard I couldn't distinguish anything. People milled around me, but I couldn't understand their words, for the pounding in my ears. Finally sirens pierced the air and broke through the muffled barrier.

"George," I said, "help's here—hang on!" I plucked his cracked glasses off the sidewalk so the medics wouldn't step on them and placed them carefully in my pocket. I wanted to lift George's head off the hard cement and hold it, but I resisted when I remembered the first-aid filmstrips from high school about not moving an accident victim's neck. So I just held his hand.

A tear dropped onto George's cheek, and I almost jumped before I realized it belonged to me. I was dabbing it with my finger, when two medics in white with red crosses on their torsos moved in and ushered me aside. One of them checked George's heartbeat with a stethoscope. He shook his head, and the other started pumping George's chest.

They repeated their actions over and over. Then they stopped.

I wiped my eyes so I could see. "Aren't you going to do anything else?"

The one who had been giving George CPR looked at me. "I'm sorry, Mademoiselle. He's gone."

"But..."

"Excuse me, who are you?" asked his partner with the stethoscope.

"I'm...his friend..." Why I hesitated, I don't know.

Next, the uniformed police showed up and started moving us away from George and organizing us into small groups. Then another car sailed in, this one with two plain-clothes cops. When one of them got to me, he also asked who I was in relation to George. This time I answered solidly that I was George's friend. He scrutinized my passport and wrote down my address and phone number. The other *mec* rummaged through George's pockets and took his passport. They interrogated everyone in the crowd who had seen the accident, and I listened in numbness.

"A speeding Renault hatchback veered onto the sidewalk, hit this man and knocked him into the wall of that building," someone said. "Then it raced away."

"Perhaps the driver lost control," another witness said.

Why did he leave? I wanted to assert. He should have stayed right here and waited for the ambulance and police.

"He probably panicked or he was drunk," someone else said, as if to answer my thoughts.

Another guy said he had the license plate number.

Finally, the police allowed the crowd to disperse, and people began to separate and drift away. I couldn't move, but I felt a hand touch my shoulder. I didn't turn to see whom it belonged to while George still remained with me. I watched the medics straighten him out and lift him onto a stretcher. They folded his arms on his chest so they wouldn't hang over the sides, I figured. A drop of blood had trickled from the corner of his mouth down his cheek. Other than that, he looked fine. No ugly face wounds like the time they beat him up. No anxiety screwing up his face. No haggard or feverish features. For once he looked calm and serene. It wasn't George. They covered him with a white sheet and slid him into the ambulance. They said something to me that I didn't understand, and then they slammed the door, and the virtual hearse disappeared down the street.

I felt a warm pressure from the hand on my shoulder, and finally turned. It was the lady who had taken George's pulse.

"Are you all right, Mademoiselle?" she asked.

For a moment I stared into her keen brown eyes, full of worry and sympathy. My brain began to shake off some of its numbness, and I asked, "What was he doing, walking or running down the sidewalk?"

"He was walking, ever so placidly. The car lost control, no doubt."

So you think, my mind countered.

"Will you be all right, Mademoiselle?"

I hesitated before nodding, and we parted ways. God knew I didn't want this to be murder. I swirled witnesses' speculations to the contrary around my mind while I wandered, not knowing what to do, until I saw a phone booth and called Thierry.

It seemed minutes before he reacted to the news. "I can't believe it," he said slowly. "...I never thought anything this bad would happen."

As I steeled back tears, I was grateful Thierry hadn't flung an I-told-you-so at me. "We can't rule out it was an accident," I said. "I mean, people speed down narrow roads everyday; it's not hard to lose control and end up on the sidewalk. Or it could've been a drunk driver."

"Some sort of base hit-and-run accident, then..."

"Right," I answered, a strange hope lifting me for an instant, and then dropping me with a thud on the ground.

"I can come over and keep you company..."

I didn't want to keep stirring up the contents of this cauldron of nightmares. I wanted to go home and close my burning eyes. "I just need to rest now. I'll call you later."

My mind went into a daze as I walked home, and I guess my body went on auto-pilot. By the time I entered the apartment, paralysis had gripped my brain again. Mechanically, I headed to the kitchen and slumped down in a chair. Instead of resting my eyes, I stared, elbows on the table, chin on my fists. I didn't think of George, I didn't think of the accident and the hypotheses concerning it—I just sat there, frozen.

Hours must have passed before my ears picked up the sound of a siren outside my open window. I started, and realized I could almost feel my brows sinking above my eyes. The knot in my brain finally started to loosen, and I stood up to look out the window. The heat of the day was melting away, and shadows had begun to darken the street. I pressed my hands to my face and exhaled a heavy, loud sigh that turned into sobs. I inhaled deeply and gripped the wide, thick windowsill to steady myself.

Then I retrieved my radio-cassette player from the kitchen counter and took it to my bedroom. *Just to escape into sleep.* I set the machine on my night table and stretched out on the bed. Sleep refused to visit me, but its nemesis, thinking, came back. As George's accident replayed in my head, I teetered between tears and anxiety. A pressure began to build in my head, alternating with light-headedness, and I thought I was going to faint lying down. I sat up in a panic, my breath cut short as if guillotined. I rose and made for the window, leaned on the sill, and inhaled air that was losing its whiff of vehicle exhaust with the retreating heat. Twilight had arrived, so I went to the radio to pick up the night stations. I couldn't take any of the frivolous music I heard. Not French pop, not jazz, not any of it. I stretched back out on my bed, head up this time, and placed the radio in my lap so I could twist the dial back and forth. Finally I landed on the BBC.

Somehow, the calm, well-enunciated English of the host soothed me, and I suddenly wanted to talk to Kevin. I hopped off the bed and fished his number out of my address book in my purse. I went to the entryway table, lifted the phone's receiver, and then stopped. What would I say to him? Where would I begin to sum up the enormity of all that had passed these many months?

I replaced the receiver and stared at the phone. I thought of Luc, only a ring away in Lyon. Then I pictured his likely outrage at my secrecy. I should have told him the whole story about the FBI and George while we remained together. We could have dealt with it. God, no wonder my relationships never lasted.

I even thought of calling Gram, just to inform her of the accident, no back story. But she would have begun worrying about me and I would have probably started crying again. I considered calling Thierry back, but it was close to midnight, and I didn't want to chance his parents answering.

I hated the apartment. If I had been at the Lux, I could have at least told Madani about the hit-and-run aspect of the accident. We could have commented on it, even moved on to small talk; it would have been natural with me living there. Instead, all night I made rounds of the apartment in intervals. I went from bed to bathroom and back. Then out to the kitchen for water. I took turns around the living room.

I had advanced deeper into the Arctic—all around me, nothing but frightening whiteness as far as I could see.

The police intruded on me early the next morning, one of the same *mecs* who came in plain clothes to the scene of the accident. This one was tall, with red hair and a bushy mustache. I indicated the armchair to him and I took a seat on the couch. He asked me about my friendship with George, and whether I suspected anyone might wish him ill. So I told him about the Iranians, mainly how they had beaten George up for befriending me, an American. I didn't want him to hear it from someone else and suspect me of holding back.

"I'm sure it's all in a report," I said, "since the police did get involved in the incident."

He didn't respond—just wrote in a little notebook. In the time it took for him to look back up at me, I had decided to keep mum about the Jenkins factor. No reason to complicate things, as this cop had already said he didn't necessarily suspect foul play, but only had to ask routine questions. And frankly, I couldn't face telling the French police I had worked for the FBI. I needed to keep as low a profile as possible, what with not attending school anymore.

I still had George's glasses, but I didn't want the *flics*, as the French call the cops, getting their paws on them. I asked the detective if George's aunt and uncle knew about my presence at the scene of the accident. If I had to turn George's glasses over to someone, it would be to them.

"Yes, Mademoiselle, they know those circumstances which have been revealed."

"I'd like to see them—give my condolences and find out what services they plan for George."

The *flic* expressed something between a smile and a sympathetic frown. "They plan no services here. His parents in Greece want their son sent home as soon as possible."

Someone might as well have dumped a load of bricks on me from the top of a building. No services—I wouldn't even be able to say goodbye.

God, my eyes burned and ached, and I had to bite my lip to keep them from tearing up. I straightened my posture and managed to ask, "Have you gotten any closer to finding the hit-and-run driver?"

The *flic's* blue eyes narrowed. "We've got the license number and we're looking for the car."

A repeat from the day before. The cops never want you to know anything more than you already know.

After the plain-clothes, red-headed *mec* left, a strange new preoccupation filled me. I returned to the sofa to analyze it, and realized my conscience was caught in a dilemma: clearly I wanted the police to catch the criminal. Run *him* down with a car, even. And yet...I wondered what that might lead to. Could an investigation trace the criminal's motive to me and the FBI? If a connection did indeed exist...?

A few days after the tragedy, I stopped by the Lux to check for mail and ended up sharing my grief about the accident with Madani.

"How devastating, Haley." Then words dried up, and Madani shook his head. "If I can do anything..."

What could anyone do? Not a damn thing. Not Madani's fault. I felt sorry for him.

"Listen," he said, suddenly bouncing back. "I'm lodging two girls from Ireland, sisters about your age. They're on holiday and looking for advice on seeing the city. You know Paris, and you're translating that guidebook. You speak their language...they're charming..."

"You'd like me to show them around?"

"You could meet them first. You'll like them, and it might help take your mind off this horrible event. If you have time, of course."

I didn't relish meeting anyone. Every time I contemplated something pleasant, guilt and its sidekick, nausea, assailed me. The thought of simple pleasures, like shopping at BHV or Samaritaine, made my insides shrivel. The idea of a jaunt to the Latin Quarter to check out music, or to Odéon for a movie, depressed me. Staying home all morning, on the other hand, waiting for translation time with Thierry, made things bleaker. Thierry had his Spanish class. I had nothing but *A Guide to Paris* to fiddle with. That even made my heart sink at one point, when I happened onto a photo of the Deux Magots where George and I had met for coffee the day the Iranian followed him.

Hell, why not put the bloody guide to use? I decided to take Madani's advice and meet the Irish sisters.

Bernadette and Kathleen Morrissey from County Tipperary struck me as out of their element in Paris. Still, they voiced solid enthusiasm about El Dorado on the Water. They were having a fine time they told me in their brogue, and yet they seemed eager to pal around with me.

Sparkling and blushing, is how Bernadette and Kathleen projected themselves on our first meeting, like opposite sides of a coin. Bernadette's eyes radiated a lively blue, a reflection of her personality as dominant elder sister, while Kathleen's darker-blue eyes leaked shyness, the younger sister in the shadow. The girls had accomplished the ordinary tourist tasks, including a climb to the top of the Eiffel Tower. They had also eaten plenty of what they called spicy French food. They didn't care for the mustard in the salad dressing, for one thing. Bernadette said they had three more days of holiday, and if possible they wanted to give their stomachs a break and let their eyes do the feasting on new sights.

I knew the solution, and got cracking with an invitation to dine at the Pub Winston Churchill. Who would believe that a meal in a place I had deliberately avoided for almost a year would boost my mood? Bernadette and Kathleen praised the Winston Churchill, and for some reason my heart rose a little, like a musical note from the bottom of its scale.

The next evening I invited them to an English-language movie on the Champs-Elysées, in one of those huge, plush-carpeted *Salles Prestiges*. Bernadette called it "grand," and I brightened a little more.

Funny, at first I'd thought I might resent their new-to-Paris status. Envy their first-time thrills. Yet, compared to the way I'd been feeling, their positive personalities sugared the air. Bernadette fired questions at me. What was Nevada like? How do you say this in French? Kathleen pitched in comments, and they both sprayed me with contagious giggles.

Saturday I spent the whole day with them. I gave them a tour of part of the Marais, and then we trekked across the Seine to the Latin Quarter. I couldn't let them leave town without experiencing Place Saint-Michel and the Quartier Mouffetard.

That's where I faltered, and failed to put the final, personal touch on *A Guide to Paris*. As we approached Place Saint-Michel's little labyrinth, the weakness and nausea I had been suppressing crept back into me. I had planned to skirt the Poseidon, but my limbs started to go limp and I couldn't continue. George's cracked glasses, still lying in my desk drawer, hovered in my mind. I hadn't been able to bring myself to give them up. To face George's uncle and aunt...

"Mesdemoiselles!" cried a hawker from a Greek restaurant on the edge of the maze. "Come feast on our brochettes..."

"No!" I said. "No thanks." I turned to Bernadette and Kathleen. "We haven't even had tea yet...can't skip that...we should have stopped before coming here...sorry..."

Bernadette gave me a quizzical look. "Tea will be fine with us, Haley. Whatever you suggest."

I started thinking about the *salon du thé* next to the Auxerrois. How George had adored their *financiers*. It would have been the perfect place to treat girls from a tea-loving culture, with its marble tables and classical crown molding. But I couldn't face that either.

So we had tea in a café, and the girls let loose more of the charms of Ireland.

"Lovely to hear you speak such good French, Haley," said Bernadette. "Ours isn't great by any means."

"Because we have to take Irish in school as well," Kathleen said.

I forced my smile back. Around Thierry I could turn morose, for he knew all about my troubles. With the girls I had to participate. "So everybody takes Irish in school?" I asked.

"Yes, and it isn't easy," said Bernadette. "The spelling's a nightmare—worse than English.

"What does Irish sound like?"

The girls giggled.

"Nothing like English," said Bernadette. "You'd be shocked. Say something, Kathleen. Your accent's better than mine."

Kathleen blushed and then jabbered something wild. "*Conas tá tú?*"

"What?" I said.

Kathleen's eyes shone like those of a child who had carried off a successful trick. "It means 'how do you do?' *Tú* is *you.*"

"More like French," I said. "I never would've thought that."

"King is *ri*, like *roi* in French," Bernadette added. "And *Dia* is God, like *Dieu.*"

Kathleen asserted herself. "All Celtic languages—Scots Gaelic, Welsh, Breton—are somewhat similar to the Latin-based languages."

"Welsh," I said. "That's what my heritage is."

"Morgan, of course. We're right across the sea from Wales."

"And I have a Parisian friend who's half Breton. His name's Thierry, and he said he'd like to meet you." The idea of us all four going out excited me. The pleasant face I forged for Kathleen and Bernadette had worked on me too. Perhaps, that's what Madani had in mind in the first place.

I called Thierry that Saturday evening, and he offered to take us all out Sunday.

"Bernadette and Kathleen would like to go to mass before we do anything," I said.

I thought he might sneer at that. Instead, he said, "So we'll all go to mass first."

Fine. I hadn't been to church in Paris since the time I patronized my Saint-Germain l'Auxerrois out of protest against the excesses of Islam.

Thierry planned more than going to an ordinary mass. He organized a drive to Chartres for Sunday service in the most magnificent Gothic cathedral in the area.

We left Paris early in the morning, Bernadette and Kathleen in the back, Thierry and I at the helm. We cruised through the countryside, its spring green full of promise and of a reminder that a year ago the best had been yet to come...and the worst. Luc...George. I repelled the stinging memories and concentrated on spying the cathedral's spires, which I had already seen on a previous visit.

It was an easy task. The colossal church dominated the entire town of Chartres. It monopolized the horizon for miles, having dwarfed everything around it for almost a thousand years.

I reflected on the soaring spires. They pierced the sky in an expression of piety, of man's yearning to meld with the divine—in anonymity, I had learned in my medieval history classes. I could never comprehend those anonymous artisans who labored their entire lives to achieve enormous, complex sculptures to God. They must have felt a part of divine creation, but they took no credit for their work, left no personal mark or symbol.

I longed to make my imprint on Paris, like Joe Dassin, Charlotte Rampling, Jane Birkin, and the rest. In the Middle Ages, an attitude like mine probably equaled excessive pride. The ancient artisans had no problem dedicating their lives to erecting a cathedral they might not finish in their lifetimes. A generation would pass on, and their progeny would continue to build and craft the palace of God anonymously. I, on the other hand, suffered from modernity. I marched headstrong toward vague goals. Instead of giving, I grabbed what I could, without thinking I might muck up lives around me.

We pulled into Chartres and parked near the church. Inside the cathedral, I wondered whether the ancient craftsmen would have actually appreciated the recognition if they had received it. They deserved it but never sought it. I yearned for it, but at this point I didn't feel I deserved it.

Bernadette and Kathleen pointed out the dazzling stained-glass windows and the towering arched ceilings. We sat in wooden pews that looked a hundred years old, the dark wood polished with wear and warped uneven.

When the service started, choir voices spiraled up through the Gothic stone arches, to the ribbed vaults. I wanted to follow them, as their echo, so they could lift me into holy air and sooth my spirit. Then the voices evaporated in deference to the priest's sonorous chants. The familiar group prayer followed, and every voice around me, Bernadette's and Kathleen's, even Thierry's, recited in unison, "I have sinned through my own fault, in my thoughts and in my words, in what I have done and what I have failed to do. And I ask the Blessed Virgin and all the angels and saints to pray for me..."

Everyone's voice but mine. I couldn't ask anyone to pray for me, or bring myself to ask for forgiveness after all that had happened.

Bernadette and Kathleen took communion. Thierry went up too. His devotion surprised me—first time I had seen him in a church. I sat back and let parishioners file in front of me to exit our pew. Then I subjected my knees to the wooden kneeler. I twisted them to where I could best tolerate bone on wood, a discomfort I figured I merited. That was the idea of conserving the old-style wooden kneelers, wasn't it? A bit of medieval self-mortification? At least I could appear to be praying, like everyone else.

I watched people line up to receive the host, and again I thought of the ancient artisans. Like them, I had constructed something of value, patiently, painstakingly, block by block. That was how I had built my friendship with George; it was also how I had destroyed it. Yes, I had used George, and so had those bastards who passed themselves off as his friends. Of course, Jenkins had used us both.

Anger enflamed me to the verge of tears. To calm myself, I reflected on more subtle means of "using." Technically, I suspected Luc, Thierry, and I had all used one another in some way, each for his own personal fulfillment, or for some dream, perhaps. Was that wrong? I observed the pious faces as they filed back into the pew and knelt along side of me. No answer came to me.

After Thierry dropped Bernadette and Kathleen off at the Lux that evening, I stayed on with them while they packed. I had gotten hooked on their cheer. They offered me an open invitation to visit their home town, Knockavilla, and stay with them. They even said their "mam" would be delighted to meet me. When I finally trudged down the circular stairs to the Lux's lobby, I thanked Madani. The man knew me better than I knew myself. Then I left the Lux, with a knot in my throat big enough to choke me.

A couple of days later, I received a call from Madame Perri. Immediately, I expected news of Luc. But no, she instead invited me to lunch at the Drugstore Saint-Germain.

The location filled me with the *cafard* again, since the Drugstore lay kitty-corner across the street from The Deux Magots. Twice, I had seen George in

The Deux Magots—the second time, right before he got beaten up. As I entered, I felt a queasiness that perhaps Madame Perri noticed.

"Have you been well, Haley?" she asked, once we got seated. "Since Luc left we've missed your company."

After her kind words and smile, I tried to look perky. "I'm fine. How are Monsieur Perri and Jeanne?"

"They're well, but now that you mention Jeanne...something's come up."

"What?" I said impulsively. Since George's demise I feared tragedy and misfortune with every change of breeze.

Madame Perri looked surprised and patted my hand. "Nothing bad, dear. Although I'm afraid it will eventually affect your living situation..."

I stared at her.

"I hope you can understand, Haley. You see, Jeanne would like to move into Paris. Commuting from Montrouge to her legal studies isn't impossible, but she would rather be based in Paris proper."

"In the apartment in rue des Archives," I said. Why wouldn't she? The Perris owned the flat.

Madame gave me a worried smile. "Yes, but Jeanne says she would be happy to share the apartment with you..."

What unbelievable luck! I hated the apartment in rue des Archives. Not only did it have too much space, it turned out to be less cost-effective than I had predicted. Utilities to pay, groceries to buy. Plus, I didn't like cooking by myself, so I ended up eating out much of the time.

Now I had an excuse to flee the Arctic. "Actually Madame, Marie, I mean, I was thinking of looking for a smaller place, anyway. I can transfer back into the Lux whenever Jeanne wants to move in."

Jeanne as a roommate merited pondering for about one second. I smiled to myself: interesting, nonetheless, her sending *Maman* to do her bidding.

Thierry helped me move back into the Lux and complained about Jeanne all the while. Then, something unexpected took place. I wasn't nestled in my room two days when I received a call from none other than the new occupant of rue des Archives herself. I took Jeanne's call in the lobby.

"I hope you're settled in your hotel all right, Haley..."

"*Oui, oui, très bien*," I said, with a touch of sing-song in my voice. "It's easy returning to the Lux."

"Good. Sorry I had to displace you. *Maman* did pass on my offer—"

"Yes, don't worry about it, I like the Lux." I wanted to puff out an impatient sigh.

"Another reason I called is you've had a couple of visitors."

"...Who?"

"Some man yesterday with an accent. Kind of Middle Eastern-looking. He wouldn't tell me his name or what he wanted. He just said you had a mutual acquaintance..."

George!

I squeezed the receiver and masked my alarm. "Was he young?"

"I suppose...about twenty-five to thirty."

I lied. "Could be someone from the Alliance Française. I knew a lot of people there, but this one doesn't seem familiar."

"I wonder how he got this address?"

My mind scrabbled. "No idea. Did you tell him I was at the Lux?"

"Of course not—"

"I appreciate that. I don't want any strange men looking me up."

I was about to sign off when Jeanne added, "The other visitor was a police officer in plain clothes. He came by a few minutes ago."

Mince! "Did he say what he wanted?"

"No, but I did give him your address."

"Oh," I answered, and went on with a half-truth. "I happened to witness a hit-and-run accident. The police said they'd have follow-up questions for me. Thanks for letting me know, Jeanne."

I hung up, just as the same cop, who had already interviewed me twice, entered the lobby. The *flic* must have floored it from rue des Archives to the Lux.

As he and Madani exchanged greetings, I took a steadying breath and stepped towards them. Madani excused himself.

"Mademoiselle, do you mind taking a stroll?" asked the smiling officer. "Such a nice day...conducive to clearing one's thoughts."

I hadn't noticed what kind of blasted day it was. All the sunshine of Nice and Nevada combined couldn't clear my thoughts with this *flic* showing up again.

We struck off, up to rue Saint-Honoré. The mustached, balding *mec* was called Brondel, and he got right down to business. "These Iranian acquaintances you mentioned last time we talked...what do you know about George Abdi's connection with them?"

I didn't have to lie. "Nothing, other than they beat George up, which I already told you. He liked talking to them about the Iranian Revolution." I shrugged. "That's about it."

"So, George Abdi was interested in Iran?"

"Yes..." I wondered what he was driving at.

"What kind of relationship did he have with these men?"

"I don't know. I've never laid eyes on them." *Bon Dieu*, the police were specialists at asking the same question umpteen ways, either trying to trip you up or pry something else out of you.

I peeked over at Brondel and saw him frowning.

"What did Monsieur Abdi say about these Iranians?" he asked. "Their names? Their business in Paris?"

"No, no names. I've never met any of them." Then I decided to feed him a certain detail, so he wouldn't suspect I was holding back. "George did say they were raising money for Iran."

The officer stopped and turned to me. "Which ones are raising money for Iran?"

"I don't know. I don't know any of their names." Thank God Jenkins never asked me to get them. On the other hand, I thought bitterly, names might be able to help track down George's killer. I vacillated over revealing the mystery visit to rue des Archives. My spine tingled cold. I hung back.

The *flic* resumed his stroll. "You will inform us of anything else you remember, Mademoiselle Morgan?"

"*Oui, bien sûr.*"

At the intersection Brondel stopped again and handed me a card with the phone number and address of the commissariat in the Fourth arrondissement. "One more thing, Mademoiselle." He tilted his head and studied me. "Why have you moved from rue des Archives to a hotel?"

I cleared my throat and coughed up a lie, just to make a long story short. "I was house-sitting in rue des Archives, but my home is the Lux."

He produced a wry smile. "I see. Also, the last time we talked, you said you were a student at the Alliance Française...correct?"

Why ask this? It seemed he had deliberately saved the trickiest question for last. I swallowed and delivered my second lie. "I'm in between sessions...but I start summer school soon."

He nodded, and his smile turned a fraction friendlier. "*Bon. Au revoir, alors.*" Then he left, looping back toward the Lux where he had probably parked his car. I realized I was chewing my lower lip and ceased immediately, hoping the *flic* hadn't noticed it as some kind of sign of guilt.

I took the long way back to the Lux, just in case Brondel decided to tarry and chat with Madani. To avoid seeing him again, I walked all the way to Hôtel de Ville where I stopped to ponder and rationalize my reticence and lies. If I hadn't fudged the truth about school, I would have risked losing legal permission to remain in France. I decided I'd better look into re-enrolling when I had a spare moment. About that visitor to rue des Archives...regardless of his Middle Eastern air, he didn't necessarily have anything to do with George's death, or his beating. No point telling the cops and embroiling myself even more. Still, I itched to share this mystery with a certain someone, as much as I loathed to think of him.

Without giving even a nod to my second favorite building in Paris, I made an about-face and headed to the first public telephone I saw.

The number rang nonstop. Jenkins had left the country, no doubt. Left me hanging over hot water. I checked my watch: another hour before Thierry returned from his Spanish class. I sighed, and like any logical Parisian, I bought a newspaper and found a café to kill time in. After reading *Le Monde* from cover to cover, I ducked into the metro at Saint-Paul and rode to Thierry's.

"I think you should tell the police about that visitor," he said, as we sat in his mother's study.

"Maybe I would, if they'd stop badgering me about my personal life. They won't stop bugging me about school, and they wanted to know why I'd moved from rue des Archives back to the Lux. The more I give them, the more they demand."

"Just don't let them know you're working without a permit."

"...Why? What would they do?"

Thierry set his pencil down and sat back. "My dad says they could force you to return to America. He said if you're in school though, you can stay here practically as long as you want." He looked embarrassed. "I wouldn't have brought it up if it weren't for the police and all..."

I thought about Thierry's father. Monsieur Kérouac never showed much enthusiasm for our translating endeavor. He was an airline man and he wanted his son to follow his path. Well, he wasn't going to discourage me. "I'm glad you brought it up," I said, and slapped the desk. "I've got to get that work permit."

Thierry didn't know how to go about it, but he said he would look into it. In the meantime, I decided to make my own inquiries.

I hadn't seen Kevin in five months, and I longed to meet him and catch up. In particular, I craved the information he might have as a foreigner working in Paris.

I skipped out of the Lux with the old spring in my step, destination Shakespeare and Company. I walked down to the Pont Neuf and onto the bridge. Mentally, I waved to Henri IV's equine statue. Good old Henri IV, smiling amount his steed. He gave up Protestantism to become king of France and live in Paris. He declared that every peasant should have a chicken in his pot. He wanted to do best by his subjects. Then he was assassinated.

I stopped to observe his statue, and I wondered how France might have fared if Protestantism hadn't been crushed after his death. I prepared to move on, when for the second time a fellow across the street caught my attention. He seemed to inch along the bridge in tandem with me. When I stopped to study Henri IV's statue, he halted and appeared to be admiring the spire of Sainte-Chapelle in the other direction. I turned away and then whipped my head back, only to catch him eyeing me. His gaze snapped back to the spire. I didn't want him to notice me staring, so I hurried on across the bridge.

Ordinarily, I wouldn't have thought twice about this *mec*. And yet…he was dark, a Middle Eastern or southern Mediterranean type. I shook my head. Christ, I felt like a paranoid moron. Middle Eastern types abounded in Paris.

I reached the Left Bank and continued along the river. I passed the famous Quai des Orfèvres, headquarters of the fictional police detective Maigret. Jenkins had fashioned himself after the *commissaire*, as if the cad could even come close to the consummately ethical Maigret. Jenkins wasn't worthy enough to light Maigret's pipe.

Now the inspector on George's case—my detective Brondel—had turned out to be much more akin to the fictional *commissaire*. Given his diligence, a little too close.

I arrived at dear old dilapidated Shakespeare and Company where I learned Kevin was off for the day. From the nearest pay phone I called him at home.

"Haley, old mate!"

I sagged with relief. You never know how people will react after a five-month absence.

"I was just doing a spot of housecleaning, but I'd much rather have coffee with you."

I suggested Kevin meet me in a café we were both familiar with, the locale where we first met on rue des Ecoles. Nostalgia kept haunting me, and I wanted to recreate the atmosphere of enthusiasm and hope that had electrified me in my early days in Paris almost one year ago.

"I'm quite glad you called," Kevin said, cradling his cup and saucer in his palm, "because I've got the best news. I was even going to come and see you at the Lux."

Then why hadn't he? Kevin had changed. His hair hung shorter, above the collar and kind of wispy. A new cut for a new decade. Come to think of it, I wore my own hair shorter now. Luc had considered it too short, but Thierry liked it.

We sat at a table on the sidewalk, just like in July of 1979. The waiter swept by with a tray of demitasses. Cups, glasses, and spoons clinked and tinkled all around me. Chairs scraped the sidewalk and a light breeze brushed my skin like a feather. Spring flirted with me, maybe even offered me a lifeline. It felt so good to just sit there as in the old days, I didn't want to break the spell by voicing my problem.

Instead, Kevin spoke. "My disco project is finally shaping up. And you'll never guess who might become my partner and help me get this bloody thing off the ground by summer's end. Guess who it is!"

How the hell would I know? Here Kevin was, on the verge of realizing his dream, while I sat balancing on the edge of a cauldron whose water boiled with police, Iranians, and my illegal work status. My head started to throb just thinking about it.

Nonetheless, Kevin was my oldest friend in Paris, so I humored him. "I don't know—Sasha," I threw out.

"Bingo!"

"Sasha Rifkin?"

"What other Sasha do we know?"

"Right," I said through a haze of shock. "Good for you."

"Yes, she's coming to Paris in June."

"Be nice to see her," I said, a touch wistfully. Then I turned to the business at hand. "Kevin, how did you get permission to work in Paris? You *are* working here legally...?"

"Certainly. I got a permit before I left England."

"I need to get a permit here in Paris."

"Hmm." He brushed back his bangs, more out of habit since they now hung so short they couldn't possibly stray near his eyes. "I'm pretty sure you have to go through the Prefecture of Police."

I froze.

"And," he continued, "they usually want you to have a job already lined up. Where do you want to work?"

"I already have a translating operation with a friend, but I don't know how long I can go on without a permit..."

"It would be wise to get that taken care of, Haley. Otherwise you can't collect benefits. Plus, you have to pay taxes and all that."

Tax delinquency. Did any words inject more anxiety? Apart from *police*?

"So I could get in trouble for tax evasion?"

"You would in Britain. And in America." He shrugged. "I don't imagine France is any different."

I nodded numbly. Jesus, that's all I needed. "Was it easy getting a job at Shakespeare and Company?"

"Well, they hire people from Britain." He screwed up his eye, his freckly cheek winding up with it. "I've never heard of anyone from the States working there. Not that it wouldn't be possible..."

"Yeah," I said, with not much hope in my voice. "Thanks for the information. Let me know when Sasha arrives. I'm really happy for you."

And I was, in a heavy-hearted way.

After I left Kevin, I still held out hope. My next inquiry took me to the Alliance Française. I hadn't seen my favorite teacher, Professor Bertalot, since I started skipping classes who knew how long ago. He had looked after my interests back in the summer and found me Madani's hotel. He was old enough to be my grandfather, and his affection toward me flowed accordingly. Maybe he could help me here.

I found him in his classroom. "You should come back to school, *ma chère*," he said. "I miss your hand waving in the air."

That made me brighten. Nothing had changed in the classroom, including the professor himself. He sat at his desk on its slightly elevated platform, wearing his signature red tie and gold cufflinks. I felt anchored, moored in my port, as I sat in a chair next to him. What I loved most about Paris was how most things stayed the same around the city. Same cafés, same restaurants, same employees I had gotten to know after almost a year. I let gush a warm, grateful smile toward my teacher.

"I plan on coming back to school," I said with sincerity. "I've just been busy..." How to broach the subject without declaring I was working illegally?

"Are you still lodging at Monsieur Madani's establishment?"

"Oh yes, it's been perfect. I still can't thank you enough for that, Monsieur." I could sing Madani's praises all day, but now I needed new help. "By the way, Professor, I've had the opportunity for a job here in Paris. Translating with a French friend, from English to French and vice versa. We already have material...but I'm wondering how to go about getting a work permit..."

Professor Bertalot's white eyebrows had arched with interest as I began my speech, and now descended into a squint. "Working in Paris as a foreigner can be problematic, *ma chère...*"

I clenched my teeth.

"Ideally," he said, "you should start the process from your home country. Then there are French labor laws that require the work for which you are applying be something a French person cannot accomplish. Your translating, for example, would fit that bill, since native English-speaking skills are required..."

I edged forward in my chair.

"However," he went on, one hand massaging his forehead and bald head, "there is a caveat. Now that the European Economic Community is in full swing, our laws dictate we give English speakers from our member countries first priority over these jobs. People from Great Britain and Ireland, and so forth. If only you had come to Paris twenty years earlier, *ma chère* Haley, it would have been easier."

I sat back in my chair. *Twenty years earlier I was only three years old.*

"The only advice I have for you is to come back to school. Part-time work permits are more readily issued to students. Once you are in school again, you submit your work application to the Prefecture of Police."

My stomach plummeted—*again the police*! Then I thought of Sasha and Kevin. "What about Americans who start their own businesses here, restaurants or clubs, for instance?"

"Ah well, they are always welcome. They inject capital into the French economy and they employ people."

"I see." The professor talked on, but I hardly listened.

I left his classroom before he could see tears of pure frustration pool in my eyes. *They are always welcome*: I couldn't stop gouging that wound. If you had enough money, you could live wherever you wanted. You were welcome, *invited* no less, to invest your money in the most desirable places on earth.

Morale at zero, I drifted down boulevard Raspail, all the way to Montparnasse. I sauntered into the Rotonde and ordered some soothing tea on the covered terrace. The big picture windows now stood open to the soft spring air. The Rotonde had been the first place George and I had taken refreshment together when I gave him the tour of the Hemingway cafés.

Hemingway. No problems for him in Paris. He needed no stupid work permit to bang out stories at the New York Herald-Tribune. The dollar reigned supreme and expats wrote their own tickets. Americans had helped the French win the First World War—an honorable war—and were feted as heroes. Now the dollar dived daily, America still bore the tarnish of Vietnam, and the Iranian debacle had smudged any shine we'd managed to recover since 1975.

Speaking of Iran, the Middle Eastern-looking *mec* was back, or so it appeared. A couple of tables down from me sat a man who looked remarkably like the guy on the Pont Neuf. Same ugly, black, butch haircut. Same aquiline nose. Lean torso. Grey leisure-suit jacket.

That was all I could glean from his profile, but somehow he looked familiar...from some place in the past. But where? How did this stranger's image get stamped in my mind? In winter when I strode through the streets head down, butting the cold wind, I only noticed the people I collided with. Now, spring air, leaves, and sounds had nudged my noggin up again, yet I usually maintained a brisk gait and acknowledged only the people who stopped to ask for directions. So why this feeling of familiarity?

Impromptu, I swiveled around. Again, I caught him eyeing me. For once I wished I had a camera, something I refused to carry to avoid being branded a tourist. I would have snapped his mug and hightailed it to metro station Vavin. Once I got the photo developed, I could have studied it at my leisure and perhaps identified the freak.

Instead, I discreetly placed a ten-franc coin on the table and rose—a little too abruptly, for I banged my table and set my cup, saucer, and spoon clanging.

I took off along boulevard du Montparnasse toward the tower. I had to perform a virtual samba to get quickly through the crowd. Then I crossed the street for good measure. Unless that butch-head had already paid his bill, he would never catch me.

When I reached the intersection dominated by the tall, black Tour Montparnasse, I cut a sharp right down rue de Rennes and wove into the pedestrian flow. At the first green light, I crossed the street and then slowed to search the crowd.

A jolt of electricity surged through me. Butch-head stood on the other side of the street, but I could only snatch a glimpse of him in the pack of rush-hour pedestrians.

A fleck of fear tickled my spine, combined with an inexplicable thrill that echoed in the beating of my heart. When Butch-head crossed to my side of the street, I slipped into the giant record shop, FNAC. There I joined the patrons who shuffled through records and cassettes. If Butch-head wanted to follow and pretend to enjoy the activity as well, so be it—he would never outlast me in a record shop.

Strange, but he didn't show up. I, on the other hand, managed to find a discounted Serge Gainsbourg cassette. I figured I deserved it.

Butch-head disgusted me more than scared me. With that grey leisure-suit jacket and his shorn hair, he reminded me of a rat. Who the heck wore their hair that way these days? Even George's conservative coiffure never looked that short and creepy.

George. They had persecuted him mercilessly. Had they now started on me? I shook myself and moved forward in line to the cash register. Harassment, that seemed their tactic for me...if something shady truly was afoot. And if Butch-head proved to be the one who had popped up at Jeanne's in rue des Archives?

When I left the FNAC, I found the nearest PTT and called her.

She eagerly described the mystery visitor. "Short black hair. I mean really short. Hooked-nose. Kind of narrow, dark eyes...close-set."

Good enough, although I didn't know whether this confirmation was a bad thing for me or not.

"Is he someone from the Alliance Française?" Jeanne asked.

"I don't think so," I answered, pretty damn truthfully for a change. I was sick of lying and misleading people.

"So where do you think you could have met him?"

"No idea." And I left it at that, so I didn't have to lie.

8: And If You Didn't Exist?

As the remaining days of May ticked by like the second hands of a clock, I peered about me everywhere I went. The city melted away. Only the people stood out. I scrutinized them with a sharpened sense of guard and the heightened sense of a predator as well. I quit lingering in cafés. I ordered my coffee at the bar, downed it, and scooted out. I combed the crowd with my eyes wherever I happened to be and searched the eyes of every man with a dark complexion.

In short, I hunted for Butch-head and felt disappointed when I couldn't spot him again. I wanted to root him out and confront him. Demand he give me the lowdown on this business. But he must have been taking a break, for May ended without a sighting.

"I'm actually starting to miss him," I told Thierry, as we indulged in one of the recommended walks from *A Guide to Paris*.

We had chosen boulevard de Courcelle, a boundary between the Eighth and Seventeenth arrondissements and a sector of Paris I had paid scarce attention to over the year.

We were the sole pedestrians in sight, and after two weeks of prowling around Paris—eyeing, spying, craning my neck to examine every passerby near and far—I finally relaxed a bit. I slid back into my old m. o. and started admiring the sculpted, limestone façades and the flowery wrought-iron balconies of classic Paris, courtesy of Baron Haussmann.

For a few strong heartbeats it seemed I perceived Paris for the first time. Ravel's "Bolero" waxed in my head once again, and I felt transported back to the summer of 1979 when I first started reveling in the atmosphere of the magnificent avenues and boulevards. The grandeur and timelessness of Paris filled my heart and lungs with an electric air, and I knew that if El Dorado on the Water didn't exist, I would have to create it.

Where would I be without this city? Just a kid whom everyone tried to tag "Hayley Mills," living with her grandmother in provincial Reno. I thought about the Joe Dassin song, "And if You Didn't Exist" ("Et si tu n'existais pas"). I'd bought the album while on the run from Butch-head. Only Joe's ballad didn't refer to love of a city—but to love of a person, of course. I was the weirdo. Suddenly a longing struck me as I strolled next to Thierry, and I looked at him with an aching inside me. I wanted to say something, but I couldn't formulate what. So I suggested we pause at Parc Monceau.

The idyllic little park, embroidered with trees, flowers, and a classical colonnade, made me feel we had wandered into the ancient Greek countryside. My heart felt lighter, and when we settled onto a bench to relax, I wanted to link my arm in Thierry's. If he didn't exist...or Luc, I would have to create them too, such a vital part they had played in the vibrant mosaic that formed my Paris. The city felt incomplete with Luc missing, but I still had Thierry. I started to reach for his arm—

"So you miss your Iranian admirer now that he's lost interest in you?"

"What?" I said, relaxing my arm. It was as if someone had let a screen door slam in my face. Why the sudden, smart-aleck reaction to a comment I'd made at least five minutes ago, and in jest? I parked my hands in my lap. "If you mean Butch-head, I'm actually glad he's lost interest, because if I see him again I might have to harass him in kind."

Thierry crossed his arms and stared at me. "What, trot after him all over Paris?"

"No, I'm thinking more on the lines of verbal harassment. I'll tell him off and confront him about what he's up to."

"Then you'd better take me along."

I studied Thierry's impassive eyes. I hated that they rarely revealed what he felt. They expressed nothing, but his comments had betrayed him all the same. I wasn't sure whether to feel flattered or offended by his offer to accompany me during a future confrontation with Butch-head. Obviously he cared about me. But did he think I needed protecting against that rat in the leisure-suit jacket, who scurried in and out of crevices around the city and lacked even a shred of nerve to look me in the eye?

"Are you getting jealous?"

Ah, a flare in his eyes! "What's there to be jealous about?" he said.

"Just joking," I said. I couldn't gauge him, and he had obviously misread me. For two people with so much in common, sometimes it seemed we hardly knew each other.

"Don't worry, I won't do anything drastic," I said.

Thierry sat back. "I know *you* won't." Then he changed the subject. "Have you looked any further into getting a work permit?"

Could he have brought up anything worse? With the tip of my shoe I lightly kicked the sand on the path in front of our bench. Then I gave him the whole depressing summary I had gotten from Professor Bertalot.

"I take it you don't want to go to the Prefecture of Police," he said.

I loved him for instantly understanding, and again I wanted to grasp his arm.

"Could we put the work permit off for a while longer?" I asked. "Maybe slip in another translation?"

"Depends on Garnier." He sighed. "My finances are getting a little tricky, what with taxes and everything. I'm going to have to report more than I make..."

I kept my arm to myself and lowered my eyes. "I understand." I couldn't bring myself to touch him now. He would think I was pitying him, or something. And yet, if I were truly serious about taking a chance on him, I'd make a move...

"They're trying to recruit me for Air France again."

"What?"

"They're hiring again," Thierry said, staring straight ahead. "Looking for people with knowledge of languages. They're especially interested now that I have Spanish."

"Oh," I said, losing my emotional footing yet another time. I managed to recover and hide my disappointment. "I guess with French, English, German, and Spanish, you can pretty much cover two or three continents."

"All continents, really, since English is the language of aviation. But yeah, the more languages I know, the greater my advantage over other applicants...I'm just exploring my options right now."

I flattened myself against the bench and started flicking sand with my shoe again. Thierry's wasn't the only future at stake. What about our translating enterprise? I didn't ask. I refused to let him think I depended on his every word, as if his decisions influenced whether I lived or died. When they didn't. Paris, after all, wasn't to die for.

Funny, after voicing that in my mind, I felt much calmer. Like admitting I was an alcoholic at an AA meeting. Paris tingled under my skin. It hummed in my blood, and probably would remain there forever. But I could survive without living in El Dorado on the Water.

Then, like the alcoholic facing the wagon, I shivered. Without money, how would I be able to even visit my favorite city? Options: I had to find my own.

"Anyway," Thierry resumed, "I have to take some tests and go through interviews again. Nothing's certain, so we might as well keep working when Garnier comes through."

He didn't repeat the work-permit business and I appreciated it. If only I had the money to start school right away. What an illusion, considering I was still on a reduced income from my grandmother and received nothing from Jenkins. Thierry's world beckoned him with opportunity, whereas I would have to ask Gram for more money if Garnier didn't come through.

Was Paris really worth all this aggravation? Back at the Lux, I sat at my bare-bones little desk and made a list of grievances I had with the city. Truth be told, certain things bugged me plenty.

My list turned into several paragraphs of venting. Little things in Paris irked me, like dogs sitting across from me in restaurants. I remembered with distaste the German shepherd I had dined across from not long ago in a pizzeria with long, picnic-bench-like tables. This oldish, greasy-haired *mec* just waltzed in with his dog and made straight for where I was sitting. Empty tables abounded in the restaurant, but he and his dog had to sit right across from me, as if it was the most normal thing in the world. He ordered two pizzas, one for himself and one for his dog, then cut up the dog's and placed it in a plate in front of the animal. I'm sorry, but watching a dog inhale his food and lick his plate right across from you, is not appetizing. That it was a *he*, I unfortunately verified when I noticed him trying to lap at his private parts as well. He almost tumbled off the bench.

Then there was that scene in the Bois de Vincennes. One day as I explored the park, I strolled toward a teenage girl lounging on a wrought-iron bench. There she sat, enjoying what seemed an innocent ice cream cone. A scruffy little Scotty dog was perched on the bench with its front paws in her lap, something that made me think of a charming Renoir subject. Then as I walked past the two companions, I caught them sharing the ice cream cone. She'd have a lick and then offer the cone to Scotty—back and forth, until I thought I'd be sick.

I raised my pen. Well, it wasn't that big of a deal, really. I understood people's love of animals could lead to extremes—a question of culture, I guess.

I returned my pen to my French, grid-style notepaper and considered the weather. Paris was heating up these days, which reminded me of how slimy-hot it could get. The city's humidity battled me a good part of the year, in fact. In winter, damp, icy air, matched with cannon shots of wind felt like an arctic onslaught. Freezing, whistling drafts slashed my nose and ears and crushed my fingers and toes in a vice if I didn't have my gloves on.

The cold had moved on by now, but I couldn't put my pen to rest without starting a paragraph on summer humidity. It could melt me to the ground if a heat wave paid a visit. Heavy, steamy air would invade every cranny of my body, and I was lucky if a tee shirt lasted me half a day. When the dreaded heat wave called *canicule* struck, I would hop from one strip of shade to another, an effort that made me perspire all the more.

No winning, especially when I recalled the summer city smells. I had forgotten about them until June returned. I guess when you're first in love, sight isn't the only sense you put on hold. Now, noxious odors began to creep back. I never knew when they were going to surprise me. I'd be walking down the sidewalk, and next thing, a blast of foul, furnace-hot air from a building vent would hit me, spewing its bad breath on my bare legs.

Sometimes I could anticipate stinky fumes. When I crossed the street behind an idling bus, for example. Bus exhaust was the hottest, most obnoxious smell of all, and I would hold my breath as I passed behind it.

Of course, I couldn't neglect listing the grates in the sidewalk. If I didn't side-step them, hot, gritty industrial air from the metro, or some other underground source, might gush up and bathe more than my bare legs. Oh, and speaking of watching my feet...well, in France you watched your step in general, because many pet owners didn't pick up after their dogs.

And let's not forget about tipping Madame Pipi, and that in boutiques you can't touch merchandise unless you plan to buy it. I added green grocers to my list, many of whom wouldn't let me handle the fruit. I had to point to the peaches I wanted, or let the vendor choose for me.

I set my pen on my desk and read my complaints. They hardly amounted to an indictment. Then, I forced myself to again face the worst thing that had befallen me in Paris: letting myself be seduced by Jenkins and his ready cash. I didn't need to record that. Of course, I had fallen prey to a different kind of seduction by Luc and Thierry, which led me to reflect on Serge Gainsbourg's song, "Maxim's." He croons about being a young man enthralled with the lush life in Paris: heady rides in his rich girl's Jag, English cigarettes and cocktails of Gordon and Pimms, rushing to dine at Maxim's. He's a virtual milord. And yet, the first line reveals a terrible irony. "Ah, to kiss the hand of a worldly woman, and skin my lips on her diamonds." The young *mec* gets the paradox of Paris right away. Why had it taken me so long? Perhaps Luc had a point about Paris not being the be-all, end-all.

Luc. Just as I had begun to acknowledge his point of view, I came to find out he now planned to visit Paris. What with Kevin announcing Sasha's visit, I felt as if two bright stars had shot into orbit just to cheer me up.

I expected Kevin to call me when Sasha arrived. Instead, my old pal herself rang me up—all the more heartening.

"I told Kevin I wanted to call you personally," Sasha said in the *salon du thé* next to Saint-Germain-l'Auxerrois. "Sorry I haven't kept in good touch ..."

"I haven't either, so don't worry," I replied, simply happy to be with someone who reminded me of my old, carefree Paris days. "You're here—that's what's important."

At my invitation, we sat nestled in the cozy, classy tea and pastry shop next to the Auxerrois and across from the Louvre. With Sasha willing to commute to my side of town (she had settled back in her four-star hotel near the Eiffel Tower), I had finally mustered enough strength to patronize it again, an effort that involved suppressing guilt over George and the fact he had loved the shop's *financiers*. It was the first time since his death, and I wanted things to be normal again.

"You look different," she said.

I straightened in my chair. "Maybe it's my short hair."

"No, I've already taken that into account." Sasha frowned. "There's something else...your eyes...they're different."

I smiled. "If you say so."

My old friend continued to peer at me with that sharp, cat-eyed look I had first noticed a year ago when we met. "Definitely, your eyes have changed. They look...I don't know...burdened, or something." She squinted. "You look older."

"Well, I am a year older." I leaned over our round, marble-top table. "Remember last summer in The Cool Tattoo? And Versailles!" Excitement and nostalgia for those frivolous days boosted my mood.

"Yeah," she said wearily. "I don't want to go back to either one."

My heart sank a little. Not that I pined for those specific places either. I just wanted to recapture *the time*, when everything shone fresh and glossy. The only way to do it, to validate the reality of those moments, was to share the memory with someone who had been there.

Sasha, on the other hand, wanted to talk about the present. "This club enterprise I've got going with Kevin has got to be unique. Nothing like The Cool Tattoo."

"But it's going to be an Anglo hangout, right?"

"Sure. We'll call it The Roundabout most likely, only we're going to make it French-friendly as well."

I placed my elbows on the table and my chin in my hands. "Then you should call it the *Rond Point* and play some French music now and then."

"We'll see about the name, but we will play the occasional French tune. Classic rock too. Mainly, we want to bring more of the new, non-disco Eighties music to Paris. Electronic stuff like *Funky Town*, and Punk hits like *London Calling*." She started bouncing up and down—"London calling, da-da-da-da-da."

After she stopped, I nodded my head politely. Her enthusiasm tired me, and my spirits started to sink again. Kevin and Sasha were poised to give birth to a new venture. Even George had gotten involved in something new before he'd died. George...

"Now I can really see it," she said suddenly. "That *burden*, or whatever it is in your eyes. Looks like you've been through a war."

"What?" I said, chin coming off my hands.

"You're acting strange. What's going on?"

Sasha studied me like an elementary school nurse, which made me squirm and sit back. "I don't know...nothing."

She folded her arms and continued to stare at me. "There's something wrong. Even Kevin said you acted down the last time he saw you. Are you tired of Paris? Homesick?"

The comment from Kevin surprised me. "I've just had some bad luck lately. Getting a work permit's turning into a nightmare."

Sasha relaxed a little. She smiled and placed her arms on the table. "Kevin said you were doing translations with a friend. Might that be Thierry? Or Luc?"

"Thierry," I confirmed. "Things are getting slow, though, and I need that permit. Luc moved to Lyon for work."

"That's too bad."

I leaned back in. "He's coming to Paris for a visit, though. Any day now, Thierry told me."

"Hey, why don't the four of us go out again?"

I had to resist the urge to frown. "...I suppose we could."

"Really, Haley, my treat!"

I finally smiled. "I'll ask them." I thought that would end her questions about my mood. I was wrong.

"Must be frustrating trying to get a work permit," she said.

I nodded. *Something you'll never relate to, Miss Investor.* I know it was mean, but I couldn't help thinking it.

"It still doesn't explain that weight-of-the-world look you have," she said.

Perceptive and sensitive, my flamboyant friend had become. She had refused to open up to me eight months ago when she was in trouble with Kevin. Now she banged at *my* personal door. I wasn't the only one who had changed. For a second I peered back at her and then looked away.

"So, what is it, Haley? And don't screw up your face like you don't know what I mean. Something's gone down here since I left in December."

I looked around the *salon du thé*. George always found it fanciful that the big vase in the corner contained a huge, colorful peacock feather. Be it that, or the delicious *financiers*, we always agreed about the tearoom's charms. I sighed and offered Sasha a feeble smile. Might as well dole out enough to satisfy her curiosity.

I sat back and began slowly. "Do you remember that Greek guy? The one I introduced you to at the American rally back in November? George..."

"Yeah, the weepy one—"

"He never wept, Sasha. Kevin told you wrong. His eyes got a little watery, that's all."

"Okay, what about him?"

Never mind, I wanted to say. Still, I figured I owed it to George to straighten out Sasha's warped perception of him.

So I settled my temper and softly said, "He died."

Sasha's eyes widened. "Died? When?"

"Last month. A hit-and-run driver mowed him down on a sidewalk in the Marais. Right after we had coffee."

Her eyes contorted in disbelief. "You witnessed it?"

"Not everything. I left the café after him...and saw him splayed out on the sidewalk. I watched him die. He was brave, one of the bravest people I've known."

"I'm sorry. Were you two seeing each other?"

"Only as friends."

"Hmm..." Sasha's cat eyes took on a suspicious air. "No disrespect, but what does bravery have to do with getting run down by a car?"

I stared at the crumbs in my plate and started chewing my bottom lip. What to tell her? Then I raised my eyes in resignation. "The day George died, he insisted on meeting me, right after a bunch of Iranian thugs had beaten him up for seeing me the other times."

"Wild!" Sasha leaned over the table at me. The curiosity in her eyes seemed insatiable. I had gone this far and now I just felt like giving in. I wanted to lie back on a silken couch, eyes closed, and let it all out—exhale every jagged piece of the tragedy that had worn me down, and then go to sleep.

I told Sasha the truth. From George's death, I narrated backwards: to his beating, to our meetings and discussions of Iran, to Jenkins and the money. I even told her I suspected George's demise was not an accident. The only thing I left out was Butch-head, because I was starting to suffocate inside.

Then a strange relaxation came over me. The tenseness in my neck slackened. My shoulders sagged, and next thing I knew, my vision blurred with tears.

Sasha's hand landed on mine. "Hey, are you all right?"

I nodded. With my free hand I wiped my eyes with my napkin. My voice shook when I said, "I feel responsible for it all."

"Listen," said Sasha, still holding my hand. "It's not your fault. You've got to get rid of the guilt—wipe it out of your Catholic *shikse* head. If you don't, it'll devour you. *I know*."

She released my hand and sat back.

"...It's hard," I said, considering her from a new perspective, wondering exactly what she meant by *I know*.

"Well, remember: you can't possibly be sure whether Iranians killed George, much less whether they did it because of you. Have the police suggested it was murder?"

"No. Not to me, anyway."

Sasha lifted an eyebrow. "It's all an unknown—an X. You're indulging in guilt-motivated speculation, and if you let it wear you down, you're verging on masochism."

I practically gaped at her. Where the hell had she learned all this?

She went on, waving her hand like a professor. "You can become trapped in guilt. Get so cozy with it, it becomes a life style. A habit you can't kick, like picking at sores for gratification."

She placed her fingertips together and touched them to her chin. "It's self-indulgent and very destructive." She eyed me cagily, sizing me up in some weird way.

I looked at my plate again. I felt ashamed—because she was right.

Sasha murmured, "I know what I'm talking about, Haley."

That brought my eyes up. "You, Kevin, and the baby?"

She nodded slowly, directing a distant look over my head. Then she focused back on me. "The guilt over that mess began to erode my personality. Anyway, I finally wised up and started looking at things realistically. You've got to forgive yourself and move on."

Forgive herself. So maybe the miscarriage hadn't been an accident. I wanted to know, but I didn't feel comfortable asking her right out. Instead, I said, "So you and Kevin have basically reconciled...?"

"Enough to work together on this club business. And who knows what else might redevelop? One should always leave a door open for love—if you feel it, naturally. Do you have regrets about letting Luc go?"

"More like doubts. About Luc *and* Thierry, actually. Thierry's thinking of going to work for Air France...who knows where they could send him. I've blown two chances."

"Were you ever in love with either of them?"

I shook my head. "I don't know...I don't know anything anymore."

"Don't jump into anything unless you feel it. It wouldn't be genuine."

I examined Sasha on the sly. How had she become such a sage? "Did all this come to you suddenly back in New York?" I asked her.

She chuckled. "Hell no! I went to a Jewish shrink. One of legions in Manhattan, who, by the way, could do a *meshugener* Catholic like you some good."

I grinned in appreciation. "I'll remember that."

"I'll tell you something else. If this club, The Roundabout, or whatever the hell we call it, doesn't pan out, I'm going back to school to become a psychologist myself."

Sasha had rich parents. Her father owned a couple of jewelry stores in Manhattan, so investing in The Roundabout, or going back to school, presented no obstacle. If only my hurdles appeared that low! I didn't hold Sasha's blessings against her, though. No, not after all she'd said to me. When we left the *salon du thé*, I almost wanted to sling my arm around her shoulder.

Luc didn't call me the whole month or so he had been in Lyon. I thought he would at least ring me to announce his arrival in Paris; but no, I heard it from Thierry. Thanks to him, at least, the Three Musketeers were back in action, if only for an afternoon.

I met them in a café on boulevard de Sébastopol, not far from the Lux, and looked forward to my friends' every word and gesture. I fished for the familiar and hunted for old times, and hoped Thierry's humor and Luc's boldness would return like the leaves fleshing out the plane trees on the boulevard. Not that we could be frozen in a rerun. Luc had a new car for one thing, and strangely, when I glanced at it next to the curb, it filled me with a touch of resentment. You'd think Luc had brought along a new girlfriend, instead of a cobalt-blue Alfa Romeo sports sedan. Deep down, I regretted the loss of the Lancia, and spinning around Paris in it with my pals.

I flashed back on one sunlit autumn afternoon on the Champs-Elysées. The three of us were reined in at a red light, when Luc pointed right. "Hey, it's Belmondo!"

"Jean-Paul Belmondo," Thierry clarified for my benefit.

No need. I knew of Jean-Paul Belmondo, actor, international French celebrity, now sitting behind the wheel of his car in the lane next to us. The light turned green and we glided forward in the Lancia. Luc honked his horn. I waved at Belmondo and netted a boyish, blue-eyed wink and smile from "Bébel." Then his car sprinted toward the Arc de Triomphe. Not to be bested, Luc gunned it, and we lunged toward the colossal Triumphal Arch, pursuing the star until we lost him in the teeming traffic of the Arc's massive roundabout.

The memory receded and my mind returned to the present, a bit begrudgingly. Luc's hair was shorter, cropped above his ears and well above his collar. A subtle line parted the left side. All in all, he looked like a budding banker.

Then, he pulled out a five hundred-franc note to pay the waiter. The *mec* looked a little older than Luc and raised an eyebrow as he fingered the bill. When he turned his back to leave with it, Luc flipped him off French style with a slap of his bicep. I let out a good laugh, like in the old days.

Thierry followed up with the low-toned zinger, "*Va te faire voir chez les Grecs.*"

"What's that mean?" I asked, frustrated I could still be stumped after a year in Paris, and yet delighted to learn new slang from my friends.

"Ha!" Luc said to Thierry. "Start explaining that one!"

Thierry turned to me, as nonchalant as ever. "You know about the ancient Greeks...their reputation for homosexuality?"

I gave a resounding yes, proud I knew that much.

"Well, telling someone to go to Greek territory would be like telling him to..."

"I get it," I answered, and started laughing again.

"Not bad," Luc said to Thierry.

The familiar feeling of "us three" filled the air. Heartened, I decided to float out Sasha's dinner offer. "It would be the four of us again," I said. "Hopefully, we'll only be drinking wine."

Thierry accepted. Luc jumped on it with such enthusiasm, I almost wished I could take the offer back. Why did he seem so keen on seeing Sasha again?

I had no time to ponder it, though, for a familiar face across the terrace caught my eye. Short, matted black hair, aquiline nose...a short beard punctuated his chin this time...still...yes, it was Butch-head.

Of all the rotten timing. I had felt so light-hearted, I even planned to ask Luc for a ride in his new Alfetta, hoping he would offer me a turn at the wheel.

And yet, I couldn't let that son of a bitch, Butch-head, continue toying with me. I wanted to get to the bottom of it. So I feigned a suddenly-remembered errand and excused myself. Luc and Thierry didn't appear surprised at all. I guess that's how good I had gotten from all my spying days.

As I made my way off, I ignored Butch-head, pretended I hadn't seen him. I sauntered down shady boulevard de Sébastopol and acted like a window shopper. "Window-licking," they say in French. Then, when I reached rue de Rivoli, I switched gears. I swung right, strode as fast as I could, and ducked into the first doorway niche.

I waited. Individual after individual passed by, none of whom turned to notice me. Then he appeared. He must have been combing the area, for he nailed me dead in the doorway.

His dark, narrow eyes widened in surprise. Just for a heartbeat, after which he took off trotting down the sidewalk. I rushed after him, staying a few paces behind. He continued to accelerate, but I had no difficulty keeping him in sight, for he glanced back every time he crossed a street. Keep running, salaud, I said to myself, I'm sticking to you like glue until you stop and face me!

At some point I expected him to veer right and try to lose me in one of those *ruelles* that led to the Trou des Halles. Obviously, he had another strategy. For some reason he stuck to rue de Rivoli, where the closer we got to the Louvre, crowds mushroomed.

The Palace of the Louvre loomed left across the street, and we plunged into the throngs of shoppers and loiterers under the arcades of rue de Rivoli. We wove figure eights, dodging tourists, crêpes stands, and rotating postcard racks. Butch-head crossed another street and looked back to check on me. I glided on adrenaline. An electric current shot up my spine each time he spotted me, and every time his eyes landed on me, I felt a beam of familiarity.

I cranked up my stride, collided shoulders with a tourist and sent him crashing into the postcard rack he was browsing. I didn't have time to apologize, barely heard the *Nom de Dieu* he sputtered. On I charged.

Then Butch-head made his move. He swerved right, onto the square of Palais Royal. *Merde!* I expected him to scurry into the metro where I would have to slow down to rummage through my purse for my pass. Wrong. He headed toward the Comédie Française, passed the fabled theater and hustled into the Palais Royal gardens. Exasperated, I wanted to shout, *assez*—enough, you coward!

I had no choice but to follow him into the courtyard where I faced a classical colonnade. Two rows of white columns filed down the arcade that flanked the gardens. The movie *Charade* popped into my mind. Would he try to hide in there like Walter Matthau and ambush me?

He engaged the thicket of columns and started lacing through them. As long as I could see him I followed. Then I lost him.

I halted. For the first time, I felt a stream of perspiration, and I realized I was alone. A flicker of doubt made me shrink inside. Until now I hadn't thought about what would actually happen when Butch-head and I faced off. I had always fantasized us butting heads on a crowded street with plenty of witnesses. Now, I didn't know.

To make matters worse, I happened to be wearing a pair of brand-new leather shoes I'd bought at a discount store in my neighborhood. The yellowish-tan loafers were pointed and boosted with over two inches of heel—and they pinched my toes. Now that Butch-head and I were alone, I also noticed that the leather soles sent an echoing "click-clack" through the colonnade every time I advanced down the stone walk. I had insisted on showing them off for my reunion with Luc. Now I wanted to chuck them into the rose bushes next to the colonnade.

I took a slow step, rocking my foot delicately from heel to toe. My mind magnified the sound, and it reverberated between my ears. Where was this *connard* lying in wait? Funny, the irrelevancies that can flit through the mind during a crisis. French had cemented itself in my instinctual responses, otherwise I would have referred to Butch-head with the English word that starts with *F*. Interesting sign of linguistic progress, I mused, before refocusing on my situation.

To continue through the grove of columns would render me a walking duck, I decided. Not much better than the sitting variety. So I tiptoed sideways, wincing at my pinched toes. Once out of the colonnade, I advanced through the rose gardens toward the central fountain. On its base I saw a man sitting with a book. The company reassured me, so I slinked back toward Butch-head's direction. Mid-way down the colonnade I still couldn't spot him. Finally, I encountered a sort of intersection of columns, a big square of them. They led laterally to an exit out of Palais Royal, onto a side street. I shook my head: that's where he must have vanished.

Now I had to limp back to the metro. I could barely face it. I had forced untested shoes on a ten-block manhunt and my feet felt destroyed. Still, catching the connection at Palais Royal would spare my crushed toes four or five blocks. I deliberated where to get off—Pont Neuf or Louvre?—and sighed at having to make a decision that had never mattered before. At Louvre I would have to walk another couple of blocks to reach the Lux—*torture*. The Pont Neuf station would get me farther east, but it dipped toward the Seine and would require back-tracking up to rue du Roule—*agony*. I chose the latter, merely to earn more time on the metro to rest my pulsating feet.

I dragged myself to the metro entrance, weight on my heels as much as possible. Then I eased down the stairs, throwing my weight on the banister. *Dieu merci*, a train showed up immediately, for every seat on the platform had a derriere planted on it. When the train halted, I was the first to flip the metal lever, climb aboard, and nab a seat.

Pont Neuf arrived too soon. When I stood, my feet felt two sizes too big for my shoes. To tell the truth, they did measure *one* size too big because the store didn't have my size. Agh, *la vanité*! I couldn't face climbing out of the metro straight away, so I stopped for a little rest on the platform's low, orange-tiled wall. Good opportunity to take stock over what a fiasco this whole Iranian, Butch-head business had amounted to. I closed my eyes, pinched the bridge of my nose, and pondered what to do about it.

"Hey, airhead..."

Up shot my eyes.

"You are quite a walker," said a voice speaking English with rolled r's.

Butch-head slid into place next to me, and I stared hard at him. He didn't startle me. I felt no fear. I didn't even want to yell at him. Because I finally recognized him. Now that he sat up-close and in-my-face, a little too close for my cultural comfort, I remembered him perfectly—the supreme jerk who had verbally assaulted me at the American rally. The creep at whom I had menaced that stupid sign. He even wore a beard again, just as he did back in November. I recalled that he'd referred to me as "airhead" then as well.

I shook my head at him. "How come I'm so special that I've got the Ayatollah Khomeini's minions after me?"

He sneered. "The Ayatollah has nothing to do with it."

"Then why this game?" I wanted to scoot away from him, but I resisted for fear of assuming my former role of prey. Plus, I didn't want other people on the platform to hear us speaking.

He leaned closer. "You think George Abdi's death is a game?"

His sharp, close-set eyes unnerved me. All it took, though, was to recall his macho attitude at the rally, and I reared up. "Your lot ran him down—you tell me!"

Butch-head leaped up to face me, feet planted widely apart. "How dare you speak such a lie!" Then he scanned the three other commuters waiting on the wall, one of whom was eyeing him. He lowered his voice. "George was my friend. You are the one responsible for his death."

His domineering posture irritated the hell out of me. "Hey!" I whispered loudly. "I was with George that day. I could've been killed too."

"That is what I mean." He spread his feet wider and pointed at me. "You are the one who put him in danger!"

I wanted to kick him in the balls, and decided it was time to get out of there. Not without the last word, though: "You Muslims wouldn't even let him think for himself. He was a mess because of you. Now get out of my way, I'm leaving."

I started to rise, but his hands fanned out to calm me. "No, please stay," he whispered. "I must talk to you." He sat back down, which made me feel a little more at ease, though his dark eyes shone like oil ablaze.

I had him on the defense. He needed me, so I took the advantage. "If you don't tell me why you've been following me, I'm informing the police. I've already talked to them several times about George's accident. I think they'd be interested to know about you."

That made him back off a little and extinguished the fire in his eyes. For a moment he watched the people on the platform. Then his face settled into something between a sneer and a grimace. "I know you were with George that day," he said in a low voice. "The police told his uncle and he told me. I also talked to his aunt, and she told me George's glasses are missing from the possessions the police returned to her. She thinks they were stolen for the frames. But I wonder about that..."

I shifted my gaze to the deep trench that held the train tracks. I knew I should've given the glasses to George's aunt. The way she had doted on him when I came to visit during his convalescence showed pure concern and love. But Butch-head—why should I trust him? On the other hand, he obviously felt close to George...

I turned my eyes to the platform next to Butch-head's feet. "So you've been following me because I might have George's glasses?"

"Yes," he grunted sharply.

"Why didn't you approach me directly?" No answer. I raised my eyes. "You wanted to punish me, didn't you," I said with a smirk.

"...Perhaps."

"Harass me the way your thug friends persecuted George. Were you all going to beat me up too?"

He waved his hand impatiently. "Don't be ridiculous. You are truly an empty-headed woman!"

"And you're a coward." Again, I started to rise, and felt my toes pulsate in pain.

"Wait," he insisted. His hand flew out, but stopped short of touching my arm. "Were you on that sidewalk when the car hit him?"

I kept my eyes on his hand. "No, I left the café after him."

"After filling his head with more American nonsense! Charming him! No wonder he didn't see the car coming."

My mind reran the scene where George placed his warm hand on mine, right before he left the café. The old iciness filled me, and I felt stranded in the Arctic again, awful, stark whiteness all around me. I shivered. Strangely, I felt like continuing my talk with Butch-head. A train started to leave, and I waited until the noise trailed off.

Then I looked him in the eye. "You weren't there," I told him calmly, "so please quit speculating." I looked at the floor again. "George had just finished telling me his latest news, which had nothing to do with me or Iran. Don't ask me about it because it's none of your business. He was happy. Happier than I'd ever seen him. Glad to be putting behind all the Khomeini disciples and moving on. I had no influence over him or his plans." Then I sighed, and felt a touch warmer and a little less alone.

"He would not stop meeting you," said Butch-head. "He was betraying our cause and making our leaders angry."

I looked up and met his eyes again. "Listen, can't you understand that I don't represent my government?" Then a wave of embarrassment washed over me as I thought of Jenkins. I shook him out of my mind and changed tactics. "George and I enjoyed each other's company as friends whether your culture likes it or not. France is a free country, if you haven't noticed."

"His Muslim friends...he was not loyal to them."

"So you all killed him?"

"Do not say that again! I would never hurt George, in spite of his disloyalty."

"You didn't take part in his beating?"

"Never!"

"But you know the guys who did?"

"I condemn them," Butch-head said, his voice straining over the roar of a blue and white train pulling in.

We both settled into silence and watched the somber-faced commuters descend while others climbed aboard, all nursing their own quiet concerns. I was glad we had finally squared off in metro station Pont Neuf. I had spent so much time underground, since the metro beat the bus in speed, I felt quite at home on the platform. The driver sounded the horn, the pneumatic doors expelled their air and locked tight, and the train pulled away, noisy as a roller-coaster.

I felt tired and oddly relaxed. "Look, George had the right to frequent whoever he wanted and develop his own ideas. Why blame me?"

Butch-head folded his arms, which complemented the severity of his expression. "George had his rights, yes. But he did not use good judgment. He spitted in the face of the wrong people, and they saw you as the source."

I vaguely noted Butch-head's mistake in the past tense. Instead I concentrated on my own errors. I never warned George he could be getting in over his head. How could I, as embroiled as I was with Jenkins? I kept leading him on because I had gotten in too deep myself. I knew my guilt, but I sure as hell wouldn't admit it to Butch-head.

"So who killed him?" I asked.

"I don't know. No one will admit to it."

I smirked. "No surprise."

"And they are not talking to me anymore."

"Because you defended George?"

He shot me a distasteful smile. "It is like defending *you* in their eyes."

"Then we really can't be sure it was murder..."

"No."

I nodded, and we exchanged significant looks. I never asked Butch-head his name, and he didn't offer it. I guess we had an understanding—neither of us wanted issues with the police. Given his outrage and protestations, I believed in his innocence concerning George. I could even understand his blaming me. I did too, in my own way. I ended up confessing about George's glasses. I told Butch-head I just hadn't gotten around to seeing George's aunt and uncle. Eventually, I would deliver the glasses to them.

All in all, a surprising but not unsatisfactory encounter with Butch-head. I still knew no names, and the less I knew, the less I figured the police would care about me.

So I thought.

9: Sand Castle

Two mornings later, the droopy-mustached *flic*, Brondel, caught me before I could leave the Lux. This time he requested I accompany him in his car to the commissariat in the Fourth arrondissement.

I couldn't get Butch-head out of my mind during the drive. What did Brondel know? He'd said he only needed me to clear up a point or two regarding the investigation, so why did we have to go to his office? I didn't ask, and Brondel limited himself to small talk the whole way.

As we crossed the station's threshold, I silently acknowledged the *planton* standing at the center desk. Evidently, every commissariat had a sentry guarding the lobby. I remembered the *planton* in the Sixth arrondissement where Thierry and I had gone to report my stolen purse: burly and bushy-eye-browed, the *mec*—a regular armoire. The Fourth's *planton* stood lanky and wiry—not as formidable, even friendly when Brondel greeted him. *As if that meant much.* I would've given anything to be in the Sixth's commissariat right now, dealing with such a relative bagatelle as a stolen purse and passport!

Brondel and I filed into his office, and he shut the door.

"*Bon*," he said, as we sat down. A polite little smile made his red mustache twitch. "Let's get this business over with so you can be on your way."

Good sign, I thought, and edged forward on my chair next to his desk, eager to comply and get out of there.

He opened a dossier. "As I said, I just want to clear up a detail or two." He sifted through the papers and lifted a sheet. "Here we are," he said, scanning it. "According to your statement and the witness reports, you left the café *after* George Abdi the day of the accident."

"Yes," I stated firmly. Why did I have to continually confirm a simple fact?

He looked up from his paper. "How many minutes after Monsieur Abdi did you leave the café?"

For about the tenth time I repeated, "I don't remember exactly, but it could only have been about a minute later."

"*Oui...*" he drew out, and returned to his notes.

What a waste of time, I said to myself, I could be—

"Why did you wait that minute in the café, Mademoiselle?"

The question came out of nowhere. No one had pitched it at me before. So why now? I crossed my ankles and tried to look relaxed, though fear of sinking deeper and deeper into this black-hole-of-a-business made me avert my eyes from Brondel. I considered resorting to a lie, but realized the truth would suit me better. When I looked up, I said, "I didn't want George's friends to see us together...those Iranians...the ones who beat him up."

"Hmm." The *flic's* light-blue eyes remained static. Then he glanced down to scribble a note. When he raised his eyes, they held the same neutral gaze. "Did George tell you he was worried about them?"

I could feel my front teeth start to sink into my bottom lip and immediately stopped them. Stick to the truth, Haley, I reminded myself. "George actually made fun of my concern. He told me he'd broken with those guys and there was nothing to worry about."

"Did he say why he had broken with them?"

"Because they beat him up. He said they weren't honorable men." I shrugged and gave a weak smile. "George had some old-fashioned expressions."

"They disapproved of his relationship with you, I believe you told me earlier."

"George and I were just friends," I said, to keep the record straight.

A sliver of a smile slipped from Brondel, almost imperceptible. "Right. Did he happen to mention which men he had broken with?"

"No, I've never known any of their names. Not one." I regretted that last addition, since Brondel might have thought I was *protesting* too much. Again, I thanked God Jenkins hadn't taken the matter further.

Brondel set his paper down and closed the dossier. "I suppose this will do for now."

I wanted to smile in relief, but I kept my expression serious.

"I *have* had to do a little inquiring about your status here, though—purely routine. It seems you had told me you were a student at the Alliance Française..."

My heart plunged like a runaway elevator. This time I had to lie. "Yes, I'm going to start summer session now. I'm just waiting for my grandmother to wire me the tuition fee..."

My alarm must have shown, for Brondel waved his hand at me like a conductor calming a section of his orchestra. "Fine, fine, I understand," he said. "Your name isn't in the enrollment at the moment is why I ask."

"It will be. I guarantee it." I felt like a desperate child, pleading not to get punished and promising to be good in the future.

"*Bon*," he said. "Now, one more question."

Holy Christ! I shifted in my chair. The office was a little box of a room, and though all the files and papers sat neat and tidy, I still felt things closing in on me. Or maybe it was Brondel whose size seemed to fill up the room.

"The last time you attended classes at the Alliance Française was back in January," he said. "How have you been occupying your time since then?"

Merde! The question I lived in dread of had now popped up like a sinister jack-in-the-box. I drew a silent, steadying breath. "I've been taking a break...trying to perfect my spoken French...studying Paris and so forth."

Brondel smiled. "Your French sounds proficient. You must have a lot of free time on your hands. Have you never been tempted to get in touch with George's friends or family?"

I clenched my teeth to resist gnawing my lip. *Butch-head.* "George's friends?" I said. "I've never wanted to meet any of them. As far as his family goes, I still feel awkward..."

"What about your income? Does it all arrive from America?"

I felt my teeth begin to chew the inside of my cheek and stopped them. "Yes, from my grandmother."

"How does that work?"

I shot him a mental insult: *common sense, what do you think!* Then I explained. "She sends me money orders, postal orders that I can cash here."

I couldn't stand it any longer. I had to divert this cop from my personal issues. My only choice remained to get him focused back on the case. So I decided to broach a subject I had already discussed with Thierry, with Sasha, even with Butch-head.

I met his eyes. "Do you think George was murdered?"

His feathery red mustache lifted in a smile, and he nodded slowly. "That's the question I've been waiting for since the beginning of this affair. Most people would have asked it much sooner."

A prickly heat filled me, working its way up to my face. For an instant I thought my eyes would pool with tears. "I...I didn't want it to be murder...I was afraid of that."

Brondel's smile faded and he studied me. "Or you suspected murder, but feared revealing the nature of your suspicions..."

The heat in me inflamed my ears and my scalp. I had to concentrate not to stammer. "After those Iranians beat George up...for a while I was afraid they wouldn't stop there...you know, if they found out we'd met again..."

Brondel's blue eyes settled into kindness again. "Don't worry, we haven't found any evidence of that."

"Have you questioned them?"

"His friends? Certainly."

So Brondel already had names. Why badger me?

"They claim to have nothing against you, Mademoiselle. Nor do they admit to beating up Monsieur Abdi. At the time of the assault, George himself reported the crime as a violent mugging." His eyes reassumed their edge. "Of course he told you otherwise..."

The Iranians' word against mine stunned me. "George tried to lie about the beating, but he eventually told me the truth. You don't believe them, do you?"

"Don't worry, we're checking everything out. Did he confide anything about which of his Iranian friends assaulted him?"

"No. Just what I've already told you." And Butch-head? What about his take on things? How none of the Iranians were talking to him—how they didn't trust him. All too vague and uncertain, I decided, and not worth mentioning. Plus, how could I bring up Butch-head now? Brondel would demand to know why I hadn't come forth with him sooner.

"*Bien*," he said, eyes still scrutinizing me. "I think we're finished for now."

For now? A sourness took hold of my stomach.

"At any rate, I know where to find you if something else comes up. You don't plan on leaving Paris, do you?"

I assured him I didn't. Where would I go? I didn't have the *fric*, as the French called "dough," to even go back to school.

Money: an embarrassing, debasing problem. I didn't have enough to resume class, and if I didn't go back to school, well, what would savvy detective Brondel think? I would either have to ask my grandmother for a supplement or wait until Thierry and I got paid for *A Guide to Paris*. I preferred the latter of course, but I couldn't bear waiting around with my nerves feeding on me. So after I left the commissariat, I decided to call Gram and sound her out about finances in general. I had let too much time slip by without calling her, anyway.

As soon as the time change permitted, I visited my usual PTT in rue du Louvre to call America. I planned to work up to my request gradually and emphasize my need for school funds. School had saved me before when Gram had her doubts about Paris...

At seven o'clock in the Reno morning, the phone rang non-stop. I wondered where Gram could have gone that early. Finally someone picked up—my aunt.

"Where's Gram?" I asked, after we exchanged a short greeting.

"We've been meaning to get in touch with you, Haley...your grandmother's in the hospital."

The phone slid off my shoulder, and I caught it on the fly.

"She's had a heart attack. The doctors say she'll be all right, though."

That was the crux of the conversation. Brain pounding, I collected all the information possible about my grandmother's condition. I never mentioned money.

That evening I had to meet Sasha, Luc, and Thierry for dinner at Au Pied de Cochon. The shock accompanied me like a snow storm in July.

Au Pied de Cochon sported a restaurant mascot, a spry piglet occupying a little pen on the sidewalk next to the entrance. The little fellow, excited by passing admirers, capered about under a June sun whose rays now stretched out until eleven p. m.

Sasha went into ecstasy. "Haley, it's adorable!"

"Yeah," I said, with diluted enthusiasm. I had seen the tiny creature before, and today it just didn't manage to raise my spirits.

Still, Luc and Sasha intrigued me. At dinner they seemed as animated as the piglet. During aperitifs, Sasha happened to mention the Roundabout, which triggered a volley of questions from Luc that continued into the main course.

"I envy you having your own business," he said. "That's my goal."

A coquettish spark flashed in Sasha's eyes. "You're not doing bad at all at your age. Not many twenty-year-olds are sales representatives." Her feline gaze rounded the table and alighted on me, as if choosing *me* to confirm her assertion.

I gave her a polite shrug.

"But it's nothing like being your own boss," said Luc.

Jesus, was he never satisfied?

Sasha sat back and tilted her head. She eyed him with a subtle smile. I remembered with distaste her sizing him up like that when they first met at the American rally.

"Listen," she said to him, "owning a business isn't all a bed of roses. At times the responsibility scares me to death."

"But you have a good partner, don't you?" Luc asked.

Sasha hesitated, before carefully drawing out, "I think so..."

That was too much for me. Why put Kevin in question? "Sure she does," I said. I had no real interest in the business aspect of the conversation, but I wanted to know what Sasha was up to. The evening of our Russian dinner drifted back to me, when Sasha had hinted at dumping Kevin. I could still remember the ambiguous smile and wink she shot me on the sidewalk in the ferocious December cold. Sasha's opportunistic streak drove me mad. "Her partner's older," I added for good measure, "and he's been planning this business for a year."

Sasha didn't comment. Instead, she pounced on Thierry. "I've heard you're revving up for the skies of Air France," she said in English.

Thierry looked privileged to be engaged in conversation with Sasha. He must have felt like a real small fry listening to Luc and her. I know I did—in between bouts of worry and guilt over Gram. I should have been on a plane to Reno instead of celebrating Sasha and Luc's return to Paris. Details, like no money for a ticket and Brondel's order to stay put, just made me feel worse. Doubtful, that my *flic* would say, "Go to your grandmother's bedside and don't give this unpleasant homicide business a second thought."

Thierry sat there narrating his Air France employment odyssey blow by blow: the competition for positions, the tests to weed people out, all the languages he knew.

I didn't care about that either. My aunt had asked when I was coming home. "Your grandmother would be thrilled to see you, you know." I told her I wanted to see Gram too and that I would look into buying a ticket and then get back to her. Who knew when that would be with twin hurdles in front of me?

"Evidently you've got all your capital together..." Luc's words reeled me back to the moment.

I looked him up and down. Christ, he acted like a bulldog with this Round-about business.

"Well," Sasha said, almost preening, "you can never have too much...additional investment could be helpful."

I thought Luc would leap across the table to her. "So there's room for another partner?"

Sasha cocked her head again. "I'll have to consult my partner, Kevin Smythe, but I imagine he would welcome another investor."

I don't think Luc granted me more than two glances the entire evening. He only had eyes for Sasha. I glanced at Thierry and we exchanged looks.

Looks that didn't escape Sasha. "What new is brewing in the translation still, you two?"

I let Thierry address our empty schedule. "Nothing yet," he said. "We've barely signed off on *A Guide to Paris*."

Sasha smiled politely. Luc looked blank. Jeez, I wished we had an interesting book to talk about.

"It's a tricky job, translating," I finally said. I looked to Thierry for corroboration.

"Right, communicating accurately..."

"While preserving the author's style."

"Must be challenging," Sasha said, perhaps to help us out.

"I'd really like to translate a novel," I said, with my first true enthusiasm of the evening. "The closest thing was that memoir, *Cold War Chronicles*."

Thierry chuckled and then drained his wine glass. "That's the book I'll remember most the day I'm flying around the world for Air France."

He couldn't keep Air France out of the conversation. That maddened me as much as Luc begging to get into the Roundabout. My mind returned to *Cold War Chronicles*. It had been our first book, and it thrilled Thierry and me like a drug. It sizzled with excitement and promise, just like Paris. God, how I wanted to begin anew. Make a better start and do things right this time...

"Hey," said Luc, "what's wrong with this party?"

His complaint jerked me back to attention.

Sasha agreed about the flatness of our festivities and slipped me a meaningful gaze. "Yes, what *is* wrong? Let's order some champagne—garçon!" This was her party, and she refused to let it bottom out.

"Have you ever tried champagne rosé?" asked Luc.

Our bottle of golden-pink brew landed on the table, and we attacked it. The restaurant itself suffered from no lack of animation. Au Pied de Cochon echoed all kinds of boisterous chatter and laughter. At the table next to us sat a middle-aged American couple. Throughout the evening I noticed they had indulged in every type of alcohol imaginable. Now the barrel-chested *mec's* voice began to swell into a braying. "So which cabaret should we grace with our presence?" he practically yelled in English.

Sasha and I exchanged embarrassed winces, and the old guy barked on. "There's the Folies Bergères and the Moulin Rouge...and what's that other famous joint with the cancan dancers? We've gotta go to a cancan club, Mildred."

Mildred had big, bee-hived hair that resembled a red helmet. She smoked as ferociously as her husband drank. In fact, she didn't even pause her puffing to answer him.

"I read about the cancan girls before we left," he said. "You know what they used to wear under those big, frilly skirts when they kicked up their legs?"

Mildred lit another cigarette while the previous still smoldered, half-extinguished in the ashtray. "I don't remember any such book around the house. How the hell should I know?"

"Come on, honey, take a guess!"

The old girl produced a smirk stamped on boredom.

"All right, I'll tell you: NOTHING!"

Mildred's eyes narrowed.

"You heard me: no underwear!"

"Keep your voice down! That's disgusting! And you wanna drag me into one of those holes?"

Sasha and I started giggling. Thierry whispered something to Luc, a translation no doubt, and they laughed too.

Mildred's desperate husband scrambled to explain. "That's the way it *used* to be, honey, at the turn of the century—not now! They still dance, but I'm sure they at least wear underpants. Damn it, I wish I could remember the name of that other cabaret! A real famous one too..."

"The Lido," said Luc in English, with a suave French accent. "The Lido de Paris. And the girls are still quite sexy there." He turned a smile on us, and Mildred went red as her teased hair.

Her hubby started stumbling all over himself. "Ah...yes, that's it...thanks." Then he quickly turned his back on us.

Sasha tossed back her pink bubbly and slapped her empty glass on the table. "After what I've just witnessed, I'll never use English as a cover again!"

"They sound like frogs," said Luc, back to French again.

"Not so loud!" Thierry said.

"Who sounds like frogs?" I asked Luc.

"They do—Americans. They sound like frogs croaking in a pond." He mimicked the speech.

"That's funny," I said. "Frogs are what Americans call the French."

"I've heard that," Thierry said with a snicker.

"Why frogs?" Luc asked

"Because you eat them," I answered.

"But you sound like them."

"Maybe we do kind of sound like frogs," said Sasha. "*That* couple sure does."

I glanced at our compatriots as they rose to leave without looking at us.

"They're from New York," I said to Sasha. "They sound like you."

"*No*, they're from the Bronx." Sasha was right. She really didn't talk like Mildred and her husband. I don't know why I made that comment.

"It doesn't matter," Luc said, and poured us more champagne.

The rest of the evening we skated around things, sticking to the edges of the ice where minimal risk lay. The highlight remained the American couple's embarrassment from which we continued to wring more laughs—pathetic. Finally, Sasha wrapped up her party. She plucked out her Carte Blanche, and Luc immediately began thanking her.

"I can give you a lift to your hotel..." he said.

Sasha snapped a quick *okay*. A little too quick, I thought.

Then Luc turned to me. "I'd like to ask Sasha a few more questions about the business. Could Thierry drive you home?"

Of course he could since we had all come on our own. That wasn't the point. I would have loved driving home in Luc's new blue Alfa Romeo, and becoming the center of attention again. The loss stabbed me in the gut.

The Lux was only a few blocks away. I could have walked back home the way I'd come. I didn't want to trudge back alone though, so I agreed to ride with Thierry.

"I don't feel like going straight home," I told him in the car.

So we drove up to the Drugstore at the top of the Champs-Elysées for a nightcap.

"It's like they're in a whole different universe," I told Thierry over a Benedictine brandy. "All they can talk about is how they're getting ahead. Sorry," I added, hating to sound like an envious loser. "I don't mean to complain."

"I can't blame you," Thierry said. "You *have* been in the straits lately, what with work permit problems and so forth."

"And I haven't told you the latest...I ran into Butch-head again."

His eyebrows shot up, as if involuntarily. "Oh...?"

I lowered my voice and started to narrate the whole episode, minus the date of the encounter. Thierry had been in the café that day, and I didn't want him to know I'd acted without him.

"So he and I are even now," I finished.

Thierry raised one brow this time. "And you'd better leave it at that."

"Of course I will. Do you think I'd strike up a friendship with him?"

He shrugged. "You did with George."

"The two cases aren't even close." I ignored Thierry's half-smile. "Speaking of George, that detective called me over to the commissariat. He's still investigating the case."

"What did he want this time?"

"Crap about George's friends. He keeps trying to corner me into saying I know some of them. Which he'll never do, since I can't even say I know Butch-head!"

"You didn't mention him, did you?"

"No, but that's not the end of it. He's been poking around the Alliance Française. He knows I haven't been in school, so I told him I'm waiting for the tuition money from America. Then he wanted to know what I do with all my time..."

"*Mer-de!*" Thierry said in two syllables.

"Don't worry, I didn't say anything about work. I did tell him I'd be back in school for summer session, and that seemed to satisfy him."

"Good! So all you need to do is enroll in school again."

I sighed. "It's not that simple. I couldn't get through to my grandmother. That's the coup that's wiped me out. She's in the hospital with a heart attack."

"*Nom de Dieu!* I'm so sorry."

"My aunt says she'll be all right, but in the meantime I can't even go visit her, because the detective doesn't want me leaving Paris with the investigation still on..."

Thierry cupped my hand. "And you didn't mention any of this tonight."

"Who could relate to it but you? Anyway, I didn't want to kill the party."

"It died pretty much on its own. You're right, you and I *are* worlds away from Luc and Sasha."

"We're odd men out," I said in English, with a weak laugh. "At least I am."

"What's *odd men out*?"

I smiled at him gratefully before I took on the translation. God, it felt warm and comfortable floating on the same wave length with Thierry. "We should just take off," I said out of the blue. "Screw Sasha and Luc. Let's go somewhere!"

Thierry cleared his throat with one of those polite or embarrassed little coughs. "Until we get paid for *A Guide to Paris* I'm a bit short on cash..."

"Don't remind me," I said, "So am I."

"But, we could have a change of scene at least..."

"Go on..."

"My grandparents are out of town again..."

You'd think Thierry had invited me to Venice or something, the way my spirits rocketed. I grinned. "For how long?"

"Until the day after tomorrow. Shall we keep their place company?"

Again I agreed to invade the elderly Kérouacs' home. The first time had been a lark, part of euphorically floating in the ether of Paris. Camping out at the Kérouacs' flat had made perfect sense, despite the fact I didn't know them from Adam. Now, a different kind of euphoria coursed through me, a desperate giddiness that took me on a strange jet ride for two days.

This time, instead of painting Paris, we picked our way through it. At times our choices clashed, especially cafés. No Deux Magots for me, no Flore for Thierry. We agreed on dinner at the Assiette au Boeuf. I didn't care that it set me back even more financially. I just wanted to keep flying, and when we returned to the flat, I practically flung myself into Thierry's arms in order to maintain altitude.

"I didn't think this would ever happen again," he murmured into my hair, in the tar-black of his grandparent's bedroom.

"I guess it just makes sense," I answered, and grasped him harder.

And it was true. Thierry and I did make sense together. I knew it in Nice when we first made love. With Luc in the picture I just didn't want to recognize how well we danced on the same wave length. This night I felt the fit so strongly, it seemed we had never been apart.

Then the sun rose, and thoughts of Gram, of my red-mustached Brondel, of Luc and Sasha, sent me into pockets of turbulence. If I had been alone, I think I would have crashed. I insisted we get out of the house early.

We glided all over town. We browsed FNAC and Lido Musique for records, but I didn't buy anything. We even breezed through a movie, at Thierry's insistence and treat. He wanted to see *American Gigolo* playing at Odéon where the plane trees provided a green screen of modesty for Danton's statue. The old revolutionary had a rough go of it as well these days, head and out-stretched arm splattered white with bird bombardments.

Once inside, the cinema cocooned me as always—thank God for some con-stancy. I settled into one of the cozy, black-leather armchairs and waited for the catchy electronic tune that accompanied the pre-film advertisements. It gave me a shot of cheer, and I sank into a comfortable slouch. The movie's dialogue echoed in the hollow coolness of the auditorium, and I drifted away in my sailboat, away from everything. Not even the Blondie soundtrack jarred me.

Before I had to return home to the Lux, we stopped for coffee in a café on my beloved Quai de la Mégisserie. This walkway along the Seine's embank-ment equaled my corner of tranquility. We sat outdoors, in view of my Conci-ergerie, and time stood still. The pet-shop birds warbled in their wicker cages just a few doors up from us on the sidewalk, and for the duration of my café *serré*, not even the knowledge that I would have to return to the Lux by myself dampened my spirit.

Just a pinprick of concern disturbed me.

As I gazed serenely over the Seine, the corner of my eye caught Thierry watching me. It wasn't the first time. He had been eyeing me off and on during these two days of our escapade. I couldn't define it as staring, exactly; rather he would hold his gaze on me after my eyes shifted. We would finish a conver-sation, and I would catch him peering at me. I didn't say anything. I just wanted to preserve the beauty of that moment in time on the *quai*.

I hated the idea of going home. I wanted to remain with Thierry, like two lovers on the run in timeless Paris. Anything, not to be alone with my thoughts. There was Gram whom I still hadn't been able to reach, to see whether she got home from the hospital. And Sasha and Kevin. Here they were, poised to "make it" in Paris, and they didn't give a damn about the city itself. A business opportunity, that's all Paris meant to them, and to Luc too.

For me, Paris now began to represent an elaborate sand castle. A life I had painstakingly constructed in a city I loved more than anybody did. It had taken me a year to build my castle by the ocean. Now, relentless waves kept wearing it down...

When we pulled up in front of the Lux, I lingered in Thierry's car. "Do you want to do something tomorrow?"

"I can't tomorrow..."

"After your Spanish class, I mean."

"Maybe in a couple of days...I'm busy until then..." Again his eyes wandered away, only to slip back and consider me.

"Sure, in a couple of days," I repeated, trying not to sound disappointed.

While we were away, we'd learned that Monsieur Garnier had called Thierry's home and announced our payment was ready.

I wanted to do something extravagant, though I knew full well it was unrealistic, so I dogged Thierry a little more. "Now that Garnier's paying us, we could have a real getaway...Venice or something."

"Don't you want to spend more time with Luc and Sasha before they leave?"

It seemed he was trying to humor me, so I aimed a sour smile at him. "Don't worry, I plan on seeing them off—if it's convenient."

"Listen, it might be a while before I can take any trips..."

"Hey, no problem. It's just a whim. Take care of your business, by all means."

"Right..." he said. Then, he did it again: watching me right after I had started to look the other way.

"What's with you?" I finally demanded.

He studied the steering wheel, giving it a couple of partial turns. For a moment I thought he wouldn't answer. "Well...it looks like Air France is going to hire me..."

I shrugged. "I've expected that."

"I might not be as available as before..."

"Don't worry about it," I said, steeling myself. "And congratulations— really."

As I watched Thierry drive off, I wondered at timing and fate, and what was missing in me. That when I finally seemed to feel ready for love, it wanted to evade me.

If Monsieur Garnier hadn't said he was finally paying us, I think I would have marched to his residence, banged on the door, and demanded our money in person. He acted awfully cavalier, the way he took his time compensating us and offering us new material. So far he had given Thierry no notice of the latter.

I waited out Thierry's busy spell, figuring he would call me as soon as he collected from Garnier. On the fourth day with no news, I went to the PTT, rue du Louvre. Any desire to chat had dried up in me, but I needed our money. What with Gram being sick, I didn't know when July's check would arrive. I slipped into a booth in the post office and dialed Thierry's number.

Madame Kérouac answered. "He's not in, Haley. I *am* sorry." She not only sounded apologetic, but a touch worried, I thought.

"It's nothing urgent," I said. "If you could tell him I called about Monsieur Garnier, he'll understand."

"I certainly will. I don't doubt he owes you and many others a phone call. "

I sensed exasperation, Thierry getting on his parents' nerves as well as mine. I rang off, with Madame Kérouac promising to deliver my message to Thierry.

Next I called Gram, since it was finally late enough not to worry about waking her up in her condition. I got no answer.

No Gram. No Thierry. "What the hell's going on?" I muttered desperately, as I left the PTT.

At the corner of rue du Louvre and rue de Rivoli, I watched the one-way traffic shoot west toward Place de la Concorde. Everybody had somewhere to go except me.

I had just decided to cut over to the Louvre for a distracting walk in the gardens, when someone tapped my shoulder. I turned and found Sasha beaming a smile. "Madani told me you were at the post office, so I thought I'd try intercepting you."

She had lucked out. I didn't really want to hang out alone, so I agreed to let her accompany me on my stroll.

"Didn't think I'd see you before I took off," she said as we crossed the street.

"I've had a lot on my mind," I said, frowning into the distance, "but I would've at least called you." I walked steadily onto the Louvre's sandy grounds. For some reason I now needed to move with a purpose.

Sasha quickened her pace to keep up. "More worries about George and Luc?" she asked.

The question annoyed me like a gnat. "No, no," I answered firmly. "I'm just wondering where the hell Thierry is with our translation money."

"He's probably off somewhere with his girlfriend."

Someone might well have stuck out his foot and tripped me. My gait relented involuntarily, and Sasha had to slow down to keep even. I didn't want to, but I finally asked. "What girlfriend?"

She shrugged. "I don't know. Luc only told me he had a girlfriend."

"Luc," I stated dryly.

"Yeah, we've had a couple of conversations about The Roundabout, and he happened to tell me. You're not jealous, are you?"

"Jealous over Thierry?" I said, dazed.

"No, I meant Luc. Nothing's going on between us. It's purely business."

Sasha had taken the lead and now steered us toward the Louvre gardens. I don't know why, but talking at cross-purposes made me erupt in laughter. I couldn't stop giggling and Sasha lost patience, which amused me all the more.

She brought us to a halt next to the huge circular flowerbeds, and faced me. "Now I really think you should see a shrink, Haley. You're freaking me out."

"Sorry," I said, trying to tame the kind of laughter that normally possessed me when I was sleep-deprived. "I don't need a shrink," I went on, after I had contained myself. "Because I don't care what either Luc or Thierry do."

I can't really claim that as truth. The revelation about Thierry had hit me like a cloudburst of cold rain. Still, I wanted to appear detached. If I willed things not to matter, maybe they wouldn't. I regained the lead when we resumed walking and guided us out of the Louvre gardens, toward the Tuileries.

"What do you really want?"

I looked over at Sasha and sighed with impatience. Why was she picking at my mask of detachment?

"You haven't been yourself since I arrived," she said. "If you want to *kvetch*, bring it on—I'm listening." She halted right in front of the huge, round reflecting pool, its jet of water rising from the center. She took a seat in one of the curvy, green-metal chairs surrounding the concrete basin of water and waited for me to do the same.

What did I truly want? I sat down and made a mental list. Let's see...I wanted the police off my back, I wanted a legal job, some new friends, and last, but entirely not least, I wanted my grandmother to get well. Oh, and if George could be resurrected that would be jolly good too. The trouble was, I didn't know whether even all that would make me happy. I stalled at what to tell Sasha. I didn't welcome any more of her psychoanalysis, well-meaning as it was. Instead of replying, I watched a little boy in tailored shorts and knee socks set his toy sailboat out to float in the pool. His father had stooped next to him and was pointing at the boat, grooming him with advice I supposed.

For some crazy reason, the scene almost made me cry. Weep for Gram, for my parents again, for the mess I'd made in Paris...

"Do you need money?"

Sasha's sudden question shocked me. I turned to face her, not knowing exactly how to answer. "Thierry should come through with my share any day now...but thanks for asking."

"If he's off gallivanting with his girlfriend, it's probably slipped his mind."

Again, the girlfriend. God, that stung. How convenient of him to keep that from me. Then I remembered him eyeing me on the sly during our second fling. In a guilt-ridden way, he might have been communicating it to me all along. If so, he was a shit, and yet we had both wanted each other those two days, even loved each other, possibly.

"If you're short on cash, I can lend it to you."

Again, Sasha surprised me. My eyes felt moist when I looked at her. "Thanks, that means a lot—it really does. But I'm sure I'll get the money."

Sasha grasped my arm, and her face expressed such sympathy that I ended up telling her about my grandmother and my dilemma with the police.

She listened intently, and then said, "I'll loan you the money for a ticket, if the cops finally let you leave."

Her gesture had touched me so thoroughly, I let her give me a further dose of psycho-babble about feeling guilty. Before we left each other, I promised I would call if I got desperate for cash, even if she was back in New York. On the way back to the Lux, I decided I couldn't ask for more in a friend, and that I had to stop resenting Sasha's success and quit suspecting hidden agendas on her part. That sharp, mysterious feline look still bothered me, but she couldn't help it. No more than Thierry could do anything about his impassive eyes, which had revealed nothing about another girl. I couldn't bring myself to tell Sasha about that betrayal. The sting and embarrassment burned too fresh. I plodded home, my heart alternately buoyed by Sasha and weighed down by Thierry. Who did he really want, and why couldn't people communicate honestly?

"Haley, two messages for you," declared Madani, as I returned to the Lux from my outing with Sasha.

I plucked the two items from his fingers: one, a piece of folded white paper; the other, an envelope. "Thanks," I said, smiling briefly at him. As I walked up the two flights of circular stairs, I felt a rush of gratefulness for Madani. By now he had become my friend, the only friend, it turned out, who had never disappointed me.

I opened the notes and read them each twice. Then I stretched out on my bed, feet up, to contemplate them. Each contained only a couple of lines. It was who sent them that intrigued me. The contents of the envelope amounted to a concise little message from Brondel in the Fourth arrondissement. He asked to see me on Monday in the commissariat. No further information, not a speck of clue as to why. I didn't know what to make of it and had to force myself to stop speculating. I would visit him after the weekend.

At least I had the second note to distract me. That one set me pondering too, only in a positive way. Luc had written it, inviting me to join Thierry and him for a drink that evening. The two of them would come fetch me at the Lux after dinner. Surely, Thierry would bring along the cash he owed me...

I mused about the three of us, the way we used to be before Luc left and Thierry duped me, or betrayed me, or whatever the hell he did now that he had a girlfriend. At any rate, in a cloud of nostalgia and curiosity, I left my room to call Luc and accept.

About ten o'clock that evening, the three of us arrived at our destination, and I felt time had reversed itself. The Tahonga had been my first taste of night life with Luc and Thierry, and our return to the intimate, glass-encased bar struck me as a sign: the symbol of a second chance; the opportunity for a miracle to take place that could mend our three-way friendship. It was just a whim; still I hoped something meaningful was in store.

Instead, my heart dipped when I saw a white *mec* at the piano in place of that sultry black singer who had enchanted me so dreamily with "Blues in the Night," now almost a year ago. Well, I told myself, Saturday might be her day off. She had a right to a day of rest, didn't she? Still, I didn't like the change.

The white *mec* sat in the company of a bassist, saxophonist, and drummer. It was Stan Kenton night I realized after we had claimed a table. I recognized cuts from one of my father's old records. Funny, though, when the pianist started hitting those dissonant, Stan-Kenton notes, I felt uneasy, kind of out of place for some reason. Normally, I loved this type of music: mounting orchestral tension, followed by a horn suddenly going flat; or a piano waxing incredibly emotional, and then dropping off-tune, like a coin clanging on the table. Those unexpected notes sent a zing of pleasure through me, ordinarily.

Tonight, they threw me off balance. They harkened back to my childhood when I would ride in the back seat of our Fifties car, and the lone horn of a distant train would weave in to accompany Stan Kenton on the radio, and then fade out to continue its lonely journey. Even then, I think I sensed how alone we are in this world.

I sat there keenly listening, and figured out the magic that discord worked on me. The odd notes would arrive unexpectedly and bestow an emotional surprise. Just as the white *mec* made me hesitate when I walked into the Tahonga, the cool, dissonant notes suggested a sudden shift in the scheme of things. As if intense, sustained beauty and harmony just couldn't endure. Something had to break, or change. Sometimes the surprise proved pleasant, sometimes not.

The three of us didn't talk much. Like butterflies, we flitted from one superficial topic of conversation to another. From music, to cars, to Luc's job. That was fine, because I thought if we just remained posed there in the Tahonga, quiet and frozen in time, rocking no boat, we could return to being the Three Musketeers. If no one made a move, nothing would change.

Idiotic, but that's how I felt; I didn't know about them. Thierry, on the ride over, had slipped me an envelope containing my money. He muttered an apology for his tardiness, but I spared him questions. Luc's boxy, cobalt-blue Alfetta was as spacious as a tomb compared to the coffin-sized Lancia. He had made the transition to four doors and five speeds. The extra room allowed him to ferry clients around comfortably, he said. The five-speed transmission stoked his personal amusement, and I could relate to that. I would have loved taking the wheel, revving up, and sending the Musketeers back swashbuckling about Paris, if only for a half hour or so. But I didn't ask, and Luc didn't offer.

Then we drove home, and each of us flew off independently. Luc would leave the next day for Lyon, and Thierry...I didn't know where he would go.

Back in my room, I felt as flat as a Stan-Kenton note. A melancholy mood shrouded me, lasting the rest of the weekend. When Monday morning arrived, I finally cast it off like a burdensome shawl, for I had to face up to my summons and trudge to the commissariat.

I sat in the chair next to Brondel's desk.

"Was my message a surprise?" he asked, pale-blue eyes clear and intense.

I raised my shoulders in a sort of noncommittal shrug and tried not to betray my nerves.

"I happened to be near your hotel Saturday, and I thought you should know our latest news...

Twenty scenarios must have galloped through my head during his pause—none of them good. I ground my molars.

"We've found the driver who ran George Abdi down. Finally, a break in the case."

I sucked in a deep, silent breath and began to speculate. Did the driver know about Jenkins and me? Did he know Butch-head? Those were my shameful concerns for the moment.

"Don't you want to know who he is?"

I started biting my lip, and by the time I stopped and opened my mouth to say something, Brondel had charged on. "A foreign student" he said. "From Portugal, of all places."

"Why...?" I asked, almost in a whisper.

"He says he was high on cocaine. Stole the car on a dare. Says he doesn't remember hitting Monsieur Abdi, though. That is more problematic for us." Brondel gazed at me with something like curiosity. "I only called you here to ease your mind. At the moment there seems to be no Iranian plot that could put you in danger. Nevertheless, I ask you not to discuss this with anyone; we still have a lot of work to do."

I remained mute, as if my jaw were frozen, although I did manage a nod.

"Until then, we still may have the odd question or two for you. I see you're still at the Lux..."

At last my jaw unthawed and my brain started to work again. "Yes, that's my home in Paris," I said with as much nonchalance as possible. I wanted this *flic* to think I found the hypothesis of involuntary manslaughter perfectly acceptable. No reason to reject it, really.

Then I remembered how my silence on the subject of murder had made this cop suspicious before. I needed to ask how they caught this Portuguese *mec* and who could have proposed stealing a car...

I didn't get the chance.

"Must be a year you've been here," Brondel flung at me. "How much longer will Paris be your home?"

I had been here a year, and he knew it. He had seen my passport and the records at the Alliance Française. What was he angling for? Did he intend to give me permission to leave? I didn't want to ask and perhaps look eager to take flight. I hadn't the money to leave anyway, since I had used almost all my share of the translating cash to pay Madani.

Suddenly he corrected himself. "Oh yes, you are planning to return to the Alliance Française...no?"

I straightened in my chair. "Right, I'm still waiting for my grandmother's check to pay for it...She's had a heart attack, you see." I floundered. "Things are a little problematic at home...but it'll work out."

Brondel lifted one side of his red mustache in an ambiguous smile. "*Bien sûr.* I'm sorry about your grandmother."

He didn't look sorry. He just peered at me with speculative eyes. When his mustache twitched, I almost jumped. "I wonder if this misfortune will make paying bills in Paris difficult?"

He had read my mind. Always one step behind my heel, this *flic.* "No," I said, embarrassed, "I'm all right. I've paid my hotel bill and that's my biggest expense."

"Well," he said, abruptly shuffling some papers around his desk, "I'll be in touch as I wrap up this affair." Then he looked up with a kind of superficial smile. "Please know, however, that when we clear you to leave Paris, if you are short on funds, the police can help."

The police can help? I said to myself, as I left the commissariat. How? By loading me onto a plane and deporting me for vagrancy, or something? No thank you, *mon cher Brondel.* If I need help that badly, I'll call on Sasha.

I didn't manage to work in a question about George's hit-and-run driver. I just wanted to slink out of there before he started interrogating me again about what I did with my time, which was a big fat zero these days. Nothing, is what I did with my time. And that needled me.

Mentally, I pawed the earth like a horse with its hoof. I longed to make some kind of step forward. I did manage to reach my aunt who said Gram would be coming home from the hospital. Even with that relief, I still had things to stew over. The breakthrough in George's case, for instance: a Portuguese student, for Christ's sake! Why!?

I started hanging out in cafés again, and not just to kill time. I went on the social prowl. I'd scan the café terraces Paris is so famous for and try to spot people to chat up. If my sights nailed someone of interest, I would have a seat nearby. I only did it a couple of times, though. Then I knocked it off after netting the attention of some damn creepy *mecs.*

I hated having my skills idle, and sometimes I played a game to compensate. I would sit at my desk and listen to music on my cassette player, with the aim of deciphering French lyrics that stumped me. I would choose a song and jot down all the words I could identify. In between, I would leave underlined blanks for those that escaped me. A bit like hangman. I'd press *play-stop-rewind, play-stop-rewind*, over and over, while I dropped words I guessed at into the gaps of the puzzle. I figured the challenge had to do me some good.

One day I pulled out a Melina Mercouri cassette to tinker with. The exuberant Greek actress's French could be incomprehensible at times. In other words, perfect for my exercise. Her stepson, Joe Dassin, had no such flaw. In fact, he had started recording songs in Spanish, Italian, and in his native English. I'd heard he even recorded a song in Greek, in honor of his stepmother. After a year in France, I still couldn't get past my envy of him, especially now that my prospects had dried up like sagebrush in a drought. *Merde*! I said aloud. Then I sighed, rubbed my eyes and focused back on Melina Mercouri's song. I loved its melody and that she sang about Greek resistance to the country's former dictatorship, a personal fight for her. Melina had committed herself to the struggle until the regime of the Colonels came crashing down. She never acted the slacker, never the passive cash machine who let others do the hard, dangerous legwork.

I knew, because I had read her autobiography. Melina had endured threats and vulgar insults from the Greek junta, and once, while addressing a crowd in Italy, a bomb was delivered to her in a gift-wrapped box. Suspicion kept her from opening the package on the spot, but it had been a close call.

Melina, the brave Greek...how could I not be reminded of George? I opened my desk drawer. In the back, behind my pens and paper, rested the bent, wire-rimmed glasses with one lens cracked. I pulled them out and set them on the desk. When my burning eyes could contemplate them no longer, I picked them up and placed them in my purse. Then I left the Lux.

At Place Saint-Michel I threaded myself into the maze of ethnic eateries. Nothing had changed since last summer: doors were flung open; hawkers worked in white shirts and black trousers; window cases displayed whole fish on ice and colorful desserts. The immutable façade of it all should have delighted me. Instead, the aroma of gyros rotating on the spit smelled bitter, and I found the hawkers irritating. I just felt tired, and when I began to approach the Poseidon, I knew that nothing could be the same again. How much time had passed? How much history...Where would I start to explain to George's uncle? As I neared the restaurant, a weakness overcame me, a hollowness inside that siphoned my courage. A hawker at the Acropolis tried to wave me in for a meal. It was way too late for lunch and too early for dinner, but I almost succumbed. Anything to stall.

Coward! I hurled at myself. Buck up! I took a moment to straighten my sunglasses and then walked past the Poseidon, barely glancing in the window. That wasn't too hard, I decided, and turned to retrace my steps more slowly this time. What I saw as I eased by the window made me halt and stare. George's uncle sat by his cash register, writing, but it wasn't he who had surprised me. It was a girl setting tables. She looked younger than me and more European than Middle Eastern. What's more, she looked familiar.

It took more courage to set foot in the Poseidon than it had to enter the solemn, foreboding halls of the commissariat in the Fourth. Nevertheless, I drew in a steadying breath, closed my eyes for a steeling moment, and made my entrance. George's uncle had just headed towards the kitchen, so I stopped near the door and slowly removed my sunglasses.

The empty locale made me queasy, like the hollowness inside me. A bunch of noisy customers would have made me feel less conspicuous. I could have tip-toed out, instead of getting caught by a passing waiter.

"Do you desire lunch?" he asked.

"I'd like to speak with Monsieur Abdi..."

"May *I* help you?" The girl with the European air had come to join us. The Afghan waiter seemed to defer to her and moved on. She smiled at me.

"Well," I began, feeling a little less tense about introducing myself, "I'm Haley Morgan. I was a friend of Monsieur Abdi's nephew, George..."

"George's friend?" Her smile—somehow I'd seen it many times before—faded from her eyes.

"Yes, I knew George. I need to talk to his—"

"Ah, it's you, the American!" *Uncle*, is what I was about to say, when the man appeared in person.

"I didn't think we'd see *you* again."

An urge to apologize for the bother and sail out of there shot through me. Instead, I shifted gears. "Maybe I should come round to your flat when you're all home..."

"What for? Have you not caused enough grief?"

That knocked the wind out of me. Monsieur Abdi looked menacing: black eyes, salt and pepper mustache, dark, creased brow. I started to give way and stepped back. "Sorry, I just wanted to have a word with you..."

"I am busy." With that, George's uncle turned and pounded back to the kitchen. Numbly, I watched his broad back disappear through the door.

"He's not very tolerant," said the European-looking girl, this time in English.

I turned back to her and studied her hazel eyes. "A shame. I should've skipped him and gone straight to his wife."

"My aunt?" She shrugged. "I don't know... you could talk to me..."

I smiled to myself. George's sister: even more preferable. I looked around the vacant restaurant. "Could you get away?"

"We're not busy at this hour. I'll tell the other waiter I'm having a break."

The girl with hazel eyes and fair skin led me to a café in the neighborhood, one I had patronized many a time, hoping to run into George. I had always sat inside during those cold days. Now we settled at a sidewalk table, and I told her to order whatever she wanted, that it was on me.

I thought I'd impress her a little and said, "*Eleni*, right?"

"Correct, *Haley*."

Her response sounded almost like a quip, and I chuckled. "Your brother told me about you."

"And through my relatives, I've learned of you. I'm surprised you know my second name, Eleni. " Her eyes saddened, and she murmured, "George always called me by my first name..."

"*Rania*," I said, "which you don't like. He told me that too." I thought Eleni might find that touching. She had occupied her brother's mind so thoroughly that he had chatted about her in France with an American.

Instead, all she did was give me a slight smile. "My aunt said you came to visit one day."

"After George got beaten up...do they think I'm responsible?"

Before she could answer, Eleni's coke and my coffee arrived. The waiter set my cup and saucer and Eleni's glass in front of us. Then he tucked the tray sideways between his bicep and torso, so he could uncap the coke, pour some out, and set it on the table. I had witnessed the maneuver countless times and still appreciated the quick, fluid art of it. The pause allowed us each to sit back and relax for a couple of seconds.

When Eleni resumed, she said, "My aunt and uncle listen to his Iranian friends...*Were* you responsible?"

Her tone rang dead serious. It was a logical question, and I felt time had come to justify myself. "Responsible," I replied, looking her square in the eyes, "only in that George's friends disliked me and any Western influence on him."

Eleni sat back and folded her arms. "Bastards! They destroyed all hope for George in Paris. He could have started a new life. Look," she added, communicating a kind of desperate smile, "he even had an American friend—a girl!"

"Just a friend," I said.

"Yes, but the point is he could have changed."

"How?"

Her eyes began to glisten. "I just think he could be more happy." She was close to tears and her English was slipping. She needed a break.

I looked away so she could compose herself. In a sweeping gesture I stretched my arm to indicate our setting: tables only inches apart and packed with customers, pedestrians on the sidewalk, some idling by, others engaged in a clipped pace, cars sprinting and halting in gusts of engine roar. Around us, trees were fleshed thick with green, here and there revealing a glimpse of lacy wrought-iron balcony. I summed it up: "So you finally made it to Paris. George told me you wanted to come, but your father and uncle were against it."

Her eyes had dried, leaving only a slight redness that made her look feisty. "They were. But I came anyway, and my father couldn't bear that I live here with no income, so he begged my uncle to give me a job."

Eleni's chestnut-brown hair flashed golden in the sunshine. She had a small, snub nose, and I could picture her acting pugnacious to her uncle's face. Still, the shadow of George filtered through when she smiled, and reminded me of what I had come here to accomplish.

I put it off a little longer. "What would you like Paris to do for you?"

She frowned. "Do you mean, what would I like to do in Paris?"

I lifted a shoulder. "If you prefer."

"I want to make a good career here—something away from my uncle's restaurant. I would like to make many French and European friends." She grinned at me. "American friends too."

"How's your French?"

She shrugged. "Fine, I studied French and English in school."

"There are some good schools for foreigners here. You could take advanced classes in the language."

"I'm getting by fine," she said in a polite tone, but with boredom in her eyes. "I'll learn from my friends." I could tell she was tiring of this conversation. She didn't even ask me about my experience in Paris.

"What's your aunt like?" I asked, to get back on track.

"Ooof! She's a nuisance. She always worries some French boy is going to take advantage of me. Sometimes she is worse than my uncle. I can't wait to move from their house."

I gave her a sympathetic nod and then asked, "Does she loathe me as much as your uncle does?"

"What is *loathe*?"

"...Hate. Does she also hate me?"

Eleni drained her glass. "I don't know if they hate you. We don't talk very much about George in these days. My aunt cries and my uncle gets, how do you say—pissed off?"

I sighed. "Right." I really wanted to talk to someone I knew. "Do any of George's friends still come around?"

"No, thank God. They're so macho!"

Cute kid. She made me smile. "There's this one fellow," I went on, "who your aunt and uncle know. He wears his hair really short and has a slight beard and kind of beady eyes. Sometimes he wears a beige leisure-suit jacket..."

"Leisure suit?"

"It's a jacket with a collar that looks like a shirt."

"Hassan!" Eleni's delight in discovery was short-lived. "He's a jerk."

I responded with a little laugh. "Yes, well, I need to get in touch with him. Could you get me his phone number?"

I didn't complete my task that day, but I got a step further.

Thierry would have said, "There you go, getting involved with another Middle Easterner." Well, I wouldn't tell him about my plan to contact Butch-head— Hassan, that is. He would never understand. Come to think of it, my relationships in general lacked mutual understanding, and trust. Not a good way to proceed in life, no doubt. Regardless, I had to take care of this detail. Perhaps, afterward, I would tell Thierry.

I made my call to George's friend Hassan and scheduled a rendezvous in the Louvre metro station. I liked the serenity of the place. Sure, *serenity* sounds weird in a bustling, echoing subway, with trains roaring back and forth. And yet, the gleam of the white-tiled tunnels reassured me. So did the little replica of an ancient Egyptian statue, standing in a niche behind glass on the Louvre station platform. I passed it almost daily, like part of my home décor. The whole atmosphere was calming. What's more, people don't usually stare at you in the metro, unlike in cafés where the patrons are out to do just that—notice people.

Underground, the law is *mind your own business and keep moving*. People looked like automatons down there. I must have too. I could feel it when I marched up and down the stairs like a robot, never changing expression. I did run into my share of perverts on the trains. Once in a while a creep would try to rub up against me from behind, or a straying hand would graze my leg. Even those *mecs* didn't look me in the eye, though. They stared straight ahead, chins up, as if they were the most upstanding citizens in Paris. Some even wore ties.

When I finally saw Hassan hop down the stairs to meet me, I didn't move from my bench. I let him come to me.

"Sorry I'm late," he said, before sitting down. A polite thing to say, I thought. A human thing—not a bad start.

"It's normal with the metro," I replied.

He seemed at ease as he sat next to me. He planted his feet far apart and rested his forearms on his thighs, while his gaze swept over the human traffic on the platform. Perhaps he was at home underground too. When he focused on me, I got to the point.

"I was wondering," I said, looking at his jacket, a Levis one this time, "if the police still contact you about George?"

"Not for a while," he said, facing the platform again. "Why?"

"They still check in with me, and I wondered if they'd gotten off your back for good..."

He turned to me with a sober look. "I certainly hope so, Haley."

That disconcerted me. Up until this day he had never uttered my name. In the past we had screamed at each other (at the American rally) and hurled insults back and forth. Now, I was "Haley" to him. It surprised me, and yet the friendly usage somehow took the edge off things.

I faced him full on. "Then you probably don't know about the Portuguese student." Why I brought that up, I don't know. Maybe I just wanted to further the friendly tone.

"What are you talking about?"

"The police called me in and told me a Portuguese driver on drugs ran George down."

Hassan stared at me as if I'd told him Martians had invaded Paris. "That's crazy."

"I know. They say he was high on cocaine, but he doesn't remember who told him to steal the car he was driving…"

Hassan stiffened and then flattened his back against the bench.

"What do you make of it?" I asked.

He scanned the platform to his left. "I don't know."

I could barely hear him, with a train coming in. I watched the people get off and on, marching like ants. After the train left, I turned back to him.

This time his eyes were on me. "There are better suspects than a Portuguese student."

"Who?" I asked.

A subtle smile slipped from Hassan, and he shook his head. "I must leave now."

"Wait," I said, wanting to grab his blue-jean jacket.

He frowned at me so intensely, I shrunk back. Then a chubby lady sat down, plopping her two bags next to him. She puffed out a loud sigh, and he whipped his frown to her.

I knew I had to back off, and the pause made me think of the purpose of meeting my old nemesis, Butch-head. Before he could rise, I said, "Do you still visit George's aunt and uncle?"

His scowl melted a little, though his eyes remained flinty. "Not often."

"Listen, I'd like your advice about going to see George's aunt. I still have the glasses…"

His eyes widened, lifting his eyebrows. "I'm sure the glasses are forgotten by now. As I told you, his aunt believes them stolen."

For a moment I didn't say anything. I just looked at the concrete floor and pictured some base punk snatching George's glasses off the sidewalk as he lay there lifeless. I almost wished it had happened that way, instead of things ending up like this.

Finally, I spoke. "But they weren't stolen and they should be returned to Mr. and Mrs. Abdi. But not by me…"

Hassan gazed across the tracks at the platform on the other side of the tunnel. A young guy with long curly hair had shown up with a banjo. He placed the open case on the floor at the end of one of the benches and stood back, almost to the wall. A couple of twangs started up, and the sound made me think of home.

"…Would you like that I take the glasses to the Abdis?" Hassan asked.

I had a hard time looking away from the *mec* who had started to play "Sweet Georgia Brown." Gram loved that song. "I'd like you to do what you think is right with them," I said. "You were his close friend."

Hassan nodded.

"Thanks," I said, and pulled the glasses from my purse. I handed them to him, and again he nodded. Then, without smiling, we parted ways.

10: C'est la Vie, Haley

Coming clean about the spectacles cleared my conscience regarding George's aunt and uncle. Hassan, on the other hand, baffled me. What was he holding back that he'd learned about George's accident?

I hadn't swept all guilt away, however. Gram still lay recovering in Reno, waiting to see me. I needed to think. A walk on a nice long street, with nothing to distract me, would help. So I headed east along rue Réamur, away from touristy Paris. I was deliberating whether to just call my aunt and tell her I couldn't find the money, when someone sidled up next to me and gripped my arm.

"Hey, kid..."

I whipped around. May wonders never cease—Jenkins!

"How 'bout a café break?"

"You're still here?" I marveled.

"I'll explain when we're tucked away somewhere discreet."

I didn't know what to say, so I followed him out of shock...and curiosity. He led me to a café in a nest of tiny lanes between rue Réamur and boulevard Bonne Nouvelle. One of his little, old-fashioned joints, it consisted of about five tables with curvy wooden chairs. Little décor, save a yellowing poster of some kind of harbor, circa 1950s. Not even a pinball machine. Just Jenkins, me, and a somber barman who never changed expressions. The *mec* plunked down Jenkins' cognac and my coffee and retreated behind his bar.

"Aren't you going to sugar your coffee?" Jenkins asked me.

I finished looking him over. His face was as veiny and florid as ever, but his light-grey summer suit hung crisp. His dull-brown hair appeared thinner and maybe he'd added a pound or two; other than that he seemed unchanged. I took care of my coffee and waited for him to explain himself.

"After your tête-à-tête with ol' Hassan, the Bureau decided to let me stay on. What the hell are you up to with him?"

I opened my mouth to defend myself and then closed it. Jenkins should have been long gone after George got beaten up. He himself had revealed that. He should have returned to Washington way before I ever met Butch-head. Instead, here he sat, entrenched in Paris and in his old habits—downing cognac and following me.

Instead of answering his question, I said, "George died, you know?"

"...Yes...pity about that." It took him forever to drag that out. Meanwhile he scrutinized me with slitty eyes. "So why the blazes are you mixed up with Hassan?"

I wanted to ask him why he was still hanging about Paris, but I reckoned he would lie to me. So I decided to play along and find out what he knew. "Do you think Hassan's dangerous?"

He took a swig. "Depends. Is he feeding you anything?"

So Jenkins still wanted information. I felt like screwing with him, telling him some bullshit about Hassan and Iran, but I resisted. Who knew how long he had been spying on me, and I didn't want to land right back in the thick of it.

I shrugged. "Hassan made contact with me. I couldn't care less about him."

"What were you two talking about in the Louvre metro?"

Or, I thought, had Jenkins been following Hassan? I wanted to ask him what he knew about Hassan, particularly any information he could have on George's murder, but I held back. Jenkins might have suspected I had some goods myself, and I'd be damned if I was going to share anything with him. I wanted to pull his power plug from me. Cut the lines to the buttons he pushed.

I would keep things superficial. "We talked about George," I said. "I gave Hassan his glasses...from when he died. He knew I had them, that's why he first contacted me. Nothing else is going on." Suddenly I resented revealing a thing as personal and private as George's glasses to Jenkins—in reality, a not-so-superficial history.

He stared at me for a long while. Finally, his blade-grey eyes blinked.

"Haley, if you've got information about Hassan, give it to me."

I turned up my palms. "Nothing."

"If you cooperate, you'll get paid again."

Jesus, I thought. What could I obtain from Hassan? The *mec* was a jerk who bit my head off when he didn't like what I said. He had already told me no one talked to him any longer. And yet he had implied he suspected someone...

I continued to play along. "What are you looking for, and who wants to pay for it?"

"The Bureau's interested—"

"No. You've been here way too long to be working for the FBI...I'm not saying another word until you tell me who's really paying you."

Jenkins gave me a condescending smile and a shake of his head. Then he let out a chuckle. "You're assigning yourself too much importance, kid."

That really angered me, so that I drew myself up. "I wonder if a certain detective in the Fourth arrondissement would agree? Know anything about my dealings with him over George's homicide?"

Jenkins' smile tightened. "Of course—red mustache and all. I'd appreciate you keeping me out of it."

I couldn't believe it. I actually had some leverage on this fox. Emboldened, I went on. "Then tell me who you really work for."

Jenkins displayed a poker face. I waited, heart thumping, for his move.

"Haley..." he finally said, a sour utterance that seemed to begrudgingly acknowledge my existence. "Top civics student who thinks she's in a Hayley Mills adventure." His eyes shifted to sweep the shabby locale and its grim-faced barman who now stood at the entrance, gazing through the smudged glass of the front window. A hot June day, and not one door or window in the place open.

Jenkins turned his eyes back on me. "I'll wager you'd prefer the French police not know you've been running errands for the CIA." A smile twitched at the corner of his mouth. "Question of unauthorized spying. Do they know about your little translating gig, by the way? Oh, don't worry," he added with a smirk, "they'll hear nothing from me..."

I suppressed an urge to sink my teeth into my lip. CIA, for Christ's sake—they could know more about George's homicide than the police. Between that bomb and Jenkins' not-so-veiled threat to expose me to the *flics*, I felt blown off the game board.

When I recovered, I said, "Why did you pretend to be FBI?"

"Simple psychology. People usually don't get alarmed when they think they're assisting a crime-fighting outfit."

"So what do you know about George's death?"

"He was run down on a sidewalk. Accidents happen. Don't mess around, Haley. Either give me the dope on Hassan and make a little cash or stay the hell away from him."

I stiffened. "Hassan told me nothing, and even if he did, I wouldn't sell it to you."

I didn't wait for Jenkins to toss his drink-money on the table and walk out, the way he had done before. This time I got to my feet, ready to exit in right-eousness. I expected him to at least grunt in amusement. But he frowned at me, a frown tinged with regret, it seemed, maybe even worry.

Marching out should have been my next move, but for some reason my in-sides softened. My head reasoned I should coolly stride out of the café, but this weakness that swirled in my stomach slowed me. Despite my resolve, I felt uneasy about Jenkins' frown. I wanted an explanation. I hated it when a seam hung loose; when I didn't know what people thought about me. Let him mock me. Let him scold me. Then I could glide away in silent dignity, with Jenkins looking the cad he was.

"Take care of yourself, kid."

That, I didn't expect. "Thanks," I replied, not knowing what else to say, feel-ing he had disarmed me with some kind of verbal judo. I had nothing left to say or do, so I turned and trudged out, head down, eyes on the road ahead.

Decisions: why couldn't they all be as relatively easy as turning over George's glasses and turning down Jenkins? Shortly after I had met with Hassan, I received an envelope in the mail at the Lux. It contained a money order for five hundred dollars and a note from my aunt expressing her hope that the sum would suffice for a plane ticket home to Reno. My grandmother was home, healing steadily, and my aunt thought seeing me would help all the more. Of course I wanted to see Gram, except, in addition to Brondel's not having cleared me to leave, another slight complication had surfaced. The envelope from America wasn't the only item I had received.

Thierry had dropped another book from Monsieur Garnier in my lap. *Vivre à Paris* was a large picture book with text. It held great potential for the tourist market according to Garnier who wanted an English version.

Thierry and I sat poring over it in the Vavin, his regular café in Montpar-nasse going back to his secondary school years.

Funny, you'd think it was my first time in the Vavin. Thierry had taken me there before, even introduced me to the owner. But this afternoon I couldn't help dwelling on the place. The way Thierry and the owner shook hands, as they did every time Thierry visited the establishment, moved me today. In Reno no one bonded like that with proprietors. You hardly ever saw them.

Here, it showed the continuity in Paris and the solidarity among its people. In the States, employees and owners alike came and went like changes in the weather. No one frequented the same café everyday—hell, cafés didn't even exist in Reno. People minded their own business and drank their coffee at home or at Denny's where no one knew their names. It was one big revolving door of cold, lonely change, and I didn't like it.

I looked back down at the book on our table. The descriptions of El Dorado on the Water were almost poetic. The photos so familiar, I kept looking for Luc, Thierry, and me in every snapshot: from the Deux Magots, its red awning stamped with gold letters, to the sand-covered *quais* along the Seine featuring the occasional fisherman. The three of us could have been photographed at any of the locations in the book, once upon a time.

"So you're up for it, then?" Thierry asked, sounding enthused.

I wanted to dive in and start swimming without a care, like in the old days, before Jenkins and the Iranians, or any of the other things that had mucked up my Eden.

Then I cleared my thoughts and focused on reality. "Won't you be too busy traveling the world with Air France?" I asked Thierry.

"No," he said, looking kind of sheepish. "I think I'll be based here in Paris to start with."

"What about my legal status and your taxes, and all? It doesn't make sense for you to work with me."

Thierry covered my hand with his, something he hadn't done since the eve of our second fling. "You're the best partner I could ask for," he answered, his dark eyes searching me.

I was on the verge of melting and had to steady myself. "I appreciate that, but my aunt's sent me the money to go to Reno to visit my grandmother."

He relaxed his hand. "What about the police?"

"Brondel hasn't let me off the hook yet, but he's got a suspect." I filled him in on the bizarre business of the Portuguese student.

"A Portuguese druggie," he said. "What are the odds of that?"

"Not great."

Thierry squeezed my hand. "Do you have enough money to go home and come back?"

I looked around the café again. Waiters in white aprons bustled about, juggling plates, glasses, and cutlery that clinked and tinkled. Exuberant voices echoed throughout the place. Conversations among people who knew one another more than casually—who greeted one another with kisses or handshakes. The people, the conversations, the feel of history and eras had burrowed into me and become as constant as my heartbeat. The longer I sat in the Vavin, the more I confirmed my commitment to this whole experience: to Paris, to Thierry...to George. To see it through.

Instead of answering Thierry's question, I said, "I don't think a Portuguese student killed George. Not on his own, at least." When Thierry frowned, I continued. "I ran into a friend of George's not long ago..."

"Who?"

I looked at our book's cover again and its photo of the Eiffel Tower from Place du Trocadéro. The lively fountains and sculpted bull's head seemed another world in contrast to my history with Butch-head.

I looked back up. "His name's Hassan, but you probably remember me calling him Butch-head. I actually first met him at the American rally back in November."

Thierry's eyes turned somber. "The stalker..."

"No, he's harmless. All he ever wanted to do was talk to me about George. He thinks someone else might be involved in the homicide, but he won't elaborate."

Thierry leaned over the table. "Listen, Haley, be careful who you get involved with again." He sighed. "Maybe you should go home for a bit. I can loan you the money to come back if you don't have it."

His offer moved me. Coming on the heels of Sasha's generosity barely two weeks earlier, it made me realize I was silly at the time to think I needed new friends.

Thierry bridged my pause. "If you have to stay there for a while, I could come visit you..."

That threw me, and made me think of Sasha's reference to Thierry's girlfriend. The news had been second-hand, and much could have happened in those two weeks. It certainly didn't merit bringing up.

Instead, I said, "I've always said you'd like Reno."

"And you still love Paris like no other city?"

"I always will."

His fingers lightly drummed the top of my hand. "It seems we belong together. Two sides of a coin."

I didn't move. I felt Thierry's fingers were sounding me out. "I've thought that before, but I never was able to tell you."

"Let's go for a walk and you can tell me now."

"Okay," I said. "Plus, I've got a great idea that's been bouncing in and out of my head since Christmas—what do you think our chances of breaking into television are? Translating silly American shows into French?"

I turned my hand up and clasped his fingers. For once Thierry's face lost all impassiveness. A warm smile spread through his eyes and he squeezed my hand.

As we got up to leave the Vavin, I said, "That's not my only project. I think you should know my immediate plan."

Two mornings later, I walked into the Alliance Française and paid cash to start a new class. Then I walked back down to the Seine and began to stroll from the Sixth to the Fifth arrondissement. I passed the Pont Neuf, the spire of Sainte-Chapelle across the river, and then Notre Dame. There, I stopped to look down at the water. The Seine rolled along as dark-green and silent as ever. At this point, I think I loved its silence most of all. It just moved on, minding its own business. Even though it carried boats and cargo and people, it never slowed to judge.

I crossed the bridge onto the Ile Saint-Louis, right behind Notre Dame, and stopped. An overgrowth of tree leaves and vines framed the cathedral's flying buttresses in a deep green. Then I continued across to the Right Bank where the commissariat of the Fourth arrondissement resided. Brondel will be surprised to see me in his office of my own accord, I thought. Coming clean and ready to cooperate about everyone and everything.

Gram was certainly surprised, when the day after meeting Thierry I had called her at home and told her of my plan. That was the hardest thing: telling her I wouldn't be buying a plane ticket home with the five hundred dollars she'd sent me. That I had to take care of unfinished business.

When she didn't respond right away to my long story of George and the police, I teared-up, and my voice broke when I said, "I'm sorry." Even though she had already reassured me she felt much better and was on the mend, burdening her with this part of my life made me feel like a heel and an ingrate. It was the first time she'd heard me cry in years. "If I pay my school fees and my rent at the Lux with the five hundred, I'll be free to make things right."

I don't know whether she was just tired or she meant to be philosophical when she sighed and said, "Haley, I don't know what to tell you. If you'd talked to me earlier, I might've been able to help you. Now I don't know what to say, except I'm sorry too. After all you've experienced, the decisions are yours now. I'm not in Paris, so I don't know how to counsel you. I can only be available to talk."

And that's how we had left it. Strange, after that I felt closer to Gram than when she had been with me in person, right here in Paris. Closer than maybe I'd ever felt to her.

As I entered the Marais in the Fourth, I felt jittery about how I would begin with Brondel. He wasn't Gram, after all, with her unconditional love. And it wouldn't be like meeting minds with Thierry, either. No, not easy, I knew. But *ease* wasn't exactly what I deserved at this point. I thought about Jenkins, and how I had turned my back on him with honesty and integrity. I would just have to do the opposite: turn toward Brondel with the same mettle. If I could weather Jenkins, I could deal with anyone.

I arrived at the commissariat and walked through the door. The uniformed *planton* on duty eyed me from behind his high desk, but instead of shrinking inside, as I did on my previous visit, I drew myself up. "*Commissaire Brondel, s'il vous plaît,*" I said with a determined smile.

In response, I received a lifting of the eyebrow and a gesturing to the bench. "Have a seat."

I did, and had to practically force myself to stop smiling. I had almost come full circle. A visit to the commissariat together was how Thierry and I had first met. How many Americans, when you think about it, have seen the inside of a Paris police station as many times as I had? I let a little laugh slip out. My, how accomplished I had become. So positively Parisian!

Afterword

Joe Dassin died the following month—August, 1980—at only forty-two years old. Luc called to tell me, but of course I already knew. Heart attack turned out to be the diagnosis, though rumors of pills also circulated. The shock was sharp, but strangely brief, considering I had obsessed over the success of this American in Paris for almost a year. Now, somehow, the news of Joe's death filled me with a sense of liberation, shameful as it sounds. As if a rival—no, more like an over-achieving parent—had set like the sun, and ceased to eclipse me. I first heard the news on FIP and then read more in *Le Monde*. After that, I put my paper down and headed off to the PTT in rue du Louvre. I owed Gram another call and an update on my new direction: my studies, my cooperation with Brondel in finding George's killer, and my continuing translating work with Thierry, along with a part-time work permit Brondel had recommended for me. I hadn't found a regular job yet, but Thierry and his parents were helping. Thierry and I were helping each other, to be precise. We still had a lot to learn in the world of work...and love.

Acknowledgments

Many thanks to Paula Riley for her invaluable encouragement and expertise in writing and publishing, without which this project would still be lingering in Limbo; to Angela Sell for her enthusiasm and the inestimable time she contributed to reviewing this novel; to Gina Akao, Callie Marriott, William Kelly Jones, Alexandria King, Carolyn Zellers, Anne Buckley, Christine Rost, and Ben Garrido for their vital critique-group feedback; to my sister Victoria Perry and my mother Marsha Kimura whose taste and judgment I highly value; to Hervé l'Hostis, Madeleine Schermesser, Anne Branger, Dana Clinton, Martine Rivière, and Henri Sellam for their precious pearls of knowledge about Paris in the late 1970s.